CHAPTER 1

WHAT WOULD YOU DO IF YOUR HOUSE SET ON FIRE—EVERYTHING you knew, owned and loved, all your memories slowly turning to ash? Suffocating smoke obstructing your vision, making you blind and disoriented. You'd get out of there, run for your life, right? That's exactly what I was doing when I landed in São Paulo, Brazil, after my family life imploded. I just didn't know I was running straight into the flames—or that this trip was going to change my life forever.

"Oh my God, you're here!" Lu's arms wrapped around me like a corset laced tight enough to reposition my internal organs, her voice a high-pitched squeak. She always looked younger when she was happy. "I can't believe you're finally here!" Her petite body and doll face bounced up and down, getting her head dangerously close to my chin and threatening to knock the teeth out of my mouth. Her excitement the perfect antidote to my twelve-hour flight tiredness.

"Can't… breathe… Lu."

She let go. "It only took some sort of family disaster for you to come visit me." A hand slapped my arm, happy quickly turning into accusatory.

I laughed. "You talk like we live in the same city. We don't even live on the same continent."

"True. We need to sort that. You should move to Brazil. You

1

should move here!" The last word a shriek, eyebrows and lips rising at the same time, stretching her face and making her look like a Disney cartoon. "You're already here and working remote, so I forbid you from leaving." Lu pivoted on her towering platforms, entwined one of her arms with mine, and started walking towards the arrivals exit.

"Very tempting. Shame I don't have a visa to be here for more than three months."

"That's ok. I'll marry you so you can stay."

The doors to the new world opened with a futuristic sensor-powered whoosh and I instantly regretted the woolly jumper I had on. The heat and smell letting me know I was on a different part of the globe; my northern British complexion giving away I was the foreign variety.

"I wonder what immigration would think of that when they realize we're not gay."

"They don't know that, and we know each other more than enough to pass as a couple."

That was true. Lu and I had become best friends during our stint at uni in London, when we lived together for three years. We knew each other's manias better than any boyfriend.

"To be fair, I would snog and marry you."

"Of course you would. I'm adorable!" She smiled and winked at me. "What on earth are you wearing, anyway? I told you it'd be hot."

"I know! Would take it off if I could, but I would have to flash you my boobs. Don't have anything underneath."

"Oooh! Immigration would one hundred percent think we're a couple. You've barely gotten off the plane and you're already trying to flash your goodies at me."

We both laughed. "I missed you so much, you little nutter." Arm still interlocked with one of hers, I pulled her closer to me. "In my defense, it was cold in London, and I always get cold on planes."

PLAYING
with Fire

PAOLA SANTANA

So Bookish

P.S. So Bookish
www.ps-sobookish.com
Liverpool, UK

First published worldwide by P.S. So Bookish
1st EDITION – July 2025
Copyright © P.S. So Bookish 2025

Cover design and illustration by Ivanna Nashkolna

A CIP catalogue record for this book is available from the British Library.

Paperback ISBN: 978-1-0684670-0-4
E-book ISBN: 978-1-0684670-1-1

Printed and bound worldwide by: IngramSpark, Lightning Source LLC and Kindle Direct Publishing,Amazon.com, Inc.
18+ content – not suitable for young readers.

NOTE TO READERS

Dear Reader,

Thank you so much for reading *Playing with Fire*. The fact you have chosen to buy my debut novel means the world to me. I hope it sweeps you off your feet and spoils you with a trip to Brazil.

There are phrases in Brazilian Portuguese throughout this novel, intended to make you feel as alienated as our main character does when she struggles with the language. But don't worry, if you want to know what they mean, you can check their translation in the 'Portuguese Translations' section at the end of the book.

Please note that this is a spicy romance with brief mentions of domestic violence, child abuse, and trauma. As such, it's not recommended for readers younger than eighteen.

Happy reading!

Paola 🩶

To Sienna Bradley. So you know that dreams can come true, baby girl. You just need to fight for them.

We struggled to get my wardrobe of a suitcase in the boot of her car and, after minutes of me sweating like the Niagara Falls, the air-con finally kicked in. The road an endless stretch of four-laned tarmac disappearing into the flat distance in a lighter, dryer shade of grey that had been abused by the sun. The occasional Brazilian flag flying proudly at dotted intervals just in case you forgot where you were. Sky so blue and vast, landscape so flat and open, that vehicles, trains and buildings felt small even though you knew they weren't. Everything washed with blinding sunlight. A lot of concrete but also a lot of green. Tall and short palm trees scattered among different foliage, reminding you you were somewhere warmer, despite the comfortable cool inside the car.

We gossiped about our old friends; how the hottest guy at uni no longer looks handsome; how I had put dancing on hold and taken a remote job so I could travel; and her new job working for her family's business.

Roadworks up ahead started to pile up the cars—a snake game eating one vehicle at a time and making its tail longer until our progress slowed to a crawl.

"So… since we still have some time to get home, tell me, what the hell happened that you decided to run away to Brazil? Not that I'm complaining or anything, but what bank did you rob, flower? Who am I hiding you from?"

She would ask, of course she would. I just hoped that it wouldn't be so soon.

"I found my father."

Lu slammed on the breaks. The car behind us held on to his horn as if he thought we were deaf.

"Bloody hell, Lu!"

"You did what?! But I thought…"

"She lied." I took a deep breath. "My whole life, she lied to me."

3

Lu's eyes reverted back to the road, blinking, trying to make sense of what I had just said. The cars started moving.

"You can't tell me that and not explain! Give me some context, flower!"

"I found out by accident. Once it was clear I wasn't going to move back to Manchester after uni, my mother found a way to move down to London. I didn't mind, you know. Mum and I were close, and the rent in London is so expensive. It took her almost a year to find a job there. But a month ago she moved down. I was unpacking. Picked box nineteen—one of the ones for my room, but it turned out to be box sixty-one—full of my mother's old photo albums and scrapbooks. One of the notebooks was her old diary from the year just before I was born. I shouldn't have, but curiosity got the best of me."

My mother's life that year was a bit of a blur, according to her. She had gone traveling in America and, apparently, lived her own version of the Summer of Love. She told me she wasn't sure who my father was. That she found out she was pregnant after she got back to the UK and couldn't be sure which one of her holiday romances was the culprit. She wasn't even sure how to find them all even if she wanted to. I remember giggling over the fact that our story was a little like *Mamma Mia*. And I believed her wholeheartedly. It had been just the two of us for years. We were a team. It was her and me against the world.

"I turned a page and saw this picture. A younger version of my mother smiling back at me next to an equally happy-looking man. I always knew I looked like my father. My freaky green eyes and caramel hair are nowhere to be seen on my mother's side of the family. And looking at that picture, I knew it was true. Because staring right back at me was a man who looked exactly like me—same eyes, same features, same color hair."

"You're joking!" Lu knew the story. We had talked at length

about how I wished I knew my father. How I always felt like I was missing a piece of the puzzle. That weird feeling of not quite belonging, that you are different from your family, but not knowing why or where it came from.

"There were other pictures too. You know how in the old days they used to print the dates on the back of the photos, sometimes even on the front of them?"

"Uh-huh..."

"There were several pictures, with the same man, spanning around four months. I read through her diary to find his name. She not only knew who he was, she dated him for months and even met his parents. His name is Ryan. He's a property developer from Denver, Colorado. She never told him about me, and she lied to me. My whole life, she lied to me."

The car went silent. I stared out of the window so I wouldn't cry. "I met him last week. He flew out to meet me. He's a nice man. I'm the spitting image of him. Even the way we move our hands is the same, Lu."

"Holy shit! You met him? You didn't mention any of this on the phone!"

I nodded. "Honestly, I didn't know what to say or think. I still don't. I'm still so angry. By chance, box sixty-one revealed my mother's greatest secrets and blew my life into pieces. I can't even bring myself to feel happy I finally know who he is. Finding out the truth kind of ruined everything." The pang of disappointment and resentment weighed on my soul. The sadness pulling me down and tainting the happiness of seeing Lu like ink being dropped into a clear glass of water. "Can we talk about this another time? It kind of puts a downer on the excitement of being here, seeing you."

Lu's eyes flicked to me. Eyebrows arched upwards in the middle, sadness and compassion written all over her face. She knew exactly what this meant to me. How it hurt to be betrayed by the person I loved and trusted the most.

5

She drove. I stared out of the window. The silence stretching a little too long to not feel awkward.

"Anyway... Felipe is coming to see you as soon as we get back to the apartment." That made me look at her. Only Lu would know exactly what to say to completely change the mood.

When I left London, I was on the run. My biggest concern was to get away, as far away as possible from my problem. It didn't even cross my mind that coming to Brazil meant I would see Felipe.

"Don't tell me you don't remember my cousin, Pepino!" She threw a sly smile at me, eyebrows arching, voice full of innuendo. "He'll be showing you around the city over the next couple of days while I'm working."

Of course I remembered Felipe. It had been a few years, he had filled out, but it's a little hard to forget someone you exchanged bodily fluids with. The first summer Lu and I were in London, he had come out to visit, and we ended up having a bit of a thing. We'd kept in touch for a few weeks after he went home, but the distance had eventually fizzled things out. Occasionally, I would like one of his pictures on social media or he would like one of mine. But we hadn't really spoken since.

"I just got here, and you're already setting me up with your cousin?" I said, trying to give her my full scowl. But the amusement in my voice gave me away.

"He volunteered as a tribute. Plus... I might be plotting to make you stay here forever. I missed you, flower!"

As we reminisced about our London romantic exploits, the city started to reveal itself in the distance. At first, just the grey outline of square shapes—the ghost of a bar chart sitting far on the horizon. As we drove, the bars got taller—a cluster here, a cluster there. The blue celestial expanse and flat landscape around them making them look small until you realized there were over ten floors piled on top of each other. Trees getting closer together and falling into line formation; traffic getting heavier. Then all I could see on the horizon was a sea of tall buildings. And before I knew it, we were stuck in traffic, craning our necks to see nothing but rows of windows rising up either side of us like giants. Street art scaled up the side of some of the buildings like giant tattooed arms. Power lines crisscrossing above us, looking like strings on a guitar, and trees standing guard at the side of the road with their branches stretched wide as if preventing the buildings from toppling down on us. It was chaotic, busy, but vibrant and buzzing with energy.

Eventually, Lu pulled up in front of some gates that opened slowly, facing a slope downwards, disappearing under a block of flats. The heat of the day a distant memory from the shadows in the underground parking.

The lift opened, closed, and pinged when we got to the tenth floor.

"Welcome home! *Minha casa é sua casa.*"

"Wow! I can see you put your interior design degree to good use."

The open plan lounge, dining, and balcony area looked like you had stepped into a magazine—modern and minimalistic but cozy. The ceramic floors keeping the whole place cool, big windows allowing light to breeze through, and the air-con making sure we weren't boiling to death in our own skin.

She smiled at me, "Come, let me show you your room." What she meant was my little studio flat. Said bedroom looked like I had booked myself into a hotel rather than couch surfing at my best friend's pad. I even had my own bathroom.

By the time I came back to the lounge, showered and feeling slightly more human, Felipe was talking to Lu. He stood up from his place on the sofa as soon as he saw me.

Pepino, as Lu called him, was a tall, male version of

Luciana. Ironically, the word also meant cucumber in Portuguese, but apparently it was not a pun on his height or his assets. Blond, brown-eyed, round nose, square jaw, and thin lips with a cupid bow that made two perfect pyramids. You could definitely see the family resemblance, and he was indeed very handsome. As a matter of fact, everything about him was almost too perfect—every strand of hair in its place, his clothes without a single crease. Even his beard stubble looked designer. He had this carefully curated easy charm.

And he hadn't changed a thing.

"I'll be damned. Look who finally decided to grace us with a visit. Never thought I'd see the day." Eyes vivid, smile going from ear to ear.

"Hello to you too." I smiled back, biting into his teasing, and held out my hand to greet him.

He laughed as he took it, then pulled me towards him, giving me two kisses on the cheeks—continental style. "How you doing, beautiful?"

Well… rather an awkward moment. I stood there like a confused plank, not quite knowing how to react to his sudden closeness and one kiss too many. And I knew, I could feel it, that my face was starting to look like someone had attacked my neck and cheeks with a ruler. Crimson heat spreading as fast as soft butter on warm toast.

"You're forgetting she's British, Pepino. Brits don't kiss everyone like we do," Lu said, winking at me. "She won't know what two kisses means either. That's so old school!" An affectionate back-handed slap hit her cousin's chest.

He shrugged. "I like when she blushes. It's cute." Felipe's eyes locked with mine, completely unbothered, waiting for my reply. An amused smile filling his face. He was as intense and forward as I remembered him.

"Ok… On that note, I'm going to busy myself in the kitchen." Lu quickly made herself scarce.

"How have you been, stranger?"

"Jet-lagged. Not that your cousin took any notice. And you?"

"Looking forward to our two days of culture and adventure." He crossed his arms, the gesture making his shoulders and biceps look bigger in his polo. Expression soft, a smile playing on his lips while his eyes scanned my face.

"Yeah... I heard she made you my designated babysitter. Lucky you!"

"I heard that!" Lu shouted from the kitchen.

"I thought you were supposed to be busying yourself," I shouted back.

Felipe laughed. His head tipping backwards and eyes moving sideways before they returned to me. "I think I'd rather call it your city guide."

I puckered my lips, raised my eyebrows, and dipped my head sideways so he could see my skepticism.

"You're only looking at me like that because you don't know the wonders I have planned for you. Have a little faith."

We smiled at each other. For a moment neither of us said anything. Memories of the way he used to kiss me intruded my thoughts. My eighteen-year-old self thought he was a good kisser.

"It's nice to see you. It's been a long time." His voice low, meant only for my ears, he uncrossed his arms and hooked his index finger around one of mine, shaking my hand gently and letting go. The gesture was familiar. He did the same when we were together in London. "I always wondered what it would be like if you were here." The smile that followed was sweet and welcoming.

"And now I am."

"And now you are." His head bounced up and down, the nod a distant echo of his words. His eyes sunk into mine, lips spreading into a smile that spelled trouble.

"What're you doing these days, anyway?" I broke the silence.

"Working for the family business. Still single."

I pretended not to hear his cannonball hint. "So you work there too?"

"Yeah… It's like military service for our family. We all must serve our time before we do other things. But I can't complain, I actually like the job." His eyes lingered on my face. "Are you excited about your party?"

The last word cut through the moment like a freight train on a track across a road. "Party?"

He raised his two eyebrows at me, mischievous smile, head nodding.

"No, she didn't!"

"Come on now, did you really think she wouldn't use this as an excuse to throw a party?" His smile got wider, head tipping to the side as if I'd missed something obvious. My best friend was a notorious party animal. Although, if you asked her, she would call it socializing.

"Let me guess, you were supposed to gently break the news to me?"

Felipe smiled and nodded. "Wrapped in a pretty little bow." One of his hands waved towards his body.

"Lu!" My bark echoed through the flat.

"Very subtle, Pepino!" she shouted from the kitchen.

But my protests were no good. In fact, they did nothing to spare me the suffering. So a few hours later, I stood in the lift, staring at the sign. Should've known two weeks of Portuguese Duolingo weren't going to cut it, but I was pretty sure it said first floor for the gym, and ground floor for the swimming pool and party room.

A party room now filled with complete and utter strangers, all apparently here to welcome my arrival. I knew for a fact there were only two faces here I would recognize.

The dull ache of a headache was banging on my temples already. Because you know... Gathering in a room full of unfamiliar people is exactly what one needs after a twelve-hour flight, and finding out your whole life was a lie. Clearly, in Lu's world, those three things went together like tea and biscuits, crackers and cheese.

But if I'm honest, it served me right. This is what you get when you run away from your problems—you jump from the frying pan straight into the fire. And as soon as the lift doors opened, I knew I stood no chance. Lu had spotted me.

Eyes straight on her target, her oversized earrings and long blonde waves swinging from side to side to the rhythm of her certain steps, she walked towards me with purpose, as if she was a rubber band on the rebound of being stretched too far. And this... was going to be just as painful. I really don't know why I bothered hoping in vain. Lu and I had been friends for years. She had never understood what 'low key' and 'taking it easy' actually meant. I really should've known better than to turn up at the doorstep of a party addict hoping for a regrouping retreat.

"Ready to meet everyone?" she said with a grin before I'd barely stepped out of the lift.

"Please go easy on me! I'm still jet-lagged and I don't speak Portuguese," I begged with as big puppy eyes as I could muster.

"Don't worry, they all speak English." Her smugness was a tad annoying. "That is exactly why they're all here—to meet you and show you the best São Paulo has to offer. Who knows? You might decide to stay and become my roommate again."

I rolled my eyes.

"I missed you, flower! You're my sister from another mister. Two years without you was murder!" After a moment of me staring at her purposedly unimpressed, she sighed. "You know, on our business module, this little exercise was called 'networking'. Put your education to good use, woman."

There was no point prolonging the inevitable. "How come they all speak English, anyway?"

"The official spill? Portuguese is not an international language, so we all have to learn English, blah, blah, blah... but really? We all just went to the same English school when we were kids."

"You mean you're all minted spoiled brats?"

Her face lit up in a grin and she bumped into me with her shoulder. "Something like that." Then she took hold of my wrist and towed me to the very first group of people for the joy of introductions and polite conversations.

Halfway through our 'networking' I saw them—a small group just outside the party room towards the swimming pool. My eyes instantly gravitated towards the guy in the middle.

Tall, dark hair kissing his shoulders, full lips, black jeans, boots, grey tee. His tattooed leather-cuffed arm wrapped around the shoulders of a pretty brunette with honey-colored eyes, who looked ever so slightly bored. As he laughed at his friends midway through conversation, his eyes met mine.

He didn't look away. Neither did I.

Skin in a shade every milk-tinted British person would envy, and facial features that almost made him look primal, gave him quite an interesting look. It wasn't just his features; it was his posture. It made me think of the wildlife program I had watched on the plane. He stood there as if he was a silverback gorilla, knowing no one would dare to challenge him, completely comfortable in his stance and the space he was taking. All the commotion happening around him while he just lounged there. His look and silence giving the impression that while he enjoyed the company, he would be just fine without it.

He filled all the Latin look clichés, but his beauty wasn't

obvious; it was intriguing. Like trying a new flavor of ice cream for the first time and, after thinking it tastes weird, realizing you actually rather like it.

That walking conundrum was staring right at me.

He lifted the corner of his mouth in a half smile, and the girl under his arm turned around to see what he was looking at just as Luciana called on me to introduce me to someone. All the way around the party room—thank God there weren't that many people—I kept on returning my eyes to this particular guy; only to find he was still looking in my direction. Like staring at each other gave us both some sort of relief from this whole ordeal.

When we eventually made it to his group, Lu introduced everyone, leaving tattooed arms and his girlfriend for last.

"This is Marcelo." She waved her hand dismissively at the guy I had been exchanging looks with for most of the evening. Her expression changing from cheerful to stoical. "Who, apparently, didn't get the memo and decided to turn up wearing a tacky neck piece."

He wasn't wearing a necklace but clearly knew what she meant, as he snorted, "Ever so charming, Lu." Then slightly lifted his head as a greeting to me.

"As always." Lu's voice was dry and stern.

Just before the awkwardness had time to hit, Felipe arrived carrying drinks for everyone. "I see you met the gang. And my brother. I apologize in advance for him."

"Your brother?"

The whole group felt silent for a beat, everyone staring at my confused face.

"What? Don't tell me you can't see the family resemblance?" Marcelo's voice was sarcastic, face bathed in the perversity of someone who knew exactly who I was but was enjoying the fact I had been caught red-handed not knowing who he was.

They were nothing alike. And when I say nothing, I mean polar opposites. The only thing they had in common was their brown eyes.

"Oh, let me guess... the soles of your feet are the same color. Because it sure as hell isn't your aura," Lu snapped back faster than stepping on a rake's head, and before anyone could say anything else, she grabbed hold of my arm and pulled me away, completely ignoring the girl Marcelo had his arms around all evening.

"I think you forgot to introduce me to your other cousin's girlfriend," I whispered.

"No, I didn't. That's Angie—Angela." She said the girl's name with enough poison to kill an elephant. "I can't believe he brought her to my place. The audacity, honestly!"

I halted to a stop and raised both my eyebrows at her.

"There is no point you meeting her, anyway. She's not his girlfriend. Celo changes women like he changes clothes. Next time you see him, he'll have some other poor victim with him."

"I feel the distinct whiff of sour grapes. She's not an old friend then?"

"Oh, please! I have standards." The words bordered on indignation; her whole face screwed into something resembling disgust. "He should've known better than to bring that slut to my party."

"Huh, excuse me!" My feigned American accent was rubbish. "I thought this was ma pary." I tried to lighten the mood but, really, I was dying to know what Angie had done to get this reaction out of Lu. Being this catty wasn't her thing. As I thought that, I couldn't help it and looked over my shoulder. Felipe was looking straight at us. Behind him, Marcelo and Angie were in some sort of discussion, no doubt over Lu's little display of dislike for the girl.

Almost as if he could sense my gaze on him, Marcelo lifted his eyes in my direction and this time... I did turn away.

"You know earlier… when Felipe greeted me, what did you mean about the two kisses?" I grasped for anything that would alleviate the increasingly awkward aftertaste.

Lu smiled like she was about to share some dirty gossip. "In São Paulo, you greet with only one kiss. But when we were kids, we used to say that if a boy fancied a girl, he would give her two kisses instead of one. It was like… like a marker, you know? You've been claimed, my friend," she said, poking my shoulder.

I nodded as I let the idea sink in. "We haven't spoken in years! He doesn't even know me that well."

"He knows you enough!" Her words were so heavy with insinuations, they sounded melodic. "I know for a fact he's been looking forward to seeing you again."

I shot her a look. Romance wasn't really part of my traveling itinerary. I was hoping to shed some complications, not accumulate more of them.

"Don't look at me like that! It's not my fault he's still into you."

♥♥♥

Felipe wasn't joking when he said he planned wonderful things for us to do. If I'm honest, it felt more like a two-day date. He had gone out of his way to line up all the things I loved—admiring street art graffitied all over the Beco do Batman; exploring the gorgeous and huge São Paulo Municipal Market; enjoying art and history at the Pinacoteca art gallery; sampling some tasty Brazilian delicacies in gardens turned into restaurants; paying our respects at the Metropolitan Cathedral; and having a picnic by the lake at Ibirapuera Park, watching life go by surrounded by skyscrapers as though they were the walls protecting the greenery.

It was a welcomed distraction. Being busy with him meant

I didn't have time to overthink what I was going to do with my life now that everything had changed.

Felipe was genuinely a nice guy. He was well-read, well-traveled, stupidly easy to talk to, and he was actually quite funny. When we had hooked up in London, he'd been a good kisser and an attentive lover even at twenty-one. He was the type of guy you would proudly take home to your mamma. If I could choose someone to fall in love with, it would've been him. I just never did.

He was so easy to love, though, that I caught myself reverting back to old habits—holding hands with him, letting him hug and touch me like we were more than we actually were. But I never let him cross to the other side of the friendship line. Maybe I should have. Problem was... I knew what I was doing. He was comforting, a known quantity. Like Lu, he was the one thing that hadn't changed from a time when my life was less complicated. And I knew that if I allowed it, I would be doing it for comfort; not because I had feelings for him. It didn't feel fair when he was such a nice guy.

After humoring me with a couple of days of sightseeing, Felipe asked me to meet him at some pool bar called Eight. The Uber driver dropped me off and, for a moment, I thought he had the wrong place until I saw the sign—a black circle with the number eight inside it. Eight as in the eighth ball, the black ball.

It looked nothing like the pool bars I was used to either. Sitting on a street corner, Eight's façade was almost completely open, spilling its tables and chairs onto the sidewalk in a modern pattern of stainless steel, set apart from the flux of pedestrians and cars by modern low flower boxes.

There was no sign of Felipe outside. So rather than standing around sweating like melting vanilla ice cream, I walked through the big bifolds that separated the inside of the bar from the outside.

The back wall was made of exposed brick and decorated with large prints of classic paintings. The lighting accentuating the texture of the bricks above the black leather booths and creating a warm golden glow. To the left, in contrast to the rest of the bar, was a mushroom-colored room with walls covered in pictures and a couple of black pool tables with greyish tops. Low lights hanging over them. The decor making the color of the balls brighter, inviting you to play like candy in a jar begging to be eaten. To the right was the bar—bottles covering every inch of the wall behind it, round stools dotted all the way around the front of it. Not bad at all for a pool parlor. Actually, rather classy.

I took a seat at the bar and had just managed to order a drink when Marcelo walked in dressed in black head to toe, his hair tied up in a top knot, the lower half of his head trimmed way shorter than the rest. He looked smart and crisp, his clothes fitted to accentuate his lean and tall physique. Like a Scotch bonnet wrapped in chocolate—sweet looking but would burn your face off as soon as you took a bite.

He stood behind the bartender and said something in Portuguese while looking at me, the server nodding and moving away. Without taking his eyes off me, he walked over and placed both his hands on his side of the counter, one to either side of me.

"It's Paige, right? I don't know if you remember me. We met briefly at Luciana's party."

"Sure." We both knew damn well I remembered him. The way he was looking at me made it difficult for my eyes to focus elsewhere. He had this weird aura about him, like a force field that stuns you motionless.

"Blackberry Rum Fizz?"

I nodded.

17

Chocolate irises held my gaze as his hands left the counter and picked up a mixer. His arm moved to behind his back momentarily and the mixer reappeared over his opposite shoulder, a hand grabbing it mid-air. His eyes moving from the metal cup to me on repeat as he poured things in and started preparing my cocktail.

"You're enjoying the city?"

"It sure is different. It makes London feel like a small town next to all these skyscrapers."

"Yeah… I believe São Paulo is the same size as London, but it has a third more people. It's the biggest city in the Southern Hemisphere."

I nodded to show I understood. "So, you work here?"

He shook his head. "I own it."

"You own this place?" I said pointing at the counter as if I meant the spot under my fingertip.

He laughed. "Why? Don't I look like a serious businessman to you?"

"No!" I was a little too quick to respond and my voice too high-pitched. "It's just… you look… too young to own a place like this."

His smile grew wider and smug. "What can I say…" He gave the mixer a tap to wedge it shut. "I'm the best." And started shaking it.

His cockiness hit the wrong cord, snapping me out of whatever trance he had put me in. "If a man thinks he's not conceited, he's very conceited indeed," I mumbled to myself.

"C.S. Lewis." His smugness was replaced by contempt. "Humility is not thinking less of yourself, it's thinking of yourself less."

I raised one eyebrow at him. He had batted my quote back with a quote of his own, by the same author, no less. "Sounds like you get modesty quotes often."

His smile came with a dismissive snort as he poured the

18

concoction into an ice-filled tumbler, garnished the whole thing with a slice of lemon and a berry, and placed it in front of me on the counter. His hands swiped the air, palms up, to either side of the glass as if he was putting his masterpiece on display, daring me to check it out for myself, then returned to the counter as he watched me take a sip.

The damn thing was delicious. And he knew it. His knowing smirk was even more irritating.

After a short interlude of standoffish staring from both our courts, he seemed to remember he was trying to be hospitable, and the conversation returned to its normal pattern. The same conversation I had with everyone I met after I landed. This time, though, I didn't mind answering the old line of questioning. Marcelo had this quiet, moody intensity, like the black hole you cannot help but be too curious about at your own peril. The kind that sucks you right in as soon as you get closer. He asked the same questions as everyone else, except they weren't really questions. He suggested my answers and I elaborated, almost as if he knew a lot about me already and was just asking to be polite. Felipe must have filled him in.

He never took his eyes off me. Didn't sit down to talk to me either. He remained on the other side of the bar, drying glasses, putting things away—clearly on duty.

"You have an American twang, but your English is really good." I took another sip of my cocktail.

Both of his eyebrows raised, as if he wasn't impressed. "Thanks. Yours is not bad either, Lewis." His voice dripped in sarcasm as he casually twisted a tea towel inside a wine glass.

I don't know if it was a Brazilian having the audacity to grade my English, or the name he was calling me—after the one criticism I had given him, but I laughed and almost spat out what I had just drank. The corner of his mouth lifted in a mischievous smile, while I unglamorously tried to contain the liquid from exiting my nostril and swallow it back down.

Hands touched my waist, and I turned to find Felipe smiling at me. "Sorry I'm late," he said, planting a kiss on my cheek. "I can see my boy Celo here looked after you." He winked at his brother.

Marcelo's eyes flicked between Felipe and I, hesitating over me for only a second. His face told me nothing. He placed his hands back on the counter, then looked at me through his eyelashes.

"Sure. Nice talking to you, Paige." Voice flat, emotionless.

I don't know why, but my stomach sunk. He'd obviously spent time babysitting me at Felipe's request.

"I've gotten you your favorite." He looked at his brother and nodded towards a booth on the far-right corner.

Felipe moved me out of my stool and, navigating me by my waist, made our way to the table.

"Thanks for taking me sightseeing these last couple of days," I told him after we'd finished eating.

"I'm really glad you came to visit." He pushed his empty plate out of the way, placed his elbow on the table, and leaned in towards me. Eyes intense, gentle smile on his lips.

"Me too. Although, I don't think Lu would've forgiven me if I went another year without delivering on one of my promises."

"Sounds like you sold your soul to the devil. What exactly did you promise her?"

"I only ever promised her two things. One was that we would be each other's conscience—always telling the other the truth. And the second was that we'd take turns visiting and always stay in touch."

"Was it sealed in blood by any chance?" His head turned slightly, eyebrows rising, smile teasing.

"Maybe." I laughed. It did sound juvenile. But after three years of living together and having an amazing time in London, my best friend and I were about to move back to our respective homes, miles away in opposite directions and across an ocean. The sadness we were both feeling at the time demanded a pinch of hope.

He smiled with me. "I was really sorry we stopped speaking. I kinda wish we hadn't."

A flash of silver caught my eye. Marcelo had flipped the mixer into the air and sent it spinning from one hand to the other in an arc above his head. His gaze met mine before my attention diverted back to Felipe.

"I was hoping…" Felipe's hand left the table and pushed a strand of hair behind one of my ears. His fingers lingering on my skin, running along my cheek and chin before returning to the table, "That we could spend some time together while you're here. You know… like we did in London."

"Isn't that exactly what we're doing now?"

He smiled. "Not really." His irises darted back and forth between mine, and he leaned in as if he was going to kiss me.

"Felipe…" I whispered and he stopped where he was. "Don't."

"Don't what?"

"Don't do that. It'll just complicate things."

"I like complicated." He leaned in further.

"I don't."

"Choppi?" The waiter turned up with the drinks we had ordered. Felipe turned his face to nod at her but didn't move, eyes returning to me just as soon as they had departed. She placed the glass stein in front of him. "Blackiberi room fizze?" The words were pronounced in a Brazilian accent so heavy and so fast that they blurred into one another; and a tumbler landed in front of me while I glanced towards the bar.

Marcelo was serving someone, but he was watching us.

Felipe was looking at me, his face still inches from mine, refusing to let go of the moment. But the waiter started collecting our empty plates and glasses, the crockery and cutlery clanging as she stacked them on her tray. And we both eventually conceded and leaned back into our respective seats. My gaze followed her retreat and settled back at the bar. Celo was busy making cocktails. His focus on the task at hand.

For the rest of the night, Felipe didn't bring the subject back up, but his hands were always touching me. His face strategically positioned close enough for me to kiss him, tempting me, daring me to.

Marcelo didn't come over. He stayed behind the bar, always in my line of sight. Every so often, I looked his way, and he eventually looked back at me while doing something else. I was always the first to drop my gaze.

It was a very interesting culture. Brits go out, get hammered, and go dancing. Brazilians go out for *choppinho*—little draft beer, and *espetinho*—little barbecued skewered meat, to chat and chill sitting outside busy little bars, or *barzinhos* as they call them. Because for some weird reason everything they say ends in the diminutive. Eventually, the dancing comes to them wherever they are. And let me tell you, the legends are true. Most of them can do a very decent job of moving their hips, even the blokes. They don't seem to suffer from our stiff self-awareness either. To them, it's just so natural to start dancing, even if nobody else is. I loved that. I love dancing.

It wasn't long before I found myself in such a bar with Lu and several of her friends. Felipe and Marcelo joining us later like a double act. Felipe budging the person sitting next to me to squeeze his chair in. Marcelo pulling a chair where he found space to accommodate himself and his new arm-candy.

Felipe leaned over, one of his arms going on the back of my chair, the other over the table in front of me, and planted a kiss on my cheek. "How was your day?" This was the first thing he always said to me. "You look gorgeous." And that was the second. I could be a flu-ridden mess, who had not bathed in days, and I'm willing to bet he would still say the same thing.

"Good, thank you. And yours?"

"It was alright. I'm better now that I'm here with you."

I laughed, crossed my legs, and shoved my two hands firmly in between my thighs. Felipe behaved like we were just picking up from where we left off. He always felt he could hold my hand or put his arm at the back of my chair. I had genuinely run out of ways to turn the man down softly. If he wasn't such a nice guy, my best friend's cousin, and I didn't know Brazilians don't have any concept of personal space, we would've had problems.

But saying this wasn't really fair. It was my fault. I had given him the space. I had turned up at Lu's door wanting comfort, and I had allowed him to give me some. Now, we were stuck in this hybrid limbo, where we were not together, but we behaved like we were. I'm sure he felt I was blowing hot and cold too. Allowing him to touch me, but not allowing him to kiss me. Spending time with him, but telling him I didn't want to get involved.

Don't get me wrong, it was very tempting. Felipe and I already had history, and he was not only fun to be around, but also very attractive. Why not have another taste, right? The problem was... he broke all the rules of engagement for a holiday romance. When you hook up with someone abroad, you don't expect to see them ever again. You also don't date them. It's not a long-term thing. In just over two months I would be leaving, and I didn't need any more complications when I was already running from some. What if one of us developed feelings? What if it went sour, with Lu's family being so close-knit? I knew better. More angst was the last thing I needed.

So I sat and soaked up the conversation and the laughter,

sipping my drink and keeping my hands firmly to myself. Eventually, Felipe's attention turned to someone else, and my eyes gravitated in a certain direction.

Marcelo's date was whispering in his ear. Tattooed arms crossed, head slightly bent towards the girl, he leaned back on his chair, utterly at ease, smile devilish. He looked at her like he was pondering a proposal, sipped his beer, bit his lower lip and, while looking sideways at her, nodded. Her face lit up in a flirtatious grin, his smile grew wider, and as his head lifted to take in the room, he came across me—staring at him.

His expression changed to blank for a moment. Then he jerked his chin upwards ever so slightly.

I greeted him back.

"Paige, have shots with me!?" Dani, one of Lu's friends, said from the seat at the head of the table.

"I would think twice, Dani, before pulling that party trick on an English girl. Lady P here can drink you under the table. I cannot tell you how many times she carried my sorry ass home." Lu was always quick to try and shield me.

"No, come on, let's do it. I'm up for shots."

"Alright! Ladies and gentlemen! Let's get this party started!" Felipe double-tapped the table, smiling, amused.

Across the way, Marcelo's eyebrows raised, a condescending smirk filling his face.

"It's your funeral, I'm telling y'all." Lu, both hands up in the air, denied any responsibility.

Seven trays of shots later, the bar getting louder and busier as the night went on, everybody's words and mannerisms started to slow and slur. On my way back from the ladies, navigating the wall of bodies, head down and distracted, I walked head on into someone.

"Careful now, you might look drunk." I raised my gaze to find Marcelo smirking at me.

"I'm English. We never feel drunk."

24

He stood there, blocking my way, smiling, eyes intent on me. I didn't move. We stared at each other until arms wrapped around his body, hands traveling south of the border until he grabbed them. He looked over his shoulder, smiled, and flipped one arm over to reveal the petite blonde he came with, tucking her into his side. I pushed my way through the crowd and left them to it before his eyes could return to me.

"Oh, the walk of shame! Where have you two love birds been?" a drunken Dani shouted a while later as Marcelo pulled a chair for his date, his hair now in a top knot, his demeanor nonchalant like he hadn't heard her.

The girl, smile as wide as a Cheshire cat, avoided eye contact with everyone. The neat glamour curls she had come in with looking on their way to frizzy, her dress different somehow, lipstick gone, make-up starting to look worse for wear. And the people on our table burst into shouting, whistling, and cheering, several people talking at once. Marcelo sipped his beer, leaned back in his seat, looked at his date sideways, and shrugged with an unapologetic smile. She flushed a shade of crimson, jerked her head sideways, and allowed her hair to hide her face from most of the table like curtains.

"Is this what I think it is?" I asked Dani.

"Yep! He has no shame," she slurred my way. I couldn't tell if she was amused or jealous. Whatever it was, it didn't last long; her attention diverted as soon as a new song came on. "I love this song!" she shouted and started to sing from the top of her lungs, swaying from side to side with exaggerated head flicks.

Marcelo stood up and guided his date to the edge of the dance floor. The music in a rhythm I didn't recognize. Not refined enough for ballroom; not staccato enough for bachata; lazier, rounder than salsa; using similar instruments to tango, but not the same. Three beats on one foot, three beats on the other, arms busy rotating each other around, bodies sometimes suggestively rubbing very close together. The dance was as sensual as the tango, almost as energetic as the salsa but much less structured, more rounded.

And gosh! He could dance!

They made quite a good pair. Steps in sync, her temple touching the side of his chin, one hand holding his mid-air, the other on the back of his shoulder. His firm hand and arm wrapped around the girl, telling her where to go, how to move, how to rub against him. He knew exactly what he was doing with her body, all in rhythm, without losing his step. People get this smile on their faces when they're dancing and enjoying it; he had that.

Celo rotated the girl over, arm wrapping around her middle, and dipped her towards the floor in front of him. Her body secured against his, head dramatically tipping back with a hair flip, one knee raising to rest at the side of his hips. He stood her back up and the dancing resumed.

Then his eyes locked on me over her head like he knew I'd be watching.

"What type of dance is that?" I asked Felipe without moving my gaze from the dance floor.

"*Sertanejo Universitário*. It's kind of… Brazilian country music. Wanna try it?" His hand extended out like an invitation and my eyes refocused then. I hesitated. "Come on! It's not hard to learn. I promise I'll be nice." While I mulled over the cost of looking like an idiot versus the benefit of learning a new type of dance, he got to his feet and grabbed my hand. With Dutch courage making me believe I was a dancing goddess, we headed to the dance floor.

Marcelo's expression changed when he saw us joining the swirling mass of bodies. His eyebrows screwed into a frown as if he was confused by what he was seeing, then his lips parted into an amused smile. He didn't miss his step.

Felipe made good on his promise. He talked me through the basics, warning me when he was about to twirl me, and as I picked up the steps, he sped things up. I was having so much fun, laughing so hard, that I didn't realize everyone in our group had stopped to watch us. Felipe was a really good dancer. Four songs in, he made me look like I knew what I was doing. The truth? I was just following his cues. The music stopped and our whole table cheered. The drunker they got, the noisier they had become, and apparently, *Sertanejo*-dancing foreigners deserved the loudest praise.

Celo was standing at the edge of the dance floor, arms around his date, watching us. More whistling and clapping ensued as we approached the table, but his face was a mixture I couldn't read. He didn't cheer.

"You did good!" Lu hugged me as soon as I stepped off the dance floor. "I feel like a proud mum!" Hands on her boobs, high-pitched voice, face in an overdramatic expression. "You're now officially a *Sertanejo* queen."

"Oh, calm down mother hen. I won't have a clue how to dance this when I'm sober."

"It's fun, right?"

I nodded.

"Now step aside and let the professionals show you how it's done."

Without looking at him, she reached a hand out to Marcelo, who let go of his date and walked to the dance floor with Lu. If I thought he had done a good job before… Gee! Together, the two of them danced faster, the dance taking a whole different level of twirling a girl around.

"You wouldn't think the two of them are like cats and dogs when you see them dancing like that, would you?" Felipe said in my ear over the music. His lips grazing on me, raising goosebumps, something he seemed pleased about.

27

I decided to ignore it. "It doesn't even look like the same dance!" And I made sure my tone was indignant.

He nodded.

"Can you do that too?"

A shrug followed a cocky smile. He had dumbed it down for me.

For a moment, his eyes locked on me, intense pupils cracking with electricity. His hand on my back, fingers rubbing up and down my spine just above my waist. His face incredibly close to mine.

"Come on, Pepino." Dani grabbed Felipe by the upper arm and dragged him to the dance floor. I didn't realize how much I was leaning into him, until his absence almost made me trip on my own feet. He turned around and mouthed the words, "Help me."

To which I raised both my hands and mouthed back, "You're on your own."

That was the first of many nights out. The weeks passing by so quickly, it sometimes felt like I was stuck on a bullet train— a blur of remote working during the day and partying at night. Lu had an insane social life. At times, it made me feel like I had lived as a hermit. I've never met people who liked to gather as much as the Brazilians. From Wednesday to Sunday, she always had something booked. It started sedate—a lunch or a coffee—then it became a couple of drinks, and by the weekend it was full on party mode. It was actually amazing that we found time to work in between.

Her social calendar also sentenced me to crush on Marcelo. Celo was Luciana's cousin—the perfect recipe to bump into him at every bleeding social event and gathering. Not to mention going to Eight, his bar. At least one night a week we'd end up there, and I'd end up unwillingly going in circles—me stealing looks at him; him not paying any attention to me once or ever; us barely speaking; both of us going our separate ways. Apart from my first visit to Eight, he didn't really speak to me at all, and that seemed to make my obsession with him even more severe.

That was exactly what it had become: a bloody obsession. I didn't know the guy, didn't like his cockiness or his womanizing; and, honestly, I had no idea why I was so bloody drawn to him, but something had clicked the very first night I landed. And the fact he was unapproachable, and I couldn't figure him out, had me hooked.

To make matters worse, Lu's description of his habits was spot on. Marcelo usually turned up babe in arms, and usually not the same one from the week before either. I had actually lost count of how many women I had seen him with. He was a compulsive flirt, but he never flirted with me. He never asked me to dance either.

And then you had Felipe, who seemed hell-bent in rekindling our holiday romance of millennia ago. His hands always on me, his presence always teasing, daring me to take him up on his offer. But for some reason, despite having done it before, I just couldn't cross that line, tempting as it sometimes was. If I was to tell the truth, I would have to admit that it probably had to do with the fact I was salivating over his brother. There were so many things wrong with that statement, it wasn't even funny.

It was just my luck. Because you know… in the middle of a turmoil, half running away, half trying to figure out what to do with my life, a pinch of man-whore is exactly what a girl needs in the mix. Like that wouldn't make my problems even worse! I was supposed to come to Brazil to find a way out of my drama, not find myself in a love triangle. Another complication that had no other purpose but to add to my predicament.

CHAPTER 2

Luciana

I KNEW PAIGE WAS GETTING A BIT HOMESICK. I REMEMBER FEELING the same when I first landed in the UK. At first everything was a novelty, then I started missing home comforts—food, music, people, even the sense of humor. You eventually feel very isolated and really out of place even if you speak the language. The *saudade* making you want to pack up and go home. A feeling so deep that there is no direct translation in English, giving a name to the sensation of missing something like a part of your body has been cut off.

Paige and I had lived together for three years at uni, and she had become the sister I never had. We were both only children and we bonded over that. Quite frankly, if it wasn't for her friendship, I'd probably have quit uni and come home. She had become such an important person in my life, I didn't want her visit to Brazil to end.

So, the trip to the *balada* club was just to try and make her feel more at home. I wanted her to stay as long as possible. If I was honest, I was actually trying to convince her to stay, period. I knew it was selfish, but I had missed her loads, and it was amazing to have my best friend back.

As soon as we walked into the nightclub, I knew it was the right call. When she heard all the music was in English, Paige's face lit up, her shoulders relaxed, and she started dancing at

30

the door, singing along to the lyrics. She hit the dance floor and pretty much didn't leave it most of the night. We were in her territory now. And that girl could dance!

That was another thing that bonded us. In the UK, because nobody dances until they're hammered, and most are born with wooden hips, I used to feel very conscious letting it rip on the dance floor. The better dancer you were, the more conscious other girls became, and that made you tone down on your fun so the others wouldn't feel threatened or self-conscious with your presence. Not Paige, though. Her mum had her in dance classes from when she was little, and dance had become what she did to blow off steam. So when I went clubbing with her in London, we cleared the floor. I wouldn't go out if she wasn't coming.

"Hello, love rat." I touched my cheek to Celo's to greet him with our standard air kiss. Not one to miss out on the fun, he had turned up after Eight was done for the night.

"Hey, *patricinha*. Looking good as always," he said in my ear as he greeted me.

Rather than trying to shout over the music, I curtsied.

Celo saluted Pepino, his hands signaling for something to drink. Pepino showing him his glass. "I'm going to the bar," he shouted in my ear on his way back. "Want to have a look at their menu. Do you want anything?" After he opened Eight, it had become a habit of his to always check out what cocktails other people were serving.

"Pina Colada, please."

"And your friend?"

"Rum and coke."

He gave me one sharp nod and headed to the bar. While he waited, his eyes swept the club like he was searching for something. If I knew him, he was looking for a victim. Celo was always on the pull.

Eventually, he came back—all four glasses in his hands,

giving them out according to the order he was holding them. All drinks dutifully distributed, Celo wiggled Paige's glass at me. I pointed to the dance floor; he scanned the mass of bodies until he found her. Then handed her glass to Pepino and pointed him in her direction.

This wasn't Pepino's or Celo's type of music, so they just stayed by the bar, drinking, and talking to each other. Celo doing his head and shoulder dance, Pepino just bopping his head to the music. Celo's eyes regularly scanning over the club and landing on the dance floor. Then he stopped and raised his glass. A pretty brunette in blue raised her glass back at him, giggling with her friends.

Celo wasn't a talker. He didn't bullshit or try to chat them up either. He talked with his eyes and body language. He would flirt with this girl all night, and by the time he got close to her, it would be to kiss her. As we say in Brazil, *ele chega, faz e acontece*—he arrives, does, and happens. He would bag them without saying a single word. Celo had learned to play to his strengths and cracked this formula when we were teenagers, and it worked every bloody time. I had to admit it was quite impressive.

The nightclub had filled to bulging. So whenever the floor got too crowded, the DJ would slow down the music and, not happy to dance to a ballad, people would leave the dance floor. After a few good songs, he started playing 'Sure Thing' by Miguel. I signaled to Paige that I was going back to the bar with Dani; she nodded, but she wasn't going anywhere. This was her jam. The ballad trick didn't work on her.

"Paige?" Pepino mouthed as we approached the bar, one of his palms facing up. I pointed to the dance floor. Both he and Celo looked across until they found her. With the floor emptying, she wasn't hard to spot.

Paige was dancing by herself—eyes closed, soft smile on her face, her head thrown backwards in pure pleasure, lips singing the lyrics. Her curves moving to the exact beat of the music; hands rubbing up and down her body, raising up to the ceiling; ponytail occasionally being flipped over her head. The whole thing lit by the club lights in different colors. Dressed in her fitted cargo pants, one-shoulder top, heels and big hoops, she looked very pretty. Add a sexy song and sensual moves, and everyone was staring at her. It was a bit mesmerizing when she did this. Maybe it came with years of dancing, but whenever one of her favorite songs played, she transported herself to this higher level of bliss. It was like she was in her own little bubble. Everyone in our group stopped to watch her performance.

"She just dances like that—by herself?" Celo leaned over to say in my ear.

"This is her jam. She would dance to this anywhere and not care," I shouted back.

He smiled, pulled a face, then nodded. But like everyone else, he watched her, mesmerized by her moves and abandon.

Halfway through the song, a guy decided to dance with her. He tried to hold her hand; she pulled it away, waved no, turned her back to him and carried on dancing. He was crowding her bliss. He, however, took that as an invitation to dance at the back of her, so she turned around put her hand on his chest and gently pushed him away while dancing. Paige wasn't fazed, but in Brazil you don't touch a woman without her permission. Here, a bloke can catcall a woman but if he touches her, he invites every family member and friend to step in and intervene.

And that was just what Pepino and Celo did. By the time Paige pushed the guy away, Celo had handed me his drink and walked onto the dance floor, standing in between her and the guy, his back to her. He didn't do anything, didn't say anything, just stared at the guy unblinking. That's what he used to do at his bar too when someone started causing trouble. He wouldn't start it, but if he had to, he would have no beef getting into a fight. When he was younger, Celo was a scrapper—acting out his frustrations and issues by fighting anyone and anything, so he was no shabby fighter. And Pepino had always been his wingman; I wouldn't mess with either of them when they turned.

With both our boys staring at him, the guy felt so uncomfortable, he raised his hands up as if to say he didn't want any trouble and left. Behind them, Paige had stopped dancing. Once the guy was gone, they both turned to her, Pepino holding one of her hands, touching her face, and speaking to her; she nodded.

Then she looked at Celo and held his gaze for a second. I don't think she realized he was here. He gave her one nod, then walked back towards me, her eyes following. It was just a second, but I could see it.

Pepino walked back to us, and Paige stood on the dance floor looking back at the bar. Celo took a sip of his drink, but he was also looking at her. The chorus started playing and she started swaying. Her eyes closed and she turned her back to us and continued dancing. When the song finished, she came back to the bar.

And once I had seen it, I couldn't unsee it. Every so often her eyes would gravitate to Celo, stay a second and move on. It was always brief, but it was definitely there. And he would look at her too, hold her gaze for the second and move on when she did, but I couldn't tell if his gazing was just a response to her looking at him. He was very good at keeping himself in check.

We had just ordered a new round of drinks when Khalid's 'Better' started playing. Celo walked to the brunette in blue, touched her hand, and she smiled at him giving him permission. He pulled her a couple of steps away from her friends, spun her around turning her back to him, his face touching the side of hers, and started dancing with her—his arms slowly wrapping around her middle. By the end of the song, he had kissed her.

Paige saw it too. She looked at her drink for a little while and twirled her straw around the glass a few times, then started talking to Dani and turned her back to the dance floor. We danced and had more drinks, but for the rest of the night she didn't look at them.

When it came time to leave, we all walked outside together. While we waited for Pepino to find us a taxi, Celo came over to say bye on his own; his motorbike was parked on the sidewalk across the street. He said his goodbyes to everyone else then came to talk to me.

"Where is your latest neck piece, love rat?" He snorted and looked away. "Do you even know her name?" We always teased each other about our conquests. It was our little inside joke.

He shook his head, buying into my teasing. "But I have the rest of the night to find out."

"You're disgusting." He grinned the most indecent grin. "You're going to wear that down like a pencil, you know that?" I twirled my finger pointing at his crotch. He laughed. "Please tell me you're at least wrapping it up and having safe sex." Just as I said it, Paige walked up behind me. His eyes went to her, his face turning serious, then came back to me.

"Of course. I'm not stupid. But thanks for the birds and the bees talk, Mom. See you later, yeah?" He kissed me on the cheek, nodded at Paige, and walked away. When he got close to the bike, the girl in blue came to him. He handed her a helmet and mounted the machine. She mounted behind him, clearly familiar with being on the back of a bike. The thing thundered to life, and they were gone.

"Should he be riding? Is he not over the limit?" Paige said behind me.

"No. He doesn't really drink. But since we're talking about him... do you have a crush on him?"

"What???" She pulled a face, almost offended with my question. "Yeah... like I want or need to become another notch on his bedpost." Her head shook, incredulity twisting her expression.

"In his defense, he doesn't date any of them."

"Exactly. He just uses them."

"And they use him. That brunette couldn't wait to get on the back of his bike!"

She rolled her eyes at me. "Of course you'll defend him, he's like a big brother to you." And before I could return to my original question, she walked away.

CHAPTER 3

Paige

"Rise and shine, sunshine!" A beam of light flooded into the room, making me surface from sleep.

"Go… away!" I groaned, trying to hide under the covers like a vampire hiding from the sun. But my shield disappeared from over me; Lu had opened all the curtains and taken all my covers.

"Come on you, they will be here by 6 a.m. We need to be ready otherwise we'll delay everything."

My head was pounding. "I wish you'd told me that yesterday. I wouldn't have had as many shots." I rolled over and tried to muster the willpower to get up. What I got was the feeling I was going to be sick.

"I told you we were going today." Her voice was high pitched. She stared at the mirror, placing dress-clad hangers over her body.

"You didn't tell me we had to be up by 5 a.m.!"

Apparently, it was *Semana Santa*—holy week—and the Easter holiday meant that we were joining the droves of people fleeing the city and swapping concrete for seaside. According to Lu, this was her family's tradition. Every year, they would collectively migrate for a week.

"Who's coming anyway?"

"Mum and Dad, us, Aunt Marisa and Uncle Rogério, Pepino, Celo, and Freddie."

"Can we not have a lie-in and make our own way there later?" I begged, starfished on the bed, staring at the ceiling, trying not to feel sick. My sleepy hangover face should have been self-explanatory.

Lu turned around, an unimpressed expression on her face. Sometimes she expected me to know things she had never told me. "Ilhabela is a four-hour drive away *if* we miss all the traffic, otherwise it's double. Are *you* gonna drive the eight hours if we get stuck in the madness?" She waited a millisecond for my response. "No, I didn't think so. This is our one big family holiday. My mum and Auntie Risa organize it every year." She grabbed my ankles and rotated me until my legs were off the bed. "Attendance is *not* optional. Even Celo has to turn up. It's the price we must pay for our luxury upbringing. And honestly"—she leaned onto the bed, both her hands on the mattress, face intent on me—"I would *not* like to be on the wrong side of those two." Then she pushed herself off. "We overslept. They'll be here in an hour, and you still need a shower. So get up and move, flower."

"That rhymed. Are you writing poetry or something?"

"Woman!" Lu turned around exasperated. "We don't have time for this! Get your ass in that shower! You reek of *cachaça*! I can't let my parents see you like this; they'll think I'm a bad influence on you."

"That's because you are."

She scowled at me and pointed her finger towards the en-suite. I made a show of dragging myself off the bed.

Two big four-by-fours turned up right on time. Strange, as Brazilians are always late, but nobody wanted to get stuck in traffic. By the time we made it downstairs, Marisa was shoving Freddie—Felipe and Marcelo's younger brother—into the second car, the boot of the first one open, waiting for our luggage.

"Mom's scared of Celo's driving." Felipe laughed.

"Bullshit. Rogério doesn't wanna drive," Celo responded from inside the car, Ray-Bans holding his hair back like a hairband.

"And they'd rather go in the more civilized car than stay in this one with you driving. Precisely what I said." We all laughed. Marcelo shook his head. Felipe loaded my bag into the boot, then Lu's.

"And where are we going again?" I asked Felipe.

"Ilhabela." The boot started beeping and closing its door. "It's an island off the coast of São Paulo, about four-hours' drive away from here, depending on traffic."

"Put some music on!" Lu tapped Felipe's shoulder as we each picked a door to get in. He instantly pulled out his phone to connect the road trip playlist; Lu and I both got in the back.

I had gotten so used to being surrounded by skyscrapers that I had forgotten how claustrophobic they actually are. As soon as we left the city center, buildings rising like imposing stalagmites in our rear view, the sky looked wide and open. As if we had broken free from the concrete jungle canopy and could now see all the blue.

Well… I say concrete jungle, but São Paulo was actually surprisingly green. It never ceased to amaze me how I could bump into a humongous rubber tree in the middle of a metropolis. It was such a bizarre experience to stand next to one of these silent old giants surrounded by congestion, horns, and sirens. If they could talk, I'm sure they would have some amazing stories to tell on how the city's flux had changed and expanded like ripples around their little islands of nature.

And if the flora wasn't enough to awe you, there was always the fauna. As Lu used to say, "You have squirrels, we have *micos*." But our squirrels looked like little English gentlemen next to the gangs of little monkeys that loved steeling your food as soon as you weren't paying enough attention. Maybe my furry fellow Brits had also heard Churchill's call to keep calm and carry on. The only respite here being that the *micos* weren't everywhere and anywhere. The furry mafia didn't travel far from the greenest parts of town.

While the city had gone flat around us, it still took us ages to escape its grasp—the roads getting wider and wider until we were on a five-lane motorway, the landscape slowly turning to green. It vaguely reminded me of the motorways at home—laned and manicured. Then the scenery started to change, going from very flat to long inclines and hills—big geometric cutouts and a sequence of tunnels allowing us to drive through them.

As time ticked by, the chatter and excitement slowed down, the holiday enthusiasm wore off, and the hangover kicked in. One and a half hours in, both Felipe and Luciana had fallen asleep. Felipe with his head against the window, Luciana with her head on my shoulder.

I caught Marcelo's eyes in the rearview mirror—he looked at me for a second, then at the road, then back at me. But apparently, he fell no need to make conversation. This was him, though—the silent assassin type.

Brown eyes gazed at me, the road, me, the road.

No words were spoken. If an expression or gesture would do it, he wouldn't say a thing. He didn't waste time talking about the weather either, almost as if his words were too precious and he only used them when extremely necessary. He barely spoke to me, but our eyes met often.

Celo shifted in his seat, sighed, tilted his neck from side to side until it cracked.

Me, the road, me.

A few more times his eyes met mine in the mirror—holding

my gaze, going back to the motorway, then coming back to me —but we continued in silence until a phone started ringing through the car's sound system, Marisa's name popping up on the dashboard screen, waking up Felipe and making Luciana jump.

"*Alô?*" While he had laughed and listened to our conversations, this was the first time he'd spoken since leaving São Paulo. Marisa's voice boomed through the car speakers in Portuguese, something about Freddie. Celo agreed.

"How long have I been asleep?" Lu lifted her head from my shoulder, my top strap marked on her cheek, her eyes still looking small.

"Thirty to forty minutes." Marcelo's voice was flat. He responded to Lu, but his eyes were on me through the mirror. "We're going to stop at the next service station. Freddie gotta go pee."

"How old is Freddie?"

Felipe looked back at me, a sleepy smile spreading across his face, and he reached out and squeezed my ankle. "Six. Mom says she doesn't know where he came from." He snorted. "Lucky little bastard gets spoiled rotten by all of us."

By the time we got back in our cars, caffeinated, fed, with joints stretched, and Freddie's energy levels depleted, Marcelo's Ray-Bans were on his face, and I could no longer tell if he was looking at me in the mirror. Lu and Felipe, now awake, chatted nonstop.

The road got greener, trees and lakes appearing between the bends, hills looking taller, and the motorway getting narrower. Two hours later, we went around a bend and the sea was right there—glittering in the sun in a dark shade of blue, surrounded by tall hills. The look of everything changing with its presence—the roads getting even smaller, the vegetation more tropical, palm trees appearing everywhere. It teased us, peaking in and out of view, and it made us wait in the queue to the ferry. But once it reappeared, it was turquoise green, and the smell of fish and salty water hit us with the cool breeze.

When we arrived at the house, it was early afternoon, and the sun was scorching. "I'm jumping in the pool!" A very excited Freddie ran out from the car, already in his underpants, and disappeared through the greenery, Rogério in hot pursuit. A few seconds later we heard the noise of screams and water splashing.

"How come the little one speaks English?"

Lu shrugged. "He goes to the same school we all did."

Clinging to the side of a hill, from the road, the house looked like a cream L-shaped block with weirdly shaped windows. But once you opened the front door, a floating staircase took you down to a sitting room completely fronted by glass, making you feel like the swimming pool, gorgeous sea views, and surrounding hills were part of a giant mural. The pool was lined by alternating palm trees and sun loungers. Inside, it was all rectangular shapes and windows. All of them placed to frame the panoramic scenery as well as to maximize the light. To the right there was an open plan kitchen. A long narrow window ran on the wall behind the dining table, surrounded by smaller rectangular ones, framing the views horizontally and vertically as if they were pictures hanging on the wall.

It was quite simply jaw-dropping.

I stood at the floor-to-ceiling windows staring at the scenery. Freddie divebombing into the pool repeatedly now dressed in a float suit.

"It's gorgeous, isn't it?" Marta, Lu's mum, stood next to me. "And sometimes peaceful too when Freddie goes to bed," she whispered, leaning into me. We both chuckled. "Ilhabela is mostly a nature reserve. Apparently, there are over forty beaches and three hundred waterfalls here. It's so beautiful."

"This place is surreal!" I just couldn't get over the view.

"When Lu said you were coming to visit, Marisa and I insisted that you came for Easter. This is the best part of any trip." She wrapped her arm around my shoulder and gave me a quick hug. Marta had always been lovely to me.

"Where do you and Auntie Marta want everyone, Risa?" Marcelo stood at the top of the stairs with Felipe, bags piled by the door.

"Marta and Pedro, Rô and I, Freddie, Felipe, Lu, Paige, and you." Marisa indicated the order of the rooms with her hands. "I know you like the one at the end of the corridor, and I need to create a buffer around Freddie."

Rogério was watching Freddie, Lu was helping her mum unpack all the food, Pedro was stocking up the drinks' fridge, Felipe and Marcelo were delivering everyone's bags to their rooms, and Marisa was dressing up the sun loungers, opening blinds, opening windows, and ventilating the house. They were a well-oiled machine, everyone jumping straight into their roles like busy little ants. I joined Lu unpacking the food.

"So… what do you think?" She smiled at me.

"Now I know why you dragged me out of bed." I laughed.

"One of the days we will do a trail, so you can see the waterfalls. We'll go to the beach too, proper holiday stuff. It will be the best week ever!"

As she said that, Marcelo reappeared and started to help Pedro put the drinks away in the fridge. His eyes passed over me for a second, then he carried on as though he hadn't noticed I was there.

"Come on, let me show you your room." Lu grabbed my wrist and towed me up the stairs and down a corridor with several doors in a line. Every room had a balcony with sea views and an en-suite, the wall facing the sea made of floor-to-ceiling glass. That was why the house was L-shaped, so everyone could get a view. "Make yourself at home. I'm just gonna finish helping Mum, then we can chill." She winked at

43

me and left. I walked out onto my balcony to take in the scenery.

It didn't take me long after I landed to realize why Lu was so homesick when we were at uni in London. Being a cynic, if I had all these perks, I would want to come home too. Who wouldn't want to live in perpetual sunshine and party mode? My best friend also got on with her family, especially her parents, which is a lot more than I could say for myself. Melancholy washed over me just thinking about it. Maybe I wasn't a cynic. Maybe I was just good old-fashioned jealous.

I started to unpack my bag.

It had taken me a week to find Ryan Miller and his construction business on Facebook; and another week to muster the courage to call him.

When I first got hold of him on the phone and told him I thought I might be his daughter, the line went dead. He flew out to the UK on the next flight and all hell broke loose. He was beside himself. Now married and divorced with two other daughters, he couldn't believe my mum had never told him. His American accent still echoed in my head to this day. I'm sure it echoed in our neighbors' heads too. The clashing of the two titans had torn our house apart. Part of me was glad my father actually gave a shit and wanted to know me. The other felt slightly sorry for my mother and wondered if hunting him down had been such a good idea. Even now, I'm not sure they were arguing just about me. Over two decades of unresolved business and pent-up emotion had floated to the surface like a rotten corpse. They haven't spoken since.

"That was a long sigh." Luciana was standing by the door.

"What?"

She laughed. "Your eyes did that funny thing they do when you go to fairyland." Her eyes converged into her nose.

"Shut up. I don't go cross-eyed." The sadness showed in my voice. I sat on the bed. "If you must know, I was just admiring the view." I exaggerated the arc of my gesture towards the balcony to make my point.

Lu's eyes narrowed. She sat next to me, her head tilted ever so slightly. "Are you sure you're ok, flower?" Sometimes she noticed things you didn't even think she had seen.

"Yeah, of course, everything is fine. Don't be stupid! I'm in the most beautiful place, with a bunch of rich people paying for everything, and my pale backside will soon be seeing the sun. Why wouldn't I be fine?"

"Oh, I don't know… maybe because your world has just imploded, and we haven't really spoken about it since you landed?" She watched my face for a moment to gauge if she was on the right track. "Is this about your mum?"

Through the floor-to-ceiling window, the sea sparkled under the sun. Little crests of white forming on top of the biggest waves, boats slowly crossing the expanse of bluey-green in the distance. "You know what really gets to me? When I was eighteen, I asked her if there was any chance that we could find him. She looked right into my eyes and told me she didn't know who he was." I pointed at the pale green discs that graced my face. "Right into the eyes that look exactly like his. Do you know how cold and calculating you have to be to lie to someone's face, looking straight into the evidence of your lie, and behave like you're telling the absolute truth?"

Lu reached for one of my hands and gave it a squeeze. "I still can't believe Kate knew who he was."

I stared at our hands. "And rather than showing a shred of repentance, she decided to give herself the right to resent me for going through her things and contacting him without speaking to her first. Resent *me*! Like she wasn't the one who lied to me my whole life!"

Lu's eyebrows raised in the middle; she gave my hand another squeeze.

"'Gosh! You are just like him! Stubborn and short-sighted

like a mule!' she told me, mid-argument, when she tried to convince me to give up traveling and follow through on my dancing career. She blames him for everything. Never mind that he wasn't the one that lied to me, or that I wasn't even going to his country, this was all my father's fault. And here's the kicker… My mum has never mentioned the likeness. My entire childhood, she knew who he was, where he was, and I'm pretty sure she secretly kept tabs on him, but she never said a word about him. And now, every time she's pissed off, she can't say it enough. Like a cruel joke, rubbing in my face the secret she has kept for so long just because she's angry. Our outbursts became so intense that, by the time I left, we were barely looking at each other's faces. I haven't spoken to her since I got here. The woman that had been my point of reference all my life is now closer to a stranger." My eyes filled up, my voice trailed off and broke.

"That's really shit, flower. I'm so sorry. You two were so close." We were quiet for a moment. "What about your dad? You said he's nice?"

I wiped the tears off my face. "Ryan calls me regularly, wanting to help and make up for lost time. You know, he has two other daughters. I have two half-sisters, met them via video call. We have the same hair, but different colored eyes. Ryan was very supportive of me traveling here. He's even given me money to help keep me afloat. My mother would kill him if she knew. I think he hopes I'll go to Colorado to meet my sisters. You know… it's funny how you can recognize yourself instantly in someone you've never met. I knew he was my dad when I saw his picture. The tall American stranger with caramel hair and green eyes that remind me so much of my own."

"That's good, no? At least there is a silver lining—you always wanted a bigger family. Now you have one, and you can start building a relationship with him and your sisters."

Lu stared at my eyes for a moment. "Did you ever ask her why?"

A head shake. "She was too busy being mad at me for finding out the truth she didn't wanna tell me herself."

"I'm sure it sounds very black and white now, over two decades later, but things rarely are black and white, flower. It's all just a big blob of grey. Maybe, at the time, she had good reason?"

"Are you defending her?" Indignation showed at my edges.

"Not at all. I'm just saying that something must have happened. Something big. Something that made a twenty-year-old woman think that being a single mum was a better option than telling the father of her child she was pregnant. And it would be good for you to know what that was, before passing judgment. That's all."

Lu watched me for a while longer, then bumped her shoulder into mine. "Just think about it, ok? Now, we're not crying today. Come on, let's go to the pool and chill for a bit. Show me your bikinis."

"What?? What is this? Show me yours and I'll show you mine?" I laughed.

"Show me your bikinis." She gestured with her hand for me to hurry up. I walked to the chest of drawers and took a couple of them out.

"Oh no! You're not wearing these."

"Why not? What is wrong with them?"

"Look at the size of this!" Lu held one of my bikini bottoms in front of her face. "You can parachute with this from my balcony, and you'd still land on your feet!" Before I could say anything, she dragged me to her room. A pile of bikinis was on top of her bed. "Now, let's find you something more appropriate. Try this one." She picked a green printed set and waited for me to change.

Living with Lu in London, I had learned that body privacy didn't exist in her dictionary. As far as she was concerned, 'we had the same bits, so there was nothing she hadn't seen before'. The first few weeks we house-shared had me screaming and covering myself every time she burst into my room. Now I had just given in to the inevitable.

My reflection glared at me from the mirror. "I feel naked."

"Nonsense. You look amazing! This one is a much better fit."

"Your uncles are here! I really don't think this is appropriate." The bikini was tiny. It rode up my backside showing my arse cheeks, with little bows hanging for dear life at the side of my hips via thin, tasseled strings. Two long triangles covered my boobs and tied behind my neck like a halter neck, giving me a killer cleavage.

"If you think this is bad, just wait till you see Auntie Risa's. That cow had two kids and looks better than both of us. It's so unfair. Here, use this as a cover-up until you get to the pool."

As they say, when in Rome…

By the time we got outside, the inflatables were out. Freddie trying to leap from one to another like a frog. The parents were nowhere to be seen, but Felipe and Marcelo were on the loungers. Both on their phones, both in shorts, tees and Ray-Bans looking like fraternal twins—one handsome, tall with short blond hair; the other sexy, less tall, with long, dark hair. One you could marry, the other would ruin your life.

Lu and I picked a couple of loungers on the other side of the pool, Felipe getting up to come see us, Marcelo behaving like he hadn't seen us at all. As the good Briton that I am, I stripped, keen to get some much-needed vitamin D and bask in the sun like a cat.

Felipe stopped in his tracks and stared. Marcelo's head lifted; he stopped texting.

For a second, nobody said anything, and all I could hear

were Freddie's squeaks against the inflatables. I knew that bloody bikini was a bit much.

Lu walked over to Felipe and pushed his chin up, closing his mouth. "You're welcome. You can thank me later." I'm still not sure if she was talking to him or me.

I made a bid for distraction. "Lu, can you put some sunblock on my back?" And sat down to hide my arse cheeks.

"I'll do that!" Felipe volunteered, grabbing the bottle off me and squirting sunblock on his hand before anyone could protest.

On the other side of the pool, Marcelo stood up, dropped his phone on the lounger, took his Ray-Bans off, and stripped to his swim shorts. Brazilian swim shorts were a lot smaller and tighter than British ones—just a wide band across the guy's hips, wide enough only to cover the bare essentials.

"Freddie, *vem cá*." He waved at the frog while walking towards the greenery and taking some distance from the pool. He was no bodybuilder, but his body had clear definition, imposing, lean, and solid. Covered in tattoos, tanned, bad boy vibes smeared all over him, he was pure punishment.

Freddie joined him on the grass. They looked at each other, Marcelo nodded, and they set off running. Celo doing a flip, Freddie shouting, "Jeronimo!" and cannonballing into the pool. The splash making its way all the way to us.

"There goes the peace and quiet." Lu rolled her eyes.

As soon as they resurfaced, Marcelo grabbed Freddie and catapulted him upwards so he would fall back into the water, screams of joy echoing through the house.

"Celo! Stop encouraging him! I can hear him all the way from here!" Marisa shouted in English, reappearing on one of the balconies, conscious that her sons were the source of all the racket.

"Did you hear that, Freddie?" Celo shouted back, water up to his chest, combing his hair back with his fingers, the muscles on his arms and shoulders gaining more definition. "Stop having fun on your vacation."

♥♥♥

Ilhabela had this very organic vibe. Every building a different color, a different style, sometimes modern, sometimes colonial-looking, nothing matching. The sea at night looked like a vastness of black, with the lights of the mainland on the other side of the bay glittering in gold. The hot humidity in the air and seawater smell clinging to your skin like a water spray. The town was crawling with people for the Easter holidays.

Felipe draped an arm around my shoulder as we walked to the restaurant. "You look so hot in that dress," he whispered in my ear. Luckily, we didn't have far to go.

As we all sat down to eat, I couldn't help but notice the difference. I was an only child, my mum was an only child; she never married and had no living parents; so family meals were always just a table for two for us. But sitting here with Lu's family was like sitting in the middle of a beehive—everyone talking at once. My mother and I had definitely missed out on something being just the two of us.

It made me think about how it must feel to be completely on your own. And for a moment, I almost felt guilty to have left my mother all alone. Before our blow up, she was a very good mum to me. And despite the fact we weren't talking, she had messaged me several times since I'd landed, trying to check in.

"So when do you go to China, Felipe?" Marta cut through the moment when all conversations had fallen silent, everyone turning to join the one discussion and momentarily speaking in English for my benefit.

"In the next couple of weeks. Dad wants to secure some investment for some big projects. I'm going to make sure it all goes according to plan." On the other side of the table, Rogério nodded.

"You are staying there for quite some time, aren't you?"

"One month."

"Are you looking forward to it?"

"I was, but now not so much." He reached for my hand on top of the table. "At the minute, I would prefer to stay put here." And he looked at me like he was giving me my cue to confirm his story. Everyone looked at our hands.

Marcelo stopped flipping his butter knife.

"I'm sure you'll have a great time. I heard China is amazing," I said, pulling my hand away from his. The table falling into an awkward silence apart from the low murmurs of Freddie's YouTube video.

"That is a big step for you in the business, isn't it? More responsibility." Lu's mum continued, politely breaking the silence and diverting the topic.

Luciana tilted her head, eyes widening and returning to normal size while looking at Felipe. He shrugged.

Celo caught my gaze and held it for a second, before going back to behaving like I wasn't there. Even though he was sitting diagonally from me, he barely looked at me or spoke to me the whole time we were out. He didn't comment on anything I said, didn't join any conversations I was part of. It was like I wasn't worth the effort.

And yet... we had these moments where he'd just stare at me like he was trying to read my thoughts. His quietness and distance only making him more magnetic.

It was painful.

"What about you Paige?" His mum, Marisa, caught me off guard.

"Sorry, Marisa?"

"It's ok. Call me Risa. Everybody does. How long have you been in São Paulo now?"

"About a month."

"Are you planning to stay?"

"Yes, she is!" Lu jumped in; everyone laughed but Marcelo.

He followed the conversation with his eyes but didn't comment. His face bearing a slightly bored expression.

"Not really sure. I promised my father I would visit him in Denver."

Celo fidgeted in his seat. Looked down at his hands and resumed flipping the butter knife on the table.

"Denver, Colorado?" Marisa spoke to me, but her eyes were on Celo.

"That's right."

"Great place. We skied there a few times."

"I was hoping you would still be here when I get back from China, though." Felipe, again, trying to make it sound like we were something we weren't.

Celo looked back at me, the muscle in his jaw moving. Beyond him, Marisa was looking at the three of us.

I smiled but didn't answer.

After dinner, Marta wanted to show me the church. So we all walked through the cobbled streets until we reached the square. White and blue, *Igreja da Nossa Senhora D'Ajuda*—the Church of Our Lady the Helper—stood all lit up at the top of a fair few steps. Colorful bunting radiating from the cross at its top and covering the sky at its front like sunrays; big, crucified Jesus at the bottom of the steps. A yellow mustard building beyond it on the other side of the square, looking like a French château. The whole thing was very colonial-looking. Apparently, it was built when the Portuguese colonized Brazil. My mum would've loved it.

We made it back to the house with Freddie asleep on Felipe's shoulder. Everyone had fallen quiet—tiredness, booze, and a full stomach catching up with us all after our early start. Freddie had the best deal. He could fall asleep whenever he wanted, there was always someone to carry him home.

For a few minutes I sat on my bed trying to decide what to do. But with the whole meaning and value of family still playing on my mind, I video called my mother.

"There you are!" She sounded tired. Her face was squashed against the cushions on our sofa at home.

"Yes… here I am."

Her eyes narrowed trying to see the room behind me. "*Where* are you?"

"Ilhabela, on holiday with Lu's family." We hadn't spoken in over a month. I was still upset she'd lied to me, and it felt awkward, but I had to admit I missed talking to her. "You should see this place, it's amazing." I walked onto the balcony and changed the view on the camera. "It's dark now, but the views are insane. This darkness here"—I added my finger to the camera shot, pointing at where I knew the water would be —"it's the sea. They also have those colonial-looking buildings you like." I flipped the camera back to me.

"Lucky you! What time is it there?"

"Eleven o'clock." The penny dropped. They were three hours ahead in London. "Shit, Mum. I'm so sorry I woke you up."

"It's ok, poppet. I wanted to talk to you. You haven't responded to any of my messages. You know I worry something will happen to you and I'll have no idea where you are."

"You can see where I have been on Instagram, Mum. Plus…" my voice dropped in volume, "we weren't necessarily on good terms when I left."

"I know. But this standoff between us is rather ridiculous, don't you think? I'm your mother for crying out loud! I can't believe we're not speaking because of a stupid diary I should've binned years ago."

There it was. "Excuse me?" I stared at her in disbelief. There was still not a single ounce of repentance or regret anywhere in her demeanor. "Is this really how you want to play it, Mum?"

"What do you mean, poppet? It's the truth, isn't it? Had you not gone digging in my things and not found that stupid diary, we wouldn't be here. Would we?"

I laughed, but it tasted bitter. "That's an unfortunate choice of words, don't you think? Bearing in mind that the real reason we're not talking has nothing to do with your diary and everything to do with the fact *you lied to me* my whole life. Why don't you try taking some responsibility, Mum? *Stop* minimizing what happened. Admit that you lied to me and maybe then we can get past this shit."

"Paige Lancaster! That's no way to speak to your mother!"

"You know what, Mum? I'm not doing this." I flicked my finger back and forth between her and me. "Until you're prepared to take some responsibility, I have nothing to say to you."

"Paige…" She started saying something, but I cut the call. Her tone was wrong, like she was about to tell me off.

The urge to scream came over me, but I didn't want to alarm anyone in the house. So I screamed with all my might, nails digging into my palm, limbs going stiff—silently. Like a horror movie on mute.

The phone started vibrating. I looked at the screen, but I already knew who it was.

"Stop calling me!" I gritted my teeth at my mother's name, then launched it from the balcony on to my bed inside the room. It landed with a thud. If I could, I would have thrown it against the wall instead.

A few more times it rang while I took deep breaths on the balcony and tried to curb my anger. Fury eventually giving

54

away to sadness. The disappointment no longer making me cry, just making me tired.

The breeze was cool, calming. I stood there for a minute, looking at the view—lights glittering in the distance; the darkness turning to green closer to the house; palm trees swaying in the breeze, their leaves creating a comforting sound. The pool lit in a blue so inviting, I mentally noted to have a late dip at some point.

As I turned to go back inside, I saw him.

Marcelo was sitting in the deck chair on his balcony. He must've been there when I walked out of my room and, distracted, I hadn't noticed.

"I'm sorry, I didn't mean to disrupt your peace. I didn't see you there."

He raised one hand as if to say it was fine but didn't say anything.

It dawned on me that he had probably heard my whole conversation and watched my hissy fit. And I became very conscious that I was wearing some skimpy silk pajamas Lu had given me as a gift to keep me cool. I had also leaned over the banisters for several minutes, probably flashing my backside all over his general direction.

"Good night then."

He offered a slow nod, his eyes closing and opening slowly with the movement of his head.

I walked back into my room, closed the door, the curtains, walked across the room and switched the lights off. The plan was to get into bed, but I was too agitated to sleep, and the curtains were only light; I could see the light from his balcony through it. So I walked back to the door, but stayed in the corner, in the shadows.

He sat there for quite a few minutes, rotating a silver box between his fingers like he was deep in thought. Then he got up, leaned against the rails with both his arms straight—head dipping towards his chest, moved his neck from one side to another like he wanted to crack it, and stood up straight. He looked at the view for a minute, his shoulders slumping with something that looked like tiredness. Then walked into his room, the light switching off a couple of seconds later and my room being plummeted into darkness apart from the moonlight.

I'd crushed on this guy for weeks, and now he was going to sleep on the other side of my wall.

When I came down the next morning, everyone was already having breakfast. The smell of coffee hitting me as soon as I got to the end of the corridor. Sunlight filling the room and making the whole house warm despite all the doors being open.

"Sleeping Beauty is finally awake!" Lu shouted when she saw me coming down the stairs. "Mum and Risa want to do the tourist thing with you."

"The tourist thing?" I sat next to Lu.

"The boys will look after Freddie, and we'll go shopping and sightseeing."

"Sounds nice."

"I'm really looking forward to it." Marisa was bringing more food to the table. "I love my boys..."—she touched Rogério's, Freddie's, Marcelo's and Felipe's head to indicate who they were—"but I'm ready for some female energy and girl time."

"We've been coming here for so long, you know. It will be nice to go around with fresh eyes." Marta also sounded excited.

Lu looked at me and raised both of her eyebrows, a mischievous smile on her face.

"Yeah, yeah. You two don't make me stupid." Rogério pointed his finger at Marta and Marisa. He sported a stronger accent than his children. "Just an excuse to get rid of us and drink cocktails in the beach. Right, Pedro?"

Pedro nodded, laughing.

"Want some coffee, Paige?" Marisa hovered a coffee pot above my cup.

"I'll take some tea, please." It was like the needle had jumped off the vinyl. Everyone's head snapped up, some confused, some with eyes wide open.

"Sorry Paige." Marta's lips pulled over her teeth in an awkward smile, her eyebrows bunching together. "We don't have any tea. I forgot you don't drink coffee."

"That's ok." I smiled; Brazilians rarely drank tea. They didn't have milk in it either. "Don't worry, I can have orange juice."

"That, we have." Felipe grabbed the jug and filled my glass.

The town center was only small. Ilhabela was better known for its beaches and ecotourism than its cultural scene. But we went back to the white and blue church to pay our respects, the hill and steps we had to climb to get there making us pay for our penance. The yellow chateau-like building turned out to be Ilhabela's old jail and courthouse, now converted into government offices. We wandered through cobbled streets looking at quaint, artsy shops and buying hippie things we didn't need. But by the afternoon, we were sitting at a bar, drinking cocktails on the beach.

"As you can tell, Ilhabela isn't quite the cultural hub." Marta giggled and sipped her Kir Royale. Her eyes telling me that Rogério was right—all along, the end goal had always been to sit on the beach sipping cocktails without them.

I giggled. "It's perfect. I'm having a great time."

"I'm seriously considering buying a place in Ubatuba," Marisa told Marta. I had no idea where Ubatuba was.

The two sisters were so similar but also such polar opposites. Marta was warm and approachable; Marisa was warm but had an edge. The two of them looked like two movie stars in their uber classy holiday clothes, big sunnies and sun hats.

"Are you?" Surprise filled Marta's voice. "But we have been coming here for so long! It's our tradition!"

"I know…" Marisa grimaced like that was the reason why she hadn't passed the consideration stage. "But there is more going on there. It's more cosmopolitan, you know?"

"Isn't the point of coming here exactly to come away from the city and reconnect with nature and our roots? No tech, no servants etc." Lu was nibbling some of the prawn croquettes we'd ordered.

"True…"

"Would Celo ever let you sell the house?" Marta joined Lu in nibbling the croquettes.

"Never!"

"Could he really stop you selling it?" I was curious. Anything with his name on it piqued my interest.

"He could. He owns half of it," Lu added in passing.

"What do you mean, he owns half of it?"

"He inherited his half from his grandfather." Lu said it so blasé, like she was talking about a pocket-watch rather than a seven-bedroom villa with sea views. Sometimes the difference between her life and mine couldn't be more glaring.

And then the details clicked into place. Marisa called Celo her son, but Celo never called her Mum. Lu had said Risa had two children, not three, and she had never called Celo her cousin or said he was Felipe's brother. She didn't say *our* grandfather either. When I met him, he had been sarcastic about not looking like Felipe. I thought it was aimed at me, but now I realised it might have been a comment on the fact they weren't really related.

"Sorry, I'm confused. I thought Marcelo was Marisa's son."

"He is my son. But I'm not his biological mother."

"So he's adopted?" I tried not to sound too curious.

They all looked at each other.

"Not quite," Marisa finally responded. "We never officially adopted him." She could tell I was even more confused. "Our families have been intertwined for three generations. My dad and Celo's grandfather were best friends. They started the business together and had a lot of assets as partners, including the house we have here. Celo's mum abandoned him when he was six and… when his grandma fell ill, she asked me to look after him. She knew I loved him like my own."

"That's a nice way to summarize it, Auntie Risa." Lu lifted her glass as though she was offering a toast. "If I had to explain it, we'd be here till tomorrow."

"Thank you!" Marisa raised her glass back at Lu and they both took a drink.

"His mother abandoned him when he was six?" I thought about Freddie. He was the same age as Freddie when it happened.

"Uh-huh. Can you imagine? That's like me abandoning Freddie. Awful stuff. I brought him up since he was eight. And to me, he's my son, not hers. But anyway… let's not bring the conversation down talking about such a sad thing. He'd hate to know we're sitting here talking about him with sad eyes too." Risa reached out and touched my arm. "Please don't mention anything to him, Paige." Her voice was whiny; she was pleading. "He doesn't like talking about it."

I nodded. "I'm not surprised." But, of course, I wanted to know more. Unfortunately for me, it was very clear the topic was off the table.

"So…" Marisa finished her cocktail and signaled the waiter for another round. "Changing the subject on to more interesting things, are you seeing anyone, Lu? Come on, spill the juicy goss."

"Now, why would I do that, Auntie Risa? I'm only twenty-three."

"So you're just playing the field a bit, I get you. It's better to do it now than after you marry."

"Yeah, but please don't go gaining yourself a reputation. Do it with some decorum." Marta also finished her drink.

"Did you see the new guy they hired for the sales team recently? The tall one? I went to see Rô in the office the other day and had to focus not to dribble. I mean, I'm a happily married woman, but dear Lord! He's a *fine* specimen."

"Auntie, you talk like you dissected the poor bastard and pinned him to a board like a rare butterfly!" We all laughed.

They were such a tight-knit family, more like close friends really. Some of the stuff they talked about I wouldn't dare say to my mother. But here they were—sisters, aunt and niece, mother and daughter—talking without embarrassment about sex, good-looking men, beauty, their plans for the future, and the difference between single and married life. I had to admit I felt jealous of their openness. It didn't come as standard for us Brits.

"What about you, Paige? Any holiday romance?" Marisa narrowed her eyes, shimmied her shoulders, mischievous smile on her face.

"Yeah! How do Brazilian men compare?" Marta's eyebrows raised twice. She too wanted in on the gossip. If only I had some to share.

"She would if Felipe gave her a break!" Lu answered before I could.

"I have noticed that! He can't take his eyes off you, hovers like he's waiting for something." Marta skewered a shrimp and casually added a nail to my coffin.

"It doesn't help that they kind of had a thing when he came to see me in London." Like mother, like daughter. The two of them talking about me as if I wasn't sitting right there.

"Is he doing the overbearing thing?" Marisa was looking at Lu.

"He's doing the overbearing thing." Lu confirmed with a firm nod.

Risa looked at me then, sipping her third cocktail. "Judging by last night, I gather you don't feel the same about him?"

Now, how on earth was I supposed to tell a mother, who just took me on an amazing holiday, that I didn't like her son?

"No, she doesn't." For a minute I was glad Lu had answered the question and gotten it out in the open. "I think she fancies Celo, though." Then I kicked her under the table. "What? It's true!" Her voice went an octave higher. "You know you would if you could." Then she dropped down to matter-of-fact tone.

"Not like that! I don't even know the guy! We barely speak!"

"Felipe can be very persistent." Marisa, eating the cherry from her drink, seemed completely unfazed by Lu's disclosure. "But if the attention is unwanted, tell him straight and tell him to back off. Until you do, he'll keep trying, and he has the patience and obstinance of a hunter. I mean, I love my boy, but sometimes, it's not his most attractive quality." Her eyes widened, her eyebrows raising up. "And Celo… everyone seems to notice him. I'd be surprised if you didn't. Although, honestly, he's so moody and crabby all the time, I don't know what makes him so appealing to people. I'd love to know how he chats up women. He hardly says anything!" Another sip of her cocktail.

"Maybe *they* chat him up." Marta offered her theory.

"No, I've seen him do it a few times." Lu was eating the pineapple slice from her cocktail. "He doesn't do small talk, so he just flirts with them from a distance. Does his moody stare thing. By the time he gets anywhere near them, he just has to kiss them. Sometimes they even come to him! Like he's thrown out the bait and wheeled them in. He did it the other night when we went out. It's quite impressive, actually. Sometimes he'll kiss them before he even introduces himself! I don't know if I'm more impressed at his flirting skills or the fact it works every time. I don't call him love rat for nothing, you know!"

Hearing her say it made me shrivel. The guy was a sleaze, and I couldn't take my eyes off him like an idiot. I didn't know if I was happy that Marisa didn't have a problem with me not returning Felipe's affection, or if I was sad that the one I had a crush on was the worst kind. Someone needed to knock some sense into me.

"It has always been like this, you know, even when he was in elementary school. All the girls used to give him the puppy eyes and he thought they were disgusting." Marisa laughed. "Then he turned fifteen and found out what girls can do. It has been a revolving door of them ever since." The waiter placed our new drinks on the table, Marisa signaling for him to set another round in train. "I told him he needs to find a good woman and settle down, now that he's knocking on thirty."

"Auntie Risa, he's only twenty-seven!"

"That's knocking on thirty to me. Anyway, do you know what he told me?" She leaned forward in her seat, eyebrows raised, face like he'd offended her. "That he likes it the way it is. And that as far as he knows, he made *all* the women he went out with very happy *for the night* and none of them ever complained." She paused to let it sink in. "I love my son, but his moral compass does *not* point due north." Closing line delivered, she leaned back in her seat and drank some of her new poison of choice. Her pose couldn't have looked more 'classic film'. I could see it in black and white.

"Sister, he's single, young, and he likes women. And as long as he's not hurting anyone, what is so wrong with that?" That surprised me. Marta always seemed so sweet and traditional, but here she was, advocating for womanizing and tarthood.

"What is wrong with that, my dear sister, is the reason why he does it. Why he lives this way. You and I know it has nothing to do with just being young and liking sex."

Marta's head tilted, her eyebrows raised, lips puckered together; she nodded. And I became even more intrigued, dying to know what they were talking about. But asking would be an admission that I was more than interested. It was also strange to hear someone talking about Celo like they were so close. He always seemed so unapproachable.

"What about you, Paige? What is your take on this? Do you think people should play around?" Marisa flipped the whole conversation three hundred and sixty, three pairs of eyes settling on me like I was under a heat lamp.

"I think everyone should do what works for them, as long as they're not hurting anyone."

"So you play around too?"

"Gosh sister, don't put the poor girl on the spot like that!" Marta came to my rescue.

I laughed, but it was out of awkwardness rather than entertainment. My face burning with embarrassment. "I play too. Just not to the same extent. I find the one hook up per week a little extreme."

"So you disapprove of Celo's lifestyle?" Marisa looked at Marta, her open palm pointing towards me like my opinion reinforced her point.

"It's not my place to approve or disapprove of anyone's lifestyle. I can only tell you that I wouldn't like to be one of his playthings. That wouldn't work for me. But if, like Marta said, nobody is getting hurt, then maybe he's going out with women who are in the same boat as him?" I shrugged.

"Oh, she disapproves. But it's only because she's interested." And I wished my eyes could sew Lu's mouth shut.

She, however, was completely oblivious to my stare. "Wait… he lost his virginity at fifteen?" Her voice had the higher pitch of nosy curiosity.

"I think so, but he never confirmed or denied it."

A gasp. "With whom? Do we know?" Lu's tone went an octave higher. Interest making her lean forward on her seat.

And I genuinely wished for a noose. I don't know if it was the alcohol speaking or if the three of them had made a pact to make me cringe. Their openness no longer looked attractive. I'd be mortified if I found out someone was talking about my sex life so casually over drinks like this.

"Angela Gurgel, I think. She has always been all over him like a rash."

Lu pulled a face like the idea made her sick. "Now, *that* is what I don't see the appeal of. That man needs to improve his taste in women."

"Don't quote me on it. He never confirmed it. He never tells anyone anything. We all know he has a different date every week, but he never talks about them, never brings them home to me. Keeps his cards very close to his chest, that one."

"I think it's the tattoos, you know," Lu added, finishing her drink.

"Yeah… I don't get that either. He looks like a comic book! I told him, he gets anymore, and I'll disinherit him. His back and arms are already covered, he doesn't need any more."

"You know he doesn't need the money, right?" Lu's head was tilted to the side, nodding like she was stating some universal truth.

"I know. But I had to try. Ladies… I don't think we can drive back after this one. Well, after the last two really. I'm going to have to call the cavalry. Who wants to bet what Rô will say when he sees us here?"

For what was left of the afternoon, I watched Lu plot and

plan a night out. Apparently, two days was her limit. Longer than that and she started getting socializing withdrawal symptoms, some of which included boredom and irritability. The result was that after dinner in the old town, Lu, Celo, and I were to walk to a place called Estaleiro Bar, while Felipe taxied everybody else back to the house.

The streets were busy, full of holidaymakers and bars, music and chatter coming from all corners creating a chaotic mixture of sounds. Facing the seafront, the Estaleiro looked like a giant cage from the outside. But once you walked through the mesh metal doors, the inside was cozy, modern, and colorful, with wooden deckchairs and tables scattered everywhere, plants hanging from exposed brick walls.

"Going to the ladies," Lu announced as soon as Celo put four drinks down on our table.

Since our conversation at Eight, he and I had never been left unattended. And for some weird reason, the idea of being left alone with him made me nervous. I don't know why I let it bother me. He never paid any attention to me, and I sure wasn't going to cross that bridge.

As expected, although he was sitting right next to me, he ignored me completely; sipping his drink and scanning the room systematically until his head had turned the full hundred and eighty and his eyes landed on me.

They landed and they didn't leave. His stare was so intense, I started feeling self-conscious.

"Your eyes are a crazy shade of green, aren't they, Lewis?" he blurted out of nowhere. "They're almost white. Like they're made of water and the dark rims around them keeps the water in."

"Lewis is not my name."

He smiled, his eyes unmoving, and started rotating the base of his drink on the table.

"I get that a lot. But nobody has compared them to water before. That's a first."

Another smile. Eyes still fixed on my face.

"Yours glow red in the sun." It dawned on me too late that I might be giving away just how much attention I paid to him. He had made one comment then said nothing else. And I, feeling self-conscious, had felt the compulsion to fill the silence with oversharing.

His eyebrows arched upwards, lips pressed together, and he nodded like he too had just realized I was paying attention. His eyes didn't waver. He looked at me like he was analyzing my face.

I fidgeted in my seat and adjusted my dress, squirming under his scrutiny, and his eyes dropped to my cleavage.

"You're not gonna find any water down there," I told him when I felt he had stared at my boobs for too long.

His eyes flicked back to mine like he was snapped out of his reverie, lips parting into a coy smile. He looked away, down to his hands, then back to me. "Sorry. I seem to get distracted by round soft things." The words were an apology, but his tone was not. Like he was just stating a fact.

Brown eyes sunk into me as if they had teeth, and he smiled, unapologetic and devilish. His flirting hitting me like a cobra strike—for a split second I was taken by surprise and stunned.

"Could've fooled me with all the sticky insects you seem to date." Now, why on earth, out of everything that could come out of my mouth, did I have to go and say that?! Something, please, swallow me whole.

He let out a boisterous laugh, amused. "First of all, I don't date them. Second of all, if you must compare them to an insect —*you*, not me, may I add—I don't like sticky insects. I prefer *Tanajuras*."

66

"Tana-what?"

"*Tanajuras*. Google it." He sipped his drink, and his attention reverted back to elsewhere.

"I love this song! Celo, dance with me." Luciana's voice came from behind us. She grabbed his hand and took him to the dance floor.

While they were off doing their thing, I Googled what he'd said. It took me a couple of tries, but I found it. Tanajuras were a type of leafcutter ant. Bigger than usual, they have generous bulbous behinds that are considered a delicacy in some regions of Brazil. It's also the slang Brazilians use to describe a woman with a generous derrière.

"Ants!?" Felipe almost made me jump out of my skin. "Didn't mean to scare you, sorry. I'm assuming the full drink is mine." He pointed at one of the beers on our table.

I nodded.

"Yes, that one is mine, or yes to the ants?" He grinned.

I tipped my chin upwards to signal the glass in question. "Yes, that one is yours."

He sat down next to me, took a sip, then leaned in, forearms resting on his thighs, both his hands touching the side of my legs, just above my knee.

"Now, why the hell would a good-looking girl like you be googling ants on a night out? That's an interesting mystery." His smile was sweet and flirtatious.

"Felipe…" I wiggled my knees free from his hands.

He leaned away from me ever so slightly. "Wow! Is it really that bad to be the center of my attention?" His words sounded insecure, but his tone was teasing.

"We both know it isn't."

He levelled his face to mine—eye to eye, nose a couple of palms away—and pulled at the end of one of my curls. "Then why are you trying so hard to resist my charm?"

"You are very charming, indeed." I squeezed both his forearms. "But in a few weeks, I'm leaving. So, what's the point?"

"Are you looking for a husband?"

His comment took me by surprise, and I'm sure shock was momentarily stamped all over my face.

His face got closer. "Then why can't we just have some fun while you're here? Like we did when I came to London."

"Fun that lasts a few months is called dating."

"Always so black and white… Sometimes it's more fun to be a little grey, you know?" His eyes narrowed and he opened a devastating smile. "But that's ok. As it happens, I'm quite happy to date you." His hands were back on my legs, rubbing circles with his thumbs.

"You don't really want that, Felipe. In less than two months, I'll leave, and we'll be where we were after you came to visit. You and I know it doesn't work." I pushed him back slightly and readjusted the way I was sitting so his hands let go of my knees.

"You're breaking my heart!" His exaggerated and overdramatic expression made me laugh. He could be such a drama queen when he wanted to.

"You're funny, I'll give you that. But it's just not a good time for catching the feels."

His face changed to serious. "Lu told me you found your dad." He took another sip of his drink. I took one of mine.

"I did. Not without damage."

"Sounds complicated."

"It is."

He leaned back in, smoldering. "Another reason to let me show you a good time. I promise I'll make you forget it all." His brown eyes rolled down my body as if they were a cat scratching a post, and he bit his lip.

It was so cheesy! I burst out laughing. "Oh right, Casa Nova. Keep it in your pants, will you!?"

He leaned back into his seat, hands and face expressing mock horror. "That was my best flirting! You smashed my heart and my ego. Thousands of little pieces, all glittering on the floor. You should feel guilty."

"Should I?" I was still laughing. "Does that cheesy shit actually work for you?"

His face twisted into an offended expression. "You should feel *extremely* guilty, then you should vow to make me feel better no matter what." His fist balled like he was giving a *Brave Heart* performance. "I have a list of how you could do that, by the way," he added as a second thought, then leaned back in—one hand on the back of my chair, the other on the table—and whispered in my ear, "I haven't forgotten that thing you do with your tongue."

I pushed him away and smacked his arm.

"Getting cozy already?" Lu had finished dancing.

"I'm trying! But she's bruising my fragile male ego."

"Ha! There is nothing fragile about your ego, Pepino."

We drank, danced, and laughed some more. Luciana flirted outrageously, and the boys sabotaged her mercilessly, running commentary on her flirting as if they were film directors.

"Leave her alone! Let the girl flirt to her heart's content!"

"Thanks, flower," she said, shooting an accusatory look at both Pepino and Celo.

"Oh! You think we are mean?" Felipe tapped the table twice then waved his hand at his partner in crime.

"She started it," Marcelo concurred. His eyes blinking once to emphasize his nod.

"Once, Celo and I went out; Celo was cozying up to this blonde when Lu arrived late with her entourage. She thought it would be funny to pretend she was Celo's girlfriend.

Strutted over and threw a bit of a scandal. It earned Celo a smack across the face from the blonde."

Marcelo nodded, shooting Lu an unimpressed look.

"How was I to know she was going to crack one across your face?" Lu's voice was high-pitched, pretending an ignorance it didn't carry.

"Come over here, girlfriend, let me give you a kiss and be all over you like a rash. That'd work a treat for your flirting tonight, wouldn't it?" Celo said, leaning into her as if he was about to kiss her.

"Don't you dare!" Her hands shot up as a feeble barrier between the two of them. "I don't want to get the romping rabies you've got."

"Come now, *patricinha*, don't you behave like you're some convent virgin. Everyone here knows damn well you're the femme fatale."

That was a fair comment. If anything, Lu and Celo had a lot in common when it came to their love lives.

"The difference between you and I, my friend, is volume. I haven't bedded half of the city. I'm not a rent-a-hunk like you are."

Marcelo scoffed, smiled, and his head and eyes rolled over to the other side of the bar, ending with an incredulous head shake.

We had a great night and danced loads, but Celo never danced with me. Every so often, though, our eyes would meet, linger for a minute, suspended in the moment and fading out the conversation, then depart back to the noise and chatter. It was as though he was watching me, especially when Felipe touched me.

And as per usual, Felipe's hands were never far from my body, rubbing circles, touching, keeping me close. It was all a bit much for someone that was supposed to be just a friend. But he did it with such naturality and tenderness, claiming on the history we shared, that it was hard to be rude about it and tell him where to stuff it.

There was something comforting about it too, I can't lie. And, I guess, I enjoyed the attention; because I probably let him get away with it when I shouldn't. Allowing him to claim an intimacy I wasn't really prepared to give him. But it felt nice, soothing.

CHAPTER 4

Paige

CASCADING FORTY METERS DOWN A VERTICAL ROCK FACE LIKE A bride's veil and landing in a crystal-clear pool of water, *Cachoeira do Gato*—Cat's Waterfall—was quite something.

To get there, we had to wake up stupidly early, charter a yacht, ship to the other side of the island, bathe in insect repellent, and hike for an hour and a half through forest, wooden bridges, and streams. But it was so worth it. Everyone was so hot and relieved to get there, that we all stripped to our swimming suits and got into the natural pool. Marisa, Rogério, Marta, Pedro, and Freddie had stayed on the boat. None of them too keen to face the forest and its infamous mosquitos. Marisa claiming that if Freddie got bitten, her life wouldn't be worth living.

Before heading back, we took turns taking pictures. Marcelo managed to stand right next to me without touching me at all. Felipe only too friendly and keen to hold on to me whenever he could. Then Lu found a place where the stream was shallow and ran over some smooth rocks. She asked me to face the waterfall and sit like a Japanese geisha in the middle of the stream with my back to her. Apparently, my bum looked great at that angle. I pulled the pose, and she asked me to look sideways. When I did, Felipe was standing at the edge of the water, Marcelo right behind him.

While Lu took the picture, Celo stared right at me—his eyes softened, the shadow of a smile playing on his lips. Then Felipe turned to talk to him and he readjusted his posture, crossed his arms. When he looked back at me, his face was different.

"That's going to be *the* shot," Felipe shouted.

It took us another bath of insect repellent and a further hour and a half to trek back to the beach. When we got back on the boat, Marisa and Rogério were nowhere to be seen.

"Where are Mom and Dad, Freddie?"

"They went down there." He pointed below deck. "Daddy said he needed to help Mommy with the bikini." He continued coloring his book, Marta and Pedro sipping their glasses of wine and giggling.

Marcelo laughed. "So *that's* the real reason you all wanted to stay on the yacht."

"No comment," Pedro replied before giving Marta a passionate peck on the lips.

"Yeah… then she says she has no idea where the kamikaze pilot came from." Felipe pointed at Freddie, also finding it amusing.

Lu looked at me, knowing what I would be thinking. "What did I tell you? Brazilians have no shame." She laughed.

When they finally resurfaced from below deck, Marisa was giggling, Rogério trying to grab her backside as she walked up the stairs, until they saw us. Then they composed themselves and finished walking up the steps like they were just admiring the boat decor. Lu wasn't lying about Marisa's figure or her bikini. They were both way smaller than mine.

"You guys are back!" Marisa started the conversation, completely ignoring the fact we all knew they had been downstairs getting frisky. "How was it?"

"Not as much fun as you guys seem to have had."

73

Marcelo's face was full of innuendos. "How is it that we get to trek the jungle, while you're having all the fun?"

"It's called marriage, son." Rogério winked at him.

Marisa ignored them both. "Paige, how was it?"

"It was beautiful! We took a lot of pictures."

"Lu took a really nice one of Paige," Felipe was quick to volunteer.

Luciana scrolled through her phone, found the picture, and handed it over to Marta, Marisa coming to sit next to her to have a look.

"That does look amazing." Both of Marta's eyebrows were raised.

"It's a really nice shot, Lu. Your figure does look stunning, Paige." Marisa was nodding.

Felipe went over to have a look, then gave me the thumbs up, one eye closed, his lips puckered together. All of them talking about my arse like they were talking about what they had for breakfast. I could feel my cheeks starting to burn. But I don't know what else I expected; Brazil is a nation famous for their *bumbum*, after all.

Celo leaned against the cabinet, crossed his arms, and looked out into the sea as though he wasn't interested. "Are we raising anchor or what?"

The crew took us around the archipelago and stopped in a spot deep enough for diving. From the boat, the sea was even more inviting, the water so turquoise and crystal clear that it was impossible to resist the urge to jump right in. The more civilized got in through the swim platform at the back of the boat; but Marcelo and Felipe climbed as high as they could before jumping in, fists pumping each other once they resurfaced.

"Come on you two! Don't be such marshmallows!" Felipe shouted at me and Lu from the water.

We climbed to the top as they swam around and got back

onboard. While we tried to muster the courage to jump—shitting ourselves—they made their way back up. The two of them waiting behind us for their turn.

"Before I'm forty would be nice." Marcelo was getting impatient, his eyes a brighter chocolate with adrenaline. We didn't move, so he jumped, doing a flip on the way down. Felipe followed.

"Oh, screw health and safety." I grabbed Lu's hand and we both jumped.

Plashing… burbling… the sea complaining about the water displaced by our sudden entry. All my senses disappearing into the muffled noises and suspended sensation of being underwater, all of them returning as soon as we resurfaced.

Lu was laughing and screaming. "That was amazing!"

Marcelo was the closest one to me. I looked at him while trying to stay afloat, giddy from the excitement.

"You might need to…" His hand raised out of the water and pointed at me.

I followed his pointing. My bloody bikini top was at my neck, my boobs had made their great escape during the dive.

"Oh gosh, sorry!" I tried to readjust everything.

Both his hands came out of the water, a gesture designed to show me he didn't mind, amusement and mischief smeared all over his face. "I didn't say I wasn't enjoying it."

He swam away as soon as he said it—strong arms coming in and out of the water in a front crawl, while Lu and I paddled like little dogs back to the platform.

"I want to jump! I want to jump!" Freddie wanted to be part of the action.

"Come on then," Marcelo shouted back at him, still in the water, "but do it from here." He pointed to a much lower ledge.

He didn't have to wait long. Freddie ran to the spot and jumped without a second thought, hitting the water like a little brick wrapped in a life jacket. He surfaced, smiling, thrilled that he could do what the adults had done, his face quickly turning into a grimace.

"You alright there, bud? Water went up your nose?"

"Uh-huh."

"Next time you need to keep your mouth closed and hold your nose like this." Celo's hand came out of the water to show him how it was done.

Freddie's frown didn't linger. "Again!" His excitement creating a splash.

"Ok. But I will jump first, then I'll swim here. You wait for me, ok? Then you can jump. And don't jump on top of me while I'm swimming. You have to wait until I tell you to jump, ok?" Marcelo showed a tenderness to his little brother that he didn't show anyone else.

We all jumped once more; this time I held on to my boobs so they wouldn't run away. Celo swam back to the lower ledge so Freddie could jump. The boys jumped a few more times—each dive becoming more elaborate, each of them adding more flips and turns mid-air—before the crew decided it was time to move on. Probably scared someone was going to break their neck.

On our way to the next stop, a pod of dolphins followed the boat, jumping and having fun just like we had done. Freddie going berserk, Rogério having to hold on to him by his life jacket so he wouldn't fall overboard in his excitement. If I was honest, I almost followed suit. They were such incredible creatures! Able to swim at a speed that was hard to comprehend when the most I could do was breaststroke. Eventually, the pod lost interest and disappeared once we got close to shore and slowed down. There were other boats zipping around that made for better entertainment.

The crew kitted us all with life jackets, snorkels, and flippers, and pointed us in the direction we should be swimming—Marcelo, Felipe, and Lu forgoing the jackets. We all had a go, even Marisa and Marta who tended to enjoy watching everyone else frolic from the safety of the boat with glasses of wine. Freddie bobbing up and down on the waves like a jellyfish.

It was so beautiful. The place was crawling with fish and the occasional turtle, gracefully gliding in the vastness of blue, so used to human presence that they all just carried on going about their business. While I joined Freddie bobbing on the surface, Marcelo, Felipe, and Lu, being snorkeling veterans, dove deeper. Lu's figure looked amazing underwater, and it was my turn to take pictures of them. Marisa kissing Rogério underwater, Pedro hugging Marta, Freddie with his goggles on his head floating on the surface; Lu diving down, Felipe and Marcelo diving around; a selfie of Lu and I in our goggles, and Marcelo sitting on the sand at the bottom like he was meditating. He could hold his breath for quite a while; it was impressive.

While I was taking the pic, he looked up at me, his hair looking like an octopus around his face. He stared at me for a while, then kicked the sand at the bottom and came up to the surface. His body looking even more defined, lean, and graceful underwater, cloaked by air bubbles.

Marisa and Marta were the first to return to the yacht, followed by Rogério and Pedro. I went back and sat on the swim platform, my legs in the water. The noise of the waves hitting the side of the boat in a comforting, relaxing rhythm, the yacht itself rocking in a lazy motion that unknotted all my muscles and made me sleepy. Lu was floating in the waves, staring at the sky. Towards the shallows, Felipe was trying to teach Freddie how to snorkel and hold his breath.

Then Marcelo resurfaced from diving, just a little way from me. He stayed in the water for a minute, cleaning his goggles, just floating and watching me, not saying anything. To escape the scrutiny, I started going through my pictures. He swam to the platform and sat close to me but not next to me.

"Are the pictures any good?"

I went to give him the phone, but he leaned in to see them while I held it, so I started flicking through them.

At some point, he stopped looking at the phone and started looking at me, his breath feeling warm on my shoulder.

I stopped swiping through the pictures and turned to him.

His eyes took in my face, my eyes, my lips, very close to me but not close enough, not touching me at all. Making a tingle run up my spine and letting me know that I very much wished he did.

Then his gaze shot to behind me; he sighed and leaned back to where he sat. We both watched as Lu and Felipe swam back to the boat, Freddie being towed by a strap on his life jacket.

"You guys ok?" Felipe placed a hand on the platform between me and Marcelo.

"Yeah, Paige was just showing me her pictures. There are some nice ones of you and Freddie." Marcelo's voice was flat. He rested his forearms on the top of his thighs, legs in the water, body swaying with the boat, hair still dripping.

"I want to see! I want to see!" Freddie was maneuvered around and pushed back onto the swim platform. He sat on my lap, and I showed him the pictures, Lu leaning on the platform with her elbows to see them too, her body half submerged.

"That's a nice one of Auntie Lu. Don't you think, Freddie?"

"Uh-huh."

"You don't say uh-huh in English, Freddie. It's yes or no," Lu tried to correct him.

"Uh-huh." We all laughed. Lu shook her head. Brazilians very rarely said yes or no. It was normally 'uh-huh' for yes and 'uh-uh' for no. Freddie was the king of this habit.

"I think someone is getting a bit tired after all this

swimming and excitement. Don't you think, Auntie Lu?" I gave Freddie a squeeze; he didn't move, seemingly comfortable on my lap.

"Oh good! You're all back." Marta's voice came from behind us. "Let's have a break and have some food."

The rest of the afternoon went a little slower, everyone taking it easy after eating and having a bit of a siesta until Freddie caught his second wind. Brazilian music was playing in the background. The sound of chatter and laughter coming from the upper deck where Marisa, Marta, Rô, and Pedro were playing cards. And splashes and screams were coming from the water where the boys were entertaining Freddie. Lu and I were lying on the seats on the lower level sunbathing, when a shadow blocked the sun above me, and I opened my eyes to see what was causing the interference.

Celo was standing over me in his swimming trunks, fresh out of the sea.

His hair was haphazardly thrown sideways, water dripping from it, down his long torso and falling next to me but not on me. The hairs on his legs flat against his skin, thighs just the right thickness.

A condescending smile spread across his face. He knew I had checked him out.

"I'm making cocktails. Do you girls want anything?" He ran a hand through his hair, and my eyes, betraying me and making me lose all dignity, went from his hands to his arms, to his V line, and down to his swim trunks.

Sweet baby Jesus! That did not conceal his bare essentials, not from this angle.

"What're you offering?" Lu responded, without moving the hat she had over her face.

"Anything you want." He answered her, but his eyes were on me, his pupils huge. First on my face, then lazily scanning down my body, returning my once over of him. I felt like he'd

79

stripped me naked. It wasn't a stretch; this bikini left very little to the imagination.

"I'll have a Pina Colada, thank you."

"Sex on the Beach, please." Oh, for fuck's sake! I literally said the first thing that came into my mind.

He smiled, his eyes shifting to the horizon, tongue licking his lower lip. The bastard was enjoying my verbal diarrhea and toying with me.

Lu removed the hat from over her face and his face changed to blank. "I'll see what I can do." His tone didn't hint at anything. He clapped his hands, rubbed them together, and walked away.

Lu looked at me, raised her eyebrows. "Sex on the Beach? Really?" A naughty smile creeping over her face.

"It's the name of a cocktail. Take your mind out of the gutter." I closed my eyes, trying to ignore the pun and the fact he could probably hear us.

"Yeah, right! Lie to me cause I like it, Paige Lancaster. I know damn well what cock tail you'd like to taste. I can cut that tension with a bloody knife."

"I don't know what you're talking about." I hoped to God the sexy bastard couldn't hear us and resisted the urge to look and check if he could.

Luciana put the hat back on her face and lay back down. "Still, he has his uses, as annoying as he is."

Felipe and Freddie came back on to the boat. Freddie running past us, Felipe sitting down next to me, his skin cold against my leg. A few minutes later, Freddie came back with our cocktails. A serviette ripped in the shape of a bow tie stuck to his neck with some sort of liquid.

"Pina Colida… and Kisses and Beach. I'm a *garçon*, Auntie Lu. Can I take the order?"

"Where is the menu? I need to look at the menu first." Lu moved the hat from her face to play along.

"Ok." He ran off saying something in Portuguese; the only thing I understood was Celo's name and menu. Not long after, he returned with a handwritten napkin.

Olives ----- R$15
Nuts ----- R$15
Pina Colada ----- R$40
Kisses on the Beach ----- R$40
(Keeping it PG for Freddie)

"You not coming for a dip?" Felipe asked, voice husky, the hand that was closest to one of my hands rubbing circles on my fingers. I shook my head, removed my hand from under his to hold my cocktail.

Lu, the traitor, lay back on her side of the seat and placed the hat back on her face, refusing to rescue me.

Felipe leaned sideways, resting one hand on the other side of me, pinning me between his body and his hand. "Come for a swim with me." Eyes smoldering full of bad intentions.

"Freddie, *vem nadar*." Marcelo's voice came from behind us. Something about swimming.

"*Não...* Celo, *minha gravata*." Freddie's chubby little fingers touched his bow tie.

"*Eu te faço outra, vem*." Tattooed arms lifted Freddie off the ground; he stepped off the back of the boat and put Freddie down on the platform. "*Pronto? Um... Dois... Três... e... já!*" Both of them cannonballed into the sea, and all we could hear was Freddie's excited screams, splashes, and laughter.

"Please, come for a swim," Felipe insisted, his eyes trying to lock mine on him.

I moved his hand from the other side of me and sat up. "No, sorry. The seawater is making my hair go funny." His expression turned into disappointment. "I need the loo."

Locking the door behind me, I was glad for the solitude and the shade. A quick look in the mirror confirmed that my hair had indeed started looking like straw. I wrapped it up in a bun on top of my head, pulled some wispy bits out so my face wouldn't look like a giant egg, and unlocked the door. Couldn't force myself to go back to Felipe, so I walked upstairs instead.

The island from here looked like a mass of green with colorful dots here and there, and a multicolored line at the shore. Now lying down on the seat, Felipe was in full conversation with Lu.

Marcelo was pushing Freddie back on to the platform, then palms flat on it, he propelled himself up and sat next to him, legs still in the water, his back fully covered with an eagle tattoo. Arms protectively held on to Freddie while he wiped the boy's face and tidied his hair. Talking and smiling, Celo's expression was the softest I'd ever seen on him. Someone once told me that you know when a person is in love with you because they look at and touch your face, and they will have a soft expression when they gaze at you. That's what Celo had—the love look. He adored Freddie.

Then Marisa went over and waved them back into the boat, Marcelo carrying Freddie back in. The sun was setting, and we were heading back to shore.

On the way back to the house, Lu had created a WhatsApp group with all of us in it and shared all her pictures. The forest, the waterfall, the boys in the natural pool, our group pictures, a few selfies... My bum did look amazing in that shot. I went ahead and shared all of mine too. After dinner, we all went to bed early. Everyone slightly sunburned and tired from a day of excitement and shenanigans. I had to add extra conditioner to my hair after all the salty water.

As the house felt silent, I couldn't sleep. Thoughts of the day filled my mind. The importance of family. How nice it was to be part of one that was so close-knit like Lu's. What I had lost not being able to be part of a bigger one. I felt so lucky to be here enjoying all these things. Never thought one day I would be on a tropical island spending the day on a yacht. Funny where life had taken me.

And, of course, Marcelo.

Who didn't talk to me, didn't touch me in any way, but whose eyes were always meeting mine. For someone who never bothered with me, he stared at me a lot.

I picked up my phone and started going through the pictures. Then clicked on the group details and found his number. His profile picture was a photo of him setting fire to a cocktail. His update said '*de férias pra páscoa*' with a link to Eight's Instagram page. Quick Google translate and it meant 'on holiday for Easter'. His personal Insta was private.

With everything so quiet, I could hear someone moving in the room next to mine. At first, I wasn't sure if it was Lu or Celo. Then a door opened and closed, and someone walked past my door very quietly. It had just gone 3 a.m. Apparently, he couldn't sleep either.

I waited a few minutes but didn't hear anything else. Curiosity got the best of me, and I left my room too, tiptoeing and leaving my door ajar so nobody would hear me. When I got to the end of the corridor, I could see him in the pool. Celo was doing laps—swimming to one end, diving under to turn, and swimming back—the glass preventing any noise from coming into the house.

Quietly, I walked down the staircase and went outside. He was swimming like a proper swimmer—cap on his head, goggles, and all. I watched as he did quite a few laps, then resurfaced at my end of the pool with his back to the door, moved his goggles to the top of his head, and stopped the timer on his watch.

"I didn't know you're a swimmer."

He jumped like I'd scared him and turned to face me, eyes huge. "What you doing here?"

I shrugged. "Couldn't sleep." Then I walked to the side of the pool, sat down on the ledge, and put my legs in the water.

Marcelo stood there, looking at me as if he was trying to decide what to do with my presence. Body immersed up to his waist, swimming cap on his head, he looked like an athlete. His eyes went to the door, back to me, then to the door as if he was waiting for others to join us.

"Everyone is still asleep."

His gaze focused on me and didn't move. Feeling the heat of his stare, I averted his eyes and started tapping the liquid with the sole of my foot, circling my legs so I created patterns in the water.

Celo pulled the cap and goggles off his head—his hair spiking in all directions—lowered himself underwater, and dove to me, taking a seat on the ledge like he had done on the boat—close, but not next to me. He wiped his face and combed his hair back. The goggles and cap had left a mark on his skin.

"I used to swim in college. Played water polo too." His voice was low, husky. That explained it all—his broad shoulders, toned legs, and his ability to dive and hold his breath for so long. "Why can't you sleep, Lewis?"

I shrugged. Wasn't about to tell him he might have something to do with it when he was giving me nothing. "Lewis is not my name."

"A man doesn't just want to see beauty, even if that should be enough. He wants to be one with the beauty he sees, to give himself to it, to be absorbed by it, to bathe in it, to become part of it."

"Are you trying to quote C. S. Lewis, *The Weight of Glory*? Because that would be a heck of a paraphrase if you are."

He smiled. His head tipping to the side, one hand swiping the air, palm up as though what I just said confirmed his point.

"How do you know that piece of writing anyway? That's a

religious essay. Maybe it's me that should be calling *you* Lewis."

Another smile. "I have varied interests." His eyes and head turned from me to the other side of the pool and glanced at the door.

"You can't sleep either?"

He shook his head, gaze dropping to the goggles and cap in his hands. He placed them in the space between us. "I don't normally finish work till late. Everyone goes to bed, I'm still wide awake. So I swim."

I nodded, lifting one of my legs out of the water and letting it drip, then lowering it back down.

His head turned, eyes watching my legs. "Are you getting in? The water is nice. Warm like a bath."

I smiled and waved my hand at my silky pajamas. I hadn't planned on swimming.

"It's bigger than the bikinis you've been wearing. You'll be fine."

"You've been keeping tabs, have you?"

He smirked. "*You* flashed me, remember?" And he jumped back into the water, swimming on his back while looking at me.

"That was an accident."

We watched each other, the noise from his movements filling the gap left by our silence. The lights in the pool making him and the whole thing look quite inviting.

Celo used his hands to splash a substantial amount of water at me. His face sinking up to his nose. I smiled but didn't get in.

He did it again.

"Ok, ok, I'll get in." I tied my hair up in a bun and slid myself in, pajamas and all. He wasn't lying, my body was instantly wrapped in warm water and the weightlessness that comes from being submerged.

He could stand where we were, water up to his shoulders. I had to bop on my tiptoes, so my chin stayed above the water.

For a moment we said nothing, just enjoyed the temperature of the pool.

"You like Ilhabela?"

"What's not to like? I'm on a paradise island with a bunch of rich people paying for everything." His lips stretched into a flat smile. "Even been on a boat today, flashing strangers apparently. Never thought I'd do that." His smile showed some teeth. "You can laugh; this is all normal to you guys, but it's not normal to me."

"Which part? Being on a yacht or flashing strangers?" His voice at a lower frequency, throaty, raspy, making something in my chest vibrate.

I raised my eyebrows at him. He knew damn well what I meant.

"It was a yacht by the way. Not a boat." He smirked, teasing at our difference in social status.

"Oh… a yacht!" I put a posh accent on, making fun of his teasing. He grinned. "What is the difference anyway?"

"Yachts are bigger. More luxurious."

"Ah… so just a posh big boat then." He laughed, and I followed. "Do you swim every night?"

He shook his head and frowned as if he was thinking about something, eyes watching his hands play with the water. "It helps clear my head."

"Clear it from what?"

One of the corners of his mouth raised in a half smile, but he didn't answer. Just kept looking at me.

"I thought you said you swim because you can't sleep."

His smile came with a snort, and he looked sideways, like someone who was caught in a lie but was more amused he got caught than apologetic. His arms started moving underwater. Then his eyes returned to me. "Do you swim?"

"If dog paddling counts, then yes." Another smile spread over his lips slowly. "But if you mean swim as in something I do to clear my head, then no."

"What do you do to clear your head then?"

I had to think for a minute. "Probably dance. I've been dragged to dance classes most of my life. Have to use it for something."

Absentminded shallow nods. "That explains it."

"Explains what?"

"Why you picked up *sertanejo* so quickly." His eyes dropped to my lips. "And how you were dancing in the club the other night."

"So you were watching?" I swam backwards, trying to get closer to the shallow end to get a better footing.

"*Everyone* was watching." He stepped forward, bridging the gap to keep the same distance.

I shrugged. "I wasn't paying attention."

We gazed at each other until his face turned serious. "You know, Felipe is really into you." He leaned sideways and propelled himself with his arm, the water making a soothing sound.

An exasperated sigh escaped without my permission. Why did he have to bring this up and spoil everything? "So everyone keeps on telling me." I could feel the waves of him moving at the back of me.

"You should give him a chance. He's a nice guy."

I snorted. So that was his plan. The day he decided to actually speak to me, he wanted to talk about Felipe.

"You already have history, no?"

"*Ancient* history. That was years ago."

Celo swam back around to the front of me—his hands and feet moving without breaking the surface.

"You not into him?" He stopped swimming, his feet going back to the bottom, and he looked at me like the answer mattered.

"That's what I keep on telling everyone. But *nobody* seems to take notice."

The corner of his lips raised. "Felipe can be very persistent."

"That's what Marisa said."

His eyes locked with mine for an instant. Then his gaze traveled from my eyes to my lips, and back to my eyes. "I can't say I blame him. Everyone seems to be a bit in love with you, even Freddie."

"Now… that one is cute. Him, I would date."

A gorgeous smile took over his face; his expression softened. Freddie was his soft spot.

We stayed in the pool, not saying anything, relaxing in the water, floating, swimming around each other. He had clearly exhausted his small talk repertoire. It might sound strange, but it was actually refreshing not to have the pressure to make small talk—unable to ask what you really wanted to know, and instead asking things you weren't really interested in. But a few minutes later, the skin on my fingers started to look like I was being cooked in boiling water.

"I think I need to get out. My hands have started feeling like prunes."

He smiled, head dipping ever so slightly to give me a nod, eyes following the motion.

I turned around to get up the steps. He swam to the side and got out, started drying his hair and face with his towel, then looked at me and stopped—his eyes going straight to my boobs. I looked down and the pajamas were sticking to my body, the cool breeze had triggered my goosebumps… and my nipples.

Marcelo walked over and raised up his towel, stretching it open in between his hands like an offering. I nodded and he wrapped it around my shoulders without touching me.

He wiped the rest of the water from his arms, torso, and legs with his hands, picked up his cap and goggles, and signaled for me to go ahead of him.

We both walked back into the house in silence—the lock on the door falling into place with a satisfying click behind him. He followed me up the stairs and down the corridor without saying a word, both on our tiptoes so as not to wake anyone. When we reached the door to my room, he continued walking. At his door, he looked at me.

Seconds ticked by.

His eyes showing something that resembled sadness. "Night," he whispered, his hand squeezing the door handle.

I nodded and he was gone.

I didn't sleep a thing. And judging by all the moving around in his room, he didn't either.

The next day, he was quiet. His eyes behind his sunglasses all day. Everyone having a lazy day relaxing in the house after all the excitement on the boat. Rogério and Pedro had decided to barbecue for lunch, and Lu and I went to town in the afternoon.

But when night came, I waited for everyone to be asleep. At 2:50 a.m. I switched the lamp on in my room. I knew he would see it from his window and know I was awake. And at 2:55 a.m. I went for a swim. This time wearing the cute green bikini Lu had given me. I'm not sure what I was trying to achieve wearing it. I had taken it off several times before coming to the pool. But I had this crazy need to make him look at me. I wanted him to look. Wanted him to want to… I'm not sure what. That is where things got blurry. I didn't want to be one of his playthings. And yet, here I was—sneaking out to pot about in a pool at 3 a.m. wearing a sexy bikini. Someone needed to slap me.

I let my body float in the water. I could understand why he swam to clear his head. Underwater all your senses were dulled. I closed my eyes. The feeling of weightlessness making everything disappear until all I could hear was my own breathing, all I could feel were the ripples of water hitting my body.

I stayed like that, floating myself into oblivion, until a shiver started running down my spine with that tingling you feel when you sense someone is watching you. My eyelids opened. Celo was standing at the edge of the pool looking at me.

My feet touched the bottom. "How long have you been there?"

He shrugged. "I didn't want to scare you." Then looked at me for a second longer before walking to the end of the pool and diving in, coming to surface just in front of me. Close enough that he could extend his arm out and touch me if he wanted to, but not too close. He wiped his face. "You can't sleep again?"

I shrugged. Didn't want to lie, but didn't want to admit I was there on purpose either. "I can move, if you want to do your laps."

A head shake, his eyes locked with mine. "You were dragged to dance classes most of your life." He quoted me word for word and waited. When I didn't elaborate, he continued "Were you part of a team or something?"

"Dance company, yes."

"Like a ballet company." I nodded. "So, you performed." Another nod but I didn't say any more. "Were you any good at it?" His tone was teasing, somewhat frustrated with my lack of response.

"By the time I was eighteen, I was earmarked for one of the top dance companies in London." I don't know why I felt the need to set the record straight and brag. He was giving me rope and I was gladly hanging myself with it, talking too much. He had done the same when we had spoken at Eight.

90

His eyebrows raised, the corners of his lips dropping downwards, he nodded. "So you're a dancer."

"I was."

His head shook, shoulders and hands rising up like he was asking why.

"It's a long story." One I didn't want to go into. After my bust up with my mother, I had decided to go traveling and put my dancing on hold. At this point, I didn't even know if I still had my place when I got back. I had claimed I needed a break for mental health reasons, but the dance company had probably replaced me, and my chance had sailed. "Did you compete with your swimming?" Before he asked anymore, I flipped the table.

A nod.

"Were you any good at it?" I said, matching his tone to me when he asked me the same question.

His smile was cocky, clearly satisfied with his own performance, and he gave me a second nod.

"Then why did you stop?"

"It was just a hobby while I was in college." His eyes didn't leave my face, arms going back and forth underwater. "What type of dancing did you do?"

"I tried different styles but settled on contemporary."

"And now that you just dance to clear your head?" I looked at him blankly, not sure what he was asking. "What do you dance to?"

I shrugged. "My favorite music… or… something fast that will make me tired."

"Like what?" He was paddling, trying to keep his feet from touching the bottom of the pool.

Another shrug. "I don't know. It depends on my mood at the time."

"Show me."

"I'm not dancing for you!" I gasped.

PAOLA SANTANA

He grinned. "I meant the music. But I'd enjoy the dancing, if you're offering." His facial expression full of undertones.

I splashed water at him.

His smile grew wider. "I'm serious."

"Shame I'm not offering."

"I mean the music."

"I don't have my phone."

Celo swam to the ledge and picked up his phone from a pile on the floor. He wiggled it at me, not wanting to bring it to the middle of the pool, and I walked to him. He handed it over as I got close, making me stop at an arm's length from him. Spotify was open.

I struggled to pick something. "This doesn't work. It doesn't have my playlists." I tried to hand the phone back to him. He looked at it but didn't take it back.

"Play your favorite song."

"I have a lot of favorites. I listen to a lot of music."

"Play the one you were dancing to at the club." His smile was full of bad intentions, seeming to know I would dance to that one anywhere.

"Nice try. I'm still not dancing."

"Play one of the ones you were playing earlier today, when you had your earbuds on." I didn't think he had noticed; he had his glasses on.

"Why do you want to listen to my music anyway?"

"Curiosity."

I stood there staring at him. The light on the phone dimmed. Without breaking eye contact, he tapped it so the screen wouldn't lock.

I played the last song I was listening to before coming to the pool—Sam Smith, 'My Oasis'. The intro started and Celo reached over and lowered the volume, then crossed his arms over the edge of the pool and lowered his chin to them—his skin stretching over his arms and back, giving me a full view of half of his tattoos. He went quiet, facing forward, trying to focus on hearing the music despite the low volume. I put the phone down on the edge close to him. But as the song started, I realized it was a Freudian slip—the lyrics giving away my thoughts without me meaning to. He looked at me when the chorus started playing and, embarrassed, I averted my eyes to the other side of the pool, pretending to be listening too. When my eyes returned to him, he was smiling. I had started swaying to the music.

"No. I'm still not dancing."

His shoulders raised towards his ears then lowered back, but his eyes were playful. "You like music with a heavy base beat. The moody type."

I nodded.

"I like the lyrics on this one." His smile was smug, eyes teasing.

Shit. He was actually listening to it and seemed to know the meaning of the words to me. I tried to change the subject. "What type of music do you like?"

"Indie rock, *sertanejo*, *MPB… bossa nova…* occasionally classical." The names rolled off his tongue like a well-rehearsed line, as if he answered this question often.

"Classical?"

"It's good for focusing. Has no lyrics."

"I didn't figure you for a classical music lover."

"Like I said, I have varied interests." A half smile, chin resting on his shoulder, eyes scanning down to my cleavage and back.

"MPB?"

"*Música Popular Brasileira*—Brazilian Popular Music. A mixture of Brazilian traditional styles and international ones."

"And B-something *Nova*?" Genuinely had no idea what that was.

"*Bossa Nova*. Mellow samba with a hint of jazz." The corner of his mouth raised, full of mischief. "This is my favorite part of this song." He meant Sam Smith's feelings getting deeper.

I tried to ignore him. "Do your tattoos mean anything?"

"Some do, most don't." He rewound the song. Crap.

"Which ones mean something?"

Celo moved to stand in front of me and looked at his arms —distracted, hair falling over his face. This was the closest I had ever been able to look at him, like really look at him, without having to pretend I wasn't ogling or being worried about other people noticing. A dusting of dark hair covered his chest and ran down the middle of his body. Three birthmarks in the shape of a triangle dotted the spot where one side of his ribs would be.

A finger pointed at a design. "That's for my grandma. They were her favorite flowers. This one is for my granddad." His whole head shifted to look at the other arm. "This one is for my mother. And these are Marisa's favorite flowers. The eagle on my back was for my time in college in America." The tattoos wrapped around his arms like lace.

Whenever he was anywhere near me, Celo always left a gap in between our bodies. It was carefully calculated so he was always standing an arm's length away from me. Politely acceptable, but too far to touch. Along our conversation about music and tattoos, the gap had shortened and, when his eyes raised from his arms, we were really close.

He stopped talking.

His eyes blinked twice but the eyelids didn't touch each other. Throat worked like he was trying to swallow something. Arms left to float on the surface of the water to either side of me.

The music was still playing. But for a minute all I could hear was my own breathing and the rivulets of water coming from the pool pump.

His gaze raked over my face like it was trying to grab me.

Lips parted. Body swaying as if moved by the water to be closer to me.

Slowly, his head started dipping towards me... anticipation pinning me to the spot, making me perfectly still, my breath catching.

I could feel his breath on my face, fast and shallow. Eyes anchored to my lips, revealing his thoughts and destination.

The tips of our noses touching... so subtle that I questioned if it actually happened. Electricity zinging up my spine, almost making me shiver.

But when I tipped my chin to cover the gap, his head dropped, his forehead missing my face by a whisker.

Celo closed his eyes, groaned, and propelled himself backwards, swimming away from me until he stood twice further than his usual distance. The gap making me feel like he had actually pulled something from my body, as if he had yanked a chain, pulled a plug, and drained all my contents. The waves from his sudden movements hitting me and almost knocking me off my feet.

When he looked back up, his eyebrows were furrowed, his eyes looked tired and sad as if he was enduring a level of pain.

A deep breath. A sigh. "*Se eu deixar, você vai arruinar minha vida, né?*" he said, eyes intent on me.

"What?" The word came out in a gasp, as though I was out of breath.

"I said I better go to bed. Freddie will be bursting into my room at 7 a.m. sharp."

I'm pretty sure that wasn't what he said. *Você* means you, and *minha vida* means my life. He put his hands on the edge of the pool and got out, wrapping his towel around his hips. I just stood there, stunned into a statue, deflated the moment was over.

"Will you lock the garden door behind you, Lewis?" Head bowed, shoulders defeated, eyes fixed on the water, not on me.

All I could do was nod. And it was feeble.

He grabbed his phone, paused the music, and disappeared into the house faster than I could say his name.

For a moment I didn't move, disoriented, confused. But left by myself, high and dry, I got out of the pool, wrapped myself in my towel and headed back inside, locking the door as I promised. Part of me was disappointed, part of me was angry. He flirted with and snogged anything that wore a skirt, but he couldn't run away from me fast enough.

"Pepino, Celo and I have decided we are going to the beach today," Lu announced as soon as I approached the breakfast table.

"Yay!!! I like the beach!" Freddie was eavesdropping.

"Sorry bud. This is for the big kids only." Felipe was quick to manage his expectations.

"Aw! Why can't I come? Mom, I want to come!"

"We're going to another beach, Freddie. One with other children, so you can play, and where the mosquitos won't carry you away." Marisa, unintentionally rhyming.

"Are you coming with me, Paige?" Apparently, Freddie didn't think I qualified for the big kids' category.

"No, sorry pumpkin." I ruffled his hair.

"I'm not a pumpkin." The corner of his lips turned downwards, and he frowned in the cutest sulk ever. I had obviously added insult to injury.

"Tell you what…" I crouched next to his chair. Marcelo was sitting right next to him, watching us with amusement. "What if I promise we can watch *Cars 2* tomorrow. Do we have a deal?" I extended my hand out to him.

"And *Spider Man*." He crossed his little arms, refusing to shake my hand.

"Gosh, you drive a hard bargain. We'd have to watch it in English, though. My Portuguese isn't very good. *Cars 2* and *Spider Man*, deal?" He shook my hand, satisfied he had gotten what he wanted out of our barter. I got up. "They train them well in that English school of yours. He's as sharp as a razor this little one."

"He must be." Felipe laughed. "I can't take you on a single date, but he just guilt tripped you into giving him two." Giggles spread across the table. He was joking, but he wasn't far from the truth.

"Sorry, you're just not as cute," I joked back. "But you are the *cutest*!" I said squeezing Freddie's cheeks and giving him a kiss. He stopped munching his croissant to smile at me.

"So… anyway… we have a choice," Lu carried on. "We can go back to the touristy beaches you have been to already, or we can go to a more secluded one. What would you prefer?"

"The quiet one sounds nice," I said, sitting next to Felipe, the only seat available.

"You look nice." His hand rubbed a circle on my back.

Marcelo's eyes locked with mine—his elbows on the table, hands covering his mouth and supporting his head—then he looked elsewhere.

"Want some juice?" Felipe's fingers wrapped around the jug.

I nodded.

"If you go to Jabaquara, make sure you take some insect repellent." Marisa was buttering a bread roll for Freddie. "Those horrid mosquitos can be nasty."

We drove a few minutes and had to walk down a path before getting to the beach, but once we got there, the sun was hot, the sand golden, and the water a pale green. A few boats bobbed up and down at a distance from the beach. Waves crashed on the sand with that soothing sound that could send you to sleep.

"Go on, you two, get us four sun loungers." Lu pointed at Marcelo and Felipe, fanning herself like a madam.

Marcelo sneered. "And when are *you* getting your credit card out, *patricinha*? What happened to equal rights?" he remarked, but he was already signaling the waiter. There was an edge to him today. He was snappier, his temper shorter, and he had gone back to not speaking to me unless extremely necessary.

"Who said I want equal rights?" Lu glared at him. "I want my human rights—to vote, own property, and make my own way—but I'm a woman and I want to be treated like one."

His laugh was dry, sarcastic. "Your human right to be a daddy's girl? You get away with murder cause you're the only girl."

"What do you want me to say? I was born wise. Made myself a queen"—she placed an imaginary crown on her own head—"rather than joining the plebs." Then waved her hands dismissively at Felipe and Celo.

"This is the crap I have to deal with," Celo said to Felipe. "Then you say I'm rude to her."

Sun loungers sorted, we all walked down to the sea. Without warning, Marcelo grabbed Luciana, carried her kicking and screaming, and unceremoniously dumped her into the waves.

"You are such an arsehole!" She laughed, splashing water at him, her smile too wide to be genuinely offended.

"Your royal highness, queen of pain in my ass." He made a show out of curtsying, his smile sarcastic.

The water was gorgeous. First, a little cold but then quickly pleasant and cooling. As Lu and I returned to the loungers, Marcelo and Felipe went to see what was happening on a makeshift volleyball court set up further down the beach.

After a few minutes, Lu moved her shades to the top of her

head and readjusted herself on the lounger, her legs taking a sensual pose.

"I know that move. Who are you eyeing up?"

"He's tasty." She pointed to a brunette standing a couple of rows away from our loungers, talking to his friends. As she pointed, he noticed. She smiled, her knee moving from side to side like she was killing time, and he smiled back.

"I knew it!" I laughed.

"Flower! We've been here for almost a week; I haven't had so much as a snog! A girl's got to get herself something to eat!"

Lu was a serial dater. She had arrived in the UK on a mission to forget an ex who had cheated on her and broken her heart. Had she not done it with such panache, she would have gained a bad reputation. But during our uni days, she complained endlessly about how European men didn't have what she called *pegada*. She'd always rated Brazilians at the top of the scale.

"Throw me against the wall and call me a lizard, you know." I'm not sure I knew. This was one of her many Brazilian sayings that didn't quite translate. Whatever the hell that meant, I always thought it sounded a little biased. True, I had had a taste with Felipe. But at that point we were just two kids fumbling in the dark. None of us had a clue what we were doing. Now, a little wiser, on full holiday mode, in hot temperatures, and surrounded by almost naked bodies, I was curious.

Unfortunately, I could be curious all I wanted. There was just no chance of me ever testing the theory when Felipe was standing guard over me like a German bloody Shepherd.

Felipe was good-looking. Looking at him now, in his swim trunks, he wasn't far from Marcelo—minus the tattoos and taller. But while the latter didn't give me the time of day and consumed my thoughts, the former was like a giant teddy bear that competed for space with my shadow. When I learned he was going to China on a business trip, I actually felt a sense of relief. We had gotten ourselves into this hybrid weird friendship that I just couldn't get myself out of. I loved Felipe, I did. He was a great guy. But he had never gotten my knickers in a twist like his brother did. Our sexual tension and romantic chances died in their sleep the day I met his brother. Sounds mean, I know. I didn't do it on purpose. It just happened. And just thinking about it made me want to go and drown myself in the sea. Could it get any more clichéd than me turning down the nice guy for a bad boy? So textbook cheesy, it was actually vomit inducing. I didn't know what was wrong with me.

As I sat there pretending not to be jealous of Lu's freedom to flirt to her heart's content, Marcelo tied his hair up, muscles on his back, his biceps, all working. The eagle tattoo between his shoulder blades urged me to stop staring with its beady angry eyes—feathers at the end of its wings just flicking over his shoulders towards the front, claws outstretched menacingly down his back. The tattoos on his arms were a collection of different things—objects, animals, flowers, women, skulls—all black and grey, like he had added them over time, one by one. He walked back to drop his shades on his lounger, and I was glad I was wearing mine. His swim shorts hung dangerously low at his hips, the waist of them sitting below the curve between his waist and his perky backside at the back, and the V line on his abs inviting me to let my eyes wander. Lu's 'throw me against the wall and call me a lizard' all of a sudden started making more sense. He half jogged back to the game, kicking sand with his feet as he went, and entered the court to play.

"Yeah... he's quite something, isn't he?" Lu's voice pulled me out of my reverie. "When we were little, I used to say he looked like a monkey. But now he's quite something. Don't you think?" She crooked her neck to one side. "Kind of an annoying something," she added as an afterthought.

"I don't know what you're talking about." But as soon as I said it, I knew I was in denial and Lu could smell it like a shark blood in the water.

"Oh yes you do. I see the way you look at him." We both looked at Marcelo as he positioned the ball in the air so Felipe could hit it on a kill shot over the net. "He *is* gorgeous. But he is also one of those wild horses you just can't tame, my friend. He will eat you up, chew you, and spit you out like tasteless chewing gum."

"Wow! That's a new one. I don't think I'll ever get used to your food vs. love-slash-sex comparisons. Gee!" I smiled, shook my head, and without thinking betrayed myself and gave Marcelo another quick look. I meant for it to sound careless and uncaring, but all I could hear was a hint of sadness.

I knew Lu was right. The same way I knew his lack of company on this holiday was just out of respect for his family. I could tell I wasn't the only girl looking at him. And as attracted to him as I was, logic told me that I would be damned if I reduced myself to one of his toys. To him this was just a game of lust and skin—a sport he was very good at—but my crush made it much more than that to me.

Whether I did or didn't, I would always walk away heartbroken. Maybe after this holiday I should go home and quit while I was ahead.

"I'm only looking after you, my sweet, naive friend. Having your heart broken is not going to do me any favors. Not to mention that dating your ex-fling's brother is a bit of a taboo. A bit of a big *problema*, flower. And you run away from problems like the devil runs away from the cross. I want you to have a good time while you're here, so you stay longer. It's no fun when my partner in crime is on the other side of the Atlantic."

I smiled, but as I did, I felt the familiar melancholy taking hold. "I know. You don't need to worry. He has no time for me. As a matter of fact, he barely speaks to me at all."

"Is that so?" Lu gazed over at Marcelo with a suspicious look. "Oh well... he's no good for you anyway." She perked up. "However... my lovely cousin Felipe, *on the other hand*, is quite fond of you." She touched my ankle with her sand-covered toes, the granules scratching against my skin. Her voice was serious, but her eyes were mischievous. "He's a keeper." She delivered her verdict with an overdramatic frown and serious expression.

At that, I had to laugh. "I'm sure he is. *But...* as you know... and as I tried to make very clear to him, I don't like him that way." I offered an exaggerated shrug and head shake that were supposed to be apologetic.

"I know. But I did promise him I would have a word... or two." She raised both her eyebrows. "I can now gladly report I've done my cousinly duties." Her smile was so wide she resembled a dodgy salesman—anything but sweet and honest.

A while later the game ended, and by the look of it, Marcelo and Felipe had lost. That seemed to have no effect on their moods as they walked down to the water, laughing and talking to the other players.

Celo ran in and lunged into the waves. Then stood up, hands pushing his hair back, wiping his face, water running down his back.

It was like the vultures could smell dead meat. Within seconds, overly keen slim bodies approached the group, the other players introducing the girls to Felipe and Marcelo, who greeted all of them with the standard one kiss. His hair slicked back, body half emerged in water, he flirted with miniscule bikinis—eyes smoldering, a smile that spelled trouble written all over his face. One of the girls, in a red bikini, moved to stand next to him—big smile full of teeth, acting all coy, touching his arms whenever she had a chance. He glanced my way for a couple of seconds, then turned back to her and laughed about something she said.

With me he was all moody silence, with her he was all smiles. I could feel my temper flaring. So, I ordered a Caipirinha cocktail.

"It's a bit early for Caipirinhas, isn't it?" Lu and her x-ray bloody vision.

"Our holiday is almost over. I think it's time I let my hair down."

"Ok…" The word dragged with suspicion; her eyes narrowed. She was just about to ask me something when the brunette she had been flirting with approached her, she herself turning all coy. He pointed at the bar, she nodded and got up. "Will you be alright for a minute?" I nodded. From what I could tell with my limited Portuguese, he had offered her a drink.

Marcelo and Felipe walked back from the sea and sat down on their sun loungers. Felipe lying down on his next to mine, Marcelo mounting his like a horse.

"You started the party without us?" Felipe pointed at my Caipirinha.

I shrugged. "It looked like you guys were busy, and Lu is otherwise engaged."

I nodded towards where Lu now sat twirling a strand of hair around her fingers, smile also full of teeth, talking to the brunette. Both Marcelo and Felipe leaned over to see what I was talking about, grins creeping on their faces once they understood.

"Poor bastard. He has no idea what he's getting himself into." Felipe laughed.

Marcelo snorted. "She'll eat him alive."

"And on that note… bro"—Felipe smacked Marcelo's arm with the back of his hand—"incoming." Red bikini was coming back. Prancing towards us like she was auditioning for

Baywatch. She walked past our sun loungers giving Celo the eye; her smile might as well have been a billboard flashing 'I'm flirting'. He looked at her for a split second, then started scrolling on his phone.

Felipe laughed and shook his head. "You must be covered in fucking honey because they stick to you like flies. And you don't give a shit, do you?"

Marcelo shrugged. "It's because I don't give a shit that they stick to me like flies," he replied, without looking at Felipe, all of a sudden really interested in his phone.

Cocky, sleezy bastard!

I drank the end of my Caipirinha in a single hit of the straw. "I'm hot." Threw my shades on the lounger and got up to go for a dip.

"Want some company?" Felipe shouted at the back of me.

"I'm good," I shouted back without turning.

The sea was a relief—cool and soothing. I swam out then allowed myself to float. The water blocking my hearing, numbing my senses. The calm waves allowing me to relax. This is what both Lu and Marisa were talking about. The guy was a babe magnet, I had seen him with other girls before, but today this was touching a nerve. Maybe it was because of last night. Yesterday he had come closer, flirted with me, almost kissed me. Today, he was chatting up some Brazilian bimbo. If I was honest, I felt like a fool—hoping, craving for someone that would only treat me like a disposable piece of arse.

My peace and quiet didn't last long. Felipe swam out to me, and I allowed my feet to touch the bottom and stood up.

"You don't mind if I join you, do you? Don't really wanna hold the candle for those two."

"Hold the candle?"

"Yeah, you know… When you are the third person with a couple."

I looked towards the beach. Red bikini had come back and

was sitting on Marcelo's lounger. He was talking to her, all smiles, but he was looking at us.

"Ah, you mean being the third wheel on a date."

"Is that how you say it in England?"

I nodded. "I sympathize. Hey, do you have shells on this beach?"

"I think so. Maybe on that other end."

"Maybe we can get some for Freddie so he can make some artwork or something. What do you say we go get a couple of Caipirinhas and go looking for some?" Since he was here, he might as well make himself useful.

"Sounds like a plan."

We headed to the bar, passing the two sets of love birds, and ordered our drinks. Then walked down the beach collecting shells and laughing, like we had done when he took me around São Paulo on those first couple of days.

"I'm running out of hands to carry your shells." He laughed. In one hand he had his drink, and I had been using the other like a basket for all the shells I was collecting.

"Here." I finished my Caipirinha, threw my limes in the greenery, and offered him my cup to put them in. He managed to lose more shells than he put in the cup. We were laughing over our disjointed effort, trying to rescue the shells we had lost before the sea reclaimed them, when Marcelo appeared out of nowhere, his eyes darting in between me and Felipe.

"*Hey, cê ainda quer entrar no campeonato de volley?*" He pointed over his shoulder with his thumb.

"*Meu, vamo lá.*" Felipe turned to me. "We are back on for another game."

I nodded and we all started walking back, Felipe to one side of me, Marcelo to the other.

He spotted my cup of shells. "You just collecting shells?" His gaze held mine, eyes scanning my face.

I nodded and looked away.

Luciana's date had also headed to the court, so she was back at the loungers when I walked back. "Look at that! *Dona Flor e Seus Dois Maridos.*"

"I don't know what that means, Lu."

"It's a Brazilian film about a woman and her two husbands. One is a sex god, the other a nice guy."

"Then I'm definitely not her. I don't even get a snog these days."

"Pepino will snog you in a blink of an eye if you let him."

I scowled at her.

"You ok, flower? You look a bit on edge. Did anything happen?"

"Nope. That's the problem. Nothing happened. This girl over here needs to eat too, you know."

Lu let out a proper belly laugh. "A bit sexually frustrated, are we?" She sat up on her lounger. "I know the feeling. It sucks to have to behave on family holidays."

"Oh yeah... cause God forbid you don't have a toy to play with for more than a few days." We looked at each other. Then she giggled and I followed, glad she hadn't taken my snappiness as offensive.

"Come on, let's go down there and show those skinny bitches how to cheer for our boys. They bloody better win."

It turned out the championship they had created involved four teams of two. Marcelo and Felipe made quite a formidable pair. Once 'the overall winner' title was up for grabs, the two of them had become very competitive. Both of them going to extreme lengths to prevent the ball from hitting the floor— diving on the sand, running off court and all sorts. Marcelo's top knot coming undone, pieces of hair falling unnoticed on his face while he focused on the ball. The muscles on him coiling and springing, the power in his arms something ridiculous. As I sipped my drink, Felipe set the ball in the air and Marcelo took two steps, jumped and absolutely hammered it into the opposite court, the leather of the ball screaming against his hand. He scored and secured their first win. Both of them high-fiving each other and bumping chests, shaking the hands of the opposing players, then walking towards Lu and me.

"One down, two more to go." Felipe was clearly enjoying the rivalry. "Come on, let's go for a dip. I have sand in places I wouldn't like to name."

We all walked down to the sea. The boys in a giddy, chatty mood talking about going back to watch the competition so they knew how to play them, plotting beach domination. As they were talking, red bikini got in the sea.

"Oh... Oh..." Lu started narrating. "Houston, we'll have contact in three..." Marcelo didn't move, but his eyes flicked to the girl, to Lu, then glanced at me. A shameless half smile on his face. "Two... one." Red bikini touched his shoulder. He switched the flirt on and turned to give her attention.

"Lu, maybe Paige and I should start counting down for you. That guy is coming over here." Felipe laughed. Lu smacked the back of her hand onto his stomach and her face opened into the most flirtations smile as soon as the brunette got closer.

"I think that's our cue to leave," I said to Felipe.

"Or we could stay?" He grabbed my hand, smile hinting at trying to move us into the same category as the other two pairs.

"I'm dying for another drink." I tugged at his hand and started walking back to shore, then dropped it as soon as we got out of the water. I had just ordered another Caipirinha, when Marcelo came over and said something to Felipe in Portuguese.

"We're going to watch the competition." Behind him, Celo was looking at me. "Can you order two bottles of water for us, please?" I nodded, and they both headed back to the makeshift court.

I brought the water down just as they were about to start their second game. Red bikini walked over and when Marcelo turned to look at her, she got on her tiptoes and planted a peck on his lips. If I understood it right, for good luck. He smiled the most indecent, self-righteous smile at her, eyes lingering over her face as a promise of things to come. She beamed with so much teeth, I'm sure she was visible from the moon. Most of my cocktail disappeared in one gulp.

"I could do with a little luck myself." Felipe turned to me, eyes dropping to my lips.

I played dumb. "I don't think she'll give it to you. She seems to have picked her champion already."

Visions of violence filled my mind. I would have loved to grab red bikini by the hair, shove her face in the sand, and make her eat the whole lot.

But I had no right. Marcelo was nothing of mine.

The more logical part of me wouldn't like to give him the satisfaction of seeing me fight over him either; although that part was currently on its way to being overridden by copious amounts of alcohol.

Felipe and Celo walked onto the court, both smiling at each other, Felipe shaking his head. Both glancing at me just before the first serve. I finished the second half of my cocktail.

"You might want to slow down on those." Lu was trying to be the voice of reason. "They're not water, you know."

"Uh-huh." And I walked to the bar to get another one. Now I understood why Freddie was so fond of the expression. It allowed you to agree with anyone and mute the subject while still completely ignoring what they were saying.

Caipirinha in hand, I stayed at the bar instead of walking back to the court. Marcelo and Felipe were playing against Lu's brunette and his friend, but Marcelo was distracted; he didn't play as well. Probably because of the peacock display red bikini was flashing on the sidelines. Despite her best efforts, Lu's squeeze lost. Probably because of the display Lu was also flashing on the sidelines. When it came to getting men to look at her, Lu was a black belt. Maybe I should actually try to learn a trick or two from her.

As soon as the game finished, red bikini jumped into Celo's arms and this time she kissed him proper. At first, he didn't respond, but then he did—his arms wrapping around her middle and pulling her close to him. I wished for anger, but all I got was deep-rooted sadness. The kind of sadness that hits when you know the outcome is inevitable and there's nothing you can do about it. Felipe walked away smiling and shaking his head. Lu walked away with the brunette. Everyone going for a dip in the sea. I ordered another Caipirinha.

Felipe came out of the water; Lu came out with the brunette's arm wrapped around her shoulder; but Marcelo stayed behind. Red bikini clinging on to him like an octopus to a rock—all tentacles. He smiled and flirted with her, but he didn't stop scanning the shore like he had lost something.

"There you are!" Felipe walked into the bar. "We were all wondering where you were." I very much doubted that.

"Sorry. It's a bit too hot for me. Skin the color of milk and afternoon tropical sun are not a match made in heaven."

His faced opened into a gorgeous smile. He did have a beautiful one. "Yeah… you've gone a little rouge." His thumb rubbed on my cheek, fingers running along my shoulders and down my arm. All the areas I would show sunburn. "Have the Caipirinhas been good company?" He pointed at my drink.

I shrugged. "They don't talk much." Another smile, his eyes fixed on my face. "Is that it now? Have you won?"

"We've got one more game against whoever has more points after the next game. But we'll have a break in between so the other team can rest for a bit."

I nodded.

Lu joined us with the brunette. "You ok, flower?"

"I'm good. Just staying out of the sun." I sounded tired. Lu's eyes narrowed, her head tilting to the side slightly. "I think I've overdone it a bit, all these days by the pool." I showed her my shoulder, trying to convince her that my reason was legit.

"Mum has a good chamomile cream that works wonders on Freddie." She went along with my excuse, but I could tell she wasn't convinced. As she was about to say something else, arms wrapped around her middle and her body was pulled backwards, closer to the brunette, a kiss planted on her neck. I was both relieved and jealous. Relieved to escape her inquisition, jealous because I wanted to be kissed like she had just been.

Felipe draped his arm around my shoulder then smiled towards the door, and I knew with sickening certainty that Marcelo had just come into the bar. I didn't turn to look. Didn't see the point of torturing myself any more than I'd already done. He leaned into the bar next to me; I turned to face the door. From the corner of my eye, I could see his face turned to me momentarily. He ordered two drinks, red bikini standing right behind him. She was pretty and right up his street— petite, slim, long hair. A world apart from me. She smiled at me. I smiled back. Sadness swallowed me whole.

"Do you mind helping me with the umbrella on the lounger? I don't think I can take any more sun." Felipe nodded and we left for the sunbeds. The Caipirinhas had started to work. I felt light-headed, my muscles relaxed.

"Do you want me to put more suncream on your shoulders?"

I handed him the bottle and turned so he could do it for me. He rubbed the cream on but also massaged my shoulders. It felt nice, comforting.

"*Vamo lá assistir o outro time?*" Marcelo was standing right in front of me. I didn't raise my gaze, but his legs were side by side with red bikini's legs, their feet covered in sand. It was as though he wanted me to look at them, rub it in my face. Like he knew I had this suffocating crush on him, and he wanted to see me squirm, drowning in jealousy, watching him get it on with someone else.

"*Pô mano, agora não, né?*" Felipe's hand didn't stop massaging my shoulder.

I wanted so bad to look up, like an addict that knows the drugs aren't good for her but can't resist the urge.

"*É o último jogo, meu. Vamo lá ganhar, depois cê volta. O quê que ela vai fazer? Fugir? Pra onde? A gente tá nunha ilha, mano.*" Portuguese had this lovely roundness, with lazy staccatos and words that seemed to drag. Marcelo's voice sounded deeper in his own language. And I gave in, addiction getting the best of me, and looked up at him. The sun behind him made me squint, red bikini was standing next to him like an adoring fan, but Celo looked close to angry. His hands had balled into fists.

"*Meu, toma cuidado com o que cê fala! Acho que ela entende mais do que a gente pensa.*" Felipe's hands stopped massaging my shoulders and gave me a squeeze. "We'll go watch the other team. See if we can find a way to beat them." I nodded, put my sunnies on, lay down on the lounger, and sipped my cocktail. "Are you coming to watch us play?"

Another nod. Felipe started walking to the court and Celo looked at me as if I had spoiled his competition. He hooks up with someone, but I'm the one that gets the stern judgmental look? Prick.

They left. I didn't go. Just sat on the lounger, drinking my cocktail.

Outside, the sky was all blue, not a cloud in sight. In my head, it was thunderstorms and gales. The winds were blowing north, telling me I should pack up and go home.

Go home for what was the question. My life in London had crumbled to pieces. And Brazil, my 'get your life back on track' holiday, had turned into a bloody mess of tangled, conflicting feelings. How the fuck did I get myself here? How many times had I told myself not to entertain the possibility?

They won. Red bikini jumping up and down like she'd won the lottery. After a dip in the sea, they all headed my way. Felipe dropping a shell in my cup of shells. Someone had written the number one on it as a medal for the winners.

Drinks were flowing, music, laughter—I felt like the person standing still in the middle of a flux of traffic—and as the sun started to cool, everyone headed to the bar. Apart from Lu, who went for a walk on the beach with the brunette.

Marcelo, across the bar from me, now in his shorts and tee, was still talking to the same girl—his arm over her shoulder, both of them standing quite close, heads almost touching. But occasionally he would look my way as if to check I was still there, watching like a torture victim. Annoyed, I had downed a fair few drinks.

Felipe had stayed by me throughout the whole thing. He had become very touchy—putting his arm around my shoulder, holding me by my waist, rubbing circles on my skin —but I didn't mind. If I'm honest, I craved it. It was calming. Then his hands snaked their way around my waist; he bent down to whisper something in my ear over the music, but when I turned to face him, he full on kissed me, his tongue invading my mouth. Out of booze and jealousy, I reciprocated. Everyone seemed to be getting some, why couldn't I? When he finished kissing me, he smiled.

"Do you wanna go for a walk?" Beyond him, I could see Marcelo and red bikini walking down to the sea, his arm wrapped around her shoulder.

"I'm ok here. Besides, we might bump into Celo and Lu."

He looked around and, realizing the two of them were

gone, laughed. Then he took my hand, and we walked around the side of the bar and under a tree. As soon as we were out of sight, he gave me a good old-fashioned snog. He was a good kisser, don't get me wrong, but when his hands started to grab too much, push too much, I pushed him away.

"I'm sorry. I don't mean to be pushy. I just... been waiting for this since you landed, you know." He kissed me once more, slowly.

And it hit me like a slap in the face. Felipe had feelings for me. I was no different from Marcelo, toying with someone that wants more, like a cat playing with a mouse. Felipe didn't deserve that. This was a mistake.

I pushed him off me. "I'm so sorry, Felipe. I can't do this. I'm going back to the bar."

"Hey, wait..." He tried to grab my hand, but I dodged him and carried on walking. "Paige!"

When I got back to the bar, Lu was back and so was the brunette. "There you are! Where's everyone?"

"I think I'm going to be sick." I rushed past her to the end of the trail. She followed, and behind her, Felipe.

"How much did she have to drink?" Lu's speech was rushed, the last word taking a higher pitch. She rubbed circles on my back and held my hair while I spewed my guts up in the bushes.

"I don't know. Maybe a few." Felipe's voice was flat, dismissive. "She had a Caipirinha in her hand all day, but I'm not sure how many she drank."

"Felipe!" And she went into Portuguese. He walked away.

"I think I need to go home," I managed to say, getting myself upright.

"Yes. But first we need to wash your mouth and your feet. Come on, let's get you under the beach shower. Honestly, I can't bloody take you anywhere!"

The ride back was a quiet one. Marcelo didn't look at me at

113

all. No doubt annoyed I had ruined his plans with red bikini. Felipe looked at me occasionally, but he looked frustrated. And Lu was sympathetic, sitting with me in the back, rubbing my hair, and keeping the window open in case I had more Caipirinha coming.

We stopped outside the house; everyone got out apart from Marcelo. As the front door opened, he reversed out of the drive. The car revving, tires skidding on the gravel.

"And what happened to you lot?" Marisa looked amused. "You look like you're coming back from the war rather than the beach."

"Paige had too many Caipirinhas." Lu, the grass, was quick to expose my shame. But she too sounded amused.

"Luciana!" Marta's voice took this specific tone when she disapproved of Lu's behavior, the 'ana' on her name gaining a whole new level of emphasis.

"It wasn't me; I promise! It was Felipe."

"Felipe!" Marisa also had a tone. Felipe's name sounded shorter when she was annoyed.

"Don't look at me! She was the one ordering them." But he looked smug and smiled when he looked at me.

"And where the hell is Celo?" Marisa was looking at the door.

"He left. I think he's going back to meet the girl he was chatting to." Felipe was eating some of the nibbles Marisa had put out. None of us had really eaten since morning. "You know what he's like."

"Has he been drinking as well?" Marisa sounded worried.

"No, he never has more than one. You know that, Mom."

It was all too much. Too much information, too much light, too loud. "I'm sorry, I need to lie down." What I really needed was to bury my face, idiocy, and misery in my room.

"Lu, take a big glass of water, two aspirins, and this"— Marisa handed her a bowl—"just in case."

❤❤❤

"How you feeling?" Marta was the first to ask once I came down the steps for breakfast.

I had woken up in Lu's bedroom with her telling me I needed to eat something. Everyone around the table was smiling at my disgrace. At least, my drunken shenanigans were amusing for some.

"I'm ok, I think. Definitely learned my lesson, though." I sat next to Lu. "No more Caipirinhas for me."

There was no Marcelo.

Everyone laughed, Felipe giving me a fond smile and mouthing, "We ok?" I nodded.

Celo didn't reappear until mid-morning. By the time he walked down the stairs, wearing the same clothes from the day before, I was sitting in the shade in my hoodie and sunglasses. The thought of him spending the night with red bikini made me sick. I drank some orange juice.

And then I was angry. Angry at myself for developing this stupid, idiotic crush. Angry I didn't crush on Felipe instead. Angry I had stayed at the beach torturing myself and gotten hammered, and now I was dying, my head splitting.

Marisa was taking something out of the fridge and laying breakfast out on the island unit for him, both amusement and disapproval on her face.

Celo's face turned towards the pool, eyes scanning the sun loungers until he found me in the shade of the swing seat, his stare keeping me still.

I didn't even notice when Felipe sat next to me. Caught off guard, I broke my staring to smile at him, and when my eyes returned to Marcelo a second later, he was back to talking to Marisa and eating his breakfast.

"So…" One of Felipe's hands hugged me around the waist, the other tried to move some of my hair behind my ear. I

115

pushed his hands away from me. He looked confused. "I thought we were ok?"

"We *are* ok. But you are my best friend's cousin, and this is a bad idea. I was really drunk yesterday, ok? It shouldn't have happened."

His arm reached out for me, his voice soft. "Hey… don't worry. Nobody would have a problem with it."

"*I* have a problem with it, Felipe." He was starting to piss me off. "I know you like me, but I don't want to hurt your feelings." I got up and went into the house.

As I walked past the kitchen, Marcelo's eyes followed me, his head turning to watch me go up the stairs. He was pissing me off too.

I walked into my room, banged the door, threw myself face down on the bed, and screamed into the pillow.

CHAPTER 5

Luciana

"Hello?"

I opened Paige's door and walked in. I had knocked but nobody had answered. A pair of legs appeared to be floating a third up from the floor like someone had buried a stiff in the wall and left the legs out, suspended in some sort of macabre decor. Paige lay on the bed face down like a plank of wood. She had stormed off after talking to Pepino.

"Are you ok, flower? What's going on?"

"Um fum um um," she answered with her face still on the pillow.

"What? I can't hear you."

Her face turned to the side. "I fucked it up!"

"Fucked what up?"

"I snogged Felipe."

"What!! When??" Caught by surprise, I laughed. "Well, it's hardly like you haven't done it before. No harm done."

"It's not funny, Lu!" She scowled at me, but her voice was whiny.

"No, it isn't." I tried my best to keep a serious face. But Paige shoved her face back in the pillow, her hair spreading all around her head like seaweed, and I couldn't help it and started chuckling. "Sorry. I thought you didn't fancy him?"

"Um dum."

"You don't?"

"Num!"

"If you don't fancy him, why did you snog him?"

She rolled over and lay on her back. "I don't know, ok!? I was drunk, everyone was disappearing for walks on the beach. I wanted someone to throw me against the wall and call me a lizard, you know? Why is everybody else having all the fun and I can't?"

I started laughing. I couldn't help it.

"Why are you laughing, Lu? This isn't funny!"

"It sounds so wrong when you say it in English."

"It's your bloody saying!" She got up and sat on the bed. "Now he thinks we're in the early stages of marriage and I can't wait for him to bugger off to China. I mean, what am I gonna have to say? 'Fuck off prick. I know I fucked you in London, but I don't like you?!' I don't want to hurt his feelings!"

I giggled. "Can you imagine?" At first, she looked annoyed, but then she started smiling too. "Well… it's not like you haven't kissed him before."

Paige shot me a disapproving look.

"So no fanny flutters then, huh?"

"None, zilch, zero, nada." Her hands followed her words in an array of gestures that all meant the same thing.

"Yeah… that's not good." I bumped my shoulder into hers and we both started laughing. "Do you want me to talk to him?"

"No. I made the mess; I should clean it up. I just need to get through today and tomorrow, then things will go back to normal."

"I'm not sure they will, flower. You might have to call him a prick and tell him you don't like him." We both giggled. "But let me know if you change your mind and I'll talk to him." I squeezed her hand. "Is that really all that's going on?" Paige went quiet, looked down and fiddled with her nails. "Because you, Celo, and Pepino are all moping."

She nodded and bumped her shoulder into mine. "What about you? Did the brunette throw you against the wall and call you a lizard?"

I laughed. "God, that really does sounds so wrong in English!" She smiled. "Nah. There was just some... energetic snogging. Although... I wouldn't have minded if he had bent me over a rock and called me a lizard."

Paige let out her more genuine laugh. "You're a lost cause, you know that?"

"You're coming back down?"

"In a minute. I need to call home."

Pepino and her mum were the two things I was pretty sure Paige was trying to avoid. I didn't really think she would be doing either, but I'd let her come out of her hut when she was ready. I had learned at uni that when she got like this, you had to give her space to process things in her own time.

"Ok. I'm down there if you need me. I brought you some more water." I pointed at the glass on the side table.

Two hours later, she still hadn't come down.

"Is she not coming back down?" Pepino had been pacing around the pool in front of me and Celo for quite a few minutes.

"She said she would, but I don't think so. She's still feeling hungover and has probably fallen asleep."

"Maybe I should go and see if she's ok." He started walking towards the door.

"Pepino! Stop being an impatient pain in the arse!" He halted on the spot. "I know you like her, but she has a bitch of a hangover. Leave her alone! Celo will tell you... suffocating a

119

girl with your attention when she wants to be alone will just piss her off."

"She's right." Celo finally decided to break his annoying moody silence and help me out.

"Thank you!" I shot him a look and threw my hands up in the air exasperated.

He shrugged.

"What the hell happened anyway? I went for a walk on the beach, then I came back, and it'd all gone to shit."

Pepino sat down at the bottom of my lounger, the reflection of the sun in the water making him squint. "She's confusing me loads. We had something good going in London. Then, ok… we didn't speak for a while. But she's been flirting with me since she landed—at the party, here, on the beach, when we went to the waterfall, you know, when you were taking that picture…" Celo's head turned. "She kissed me on the beach, all fiery and really into it, said we were good at breakfast, but now she is all moody and shit." He was frustrated. And I don't think it was just with the situation.

As if the conversation bored him, Celo sighed and sat astride his sun lounger, arms resting on his legs, fingers intertwined in the middle. "From what I saw, *you* kissed her. *You* were the one flirting with her." He said it slowly, his timbre low, voice smooth like butter. His tone was calm, but everything about him screamed confrontational. It was the calm before the storm.

"So you saw it?"

His head turned to me slowly, nodded once, and went back to facing Pepino. The way he was moving made me think of a snake when it's ready to attack. At first it coils its body slowly, making itself small as though it doesn't mean any harm, but when you least expect it, it propels its whole length at you and bites you.

"Yeah, maybe, but she was into it. She came for a walk with me, and we hooked up."

Celo's face had no expression, his eyes hidden behind the Ray-Bans, but the corner of his jaw poked out, he cracked his fingers, and his head turned to face the pool.

I tapped his leg with my toes. "Did you see that too?"

He shook his head without looking at me. "I left them to it, had my own date to worry about." His voice was low and flat, the words coming out through his teeth.

Pepino was looking at both of us, completely oblivious, still waiting for an answer.

"She was drunk, Felipe!" I blurted out. He was being such a blind idiot. "Like… paralytic! She's English which, by the way, means she was conceived in beer rather than amniotic fluid. Do you know how much that woman has to drink to throw up? If it was one of us, we'd be in an alcoholic coma. She has the mother of all hangovers! And you… if you're honest, you know you took advantage. You've been trying to get back into her knickers *for weeks* and she never gave you the space. If you cared about her that much, you wouldn't have made a move when she was that drunk."

Celo's head turned towards us. Pepino didn't respond, but he started to blush from the neck up. He knew I was on to his antics.

"Stop deluding yourself that this was anything more than a quick thing. You got what you wanted, didn't you? Now give her some space and get out of her hair."

"She was that drunk and you went for it anyway." Celo's voice was low, husky. It wasn't a question; it was full on disapproval and reproach. "Then you sit here like a fucking moron, wondering why she's moody and doesn't wanna talk to you."

"Don't give me this shit, both of you. Paige and I have hooked up before. I know her, ok? Yes, she had a few drinks, but she wasn't out of it. She knew what we were doing. I didn't force myself on her if that's what you're both getting at. She let me do it. She was into it as much as I was. I would never do anything she didn't want me to."

Celo looked away, shook his head. Then inhaled a deep breath and sighed, as if the whole thing was boring and he was losing his patience. His leg flicked over the lounger and he stood up. "Does anyone want a drink? I'm getting a beer." But before we could answer he walked away.

Paige didn't come out of her room till dinner. She emerged from the corridor ten minutes late like a flipping phoenix rising from the ashes. Dressed in a figure-hugging red dress as her body armor, her hair tied up into a long sleek ponytail with little bits loose at the front of her face, big pearl hoops in her ears. Red lipstick and black eyeliner as her war paint. She never looked more like an English rose or more model-esque.

It was a complete and utter overkill.

Everyone stopped. Celo looked up from his phone and did a double take, his eyes widening, unable to look away. And I'm pretty sure Pepino stopped breathing.

I love that girl! Nobody could bounce back with a vengeance like her. What is it the English say? Hell hath no fury like a woman scorned?

"Oh, my goodness, Paige! Risa, hold on to your husband!" My mum, as always, breaking the arctic icebergs.

"I know, right! Darling, you're not allowed to look this good. You make Marta and I look like two old hags."

Paige laughed. "Like that is even possible, Marisa. You two always look amazing. If anything, I'm just trying to keep up."

"That's true." Uncle Rô wrapped his arms around Risa. "You always look amazing." Dad looked at Mum fondly.

"Sorry I'm so late. Those Caipirinhas really did me in. Plus, I think those mosquitos got me." She even sounded convincing. The woman was a pro.

"You were in your room for ages!" Freddie bridged the gap with his booming voice. Everyone laughed.

"I know. Sorry, Freddie. I wasn't feeling too good, but I haven't forgotten our deal."

"I only go to my room when my mom sends me. When I've been naughty." Conditioned by Risa to never leave the house on his own, he automatically held on to Paige's hand and started walking up the stairs towards the car. "Have you been naughty?"

"And just like that, the six-year-old gets the date," Pepino joked. Everybody laughed. "The kid has the moves, I'm telling you! High five little bro, you're the man!" Freddie high-fived Pepino, then Celo, and me.

"Mommy, I'm the man!" he said, climbing into his car seat.

"Yes, you're the man on the booster seat. Now, stop wiggling so I can buckle you in." Auntie Risa, as always, trying to herd the cats.

The drive to the restaurant was subarctic. Celo was pretending not to be interested in anything, Pepino was trying to make conversation with only me responding, Paige looked out of the window.

We walked to the restaurant with our parents walking ahead, Paige and I in the middle, and the boys falling behind walking at Freddie's pace. Paige was attracting a fair amount of attention. Every bloke stared, every girlfriend frowned and unconsciously held on to her man tighter. A group of guys went past and whistled at her; she not only gave them eye contact, but smiled at them flirtatiously, the whistles only increasing. Our parents looking amused by the commotion; Celo, Pepino, and even Freddie sporting the faces of thunder.

"Celo, why did those boys do that?" Freddie, as always, pointing out what nobody wanted to say out loud.

"I don't know, bud." Liar. He knew damn well.

"You need to stop that." I giggled, intertwining my arm into Paige's.

"Stop what?"

"I mean, don't get me wrong, I enjoy watching them squirm. Both of them have been a bit of a dick, but even Freddie is getting jealous now. This is like the *Legends of the Fall*."

"Is that the movie with Brad Pitt we watched the other night?"

"Yep. Three brothers—the little one, the nice guy, and the sex god—fall in love with the same woman."

"Wait, wasn't that like a really sad movie? The young one dies, the woman kills herself, and the sex god becomes a loner?"

"Exactly. Freddie is only six. He has his whole life ahead of him. Have mercy on his little soul."

"That makes no sense at all!" She laughed.

"No? Look back for a minute." Paige looked over her shoulder. All three boys were looking like they were walking to a funeral.

"I see…"

"I'm loving the revenge dress up, but take it easy on the little one."

"Uh-huh."

We both laughed. "You're spending too much time with Freddie."

"Did you hear that, Freddie?" Paige stopped walking and extended a hand out to Freddie, who was only too happy to leave the two clouds of gloom and join her. "Auntie Lu thinks I have started talking like you."

♥♥♥

Our last day was like a Mexican telenovela. If I didn't have a bad feeling about it all, it would've been funny.

Mum and Auntie Risa hung around the pool looking like two silver screen goddesses—in their floating coverups, big sun hats, and glasses of fizz. Paige was lying in the shade in a super cute bikini pretending to read her book—she always dressed up when she felt shit. Pepino was buzzing around her like an annoying bee, trying to have more of her honey. Celo had become a grumpy mute, hiding behind his sunglasses, pretending he hadn't noticed anything, but he was watching everyone. Freddie brought the comic relief, wearing Risa's sunglasses and floating on top of a giant pineapple, a bottle of juice in the drink holder, like a mini pimp. And dad and Rô were completely oblivious to it all. Sometimes I wondered if they were from a different planet.

I had suspected Paige had developed a crush on Celo. She always denied it. Probably because he was a love rat, and she knew it was a bad idea. Or maybe because if she said it out loud, it would become real. But on the beach, it had become very clear that her crush was jumbo jet size. How Pepino didn't notice was beyond me. She couldn't take her eyes off him. And as he flirted with the girl in the red bikini, she had become quiet, sullen and started drinking.

The irony was that Celo was different too. I couldn't quite put my finger on it at first; he was a poker face pro. Went around as cool as a cucumber, planning on everything he did being ambiguous enough that you couldn't call him out on it, but this holiday, he was quiet and his shield was up. He didn't flirt with anyone, didn't go off on his tail hunting escapades, and watched Pepino and Paige with great interest whenever he thought no one was looking. Had the girl with the red bikini not thrown herself at him, quite literally, he wouldn't have done anything. And even when he did, I could tell he wasn't trying. He was off his game; it was weird.

Everyone was enjoying the last day of sun outside, but Celo walked into the house and was gone for a while. When I walked into the kitchen, he had his back to the pool, hands on the counter, and he was tapping his head against the cupboard on repeat.

"You ok there, love rat? Need your medication or something?"

He pushed himself off the counter. "Awesome. Making some cocktails. Do you want anything?"

I leaned on the island unit while he got everything ready. "Pina Colada, please. What is going on?"

He nodded. "What is going on, what?"

"You're moping."

His head jerked backwards, a deep frown taking over his forehead. "I don't mope." He started pouring things into a mixer.

"No, you just become a grumpy mute that bangs his head against cupboards."

He scoffed. "No change there then." But he didn't look at me, focused on his hands instead.

I changed tact. "Do you like Paige?" Sometimes the best way to crack his armor was to ambush him.

Celo looked at me then—no expression once or ever on his face—closed the mixer, gave it a smack, and started shaking it. "What kind of stupid question is that?" His eyes went back to cocktail making; he smacked the side of the mixer, pulled a glass towards him, and started pouring my Pina.

"You didn't answer it, though." He added a pineapple slice and a cherry to the top of it and pushed the glass to me, then went over to the sink and rinsed the mixer. "Are you going to answer it?"

"Everybody likes Paige. Especially Felipe." He didn't look at me but poured more things into the mixer.

126

"I'm asking you if *you* like her." I sipped my cocktail. "Nice Pina, by the way."

An exasperated sigh came out of him. "What you're getting at, Lu?" And he started shaking the mixer.

"Why are you avoiding my question?" Celo was many things, but he wasn't a liar. If he didn't want to give you an answer, not to lie, he would deflect it.

His eyebrows screwed into a full-fledged frown. "Because it's a stupid question." He started pouring the orange mixture into a glass.

"Which means it's an easy answer."

He carefully poured a red liquid down the side of the glass, making it sink to the bottom. "What difference does it make if I like her, Lu? Felipe is in love with her, and she'll get on a plane and go home soon. So…" His eyes returned to me. "Your question is pointless." He added a pineapple slice to the top of the glass and pushed it my way. "There, for your friend."

"Sex on the Beach?"

A sharp nod. Hands rested on the counter. Stare made of steel.

I smiled at him. Knowing, waiting for him to remember why his mind had gone straight to this cocktail when he thought of Paige. His head lifted ever so slightly, muscles at his jaw poking out, resolute not to admit to it but knowing damn well that I knew.

"Should that not be an orange slice?"

His eyes narrowed and he stared at me for a minute. I'd touched a nerve, and it wasn't just with the orange comment. Then he sprang into action—picked up a knife, walked to the fruit bowl, cut an orange slice, threw the pineapple slice in the sink, threw the orange slice in the glass, and turned his back to me to wash the mixer. I was surprised he didn't cut one of his fingers off in his strop.

He did like her, but he wasn't going to do anything about it.

127

Part of me felt a sense of relief. This was more complicated and delicate than a spider's web. The other part of me felt sorry for the three of them. Paige had just watched the guy she liked make out with someone else. Celo had just spent a week watching his best friend and brother hit on the girl he liked. And he never liked anyone. And Pepino had spent weeks trying to get with this girl, only to eventually realize she was into his brother. Love is indeed a mean bitch, and she serves dinner cold. That's why I'd never invite that cow to mine.

CHAPTER 6

Paige

I was glad to be back at Lu's flat. Who would've thought I would be so desperate to leave a paradise island? Guess the saying is true—you can have too much of a good thing. I had actually looked forward to being back in the city, to sanity and feeling normal.

Except… nothing felt normal anymore. I thought running back would fix everything. It didn't.

I was ok during the day, but at night I sat awake looking at the pictures, playing things in my head—the drive, the boat, the late swims… Trying to find some sense in it all, but I just felt like I was going insane and seeing things where there was nothing to see.

During the holiday, Marcelo had gone from not speaking to me to flirting and almost kissing me in the pool. Then he hooked up with some other girl on the beach and for the last two days didn't speak to me at all. Nothing had really happened, yet everything had changed. Funny how something that never was can completely knock you off kilter and consume your thoughts.

Most of the nights I was awake, he would also show as being online on WhatsApp. And as I thought through every conversation with a fine-tooth comb, and sat there overthinking everything, I knew there was no rhyme or reason to it. He was just a player, a cat toying with a mouse for entertainment, and I got played.

The whole thing filled me with gloom and made me want to run. I considered going to see Ryan in Denver, even searched for flights. But when it came to booking the tickets, I just couldn't press that confirm button.

I had no reason to stay, but I didn't want to leave. Told myself I didn't want to go because of Lu—she would be really upset if I cut my trip short—but in reality, I didn't really know why I wanted to stay.

Felipe was another issue. He had tried talking to me about our kiss on the beach a couple of times after we came back. Every time he mentioned it, I cut the conversation short. Lucky for me, he was going to China soon.

When his farewell party came around, I was actually relieved. It was nice to get out of the house too. I had been hiding in Lu's flat for a week claiming to be busy with work, but I had started getting cabin fever. Maybe Lu's busy lifestyle had rubbed off on me and I was missing all the excitement of a busy calendar. Maybe that's where I was going wrong. Rather than sitting here sulking, I should be going out and enjoying my life.

Felipe's leaving do was buzzing. There were so many people, I was surprised he managed to fit everyone in his flat. All the usual culprits were there and then some. You would be forgiven if you thought he was relocating rather than just traveling for a month.

Then Marcelo turned up.

For once, without some adoring fan hanging off his neck like a chinchilla. Not that it made any difference. I shouldn't care. It sure didn't look like he cared. And, of course, as soon as he walked through the doors, the bastard had to open the most devastating smile, greeting the first group of people with boisterous handshakes, hugs, and laughter. He clearly knew most of the guests, as he worked the room greeting the men and kissing the women.

But after a few minutes, he stopped with his back to the door, eyes scanning, searching for something until he found me, and he went very still, his eyes focused. He looked at me for a long while before offering a slow nod. Eyes unmoving, keeping me equally still.

I had not seen him for a week. His hair was in a top knot and the low buzz bit underneath looked fresh, like he had just had it trimmed. All his tattoos were hidden under a polo shirt buttoned all the way up. His high tops matching the color of the logo on his chest. I hate to admit it, but after a week of seeing him every day and a week of not seeing him at all... I had missed him.

Dani spotted me and came screaming to hug me. By the time my eyes went back to him, he was already engaged in conversation with a group of women. He had come alone, but it didn't look like he was going home that way.

And just like that my butterflies turned into stomach-ache —my mood shifting from sunny to rain like the good old British weather.

He never came to talk to me, not even to say hi. Always keeping his distance, unlike Felipe who was always finding ways to end up in conversations I was in. But every so often his eyes would lock with mine from across the room. He would look at me until someone demanded his or my attention.

And I could feel it stronger than ever—the pull of upset. That sadness that just comes over unannounced and makes you not want to do anything at all. Maybe I should just go home. I'd had my fun, caught up with my best friend. Maybe it was time I faced my problems. Or maybe I should make good on my promise and go visit Ryan.

It was hard not to feel I was being punished. Punished for

running away from my troubles rather than facing them head on; for giving my mother the silent treatment and leaving her all alone. I had done it to her, now someone else was doing it to me. Maybe this was karma. Maybe the universe was trying to teach me a lesson.

"You ok there, flower?" Lu was worried about me. She had repeatedly asked me this same question every day of late.

"I'm good. Just catching up with everyone."

She interlaced her arm with one of mine. "Is it weird to be back out in the wild?"

"What?" I laughed.

"You haven't been out of the apartment for a week; now you're back out partying. Whoop! Whoop!" It never ceased to amaze me how nothing escaped Lu's notice, even when she wasn't there, and we hadn't spoken about it.

I gestured sarcastic excitement with my hands. "On that note, I'm going to go and get myself a drink. Would you like anything?"

"Not if it's Caipirinha, you're not."

I scowled at her.

"I know your M.O." She pointed two fingers at her eyes then at me.

My stare was unimpressed on purpose.

I didn't want a drink. I just wanted to escape her scrutiny. Lu sounded uncaring, but she was actually keeping tabs on me, worried that I was feeling a little blue. She wasn't wrong, I just didn't want to have to explain.

Didn't feel like partying or making polite conversation either. So instead, I took the back steps up to the mezzanine floor, eventually finding a little corner hidden by a group of people, where I could still watch what was going on, but no one could see me unless they knew where to look. The perfect spot to weather out my current annoyance at everything and nothing. And as I sat there sulking, I was painfully aware I was behaving like a child hiding under the table.

I had started to wish I'd never come to this party.

Although he never stopped talking and socializing, or flirting, Celo was not still. He was forever turning around, scanning the room midway through his conversations, never settling his attention on anything or anyone. For a minute, he looked up and I thought he had spotted me on the mezzanine, but then his eyes moved elsewhere and didn't return. Felipe joined him. Questions being asked, shoulders being shrugged. Eventually, Marcelo wandered off and moved out of my line of view.

Music mixed with chatter and laughter. Up on the mezzanine the noise felt louder. Lu was twisting a strand of hair around her finger, eyes intent on her target, sitting far too close to a guy I had never met. And I'd had enough of hiding up here like a stalker.

I was going home.

Should've sneaked out, but being an over-polite Brit, I approached Felipe to say goodbye. He had his back turned to me, and as soon as I touched his shoulder and he turned around, I realized he was talking to Marcelo.

"There you are! Where have you been?" His voice had the low pitch of annoyed worry. Behind him, Marcelo crossed his arms and rearranged his stance—chin elevated, eyes looking down at me, in a straight, stiff posture.

"I hope you don't mind, but I'm not feeling too good. I think I'm gonna go. Have a fab time in China," I said, leaning in for a goodbye hug to reinforce my point.

"But the party hasn't even started yet, you can't go home!" He accepted my hug but kept a hand on my back. "How are you getting home anyway?"

"Walking, I think. The fresh air will do me good."

"That's not really a good idea. Are you sure you can't stay?

You can lie down upstairs in my room if you want. I was hoping we could catch up before I left." His hand went down to my waist.

Marcelo looked away, the muscles in his jaw poking out.

"That's really nice of you, but I really just wanna go back to Lu's."

Celo's gaze returned to me; his smug half smile told me he was enjoying something a little too much.

Felipe sighed, disappointed, his hand moving from my waist and giving my hand a gentle squeeze. "Ok, I would take you myself, but that would make me a really shitty host."

"Don't worry about it. It's all good. It's not that far, I can walk."

"I tell you what… Celo can take you. He was just leaving as well, right?"

And there it was. Felipe gave Marcelo that look that says, 'I didn't ask you, but you have to agree with me,' and my eyes went straight to him.

Celo, on the other hand, looked at Felipe like he had announced he'd seen Santa Claus parachuting naked from his balcony. After quickly recomposing his face, he looked at me, then back at Felipe, and cleared his throat. "I'm not sure that will work. I'm already running kinda late." Voice cold, matter of fact.

"Bullshit! What is the point of being your own boss if you can't get in a couple of minutes late? It's on your way, anyway." Felipe turned to face me full on. "You don't mind if he takes you, do you? He's a bit weird, but he's alright." He tried to make me laugh, grabbing my shoulders and gently shaking them.

Behind Felipe, Marcelo rubbed the back of his neck a couple of times, the muscles in his jaw fighting each other underneath his skin.

I decided to let him off the hook. "Felipe, honestly, it's fine.

It's only a few blocks, my legs aren't broken, I can walk, or I can call an Uber." But my voice couldn't hide my disappointment.

"No way. I'm sure Celo won't mind." Felipe placed his arm around his brother's shoulders and gave him a firm tuck. My eyes met his and, embarrassed, I looked down, bit my lower lip, and shifted on my feet—something I know I do when I feel put on the spot, but can never stop myself.

A silence too long to be comfortable and too short to be awkward followed, all the noise around us seeming to fall away. And all I could do was mentally beg my cheeks and neck not to betray me and broadcast my keenness.

Marcelo stared at me; eyes twitched like he was trying to blink but couldn't. Then he nodded. I looked at him, surprised, looked at Felipe, looked at the floor, bit my lips to buggery.

Felipe escorted us to the lift. The music from his party echoing down the corridor. "Will you still be here when I get back? Tell me you'll be here." His arms wrapped around my waist, and he looked deep into my eyes, trying to create a moment.

Marcelo's head turned, watching us from the corner of his eyes.

I smiled but squirmed free by pushing against Felipe's biceps. "I wish I could say yes. But I promised my father I was going to Denver. Maybe we'll overlap, though, for a couple days when you get back."

"I hope we do." And he planted a kiss on my cheek. "Look after her for me." A finger pointed at his brother. "No funny business. Make sure she gets there in one piece."

Marcelo gave him an unimpressed, almost angry look and walked into the lift.

"Ignore him. He's always this overwhelming ray of sunshine, don't take it personally."

Off we went to the underground garage without

another word, moving around each other in orbits so he could keep me just like always—at an arm's length. Perfectly distant. He couldn't help himself flirting with anything sporting a pair of boobs, but with me... it was like I had some terrible disease and was bloody contagious. The lift ride all of a sudden seemed crowded with only the two of us in it.

A little rude, he walked out of the lift first and ahead of me. His car sat in the underground garage—mean looking, wide tires, black glossy paint. A red line running over the door between the front and back tire like the flatline on an angry heart monitor.

"A 1969 Mustang?"

"You're into cars." It wasn't a question. It was more like he thought it was highly unlikely.

I shrugged off his comment. "I was surprised to see quite a few of them here. But then again, you drive on the same side of the road as the Americans."

He raised one eyebrow while looking at me, like he was completely unimpressed. His eyes dropped to my lips and, without another word, he got in the car. I followed.

The Mustang roared to life, the whole garage echoing with the noise.

"Thanks for the lift," I said after a moment of awkward silence while he maneuvered up and out on to the road.

"It's hardly like I had a choice." The words came out through his teeth, resentful and cold.

My anger spiked. What was his problem? Was it necessary to be always such a prick?

He drove along without affording a single look in my direction. And I scowled at everything outside the window. Eventually, we pulled up in front of Lu's building. At the risk of twisting an ankle, I jumped out while the car was still pulling to a stop, banging the door shut as hard as I could behind me. Before I made it to the gate, tires screamed against the pavement.

He had graduated from ignoring me to being outright rude. Come to think of it, I didn't really know why I liked him so damn much. He had mostly just been an arsehole and done nothing to deserve my obsession.

❤❤❤

Lu jumped on my bed, head almost hitting mine—a habit she had acquired at uni. "Right! You little party pooper! I can't believe you left me without even telling me you were going!"

"You were enjoying yourself. I didn't want to burst your bubble."

"What's with the long face anyway?"

I shrugged as though I didn't know what she was talking about.

"I'm taking none of that moping. Tonight is Pepino's last night before he jets off. You more than anyone should be celebrating." She poked my shoulder. "He'll pick you up around nine and we are going to Eight. Celo has this new live band thing going on, and we're all going to support the gig."

Of course! Bloody perfect with the sour taste of yesterday's rendezvous still lingering in my memory and my temper.

"And why are we not going together?"

Lu smiled wider. "I have a date," her shoulders rising with the last word.

"The guy from the party?"

Enthusiastic nods. Eyebrows rising.

"Already?"

"You know me! I'm no time-waster."

I laughed. "And how long is this toyboy going to last?"

"Well…" Lu sucked air through her teeth. "So many men… so… little time."

"You're terrible, you know that?" My laughing gave away that I found it entertaining.

"We always knew you were the sweet one. I'm just making up for your karma." Lu shrugged, the words reaching their climax in a high-pitched tone. "You have your heart broken by them, and I avenge you." One of her fists raised; eyes narrowed.

"I see. Quite the honorable heroine then, huh?"

"Absolutely! Now come on. You need to help me look hot for my date."

"You don't need my help."

"No, but you need mine. Chop chop!" Her hands clapped in rhythm with her words.

As we walked through the doors, Eight was packed. So much for needing support for his gig! After fighting our way through the masses, we finally made it to the bar where Felipe hugged his brother throwing both hands in the air as if to say, 'what the hell'. Then he moved aside and pulled me towards the counter.

Marcelo's eyes were instantly on me, down my cleavage, then back to my eyes. I had wondered if the high-waisted sailor pants with the crossover top was a good look, but that little sneaky peek down my cleavage answered my question. He might not like me, but he wasn't immune to a little flesh.

Celo jerked his chin upwards, eyebrows raising—his usual greeting for me. Because God forbid he actually wasted his breath on words. I returned the greeting and looked away, trying to come across as unimpressed as I could.

I thought we would wander to our regular table, but Felipe apparently decided that the solid wall of bodies was too much to work through.

The music was good and the atmosphere electric. Eventually people started dancing. Nothing in Brazil seemed to end without a little bit of a dancing thing going on. I just watched, fascinated by the rhythm and energy.

Every so often, I caught a glimpse of Marcelo—rushing behind the bar, making a show out of throwing shots into a mixer, flipping bottles in the air—and every once in a while, he glanced back at me.

This is what I found so frustrating. For someone who didn't like me, he did seem to waste a lot of time keeping tabs on me.

The phone vibrated in my pocket. Luciana. She was over two hours late. To be able to hear her I had to step outside and turn the corner. Surprise, surprise… she was caught up on her date and wouldn't be coming to Eight. Excellent. Once more I was stuck with Felipe. Sometimes I seriously wondered if they did it on purpose.

I switched the phone off and looked around. The street had gone quiet. Odd for a city as busy as São Paulo.

Just as I started moving back towards the bar, a man caught me by the arm. Drunken words stumbled out of his mouth in a Portuguese so distorted, I couldn't even try to understand it. I moved back a little, and he came out from under the shadows. Well dressed, my age. Just disoriented by one drink too many.

I tried to explain I didn't understand what he was saying, but as soon as he heard my accent, his demeanor changed— eyes became clear, focused. I realized seconds too late that he behaved drunk, but he didn't smell of booze. His appearance too pristine, stance too steady for someone who had supposedly been hitting the bottle all night. I tried to set my arm free, but the more I pulled, the tighter he held on.

Panic started rising up my spine. Talking on the phone and distracted, I had gone too far around the corner and was too hidden for anyone to see me, the noise coming from the bar too loud for anyone to hear me.

The stranger noticed. For a second, he smiled.

Then his face twisted.

Several things happened at once. He yanked at my arm—my back falling on to the front of him like a plank of wood, my arms pinned by his, his face right next to mine. My necklace was snapped from my neck. Feet lifted off the ground—body being dragged into the shadows. Now in full panic, I started screaming, kicking, my movement knocking him off balance enough for me to get loose. I tried to run and almost fell backwards when he pulled me back by my hair. My arms everywhere—pushing, hitting, and scratching blindly. His grip intensified—constricting, immobilizing. As I lost ground and he pulled me into the darkness, fear really set in, and I screamed like my life depended on it.

Out of nowhere, a hand came down on the man's arm, and a punch connected to his face with a sickening crack right next to my head, while a body forced its way in between us, and the commotion set my arms free.

Marcelo stood in between me and the man.

After quickly getting back on to his feet, the stranger jerked his hand to the side—the silver of a blade hitting a spot of light. His back turned to me, eyes fixed on the man, Marcelo used his arms and body to push us both backwards towards the light near the bar's back door.

Taking stock of what had happened, the stranger seemed to weigh up his options, grabbed my phone and necklace from the floor near him, and set off running. Celo's body faced the man, his eyes not moving from the running figure until he was satisfied he was far enough not to be a threat.

"Did he do anything to you?" He held out my arms, eyes frantically scanning me. "Are you ok?" Voice sounding anxious, he stood so close, I could feel his words on my face.

"He took my necklace… and my phone." I felt cold.

Celo glanced back to where the man once stood, then moved my hair aside to look at my neck. "It doesn't look like it cut into your skin." His eyes focused on me, and a thumb rubbed the spot just above my wrist where mere minutes earlier the stranger had grabbed hold. "You're ok. Everything is fine." His reassurance was almost a whisper, forehead nearly touching mine. A hand lingered at the side of my neck, and he just stood there looking at me, eyes searching my face for something.

I nodded, but I couldn't stop staring at where the man had set off running.

"He's not coming back. Everything is fine."

"There you are!" Felipe shouted from behind us. As I startled, Marcelo let go of me and stepped away. "I was wondering where you'd gone."

"I was on the phone to Lu." The words almost didn't make it out of my throat.

I looked back at Marcelo; his posture had changed. Chin up in the air, hands tight into fists close to his body, he looked something close to angry.

"Am I interrupting something?" Felipe's finger pointed from Celo to me repeatedly.

"Some asshole just attacked her." Marcelo's voice was cold, sharp.

"What!?" Felipe was now at my side checking me over himself. "Bastard! Did you get a good look at him?" He hugged me, trying to comfort me.

"He took her phone and her necklace. You shouldn't let her wander off on her own, Felipe. She's just a stupid foreigner, but you should know better. Do yourself a favor and take her home." He wasn't just angry; he was outright furious.

It stung. Even Felipe looked shocked.

Before either of us could say anything else, Celo touched a card to the pad by the door, the lock announcing its release with a click, and he shut it behind him with a vicious bang.

CHAPTER 7

Marcelo

THAT DAMN CHICK WAS GETTING UNDER MY SKIN, MAKING MY LIFE a lot more complicated than it needed to be. It was like she was some sort of personal demon—here to torment me, make my life hell. I had to find a way to cast her out.

It was past lunchtime, and I couldn't think of anything else. All night I could think of nothing else. Every second my mind wasn't occupied, she filled the gap like expanding fucking foam.

Paige had walked out on her phone, but I couldn't see her through the front doors and Felipe was distracted talking to someone he knew, so I watched the monitors. People usually didn't notice, but facing the bar, hanging from the ceiling, were three big CCTV screens. I watched her walk out of one monitor and into the other, down the side street. Then in circles while she had the phone to her ear and almost out of camera shot. As she came off the phone, someone in the blind spot grabbed her arm.

I don't think I've ever moved so fast in my life.

I had barely opened the back door when I heard her scream. She made it like she was going to run, then her head jerked back, and she was pulled backwards into the alleyway. The sound of her screaming was still echoing in my head; it was pure panic. When I saw her trying to get away and that piece of shit holding on to her, I saw red. If I wasn't worried there was more than one of them, I would have beaten that asshole to a pulp.

I rubbed my face and tried to breathe the anger out of my system.

There was no need for him to grab and drag her. He knew where the blind spots on the cameras were. He was hunting and she was prey. It wasn't just a mugging. Just thinking about it filled me with rage. I wanted to smash his face. I needed to adjust the cameras outside to cover a wider angle.

When I could finally look at her, she was whiter than paper, a sickly type of white, shaking so bad you would think she was freezing to death. Her voice was weak, hair all messed up and sticking to her face, eyes wide, clothes out of place. She looked confused, lost, like a rabbit in the headlights.

I wanted so bad to hug her, comfort her, to make her feel better, and I almost did. But I didn't have that liberty. I had never touched her, not even to greet her in all the weeks she'd been here.

Then Felipe turned up, and despite having done fuck, claimed without even blinking the comfort I wanted to give. My blood boiled just thinking about it. I loved the guy like a brother, but sometimes he could be such a moron.

As soon as he knew she was coming, he'd claimed her before she'd even landed. The only thing he could pin his claim on was a bump and grind the two of them had while he visited Lu in London, years ago. And at the time, I couldn't care less. Now, I was desperate just to see her.

I rested my hands on the counter, did push ups against it— rocking my weight up and down. Looked at the ceiling, took a couple of deep breaths trying to get rid of the angry energy. Being behind this bar was starting to feel like confined space.

This was so fucked up. Felipe was the closest thing I had to a brother. And since when did I overthink and give so much of a shit about just touching someone?

I turned up the music, didn't want to think about any of it anymore. But the thoughts screamed even louder. I couldn't help it, my mind had legs of its own. Paige in the pool—her green bikini and the pool color making her eyes so light, it was almost freaky. Her hair looked darker wet, and when her body was emerged in water, her breasts looked rounder and fuller at the top. Felipe trying it on. Her silence to my rudeness, the door of the car banging shut, the glass vibrating.

I'd been like a drug addict at the party, trying to get my fix after not seeing her for a week, looking for her, staring at her at every opportunity. It was a good job the room was packed. Had it been a smaller group, I don't think I'd have been able to hide it.

Driving her home was torture. And I was so mad. Mad I could smell her perfume, and my car would smell like her. Mad she hooked up with Felipe, but I wanted it to be me. Mad she disappeared for a week and took away the only thing I could do. Mad I had missed seeing her. Mad she was leaving. Mad I was almost in physical pain, and she was destroying my sanity. I hadn't gone anyplace near her, and she was ruining my life.

But this is what this sickness did—it made you lose your mind and fuck up everything like an addiction.

I had to crush the shit out of this thing. I had to get her out of my system. In double time. Maybe I could drop by Angie's. Or Inara's. The best way to get over a woman is to be under another, right? Isn't that what they say? But as I went back to slicing lemons, I was just not feeling it. Fuck me! Not Feeling it?! What kind of pathetic excuse was that?! I was so completely screwed.

I don't even know what was it about her that had me by the balls. She wasn't my usual type. Paige not only had curves, in all the right places mind you, but she was also tall—only about half a head shorter than me. Her freakishly pale skin, long hair I couldn't figure out if it was dark blonde or light brown, big eyes in such a light shade of green that they were close to weird, and killer lips had definitely grown on me. Her lower lip was slightly fuller than the top one and her nose could almost be too big for her face, but all her features seemed to be in perfect harmony somehow. Even the dimple on her chin didn't stand out as much as it should. It was almost as if they were part of a carefully balanced picture—one thing complementing and balancing the other when individually they would look quite odd.

Fuck! I'd spent too much time thinking about this. And clearly stared at her face for long enough to fucking know all these details. She was a dangerous one too—the sweet girl next door type everyone falls in love with.

I rested my head on the edge of one of the shelves and put my weight against it until I felt a level of pain. It refocused my brain and it was better than driving myself insane, going in circles in my head.

"Are you ok there?"

My eyes snapped opened. I froze. You gotta be kidding me.

One look over my shoulder… Paige was standing there. I had finally lost it and started seeing her ghost.

I turned around, automatically drying my hands on a cloth. In one long motion, she looked down, tucked her hair behind one of her ears and looked at me. I looked over her shoulder expecting to see Felipe or Lu. Paige was never alone.

"Nope. It's just me. No babysitters today." She pressed her lips together and rocked on her feet. Her arms following the movement until they slapped back against her thighs. Fingers crisscrossed into each other, her hands twisting like she wanted to snap them off.

I placed my hands on the counter. She didn't come any closer.

"I don't want to bother you. I just came to say thank you." Her eyes dropped and she blinked like a memory flashed behind them. Fingers unconsciously rubbed the bruises on her arm. From where I was, I could see the shape of four fingers. "For yesterday."

Paige rummaged inside her bag, showed me a black box, gave a step forward, put it on the counter in front of me, and stepped back to where she had stood.

"So... thank you." Her voice failed as she finished the last word.

I dropped the cloth on the counter and opened the box. A little card sat on top of a leather cuff.

Thanks for saving my
stupid foreign arse.
Paige

I meant to smile, but it came out as a snort.

"I noticed you like those."

I stared at her like a moron. In this light her hair was caramel, and her pupils were huge, like the eyes of a cat. She nodded and started to turn away.

"You didn't have to do that." She turned back around. We stared at each other. "I didn't mean to call you a stupid foreigner either. I was just... pumped, I guess." Had forgotten I did that.

She stood there nodding. The bar was quiet. I unfastened the leather cuff I had on and tried the one she gave me for size. Not bad, bearing in mind she knew nothing about me. Paige smiled when she saw me putting it on.

"Would you like a coffee?"

Her smile got wider. "Do you have tea?"

"Only fluffy tea."

Her eyebrows dipped towards one another. "Fluffy tea?"

"Herbal." She laughed and shook her head in disapproval. I laughed with her. The back of my neck itched; I rubbed it. "No entourage for you today?"

"I made a run for it. *Mission Impossible* style."

"Suffering in the penthouse, were you, Lewis?" I snorted.

"You have no idea." Her voice serious, as if she actually meant it. Then she recovered. "I get fed, swim and sunbathe all day. Subhuman conditions really."

"The sunbathing doesn't seem to be working."

"Exactly. I need to make a complaint. The sun isn't hot enough to burn me to a crisp. Not even when I'm on a yacht. I thought this was Brazil! Completely unacceptable."

We both smiled. I stared. I remembered the yacht. Her body stretched across the seats, all cream and freckles like chocolate sprinkles. She had asked for Sex on the Beach. Over the last week, I had pored over those memories like I was Gollum, and she was 'my precious', going through all the pictures and her songs on repeat. Unable to stop driving myself insane.

"You never said if you wanted the herbal tea."

Before she could reply, her stomach growled. "Excuse *me*!" Hands flying to her waistline, eyes wide, face going pink. "Sorry. Fugitive on the run here." She pointed at herself.

"Do you like sushi?" The words escaped my mouth before I could think any better. Yeah. I, apparently, enjoyed digging my own fucking grave.

CHAPTER 8
Paige

I MUST HAVE BEEN STARING AT IT LIKE IT WAS ABOUT TO SWALLOW me whole, because he grinned the most indecent self-righteous grin I've ever seen on him. Why, oh why, out of all days, today had to be the day he was riding rather than driving?

Thin tire at the front, fat one at the back, chrome pipes shining like new, red-orange flames licking the black paint on the petrol tank—the bike spelled dangerous loud and clear.

"Have you ever been on a bike before?" he said mounting the thing, looking ridiculously dangerous himself.

I shook my head.

His grin grew wider. "This is a Harley. It's more of a cruiser. So don't let the noise scare you. All you have to do is keep your shoulders in line with mine. When I lean, lean with me, but always keep your shoulders in line with mine. Your feet will go on these. See this tube here? It will get pretty hot, so don't touch it with your leg at all costs, ok? And always keep your arms in, don't stick them out to point at anything. It's not safe," he explained, offering me one of the helmets. "There is comms in there, so we can talk to each other."

I nodded throughout his explanation, but I was sure my smile was painted on.

Celo helped me fasten my helmet—the inside of it squeezing my face, nullifying my hearing. Then we tested we could hear each other, and he showed me how to mount behind him, giving me his arm to steady myself. He checked my feet to make sure they were in the right place. I looked for somewhere to hold, but there wasn't anywhere, so I had no choice but to wrap my arms around him. Not that I didn't want to, mind you.

"You ok back there, Lewis?" His voice filled my helmet while he maneuvered the thing out onto the pavement, waiting for a gap in the traffic. "If you want me to stop at any time, just tap me three times, ok? We'll go after this red car."

As he whizzed his way through, squeezing between cars when he could, the bike thundering underneath us, my casual hold became a bear hug. He placed his hand on top of mine and gave it a gentle squeeze, trying to reassure me. "We're almost there. You still ok back there?" At a couple of traffic lights, he squeezed my knee and turned back to check I wasn't losing my shit.

As nerve-racking as it sounds, it was also exhilarating. And it felt amazing. The rush of adrenaline, combined with the physical contact and his voice in my helmet, was a heck of an experience.

We walked into the sushi restaurant and for a moment all I could see was the light coming from the other side. Then my eyes adjusted, and I realized a big window framed a Japanese garden at the back of it—sculptured greenery, white gravel, and yellow boulders. The black glossy furniture dimming the light inside and making the garden stand out even more. Square angles on everything giving the whole place a very oriental feel.

Marcelo asked for a table at the back, hidden out of the way, overlooking a peaceful pond filled with bright orange and white carps. Good job the ride on the Harley had destroyed all my nerves. There weren't any left to think of getting nervous while out for food.

He smiled. We both had our arms over the table. If I moved my fingers, I could touch him. He followed my eyes to our hands.

"You're bruised." His thumb rubbed where the man had grabbed hold of me.

"Yeah." I looked at the thumb mark I could see on the inside of my arm. "One of the many benefits of having skin the color of milk."

The corner of his mouth lifted in a half smile. "It suits you. Is your neck bruised as well?"

"I don't know. I can't see." I moved my waves out of the way, tilting my head so he could tell me.

His hand went under my hair, cold fingers brushing my skin, thumb rubbing at the base of my neck where the necklace would've been. "Just a little."

Goosebumps spread down my body.

He noticed. "My fingers are cold, sorry. It's the glass." A finger pointed at the cold beer he'd been holding just before. I would've erupted in goosebumps whether he held a cold glass or not, but I wasn't about to admit to it. "Are you ok? About what happened, I mean."

"I'm fine." My voice broke, it wasn't convincing. I'd barely slept remembering how close I had come to God knows what. But I didn't want to admit that either.

"No, you're not. That was too close for comfort." Voice low and smooth, angry. Eyes searching my face, shoulders, and hands as if he had never seen me before and wanted to commit the details to memory. "I'm adding a wider angle to our cameras." He took a deep breath, the muscles on his jaw clenched. "The guy who attacked you… he knew where they were. He didn't try to knife us because he didn't want to be on camera. We were lucky he didn't have a gun. If you're going to wander around São Paulo you need to know what to watch out for. That's why none of us ever lets you wander around on your own."

Celo fidgeted in his chair, rubbed his neck, then rolled his head from side to side until his neck cracked. The anger slipping out of his eyes slowly as he gazed from my eyes to my lips and back.

"You didn't answer my question."

I took a deep breath, laced my fingers together and squeezed them. "I don't really want to think about it too much." I couldn't look at him. "I'm not stupid. God knows what would've happened if you hadn't turned up. But I don't really want to think about it."

"Did you tell Lu?"

"Felipe did."

"Felipe didn't see anything. Did *you* tell Lu?"

I shook my head. Stared at my fingers; they were going red with all my rubbing and squeezing.

He sighed. "And yet here you are. The girl who is never alone. On her own."

"I'm not alone. I'm with you. And it's two o'clock in the afternoon, bright daylight. If I let it scare me in the daylight, I will never leave the house." I still couldn't look at him.

"So you go shopping?" There was judgment in his tone. That made me check his face, his eyes were amused.

I shrugged. "Retail therapy."

He exhaled a quick puff of air, his head shaking from side to side.

I tapped the leather cuff. "You don't need to wear it just to humor me. I'll understand if you don't like it."

"I like it." His eyes didn't leave my face. I started to wonder if I had something stuck somewhere about it. He looked at me with such intensity, it made me feel like something was bound to be out of place.

I decided to change the subject. "What is with you and all

151

the American stuff?" He looked momentarily confused but quickly adjusted his face. "Mustang, Harley... Are you trying to live the American dream or something?"

His smile came with a pant, but the corners of his eyes crinkled. "Maybe. I lived over there for a while. Guess it stuck with me." He shrugged. "I never stopped to think about it that way."

For a while neither of us said anything, his eyes analyzing my face like he was looking for something.

"You said your father is American." I nodded. "From Denver." Another nod. "Colorado is a beautiful place. Have you ever been?"

A head shake. "I only speak to him on the phone. I didn't know who he was until recently." My eyes dropped to my hands and my mind went back to the handful of times I had ever seen Ryan.

"Was that the conversation you were having on the phone in Ilhabela?"

So he did overhear it. "You were eavesdropping."

He frowned, his head jerking to the side slightly in contempt. "You walked out on my peace and quiet, remember, Lewis? And before I could make myself known, the conversation had gone south. I didn't feel I should intervene just to tell you I was there."

I stared at him for a minute. He had never been approachable. But now he was here, asking me about my family, sitting across the table from me like we were friends. And something about his openness and relaxed poise made me spill all my guts.

"The year before I was born, my mother went traveling in America. My whole childhood she told me she didn't know who my father was because she found out she was pregnant after returning to the UK and having a bit of a wild summer. Then I stumbled across one of her old diaries and discovered she had dated my father for over four months. She knew exactly who he was and had lied to me about it my whole life."

Celo nodded, eyes dropping to our hands on the table. "Sounds shit."

"Shit is that she refuses to admit she lied. Even gave herself the right to be pissed off at me for contacting him and letting him know I exist."

He frowned, his chin jerking upwards; his eyes darted to the side for a moment, then back to me. "Did she tell you why?"

"No. We were too busy trying to rip each other's heads off."

He looked pensive for a moment, his eyes narrowing. "Have you spoken to her since?"

"No."

"Were you close? You and your mom?"

"Very."

His middle finger started rubbing small circles on the table right next to my hand; his eyes didn't leave my face. "Are you really going to Denver?"

"Not really sure. That would be like declaring World War III on my mother. I don't know if I want to make things worse than they already are."

"That bad, huh?"

I raised my eyebrows and nodded. "What about you? Rô and Risa seem really nice."

His demeanor changed. "They are. But I'm sure by now you know they're not my parents." He cleared his throat, looked away, leaned back into his chair. His hands moving away from the table and taking something out of his pocket. A silver lighter. It didn't look like he wanted to elaborate on the subject of his family.

"That bad, huh?"

He looked at me for a beat, like he was pondering

something. Then out of nowhere he started talking. I guess he figured he would trade a secret for a secret.

"I don't know who my father is either." He flicked the lighter over and over in between his fingers, still looking at my face, but now all the way back from his chair. "The man I grew up with wasn't my father, and he made sure I knew that. My mother… wasn't much of a mother either." His eyes dropped to the hand flicking the lighter above the table. "She was a junkie. More concerned with her next fix than with her kid." Narrowed, focused eyes flicked back to me, watching my face as if he was taking my temperature.

I tried to keep as neutral an expression as I could, remembering what Marisa had said in Ilhabela: that he hated people feeling sorry for him.

"Some people are really fortunate. They go through some shitty situation, and they forget everything. For self-preservation their brain hides the memories away from them. But my brain hides nothing from me. I remember everything. I'm lucky like that." His voice was dry and sarcastic, his tone low.

"Maybe it thinks you can handle it."

He smiled. The tension in his shoulders dissipating.

"You remember everything? Like what?"

His gaze went back to the lighter and he was silent for a moment. "The day I turned six, my mother's boyfriend tried to push me around. And I went for him, punching, biting, retaliating. I was an angry little kid. My grandmother used to say I was feral." Up to the mention of his grandmother, his face was sullen. But the mere mention of her and his expression filled with fondness. His eyes bounced back to me, and he smiled.

"I'm not surprised. Sounds like you had to be."

"My mother wasn't happy about that. So the next day, she packed some of my things, and we took the bus to this big house where she introduced me to my grandparents. Then she left and never came back." His flicking of the lighter intensified. "I waited for her every day. But she never came."

"Sounds like she did one decent thing for you, at least."

He laughed, but it was full of sarcasm and his eyes didn't leave the lighter. "When I got old enough to know, Risa told me my mother asked for a substantial amount of money to grant my grandparents custody. And they paid. Because they didn't want her to take me. She basically sold me." The last sentence came out through his teeth. Voice low, disgusted.

He noticed the shock on my face before I could hide it.

The smile he gave didn't touch his eyes. "Before you feel too sorry for me, I had amazing grandparents, and Felipe's family more than made up for my shitty mother."

"I don't feel sorry for you. If you ask me, you got out of that deal on top. Two new families, a place in the city, and a villa on a tropical island. If I'm going to feel sorry for anyone, I will feel sorry for myself, who walked out of my deal poorer and without a roof to live under."

He burst out laughing. His head bopping up and down in a nod.

"I didn't know you smoked." I pointed at his lighter.

"I don't. Anymore. I used to. Never liked smelling like an ashtray." A smug smile spread across his face. "It's not a good aftershave."

And there it was.

"Yes, there is that." He was joking, but it hit me like a kick in the teeth. He was a womanizer and here I was… falling for it like a bloody autumn leaf. "I've noticed you do quite well with the… ladies. God forbid something spoils your cool." Sarcasm dripped off my words strong enough to hint at my jealousy. I looked down at my hands before he read it on my face and leaned back on my own chair.

Slowly he moved forward, resting into his elbows, arms

outstretched towards me, fingers turning the lighter in circles, eyes right on me. "I don't know about that."

I smiled unconvinced and looked out of the window. Sure he didn't. An exasperated sigh escaped without my permission.

"If that was true, I wouldn't have upset you the other day."

I turned towards him. "And all the other times." My voice was flat. It came out like an accusation.

"And all the other times." His smile looked more guilty than amused. A hand ran through his hair, he leaned back, crossed his arms. "Look, I know I've been a bit of a jerk." His gaze stayed on me, his eyelids twitched but he didn't blink, looking sad all of a sudden. Then he looked down, cleared his throat, paused like he was considering the meaning of life. "I was trying to stay outta Felipe's way. He's kinda... on a mission." He smiled but became distant, silent, his thoughts taking him elsewhere.

"And what does that have to do with you being rude?"

He looked at me for a long moment, half smiled, uncrossed his arms, and placed the lighter on the table, but didn't answer. The food arrived.

Our conversation had pauses, long moments of just reading each other's faces, but he told me about his time in America, why he came back. And I told him about London, how I had landed a place at an amazing dance company but had shot myself in the foot traveling. He taught me some Portuguese.

I finally figured what made him so bloody magnetic. Making you high on anticipation, that was his game. Body language toying with you, getting close enough to jolt electricity, but not touching. Eyes intense, licking your skin like fire keeping you warm, heavy with meaning, whispering to you while his lips said nothing. By the time he broke the silence and tried to be charming, you were happy to burn.

"Ready to go?"

I wasn't, but I nodded and moved to leave the table. As he opened the door for me, he placed his hand on my lower back to let me walk ahead of him. He barely touched me, not for very long either, but warm seared through my clothes and up my spine.

We rode 'the beast' back to Luciana's building. Marcelo stopped and switched the bike off while he waited for me to dismount, giving me his arm as support. I made a bit of a show of shaking my hair, praying to God I still looked presentable after squashing my waves under the helmet. He ran his fingers through his own hair but stayed on the bike.

So this was it. Our date was over. We just stared at each other—him on the bike, me standing on the curb holding the helmet. And I started fidgeting. He was clearly trying to make his mind up about something.

I handed him the helmet back. "Thanks for the sushi."

He smiled, rubbed his neck. "There is this great Italian place in Campo Belo—Leona. Have you ever been?"

Anticipation was making my stomach turn. I shook my head, bit my lip.

His gaze dropped to my mouth for a second before he continued. "Best pizza in town. Wood oven. Pick you up tomorrow at seven?"

All I managed to do was nod.

"See you later then, Lewis." He looked at me for a couple more seconds, then pointed at the gates to the building. He wouldn't leave until I was safely delivered.

Now used to me, the porter opened the gate without asking any questions. Marcelo put his helmet on, and the bike roared to life. As I walked past the first set of gates, I could hear the low rumble leave the curb.

CHAPTER 9
Marcelo

THIS WAS A BAD IDEA. TRUTH BE TOLD, I COULD NOT DEFEND WHAT I was doing.

All day I had tried to psych myself up to cancel this date, meal, whatever the hell it was. But every time I thought about cancelling, I looked down at the leather cuff she'd given me and came out with some bullshit excuse not to. I had settled for telling myself this was to flush her out of my system.

After weeks of having her in my head, she was bound not to be what I imagined and that would be the death of this stupid crush. It always was. They were never that interesting—usually self-absorbed, entitled, shallow—and like them, what I had with them was also shallow. But even as I told myself that, I knew I was full of shit. I had spent a week on vacation with her. I knew she was nothing like that.

This was a well-rehearsed routine for me. But for some stupid reason I caught myself flapping like a fish out of water. Struggling for something to wear—too casual, too formal, too arrogant, too pimped. Ended up giving up and going all black with jeans, t-shirt, jacket, and boots. An hour to go and I was dressed and procrastinating around the house not knowing what to do with myself. Should have left work an hour later. Instead, came home like an eager teenager panicking about his first date ever. Fucking pathetic.

I started going through the vacation pictures. This had also become part of my routine. She looked incredible in all of them but smiled the widest in the ones with Lu.

I knew who she was. I had seen Lu's pics on Instagram when she was in London. I had heard the stories too. And I looked at her, of course I did. She's a hot chick, any warm-blooded male would have looked. But I knew I was playing with fire when I was told they were coming to Eight, and I realized I was watching the doors, waiting to see her. And I knew I was in shit up to my neck, when I saw her dancing, Shazamed her song, and used it later with the girl I actually took home. Fifty shades of fucked up.

And now I was here, counting the minutes to take her to Leona. A damn car crash in slow motion.

The porter opened the gate, and I asked him to call Lu's apartment and let Paige know I was downstairs. For a minute, I wondered if she'd gotten a new phone. I was hardly keeping a low profile buzzing the whole apartment and announcing my presence.

What the hell was I talking about? I didn't need her number. This madness would be finished after tonight. I was just scratching the itch and getting her out of my system.

I waited in the foyer, and leaning on the wall opposite, watched the elevator floor indicator like it was bringing me nirvana. Lucky for me she didn't take long, must have jumped on it straight after I buzzed. The doors opened and as soon as she saw me, she smiled. I let her walk to me.

"Well, well, well… fancy finding you here." She got close enough that I could smell her perfume—flowers, wood, and oranges. I just stared at her like an idiot. "Coming to break me out of penthouse prison?"

I couldn't help but smile. "Something like that."

Detaching myself from the wall, I motioned for her to go ahead of me, the breeze coming through the doors flicking her dress, her hair, and hitting me with her perfume in double measure.

I asked for a table at the back, tucked in the corner by some greenery. She was wearing a short green dress that seemed to drape off her shoulders and tug to her curves in all the right places. Made her hair look light brown and her eyes a different shade of green. It also gave me a very generous view of her cleavage and its roundness. She did it on purpose, and it was mean. She knew damn well what she was doing. Adding a nail to my coffin, that was what.

Paige was stupidly easy to talk to, funny, smart. It didn't make my life any easier. The first time we had gone out for food just the two of us, she had me spilling all my family secrets. It was scary how quick and easy things I never talked about came out. Like we were swapping funny stories rather than our families' dysfunctions.

"I have a question for you." A hand rotated the straw around her glass.

I placed my arms on top of the table and leaned forward. "Shoot."

"I'm trying to figure out what is going on." Her eyes focused on her glass, head tipping to the side. "Yesterday you said you were trying to stay out of Felipe's way. What did you mean?"

I leaned back into my chair, crossed my fingers under the table. "I've been meaning to ask you about Felipe."

"What about him?" A hint of annoyance seeped through her voice.

"What's going on with you two? What's the deal?" Her eyebrows screwed into a frown, her head jerked back, and she looked straight at me then. "He talks about you like you're almost becoming an item, and you two behave like you're a couple. You said you weren't into him, but you kissed him." It was a full accusation.

Jealousy had eaten me alive on that beach. Felipe had laid the moves down thick and fast from breakfast, full of fingers, rubbing her back, taking her for walks, massaging her shoulders. I told myself I would let it run, even found myself a distraction, but I couldn't. Every time he disappeared with her, I had come looking, running interference. My neck itched; I resisted the urge to scratch it.

She snorted, leaned back into her chair, and looked sideways. I could tell she was measuring her words. "Look, I like Felipe. He is a really nice guy, and he has been very kind and generous to me. But we're just friends. And that is *all* we are *ever* going to be, despite everyone trying to set us up. Trying to set *me* up." One of her nails tapped the side of her glass. "Is that what you're doing here?"

I shook my head. "I'm not that nice." Thinking about the beach made me mad. Feeling jealous wasn't something I was used to. It was like a devil on your shoulder, telling you to act a fool. "Do you kiss all your friends like that? Do they all touch you all over on the regular like he does?"

Her demeanor changed, her eyes piercing me, her head tipping to the side slowly. "Gee, I don't know! Do you neck every woman that throws herself at you?"

"Did you sleep with him?" The words came out of my mouth before I could edit them. It was something Lu said by the pool the day after—that he wanted to get into her knickers, and he got what he wanted.

"What!?" She scoffed, her face twisting into a grimace.

"Did you sleep with Felipe? In Ilhabela?" It was too late to take it back, so I might as well get my answer.

She crossed her arms, her eyes narrowed. "No, *I did not*. Where the fuck did this come from? Did he tell you this?"

I shook my head. "He said you hooked up. It was late when I got back, the door to your room was open, and you weren't in there. It's not like you haven't slept with him before."

She went quiet for a minute.

Then I got a full taste of her temper. Her voice was low, her face hard, her words calm but sharp enough to cut my throat; and if her eyes could throw daggers, I would be dead. "That is because I was drunk. Lu kept me in her room so she could keep an eye on me. That's where I slept. Now… I find it a tad little ironic that you don't see me in my room one night and assume I'm fucking Felipe. But *you*? You turned up the next morning in the same clothes from the day before. Who were *you* fucking? How *dare* you question *me*, when you are the one that turns up with a different woman every week."

We stared at each other without saying anything. She was mad, but I was relieved. The thought of her sleeping with someone else had killed me since Ilhabela.

"I didn't sleep with that chick." Her face didn't change. "I needed to think, so I went for a drive. When I came back, everyone had gone to bed. I had same clothes on because I fell asleep in them."

I'd considered it—going back to the beach and fucking someone else until I was oblivious—I'm not gonna lie. But I didn't have it in me to flirt and play games. The dark haze that descended over me made being nice a step too far. What I had actually done was drive down the road, so I could kick the hell out of a palm tree. Then sat on the beach until I was calm enough to drive back.

Paige continued to look at me, irate, not saying anything, and I felt the compulsion to justify my behavior and explain my life away. I was so screwed. "The women I went out with, they were always aware of what it was. I never lied to them, never promised them anything, never asked them for anything. We were just two consenting adults getting what we needed at the time. That was all."

At first, Paige said nothing, just stared at me. Anger still rolling off her and hitting me in waves. Then she leaned forward on the table, one arm across the top of it—her breasts pushed up and over—the other propped on it holding her chin. She had two perfectly round birthmarks on her cleavage, one bigger than the other. I'd noticed them in Ilhabela, and she had caught me staring.

"And what are you doing here, Marcelo? Half the time you behave like you don't even like me. What the fuck do you want? Another consenting adult?" Her voice was sharp. The last question high-pitched, sarcastic, like there wasn't a chance in hell I was going to get it if that was what I wanted. As she got closer to the spotlight in the middle of the table, her pupils got smaller. Her eyes were all green.

The correct answer would have been anything else. I could have given her enough rope to hang herself with and she would've hated my guts and not looked in my direction ever again. But with her green eyes burning into my soul and her breasts almost spilling out of her dress, I had no willpower to lie, so I leaned forward and returned her stare.

"It's not that I don't like you. I like you too much. And so does Felipe. That's the problem." Saying it sucked all my energy. I leaned back into my chair. There was no denying it now. I'd run all my life but now had the damn virus. Was sick needing some urgent dose of get a fucking grip.

Paige's back straightened, her face going blank, her eyes big green discs as if my admission had caught her by surprise.

The waiter came over suggesting puddings. A blessing that. Nothing good would come out of this conversation. My phone buzzed several times in my pocket and, glad for the distraction, I reached in to get it. Angie was reaching out, but as if he could hear us and his ears were burning, Felipe had also WhatsApped me.

> **Felipe**
> Next time you see Paige, you need to apologize man. You were a jerk to her the other night. It was uncalled for, and she was really upset after that whole thing. You know I like her bro! Don't make me look like an idiot.

Like that wasn't on my mind already. I ran a hand down my face.

"I'm ok thanks." I heard Paige try to explain to the waiter in broken Portuguese.

"*Nada pra mim, obrigado.*" Before she could elaborate on my statement, I beat her to it. "Are you ready to go? I'll pay on our way out." She looked at me for a second too long but nodded.

It was a good job Leona wasn't far from her place, but in São Paulo's traffic that still meant a good half an hour trying to avoid talking about my admission. I really didn't think this through. Her presence, in that little green dress, had turned me into a certified imbecile with a membership card for life. We both stared out of the windshield in silence.

After a few minutes, she broke the quiet. "There is *nothing* going on between Felipe and I." Her stare burned the side of my face. I kept my eyes on the road. "We're just friends. I told him that before *and* after Ilhabela."

I could feel the frustration starting to build. "It makes no difference. He still has feelings for you." And I made sure I didn't look at her. Couldn't risk her cracking my resolve.

"You said so do you."

The mention of it made me uncomfortable. "It still makes no difference." The bleakness of the situation started breeding irritation like prolific bacteria, corroding my veneer of calm and turning my frustration into acid. I moved my neck from side to side until it cracked, to break open a valve and release some of the pressure.

Red. The traffic lights made us stand still. My damn luck that. No escape from this purgatory.

"What if I feel the same for you?" she whispered, just loud enough for me to hear it.

I looked at her then. In the dim light her pupils had dilated to their maximum. The pale green around them relegated to the rim at the edges. Eyes big and earnest, sad and hopeful, all at the same time.

I knew she liked my carcass—she watched me just as much as I watched her, but I wasn't sure she actually felt something more than curiosity. Not until now. My frustration morphed into resignation and anguish. The whole thing suffocating me, draining me of life and color.

I shook my head, but I couldn't look her in the eyes when I did it.

"Don't I have a say in this?" Her voice cracked.

Another head shake. "None of us do." It came out rasping. My eyes superglued to the dashboard on her right.

Green. The lights finally opened.

"How is that fair?" She crossed her arms and stared out of the window.

"It never is." I dragged my eyes back to the road.

Neither of us said anything else.

The rest of the way back I told myself that I wasn't stopping. If I stayed in the car, Paige would get out and that would be it. This time I would keep my mouth shut and not extend the invitation. This had gone far enough.

Yet, as I pulled in front of the apartment block, I killed the engine and found myself not only walking her to the gate, but all the way to the foyer and the elevators. I don't know how the hell I got myself in this situation. The whole day I told myself I would cancel. I didn't. The whole night I told myself I would stay in the car. I didn't. To top it off, I had shoved my foot through my mouth, lost my grip and upset her over dinner. It was like my body had disconnected from my brain. I was losing my damn mind.

I leaned over and pressed the button for the elevator.

She smiled but looked disappointed. This was goodbye and she knew it. The same way I knew that after today, I was going to have to put as much distance between her and I as possible until she went home. The prospect made me numb and tired.

In Ilhabela, and now, I had been playing with fire. Unable to resist getting close, trying to be near her without crossing the line. I should've known better. For her, I was just a holiday romance. Much like Felipe had been. But for me, she was my undoing.

Her whole body turned to face me. "I guess this is good night then, Lewis."

It made me smile. Originally, I had called her Lewis because of the quote she'd thrown at me. But then it became the only thing I could have from her that was only mine. And I kept on using it, like an idiot. Now, she was using it as a nickname for me.

The elevator doors opened. It was empty, but she didn't get in, just stared at me.

"I guess it is. Night." I leaned forward, one hand on her waist, to touch my cheek to hers in a standard greeting. I'd never done it before, I know, but I swear that's all I thought I would ever get.

The kiss lingered, my face staying next to Paige's longer than it should have. Her head turned just a fraction, lips brushing the side of my face to the corner of my mouth... and it all went to shit. My resolve—and its goodbye—crumbling to dust as soon as her lips touched my skin.

I was so tired of trying to do the right thing and resist.

Before I could think, I kissed her.

For a split second, I wondered how British women liked to be kissed, and I told myself to be gentle, respectful. But she found the hem of my t-shirt, her nails dug into me, she pulled me, got her fingers in my hair, bit my lip. *She* wasn't being gentle.

It was like a whole can of gas got thrown in the fire.

I lost it and it became desperate. There was just her, her lips, her skin, and the little green dress she was wearing. My arms wrapped around her waist, and I pushed her into the wall.

She was pulling me closer, kissing me harder, her hands were everywhere, touching everything, rubbing me, sizing me up. Like I needed her to drive me more insane. I was already turned on like a damn flagpole and she was rubbing her body on me.

The elevator pinged and the doors slid closed. I held her neck in place so I could kiss down her jaw line, her neck, the flesh she was flashing with that dress. She was all curves and softness.

I kissed down her cleavage. Those two damn birthmarks had teased me all night. Her head tipped back, breath coming out in one long huff.

She liked that.

It turned me on even more. Made my kisses get wetter, teeth nibble on her skin, and hands wander everywhere—her hips, her waist, the curve under her breasts, pushing them up closer to my face. Around and down her back, the curve of her ass, up her dress, grabbing hands full of her thighs like I could take some home. She was like a coke bottle.

I pressed her so hard against the wall that the elevator doors pinged opened. And she bit my neck, pulled my collar, bit my shoulder. Pulling me to her harder, nails scratching my skin, hands bunching my clothes, grabbing at my hair. Matching my heat with a whole hell worth of fire of her own. The elevator doors closed.

"Oh, for fuck's sake! Get a room! There are kids in this

building!" Luciana's voice cut through the kissing frenzy like an icy bucket of water.

Paige jumped, pushed me away, and stood in front of me. A blessing that.

"Hey Lu!" Her voice was strangled, like she'd been jogging. Hands adjusting her dress.

"How you doing?" Behind her, I waved with one hand, while trying to adjust myself with the other. Saved by the fucking bell.

Luciana pressed the elevator button multiple times, scowling at me like her eyes could incinerate me on the spot. The doors opened and she got in.

Paige turned to me, raised her eyebrows, hiding her face with her hair, trying not to laugh. For a moment we were two mischievous school kids, caught red-handed, trying not to find the scolding funny.

Lu stared right at us, eyes like slits, still trying to laser beam my sorry ass into inexistence, a hand pressing the button that held the elevator doors open.

Without thinking, my hands pulled Paige closer to me, my arm wrapping around her waist like it was the most natural thing ever, as if I'd always done it. "Hey, I won't be able to get away tomorrow," I whispered just for her. One of my hands slid under her hair, fingers grabbing at her neck, thumb rubbing her cheek. Her pupils black like two sink holes, almost innocent looking. I felt high. "But I have a band playing again, maybe you and Lu could drop by, if she forgives you by then?" That was loud enough for Lu to hear me. I shot her a look. Paige looked over her shoulder.

Luciana scowled. "Are you getting in or not, Paige?" She clearly didn't find it as amusing.

Paige turned around and giggled, biting her lip. Man... I loved when she did that. It was endearing, if not hot as fuck.

But I raised both my eyebrows at her; she wasn't exactly helping my case.

"Guess I better get going then. I'll see you tomorrow, Lewis." I grabbed her by the neck with both my hands, thumbs lifting her chin, and kissed her—one strong kiss, then walked away.

I could hear Luciana as the elevator doors closed. "Were you seriously shagging him in the bloody foyer?" She wasn't impressed. Her verdict was out long before the latest developments. Finding us making out in the hall clearly ruffled her feathers.

"That wasn't a shag. That was just some… really energetic snogging."

"Could've bloody fooled me! Did you even hear what I told you about him?"

What the hell was a shag and a snogging? I was gonna have to Google it. It wasn't funny, but I smiled. Luciana had her reasons, and I didn't necessarily disagree with them.

I adjusted my clothes. This level of excitement in these jeans was going to cost me. So much for saying goodbye and keeping my distance.

I didn't plan on kissing Paige. Hell, I tried my best to not put a single finger on her ever. I knew damn well that once I did, there was no keeping this train from derailing, and I was still weighing up the whole situation with Felipe. But Paige was like a tide that pulled me out to sea without me noticing— before I knew it, my feet could no longer touch the bottom. I didn't know how long I'd kissed her for, but it wasn't long enough. I was hooked like a crack addict. Sinking to the bottom, royally screwed, and painfully turned on about it.

CHAPTER 10

Luciana

BUSY DIDN'T QUITE COVER IT. THE BAR WAS HEAVING WHEN WE finally got there. The band was well known in the indie circuit, so maybe it was no surprise. Placing them inside the pool room had been a stroke of genius. The sound traveled, and everyone could see at least a part of the band from wherever they stood or sat.

Yeah, I caught that. That smitten smile that creeped onto lover-boy's face when he saw Paige. Lucky that Pepino had literally just gotten his arse out of town. This was a car crash in slow motion; it would've been so damn obvious.

Not long after Celo had clocked our arrival, Leo—his second in command—approached us with our usual drinks. Celo giving Paige a two-finger salute and a big smile. He couldn't leave what he was doing to come talk to her, but he was looking after her all the same.

"I could get used to this V.I.P. treatment. If I knew all you had to do was snog him, I would have done it myself."

She rolled her eyes.

I scanned the room looking for somewhere with a little more space. The place was so busy that it had started to feel like we were sardines in a tin. Eventually, we agreed to move a little closer to where the band stood.

The music was good! Whoever they were, they had a

decent sound. The singer had this sexy, husky, but smooth voice, and as he sang a cover of Maria Gadu's 'Lounge' it sounded even sexier.

I could only see part of him from where we stood, but he didn't disappoint. My eyes could always do with such eye drops. He sang with his eyes closed, hands sliding up and down the arm of his guitar like a caress, the sexy beat spreading like smoke, relaxing your body. He wasn't quite my type, but boy, he looked good enough to eat.

"I know that look." Paige nudged me, shouting over the music, "You found your next victim."

I smiled, flirting with her. "You know me so well…"

"Who is it?"

I pointed at the guitarist standing by the microphone.

"The singer?!" Incredulity raised her eyebrows.

"What? Is that supposed to mean you think he's out of my league?"

"Nothing seems to be out of your league!" she said, laughing. "Isn't he just a little too rough and ready for you, though? Don't you usually go for cute, mummy's boys?"

"I'm branching out."

"He's cute, don't get me wrong. I just didn't figure you for a groupie." She clearly thought it was funny.

"I'm not," I shouted as they started playing 'Fácil' by Jota Quest. Everyone started singing with them, the singer chanting 'I can't hear you', so the voices got louder and the whole bar seemed to sing along to the music.

"Everyone knows this one." Paige was looking around, curious.

"It's kind of a Brazilian classic."

I could tell she wished she could understand the lyrics. So I started translating for her. The music about when you fall in love with someone, the feelings you get when you gravitate towards them without thinking. And how sometimes, you can only explain it in a song.

When they got to the chorus the voices increased in volume and Paige looked around, amused by the cacophony. The singer put his hands above his head and started clapping in rhythm to the music, getting everyone to clap along with him.

As the voices escalated to a climax, I couldn't resist and started singing along myself, bopping along to the music, Paige bopping with me even though she couldn't sing the words. The instruments stopped, but the voices continued to sing the chorus, everybody's clapping creating the rhythm.

"Wow! That was beautiful! You guys can take my job," the singer said in Portuguese. He drank a little water from a bottle on the floor, letting it all sink in, then counted down to the next song.

"You are definitely a groupie." Paige laughed. "That was amazing! In England people only sing like this in a pub when they're pissed."

Celo appeared out of nowhere. Big smile on his face. His hand instantly around Paige's waist as he whispered in her ear. She shrugged. He whispered some more. She smiled, then nodded. He pulled at the tip of one of her curls, smile wide, eyes vivid with interest, before picking up some empty glasses and heading back to the bar.

"What was that all about?"

"You're in luck. He wanted to know if we would stay till the end. He's taking the band out for some food after, and he wants us to come with." Paige's eyebrows raised in unison with her mischievous smile.

I looked at the lead singer. "You better have said yes!"

After what seemed like a manic spell, Eight slowly started to calm down, to the point that eventually we could go back to sit at the bar.

It was strange to see the dynamic. Celo always had girls

around him—as a matter of fact, some of his conquests were in here tonight—but he never paid them a huge amount of attention when he was working. Work first, play later—that was his rule. Whatever attention he gave one of his girls was always very professional. He treated everyone the same and there was no fooling around while he was working.

With Paige he wasn't like that, though. His eyes were always on her. And every time she looked at him, he'd smile. Not an 'I get you' beam of teeth, more of an 'I hope I see you naked soon' little turn at the corner of his mouth. He talked to everyone, sorted every issue, but he hovered around her like a hummingbird around flowers. His mood the lightest I had seen in ages. It wasn't like he touched her or came over to talk to her, but his eyes were so intent on her it was like they were having a conversation. He was always aware of where she was; it came so naturally to him.

I had been right. He had been hovering around her for a while, just not acting on it. Now he just didn't have to disguise it, and it was painfully obvious just how much he was attracted to her.

I caught sight of Angie on the other side of the bar, sitting in one of the booths, watching the dynamic just as I was. The bitch was a man-eater, but Celo was the one man she never quite managed to get under her spell. He would have his fun and move on, then when he wanted, he would check back in. It had been like that since we were at high school. She was one of his friends-with-benefits, but that was all she ever was, and I could see the green envy and jealousy in her face. She had never had his devoted attention like that.

To make a point, she strutted over to the bar, leaned over seductively, and called him over with her fingers and a smile. Paige started rotating her cocktail glass on the counter, she had clocked it too. You didn't need to speak Portuguese to know what the viper was up to.

"You alright there, Angie?" Celo walked her way, hands flipping the cocktail mixer.

As he got closer, she hooked her index finger onto his collar, pulling him towards her.

He removed her hand from his shirt and placed it back on the counter. "Can I get you anything?"

"Later, I'd love my usual." She leaned over the bar, her head tilted like she was offering her lips for a kiss, and bit her lower lip. Her flirting was so exaggerated; she was just being a plain tart.

"Sure, I will get Leo to bring you a Porn Star Martini. Any other drinks?"

"And later?"

"Later what?"

"At your place or mine?" She leaned further onto the bar, her arms squeezing her boobs together, trying to tease him.

"I'm not home," he said, matter of fact, turning his back on her. "Porn Star Martini coming right up." He reached for a bottle, flipped it, started mixing her drink. It was a pity rat poison wasn't part of the cocktail recipe. He looked at Paige, gave her a wink. She smiled unconvinced and took a sip of her cocktail.

"Now I know why you don't like her," she said leaning her elbow on the counter, resting her head on her hand, hiding her face from the two of them with her hair.

I snorted. "You have no idea. But hey, on the plus side, I think today you avenged me for a change. I will give your lover-boy some brownie points." I raised my glass in a salute and took a sip.

Paige laughed. "How come?"

"Do you remember Alexandre? The arsehole I was besotted with until he cheated on me?"

"Nooo!" The word dragged, eyes wide open as she connected the dots. "That was *her*?"

174

"The very one." My voice dripped in resentment; I couldn't hide it.

"How do you do it? How can you stand her?"

"I don't."

Celo came over, pulled the tip of Paige's hair and she turned to look at him. "You ok?"

Her head jolted to the side, eyebrows raised, but she didn't smile.

He crossed both his arms over the counter, placed his face at her eye level, and stared right at her for a couple of seconds before pulling a funny face. She cracked and smiled.

Sick of all their sappiness, I turned towards the band, my elbows resting behind me on the bar. Now that some people had moved, I could see them in full glory. The cute lead singer was halfway through a guitar and voice solo of 'Umbrella' by Rihanna. He lifted his eyes to look around and found me. Staring right at him. I crooked my head, giving him a full and slow up and down once over. He looked at me for a moment, then frowned slightly with a playful smile. His eyes dropped to his guitar then lifted back to me. I hadn't moved. He finished his solo staring at me. At the end he grinned. I smiled. He knew I was into him.

Eventually, the band made their way over to the bar and we were introduced. He leaned over the counter on his elbows, face turning my way, narrow almond eyes giving me the once over just like I'd given him. I smiled, full on flirting. He was game.

Black t-shirt, blond hair in a short, faded Mohawk haircut; straight thick eyebrows—a bar running through the corner of one of them; lips so juicy they looked like they had been penciled on him; a tattoo snaking up his right upper arm and disappearing under his sleeve. Gabriel—the name of an angel in a body built for sin. This would be fun.

Celo left Leo in charge of closing up, and we all headed to

175

another bar and restaurant that closed even later. A good number of the people who worked in the restaurant industry ended up there. It was one of the few places where they could actually have a social life, bearing in mind they tended to work late most weekends.

Gabriel turned out to be quite interesting. He was a lawyer who had jacked it all in for his love of music. And as we talked, and flirted, his arm went over the back of my chair, fingers running up and down my upper arm. My hand rested on his thigh, and I leaned in. Eventually, we were whispering in each other's ears, talking so close that we were almost kissing.

Even with all that distraction, I didn't miss when *sertanejo* started playing and hell froze over. Because Celo got up and asked Paige to dance. Her face looking surprised for a beat before agreeing and letting him take her to the dance floor.

He had *never* asked her to dance before. And when I had asked him to do it, he had outright declined it. I had originally thought he was trying to help Felipe, by making him the only suitable partner for her. But looking at them dance now, I knew it was because he knew he wouldn't be able to hide the chemistry between them.

You normally danced it with your heads touching at the sides and a level of distance so you could do all the tricks. But he danced it with his face turned towards hers, foreheads touching like he was about to kiss her. And the moves he chose to lead her with were all closed, keeping her as close to him as possible, rubbing on his body. His arm wrapping around her tighter than necessary, hand sitting lower down her back than normal. By the second song, she had gotten the hang of his leading and he started pulling moves with her. A couple of them caught her by surprise, but Paige was a dancer; she automatically bounced back to the basic step, and Celo had figured out he could push her as long as she landed back on that. Whenever she missed a step or misunderstood his lead, they would laugh and he would land a peck on her lips, as if he found her mistake cute or was apologizing for pushing her too far.

They laughed and smiled at each other with so much infatuation, the whole thing was a little sickening to be honest. Made you feel like you were peeping through the windows on a private moment. As if you shouldn't be watching. Celo's face was so happy, his expression so light and soft, it was almost disturbing.

"They're quite something to watch, aren't they?" Gabriel whispered in my ear. "Dripping in chemistry and sexual tension."

"It's new. This is the first time they dance together."

"I've known Celo for a while. He's quite the ladies' man, but that…" He jolted his chin towards the two of them. "That is something else. He's got it bad; you can tell. She's got him wrapped around her little finger."

I locked eyes with Gabriel. My side was leaning on his chest, and his arm was around my shoulders. "I'm not really interested in them."

He smiled, eyes bouncing in between my eyes and my lips, then took the closeness of our faces as an opportunity to plant a kiss on me. And gee! He was a hot kisser. Before I knew what was happening, my body had turned to him in full and both his arms were wrapping around me and pulling me into his lap.

CHAPTER 11
Marcelo

I walked Paige to the elevator of Luciana's building, hands in my pockets, not touching her. We'd met almost every day in the last week, and this part of it was always awkward. Neither of us wanting to walk away, me having to.

"Do you want to come up? For a drink?"

The smart answer would've been no. Despite all my sins, and the mind-blowing amount of 'energetic snogging', I had avoided coming up to her apartment like the devil avoids the cross. Felipe was still out of town, and an unwritten bro code meant I had already gone far enough without settling the score with him. I didn't want to have the conversation over the phone, when he was halfway around the world on an important business trip. It would be a dick move. But Paige was doing that thing, when she looks at me and the green in her eyes becomes hypnotic, popping out like a lasso, my brain and willpower turning to mush.

And I nodded.

I followed her to the apartment, riding the elevator, down the corridor, waiting for her to unlock the door. Not saying anything, not touching her, just smiling at her whenever she looked at me.

She walked in—I closed the door behind me—and walked straight out onto the tenth-floor balcony. The silky strappy top she was wearing clinging to her breasts, the lacy hems teasing against her skin at the top and floating around her hips at the bottom.

I was trying to control my thoughts, my needs, wants. Coming up to the apartment had not been the smartest thing to do, but Paige bent over, leaning onto the banister—her tight jeans making her ass and legs the shape of a pointy heart—and I couldn't really remember why I thought this was a bad idea.

The sound of my shoes produced a rhythm as I walked to her.

"I always like coming out here and looking at the view at night. It's quite humbling, you know? All these lives, this energy... something a lot bigger than me."

"Yeah. It's a good view." I wasn't looking at it. Paige smiled, looking at me from over her shoulder. "I know what you mean. It can be quite interesting," I said, taking in the skyline of busy streets and buildings—lights slipping through, leaking like water from holes in a pipe, revealing life inside apartment blocks, and an endless stream of cars rushing on roads like blood in veins.

"What floor do you live on? Do you have this kind of view?"

"No. I live in a house, only two floors." I leaned against the banister too, my arm touching hers.

"That's strange for São Paulo. I thought everyone here lived in skyscrapers."

My laugh came out in a sigh. "No, you should drop by some time." I surveyed the movement in the other buildings.

Paige pushed away from the banister and went over to the drinks' cabinet. I watched the corners of her back pockets disappear and reappear from under the lacy hem of her top, her hair bouncing against the small of her back.

"So, what's your poison? We pretty much have

everything." She looked amazing in those jeans. I stopped just behind her as she chose a couple of glasses.

My body had a mind of its own and my conscience had been shoved in some backroom in my brain. I brushed her hair over one shoulder, fingers resting on her neck, holding her long waves out of the way, and kissed the tip of her shoulder. My other hand sliding its way around her waist—the silk of her top feeling slightly cold under my fingers—gently bringing her closer to me.

I worked my way up to her neck, goosebumps appearing on her skin, her head tipping to one side, her eyes closing, breath faulting. I knew she'd like that. When I got to the end of her jaw just below her ear, I whispered, "I don't want anything," and went back to kissing her neck.

Paige turned around to look at me, rotating in my arms, glasses still in her hands. "So why did you come up for a drink then?" Her voice was raspy. It wasn't convincing.

I ran my fingers down her hair, taking in her face, committing to memory the sprinkle of freckles on her skin, and let them rest on her neck, a thumb rubbing her lower lip. Then I kissed her—soft, slow little brushes all over her face—while my hands traveled down her arms to the glasses, taking them off her and placing them back on the cabinet behind her.

"I came for you," I whispered into her face, our noses touching. And then I kissed her like she was food and I was starving. My body pressed hers against the cabinet, crystal glasses chiming in protest. My hands traveled across her shoulders and down her sides—palms flat, fingers spread wide open, grazing a little too much without touching anything. Down her waist to the top of her thighs where I pulled her closer still. More chiming.

It wasn't meant as a light caress. It rubbed, it pulled, it had want in every fingertip. While my intentions were very clear, I didn't touch her in an abrasive way. My hands traveled up and down her body, fingers lingering but showing some respect. She was all soft—soft skin, soft hair, round curves. I wanted her so bad, it was driving me insane.

She could have pushed me away and wished me good night and I would have left. In physical pain, but I would have left. That would probably be for the best, but I really hoped she didn't. I had waited and resisted, I had done my best to be respectful, but right now I just wanted to be right damn dirty, as dirty as they come.

Paige bit my lip, her hands gathered my shirt pulling me to her, fingers finding the hem, nails scratching the skin on my sides in a big 'V' towards my stomach. It sent shivers up my spine and down my legs. I have no idea where it came from, but I literally purred like an animal. I kissed her harder, hugged her tighter, pressed my body against hers. The glasses in the cabinet dangerously close to being knocked off.

Did she understand what she was doing to me? The situation she was putting me in?

Paige pushed us both away from the rattling glasses and, pulling me by the waist of my jeans—two fingers inside them, rubbing where she really shouldn't—she back walked her way into her room. I followed, kissing her still, holding her to me with one arm, feeling my way along the corridor with the other.

The door shut behind us. Her arms were on my shoulders, hands tangled in my hair, her kissing getting even deeper, wetter, more desperate. Her body pressing into mine like she was trying to merge us into one.

"I know I don't have anything. Do you have anything?" she gasped in the middle of the kissing frenzy.

"What?" I was so absorbed with kissing her neck, with her body rubbing on me, that my mind didn't quite catch what she was actually asking.

Her two hands held on to my face and she looked me dead

in the eyes, her pupils huge as if she was high. "Do you have a clean bill?" The words coming out like she was out of breath.

"Yeah, I got condoms." I tried to kiss her, but she pulled back slightly, holding my face in place.

"That's not what I asked." Her lips grazed on mine, noses touching, but she didn't kiss me.

It took me a second to come down from my heat haze and have the conversation she wanted to have. "Yeah. I test every three months and don't ride bare back. I tested just before Ilhabela. Haven't been with anyone since. You?" My hands continued to rub and claw at her, my body unable to concentrate on anything else but what it wanted.

"Tested when I did all my vaccines to travel. Haven't been with anyone since."

Paige relaxed her hold on my face and my kiss landed. "We're all good then." The words barely coming out of me, intertwined with French kissing. Now, I was the one that sounded out of breath.

And I hugged her tighter. Palms full of her ass, pushing her hips into me. Wanting her to feel me, feel what she had done to me. Turned my cock into concrete, that was what. My hips moving towards her on autopilot as if they had a mind of their own. Clothes or no clothes, all I wanted to do was rub it all over her if she let me. A promise I was now hell-bent on delivering, despite my better judgment.

I wasn't the only one. Paige was pushing herself on me just as hard. Her fingers working to get rid of my shirt and giving me the green light to do away with hers. Mouths, tongues, teeth going everywhere they could reach.

She started to unbutton my jeans—just as hungry for it as I was. But I had waited for this for far too long and I wanted to make it last. I wanted to taste her, touch her, commit it to memory. I needed to slow it down.

This amount of tension would have me bursting at the

seams in no time. Especially after three weeks of nothing. Yeah, I *was* counting. I had turned into a fucking monk since Ilhabela. But I'd had plenty of Paige working me out and turning me inside out over the last week, and I needed to slow this down, or it would be my shortest performance ever. And I'd waited too damn long for it to be done in five minutes. I was going to enjoy this, savor the moment.

I took hold of her wrists and, kissing her still, walked her towards the bed until I could lie her on it. She watched me as I took off my boots, then her sandals. Her breath catching when I reached over for the button on her jeans and unzipped it. Hands reaching in and peeling them off her legs. Her green eyes on mine the whole time, pupils two wide discs.

She was wearing this gorgeous blue set of bra and panties. Man… embroidered lace… sexy as hell. Made it look like someone had painted the chunky pattern on her skin.

She had put that on for me.

No woman wears that kind of expensive lace just to go out for food. As if I needed any help getting a hard on. She *was* trying to drive me over the edge.

I lay down next to her, my forehead touching her temple, and I ran a single finger alongside the inside of the waistband on her panties—her skin erupting in goosebumps, her breathing getting faster; up her stomach, her muscles contracting. She watched as I ran my index finger on the inside of her bra—down one strap, the lace, up the other side, pulling the other strap off her shoulder.

When someone does something nice for you, you should show appreciation. And I have manners, even when I just about remember I have them.

"I like this, Lewis." I said in her ear while tracing the pattern on the lace with my fingers, running over her breasts, her nipples—her goosebumps reappearing. "I like it a lot." Gliding down her stomach, tracing the pattern on her panties,

183

kissing her neck—her lips parting, eyes closing and her breath coming out in a gasp.

She lay there, letting me do it, but when my fingers got into her panties and touched skin, it was as if I had pressed the on button. Paige exploded into action—rolling to her side, kissing me deep and wet; pulling at my jeans, hands inside my pants, drawing me out, rubbing on me like she needed it for living.

I cannot tell you how good it felt to have her come at me like that, all guns blazing, but I wanted more. So I rolled us over, her legs wrapping around my waist, and held both her wrists above her head. At first with two hands, while I kissed her, rubbing, pressing myself on her, promising what was to come, throwing more gasoline on the fire. When she got the message, I let go, but her hands stayed where I put them.

I worked my way down her neck, hands touching everything, caressing, kneading, squeezing her curves, her thighs, her ass, getting under her bra. As far as I'm concerned, there are only two other things more satisfying to touch than having palms full of a woman's curves in your hands.

Paige's head turned and her back arched like she was offering me her breasts for the taking. So I unfastened her bra, kissed her breasts, rubbed my face on them, measured them against the size of my hands. Biting, sucking at her nipples. They had this sexy pink color and raised up like two little berries against her skin.

Left a trail of wet kisses down the middle of her cleavage. Kissed, licked her stomach, pulled her panties down a little bit, kissed a horizontal line underneath her belly button. It was a tease. I wanted her on fire, dripping wet and begging for me to take her. Because that was what she did to me. By the time I got anyplace near her, she had me begging on my knees.

I kissed her hips, the inside of her thighs, the crease on the top of them. Pulled her panties down a little bit more. Her breathing getting deeper, her hips raising towards my face—offering, asking me to play with it all.

I came off her and stood at the end of the bed. Her eyes locked with mine while I took my jeans off, breathing shallow and fast, arms still above her head where I put them. I stood there looking at her, letting her look at me. Giving myself a minute to remain in control.

When I came back down on her, she kissed me like she was ready. Her legs wrapping around me, her hips thrusting against my cock like she wanted it bad, her hands grabbing my hair.

I kissed down her body and stood back up. Pulled her towards the end of the bed, dragging her down the sheets. Rubbed my hands up her thighs to the side of her panties and pulled them down slowly, raising her legs upwards towards the ceiling to get them over her feet. Her legs falling on my shoulders on their way down.

I worked my way to the center of her body, kissing the inside of her legs, rubbing my shaft on her, until I was kneeling on the floor. And I just stayed there. Blowing my breath on her skin, anticipation making her breathe harder. She smelled incredible. Some women have this scent when they're really turned on; it smells and tastes amazing.

It was just a second or two, but by the time I ran my tongue on her skin, she was going insane. And as soon as she felt it, her body was arching, she was moaning, gasping, grabbing at my hair. She did taste incredible, all pink and soft. And I was going to take my time. I wanted to see her out of breath, body pulsating, toes curling. Losing her sanity, her composure, eyes rolling to the back of her head. Like she was doing to me.

And she did. Her back arching upwards, head tipping back, gasping, her nails digging in my back.

Her hands pulled me up, body shimming up the sheets to make room for me. Done with my teasing, she grabbed hold of me and guided me in. I did try to go for slow, but she was kissing me deep, the inside of her squeezing me in waves.

Self-control slipped through my fingers like water. I wish I could say I was considerate, but I wasn't. She was so wet and on fire, and I was out of control. The bed was creaking, and my thrusting sounded like the drum base of a song against her skin, but she was pulling and pushing me faster than I was moving.

Release came with a grunt from me and a moan from her. Nails dug into my back, pain mixing with pleasure in a dangerous combination. And I did the one thing I never do. The one thing I told her I didn't do.

I should have wrapped it up or taken it out, done it on my hand, but the craving was so strong—I wanted, needed to own her. I wanted to know I was on her body, in her body, taking part of her soul. That's what she was doing to me. Consuming my mind, my soul while I was still awake and feeling everything.

I let myself stay on top of her, my head on the hollow of her neck, sweat running in between us, sticking us together, both of us panting. She moved my hair away from my face and blew long puffs of air on my neck as if she was trying to cool me down. Her breath hit me, rolling over my shoulder and down my back. Mixing soothing with pleasure to create a type of ecstasy, giving me a hell of a natural high. My whole body relaxing. If I'd died there and then, I'd die a happy man.

Then I remembered I was heavy; I tried to move but she didn't let me.

"Stay. I like to feel the weight," she said, locking me in place with her legs and arms.

Apparently, I wasn't the only one that felt the need for possession.

♥♥♥

I opened my eyes to the sight of Paige sleeping on her stomach —face turned towards me, half hidden by her arm, messy hair everywhere, a strand falling in front of her face. The sheets tangled around her legs covering her hips up to her thighs but leaving her back bare. Smooth, creamy, freckled skin like an invitation, beckoning my hands.

This was usually where I got up and started getting ready to leave. But looking at her asleep and smelling the scent of skin and sex, leaving was the last thing I felt like doing. I had thought about this, then tried not to think about it, so often that if I left, it would be like it wasn't real.

Flashbacks filled my memory—her smooth skin under my fingers; my palms grabbing, pulling at her curves. The way she gasped, tipped her head back and her eyes closed every time I kissed her in the right spot. Her body arching towards me, submissive but more in control of me than I was.

We hadn't talked much. The things she did to me set me on fire and the way she reacted to me told me all I needed to know. Sex was sex; I got it often enough and always made sure the girls were satisfied, but this… this was something else. It was hard to explain. It was soothing and harsh all at the same time.

The memories tingled my senses like she was touching the end of my nerves. It numbed my mind, stilled my thoughts. There was nothing else, just a raw need for her skin—as much of it as possible, as bare as possible. She had given me a run for my money. I was tired, my body felt like jelly, things ached, but I was on some sort of high. Whatever it was, how was I supposed to leave it?

Slowly, trying not to wake her up, I reached over and moved the strand of hair that was falling across her face. The light was warm but dim and I couldn't resist, my hand reached for her and pulled her closer, molding her to me.

Paige let out a sleepy moan and lifted her head so my arm

could go under it like a pillow. A kiss was planted on my shoulder before she found the nook where her head fit perfectly just under my chin. One of her hands rubbing soothing circles on my nipple in a hypnotic rhythm that got slower and slower, eventually stopping as she started to doze off. Her breathing resuming the rhythm of sleep.

I could have stayed like that all morning, but just as I was about to fall back into sleep, her stomach growled.

She groaned. "I think I need to get up."

Before I had time to reply, Paige moved away from me and stood up. My arms feeling empty, the bed getting colder without her body heat. She looked around for something to wear. Her figure stretched in its full glory while she tied her hair in a messy bun above her head.

I'd seen my fair share of naked women. They all had they hang ups, even the fitter, leaner ones, but here she was— curvier than most of the chicks I'd gone out with, and she didn't care that I was looking. Didn't even notice that my hungry eyes were eating every curve. She rotated in a pivot looking for something in particular, giving me a three-sixty degrees view of her body. Apparently not finding what she was after, she grabbed my shirt and buttoned it up while smiling at me. It just about closed right under her breasts.

"Do you want some tea?"

Tea. Such an English thing to ask people if they wanted tea. "Black coffee would be great, thanks. Three sugars, please."

"Oh, yeah. Sorry." She smiled, scratched her forehead. "I forget you people don't really drink tea." Her hand lowered with a muffled slap to her thigh, and she stood there looking at me. Messy hair in a bun, wearing my shirt, breasts barely contained in it, fresh out of bed… comfortable and at ease, she looked like a picture. "What?" Her voice pitched higher, and she smiled.

I grinned. Shrugged.

Paige crawled on to the bed, leaned over and kissed me. "What you thinking?" she whispered, looking right into my eyes, a half smile playing on her lips. More kisses.

It was bribery. Her kissing me, while I was still processing the night before, would've had me admitting to murders I didn't commit. "You look easy."

She frowned, pulled her body slightly away. "Easy?"

I cupped her face in my hand, rubbed the crease in between her eyebrows with my thumb. "Yeah." I pulled her to me. "Like you're not naked, like déjà vu."

"Déjà vu?"

"Yeah." I kissed her forehead and cuddled up to her like I could go back to sleep now that she was back in bed with me. "You look like I saw in my head." My eyes were heavy.

"Like you saw me in your head?" She was quiet for a moment. "Oh!" The word came out slowly. "You mean you imagined me naked?"

I heard the grin in her voice, opened my eyes slightly. "Something like that."

Paige shook her head in mock horror, sucking air in between her teeth. Then grinned wider.

"Give me some credit. It was a little hard not to imagine you fresh out of bed when you're parading around showing me your skin and I couldn't do anything about it. It was very mean, Lewis." My voice sounded husky, lazy. I pulled her closer, settling back down for some more sleep, and closed my eyes.

"What am I doing when I'm in your head? Naked." Her voice had a naughty tinge to it.

I shrugged, eyes still closed. When I didn't respond, she double tapped my chest. "Before... just talking, hugging, kissing. Your skin, your hair..." My words slurred with sleepiness.

"Before what?"

I squeezed her to me to make my point.

"And what do you reckon I will do now that you have…" She squeezed me back.

My eyes focused on her then. "You're not in my head. You're here." I combed a stray curl backwards. "Although, the one in my head *is* getting really dirty." We both laughed.

I closed my eyes again.

"Right… coffee. I'm starving!" She was out of my arms before I could disagree. The bed moved, I heard the door open and close, just about heard Paige's first steps down the corridor.

The bed felt cold without her. I couldn't go back to sleep, and I couldn't really settle either. The sheets, the room, it all smelled like her skin, like sex. This high must be what you get when you have to wait so long for something. Or maybe it was because I thought I would never have her. I started to fidget. It was obvious I wouldn't go back to sleep.

So I got up, put my jeans on, walked into the en-suite, washed my face, sorted my hair, checked my watch, my phone. Paige was taking forever with that coffee. But I knew it wasn't the coffee I was waiting for. I would have to leave soon, and it felt like every minute she was away was a wasted one. We were heading for the weekend, and I knew I wouldn't see her for a couple of days. Eight always got really busy, it was an all-hands-on-deck thing.

I stepped out of her room and could hear Paige's voice someplace down the corridor, so I followed the noise to the kitchen.

"Pepino will be seriously pissed." It was Lu.

"Felipe doesn't own me. How many times am I gonna have to say this? We hooked up a millennia ago and it was done and dusted then. I'm *not* going out with him. There *isn't* and there *never was* anything going on in between us. I can go out with whoever the fuck I want." Paige was clearly getting irritated.

"I'm just saying. You're gonna have to tell him eventually and he won't be happy."

"I don't have to tell him a fucking thing. He's not my father. I don't need his blessing, approval, or his permission. It's *my* damn life."

My stomach turned and my temper flared. Lu was spoiling everything, killing my damn high.

Stepping through the door, I found Paige standing just inside it, Luciana facing the basin. I wrapped my arms around Paige's waist and kissed her right below the ear. And I wanted Lu to see this, wanted her to know I was there, wanted her to see Paige was with me, not Felipe.

"Everything ok?" I asked, looking straight at Luciana.

"Yeah, fine. I was just saying hi to Lu." I could tell the exchange was bugging Paige as much as it was me. "Come on, we can have this in bed." She picked up a tray full of breakfast and walked out of the kitchen.

I stared at Lu as she turned to scowl back at me.

"Luciana." Stupidly, I wanted to make sure she acknowledged me. Me being here. With Paige.

Lu crossed her arms and continued scowling. "I hope you know what you're doing. This is not gonna end pretty."

"Keep out of it, Lu." It came out between my teeth. She was starting to get on the wrong side of me.

"She's *not* one of your bedpost notches, she is my *best friend*. And Pepino is like a brother to you. I hope it's worth it for you; I mean, when are you thinking of telling him?"

I crossed my arms and stared at her. I didn't have to tell her a damn thing, I didn't have to explain myself to anyone.

"Oh! You're not! She's just one of your week-long playthings, is she? You figured it'll all be over before he comes back. Well, that's rich." Her voice dripped in sarcasm.

"You don't know a fucking thing," I half growled at her. If

191

she were a man I would've broken her nose, but instead, I turned my back on her and walked away.

It's not that I couldn't understand her worry, I had worried about the situation with Felipe every time I met Paige, even before all this. Back then I'd tried my best to keep my distance. I'd even considered not taking it any further after we started going on dates, but it wasn't that clean cut. Once I got a taste, it had become impossible to walk away.

I knew Luciana was worried about her friend too. Even worse, I knew she had good reason to be, but that didn't make me any less mad. She had spoiled a perfectly good mood. The memories of the night—the kisses, the sex—were all tainted, replaced by irritation and worry.

I walked into the bedroom to find Paige sitting on the edge of the bed picking a croissant to pieces. She didn't look at me and I knew, like someone had sucker punched me, that she'd heard Luciana's comments. Lu had spoken in English; she wanted Paige to hear and understand it. Now she had really pissed me off.

"I'm gonna jump in the shower," Paige announced, putting the destroyed croissant down. "You can go if you want." The rest of the tea and food untouched.

As she walked into the bathroom, the door was left ajar, and I could see my shirt draped over the edge of the basin. The shower turned on. This would probably be a good time to leave, if I wanted to close the door on it completely. Felipe would never know, and to Paige it'd look like Luciana was right.

Lu had a point—this *was* gonna get messy. I knew it and Paige knew it too. She walked into the bathroom knowing damn well she was giving me my cue to leave.

Vapor started to escape through the gap in the door.

I pushed the door open, picked up my shirt, shoved one arm in it. Through the frosted glass I could see the back of her.

While she had gotten in the shower to give me an opportunity to walk away with no questions asked, she was also washing away any vestige of me. Cleaning away any kisses I'd given her, any lingering smell or sensation. She would walk out of the shower ready to find me gone. And by the time she changed the bed sheets, it would be like I was never here.

I watched her through the glass for a couple of minutes. It looked like she was just standing under the shower, letting the water loosen her muscles, letting the water wash me away. Maybe that was exactly what she wanted. I made for the door.

Halfway through, hand on the doorknob, I stopped. I should walk away, but I didn't want to. So I took a step back, closed the door, undressed, and got in the shower.

Paige's hands were on the wall, her face turned upwards towards the water. With her head tipped backwards, her hair reached the curve between her waist and her ass. I used one of my hands to lower one of her arms, and the other to wrap around her waist and hold her to me, turning her until I was under the water.

I let it wet my face, my hair, but I held her to me. Then I looked at her, really looked at her, right in the eyes. And I put my forehead to hers, wishing I could transmit into her head the things I couldn't put into words because I couldn't make sense of them myself.

Everything else was complicated and fucked up enough to make your head spin. But my hands on her skin wasn't. Her skin on my skin was what we both wanted. My lips on her was exactly where I needed to be, and her body pulled mine like a magnet. The simplest, most natural, raw thing in the world.

I used my free hand to run the length of her face, from her forehead to her chin, my thumb rubbing on her lips.

Her eyes closed.

I did it again. But this time my hand ran from her chin, down to her neck, over one of her breasts, her stomach, and the back of her thigh, where I lifted her up, hoisting her to my waist with her back against the wall.

We started in the shower and finished with her sitting on the basin countertop. And I wished my eyes could film what I saw in the mirror. Not because it was fast, hot or acrobatic, but because it was the opposite—slow, deep and loving. Her skin and mine, cream and brown, intertwined together like streaks in a piece of marble. What I wanted wasn't a marathon medal, it was closeness. The closest I could be, the closest I could get to her.

Today was not going to be the day either of us forgot I was here.

CHAPTER 12
Paige

I HAD PROTESTED THE IDEA AT FIRST, WHEN LU INVITED ME TO JOIN her and Gabriel on a weekend away. Who wants to be the third wheel on somebody's dirty weekend? But the prospect of exploring a new city and dipping my toes in the Atlantic again was just too good to miss.

I don't think I could ever get tired of this tropical lifestyle. Although Lu would annoyingly correct me and say São Paulo wasn't really tropical. "Wait until you go to the northeast," she would say, looking at me like I was crazy. It always felt tropical enough to me. I think sometimes she genuinely forgot I was British. It always made me laugh when they talked about doing things before 'it got cold'. Like thirteen degrees Celsius was a subarctic temperature. While Brazilians would wrap up and moan about the cold, us Brits would slap on our shorts, get our sun-starved limbs out, and call it a beautiful spring day.

Our journey to the seaside didn't disappoint and was also full of wonders. We were in the same state, but we might as well not have been, as the scenery was completely different from when we went to Ilhabela.

Green growing on top of green, tall electric cables covered in vegetation draping like green curtains. Palm trees peeping through every here and there to remind you of where you were. The motorway snaking at places suspended on top of green covered hills or in tunnels in their underbellies, swaying by rivers and waterfalls, and looking so completely out of place, you couldn't help but feel like an alien. The greenery here growing so wild, it made the British countryside I loved look like a manicured cottage garden.

That's the thing I liked the most about Brazil. It was chaotic elegance. Nature rebelling against the city, growing wild and giving the concrete a taste of its own medicine. Even though I was in a city busier, noisier, more crowded than my own, it somehow managed to feel more grounded and earthy than the cities at home.

Sitting on the coast of the São Paulo state, Guarujá was much like São Paulo on a smaller scale. Skyscrapers rising up like mountains at the edge of the road. Then one side of the street just opened into a vastness of gold and bluey-green, the beach stretching across the bay almost like someone had taken a wide brush and painted it there in a long, endless stroke. The Atlantic waves kissing the sand quite a distance down the beach in a hypnotic lazy rhythm. The view broken by the occasional kiosks, trees, and parasols.

Gabe had pulled out all the stops and got us booked in a hotel overlooking the gorgeous views. And for a moment, hearing the sea, sinking my toes in the sand, I couldn't have cared less that I was the third wheel on their date. Me and all his bandmates. We were here because Gabriel's band was performing at a private event.

For someone who tried so hard not to look like she was in love, Luciana couldn't look more smitten standing on the beach, toes in the water, Gabe's chest touching her back, his arms around her, his chin resting on the top of her head, big smile on her face, laughing at something only the two of them could hear. She glanced in my direction, looked at me for a second, then tapped his arm; he let her loose and she started walking my way.

"Hello there." Her bum bumped into me. "I told you it wouldn't be so bad, huh?"

"You did indeed."

We stared out over the sea, the wind messing both our hairs. Guarujá was very different from Ilhabela. The sea here was a shade of emerald green and the waves were bigger. In Ilhabela the water was turquoise, and the beaches were sheltered, sandwiched in between the island and the mainland. Guarujá looked out into the Atlantic.

"I hate to break it to you, but you, my friend, are smitten."

Lu let out a loud laugh. "More like dick-hypnotized."

At that, I had to laugh. "That isn't even a word! There are *so* many things wrong with that statement!"

"Well, we will have to agree to disagree. Come on, let's get ourselves some cocktails."

While the band set up and sound checked, Lu and I got ready in my room. Halfway through our priming and plucking, my phone rang. Marcelo. He never called, he always texted.

"Oh, look who is missing me already!" I answered on loudspeaker while slapping on the paint.

He laughed. "More like annoyed that I have to work." Gosh, even his voice on the phone was seductively moody. "Having fun?"

"Obviously. Gabe is playing at the… I can't say the name of the hotel, but it's a Sofitel. Jacque something."

"Jequitimar. Nice. Right on the front."

"Yeah, that's it. His bandmates are so funny! And Lu is trying very hard not to look smitten, but she so is." Lu stopped applying her make up to scowl at me through the mirror.

The phone went silent for a moment. "You're with the

197

band? I thought you and Lu were going separately." His tone was different. Lu's lips rounded, her eyebrows both raised.

"No, we came on the tour bus. I don't normally like buses, but it was actually really good fun. Caio, I think he is the one who plays the base—"

"I know who Caio is."

"—he showed me some really nice Brazilian music by a couple of singers, Ana and Victoria."

"Anavitória." His voice was sharp, deeper.

"Yeah, them."

The other side of the line went silent for a couple of seconds. "Right…" The word dragged. "What else did Caio show you?"

I stopped rummaging through my make-up bag. "Is that a hint of jealousy I hear?"

He went quiet, like I had caught him by surprise. "Truth be told, I'm not sure." His voice was hoarse, pensive.

I broke another spell of silence by changing the subject. "How is the bar?"

"Busy. All hands on deck."

"Don't go having too much fun." I tried to be light, but memories of Angie trying her luck the last time I was there made me instantly sour.

"Says the one surrounded by a boy band." There was no hint of humor or sarcasm.

"Says the one that was getting hit on last time I was there."

I heard him snort. "Is that a hint of jealousy I hear?"

"I don't know what I am, to be honest."

Lu smiled amused, made a claw with her hand, and silently growled at me.

"Touché." More silence. "I need to go back to work. But hey…" He took a deep breath, the phone going quiet for a couple of seconds. "Don't forget you're already busy, Lewis." His voice sounded almost sad.

"Am I now? I thought I was on a weekend away."

"Yes, but you're already busy *with me*." He went a little husky at the end.

"Oh, is that what you call it?"

He didn't respond.

"I'll speak to you later then, Costa." I called him by his surname.

"Laters, Lancaster." He called me by mine. The call disconnected.

"I hope you realize you have just bled a stone." Lu had her chin pointing upwards while she applied some mascara. "I never thought I would see the day love-rat Marcelo had a fit of jealousy."

I snorted. "That wasn't jealousy. He doesn't even think he misses me."

"No, flower, he said he didn't like that you were here, and he was not. Besides, *he* was the one calling. He never calls unless it's urgent. He clearly wanted to hear your voice."

"You know that is a bit of a stretch from 'I'm miffed I have to work', right?"

"Fine!" She threw the mascara back in her make-up bag. "Then explain why his tone changed as soon as you mentioned Caio. He definitely wasn't thrilled with the idea of you being on a tour bus full of good-looking men." She turned to me, smirk on her face, one hand leaning on the vanity unit, the other on her hip. "Well done you for giving him a taste of his own medicine and putting him in his place. 'You are busy', you are busy my arse. Until he officially asks you, you are as free as a little bird to whistle at cute men."

"What?" I laughed; Lu always managed to 'Brazilianise' English sayings. "What do you mean, 'until he officially asks me'?"

"Listen, this isn't the UK. In this splendid green land of mine"—she held one hand to her all of a sudden patriotic

199

boobs—"you are not dating someone and off the market until they officially ask you to date them or say you are their girlfriend. And it's then up to you to accept or decline. Until then, you're fair game." She went back to the mirror with some lip gloss. "I mean, if I were you, I would decline. But you know damn well what I think about this madness."

"Like he would ask me." I laughed. "I thought you said he didn't date." I was trying to come across unconcerned and uncaring, but I could hear the insecurity lurking underneath.

Lu took a deep breath, put down her lip gloss, and turned to me, serious expression on her face. "Look, I hate to admit this, but I know he's really infatuated with you. To be honest, I had my suspicions when I realized he was avoiding you like the plague. And…" She rolled her eyes. "I might have caught him staring at you. More than once." Her head tilted side to side in rhythm with her words, eyes wide open. "I mean, I love to hate him, but he's family. We've known each other since we were kids. We still go on holidays together; he's basically like a very, and I will say that again, *very* annoying cousin or brother of mine. He knows he's buying a fight with Pepino. Those two have been like nail and flesh since they were seven."

"Nail and flesh? Is that a Brazilian thing?" I laughed.

"Thick as thieves, I mean. My point is… he wouldn't do this if he wasn't smitten. But this is new territory for him, flower. Celo doesn't do *boyfriend*." She marked the word with her fingers. "And there is a reason for that. He lost or was abandoned by everyone he loved. This is his coping mechanism; this is how he survived. If you are going home soon, you really need to think if you want to do this." There was hurt and mercy in her eyes. She was pleading.

"What do you mean?" It came out a little louder than a whisper.

"Don't tell him I told you. He'll *not* be happy with me." She stared at me, waiting for a promise.

I nodded.

Lu sighed. "Celo came to live with his grandparents when he was six. His mum had fallen with the wrong crowd and became a junkie in her teens. When they tried to have her committed to rehab, she ran. A few years later, she came back with her little boy, saying it was his birthday and she wanted him to meet his grandparents. Then she left and never came back. I don't remember, I was too little, but Pepino says Celo was covered in bruises and incredibly skinny. When he started school, he was this angry little kid that fought with everyone, but Pepino made friends with him. And they were inseparable. Then his grandmother died when he was ten after fighting cancer for years. It was horrible… She looked so ill and frail, you know? Celo was heartbroken. A little while later, his grandfather got ill, and he lost him too when he was twelve. I think it was all just a bit much for his granddad, you know… losing his wife, his daughter being a nasty piece of work."

Lu frowned, her eyes dropping to the invisible thing she was picking on the vanity unit.

"He had no one, Paige. He was twelve and he had no family. He was all alone."

Her eyes turned to me, the weight of her sadness imprinted on her eyebrows.

"Can you imagine what that was like? He was just a kid! And he had lost everyone."

I thought about me and my mother. What would've happened to me if something had happened to her and I had no other family? For a second I felt devastated, but then I was angry. This was exactly why she should've told me. If anything had happened to her, she would've left me without anyone.

It would've been bad enough for me, but Brazilians were all about family. Everything they do involves siblings, cousins, parents. It would have been so hard living in this culture having lost the people you loved and knowing the only other

201

person you had in the world didn't want you. That had to have left a scar somewhere.

"When his granddad got ill, he made Auntie Risa and Uncle Rô his guardians. He used to spend a lot of time with them already because when his grandma got ill, Mateus—his granddad —spent a lot of time in the hospital with her. After he finished school, he went to the States to study and was out there for a good three to four years. He came back; I had just gone to London. His grandfather left him everything, including the house he lives in now. Since then, Pepino and his family have been his constant. But he keeps everyone out. Nobody really knows what is going on with him. And he keeps himself from really"—she searched for the word, her hands waving in circles as if she was cataloguing her options—"getting involved with anyone. I think he figured that if he doesn't get attached to anyone, he has nothing to lose, and it won't hurt him. I can't say I blame him. I don't think I would want a repeat if I was in his shoes."

She stared at me, trying to gauge if I really understood.

"So you see, I know he wouldn't fight with Pepino if he didn't mean it. But when I warned you off him, it's not just me being mean. Even though he doesn't acknowledge it, let alone accept it, Celo's kind of broken. Damaged goods as they say. He will mess this up just because he doesn't know how to handle it, and you can destroy him by just getting on a plane. So you really need to think if you want to take this any further. He's buying a fight with the only family he has left because of you. What is going to happen when you have to go home? He will be in bits. This isn't just about Pepino. Do you understand what I'm saying?" There was a fragility to Lu herself. She didn't just know the reason behind why Celo did what he did, she seemed to really understand it. As though she felt it on her own skin.

"Why didn't you tell me?"

"It's not my story to tell." She turned back to the mirror. "On the plus side, you should be getting a very decent shag. I heard down the grapevine that he is great in bed and well equipped." She winked at me trying to lighten the mood. All roads led to sex with Lu, especially if she felt self-conscious. It was her cop-out.

I laughed. "I thought you said he was like a brother to you."

"You're forgetting where you are. This is Brazil, flower. We talk about sex at the dinner table." She pushed her boobs up trying to readjust them. Her eyes no doubt judging her scale of hotness. "Just one thing, though"—she went back to leaning against the vanity unit—"who the hell is Lewis?"

My phone vibrated, Celo was off and wanted to watch a movie. I had piles of work to do, but the offer of spending an afternoon with him was so seductive—it was a no-brainer. Especially after being away. I would deal with my deadlines later, blame it on the time difference. Naughty but worth it.

It had started to rain as he picked me up. Lu always joked that she moved from one rainy place to another when she moved to London. It used to make me laugh. But this was no shower; this was torrential rain. I could barely see where we were going, and the whole journey, I counted my blessings that he was driving not riding. I really had no interest or business trying to find out what this would feel like on the back of a bike.

He turned off the main road into a residential street and stopped in front of what looked like a white wall so high, I had no idea what was on the other side. He pressed a clicker and part of the wall started flipping upwards. A short ramp lay inside the gates, leading to a covered garage space attached to an ultra-modern house.

Straight lines formed a rectangle divided in horizontal halves. The top half seemed to be covered in wood with a long balcony. The bottom half covered in what looked like shutters, now rolling up to expose floor-to-ceiling glass with a door in the middle. To the left of the empty space in the garage, his Harley faced the gates. To the right, a neat footpath led to the front door. A palm tree stood in the middle of the front garden dripping with rain, exotic foliage and flowers growing against the massive garden walls, grass covering everything in between, and a pebbled path heading back down to a pedestrian gate at the front.

It wasn't the same, but it had a similar style to the villa in Ilhabela.

"I thought we were going to the cinema?" I asked, taking in where we were, absorbing every detail of the place.

"I said we were watching a movie. I have a killer flatscreen and a really good sofa." Marcelo smiled mischievous.

So this was his house. I was so used to seeing him at Eight or eating out, I had unconsciously started to think he lived at the bar. Like a kid who thinks her teacher lives at the school. He pulled the car into the shelter of the garage.

"So this is where you hide. What part of São Paulo is this?"

"*Butantã.*" He unbuckled his seatbelt and opened his door, minding not to hit the bike. "It's across the Pinheiros River from where you live. If it wasn't for the traffic, it would only take twenty minutes, but the traffic here is always shit. If you walked, it would probably take just over an hour."

The rain was so thick, I hadn't even noticed we had crossed the river.

A side door led us to the sitting room without getting wet. Although it was still daytime, the rain had dulled the light, so Marcelo flicked a switch, and the room was filled with mood lighting. Across the open plan space, through a double-door opening, was a glossy sand-colored kitchen—light slipping through the glass-fronted cabinets exposing fancy wine glasses and see-through plates. Everything in its place and polished to a blinding shine. Stools surrounded the island unit, evoking a little of the atmosphere of the bar at Eight.

To my right, a spacious sitting room was dominated by a single cream L-shaped sofa, a designer reclining chair, and a big square footstool in the middle of the room. A bookcase covered in books, vinyl, and memorabilia on the wall behind it, a gigantic flat screen resting on the wall opposite above a modern fireplace, big speakers at its edges. The walls all around covered in memorabilia—a signed baseball bat, signed football shirts, a vintage looking movie poster with two American motorcycle troopers and their bikes, among other things. An open staircase perched at the corner of the wall to the garage, leading to the floor above. The whole room appeared to be open to the elements because of the huge wall of glass facing the front garden. It was not what I expected.

Not what I expected at all. Marcelo's car, bike and even Eight was predominantly black in color, but his house was all cream, sand, wood, and glass.

He walked across the room and dropped his keys on the top of the kitchen island, opened the fridge, and started putting a tray of food together. I walked around, hands behind my back, looking at everything—family photographs, books on the shelves—like they would let me in on his secrets.

"You look like you're visiting a museum. I'm sure I'm not that interesting." There was humor in his voice.

"Are these your grandparents?" I pointed at a picture on the shelves, turning so I could see him through the doorway.

His head turned my way. Small smile, short nods, but his attention quickly diverted back to the tray he was putting together.

His grandfather looked European. Light complexion, dark brown hair, happy smile that didn't show any teeth. His grandmother had gorgeous dark skin and dark wild curls that surrounded her face like a lion's mane. Smile showing beaming joy. Celo stood in the middle, a latte combination of the milk and coffee standing to either side of him. Serious face that looked a little confused.

"You were a cute kid, Lewis." He had inherited his grandfather's looks in a lighter version of his grandmother's colors.

"I'm still cute now, no?" His face lit up in a smug smile.

I scowled at him. Once a cocky bastard, always a cocky bastard. "Is that a CHiPs poster?" My finger pointed at the biggest poster in the room.

"How do you know that? That's from the 80s," he said, leaning on the counter, a habit of his.

"My mum used to love it. She says it was the best TV show she watched in America. Are you into architecture?" I crooked my neck to better read the book titles on the bookshelf.

"They were my grandfather's. He was an architect; he built this house." I nodded. It all made sense now. "Are you done analyzing me? All that is missing is a pair of eyeglasses hanging down your nose and a note pad." His voice was serious, but his eyes were amused.

"I don't think you cook in that kitchen much. It's too tidy," I teased. His house was amazing. "I'm hoping you have popcorn. A movie is not a movie without popcorn."

"You're a hard woman to please, Lewis. But…" His index finger came up and he wandered to one of the kitchen cabinets, opening a cupboard and producing a box of PG Tips. "I have that crappy tea you like to drink."

"Hey! Respect the mighty English tea." I walked towards him and snatched the box from his hand. "Where did you find

PG Tips?" Then I hugged the box to me. "I missed you so much PG! Don't listen to him."

One of his eyebrows raised. "Are all English people this weird, or is it just you?"

"No, seriously, where did you find this gem?"

"If I told you, I would have to kill you," he said, smoldering at me.

"You bought it online, didn't you?"

"Yep." He headed towards the sitting room with the food tray, placed it on the footstool, and switched the TV on. "What do you wanna watch?"

After the film was over, I stood up and started stretching. "You're staring at me with that weird face again."

"What face?"

"Like your mind is a hundred miles away," I said, sitting back on the sofa next to him and sipping my third tea.

"Nah. I'm right here." His eyes focused on me, his hands automatically playing with the ends of my hair. He brushed a thumb over the freckles on my cheek. "I have something for you."

I stopped sipping and frowned.

Marcelo reached behind him for a little bag at the back of the armrest in the corner of the sofa. He held my palm and placed the bag on it. I looked at it for a minute, unsure what to expect.

"Don't look so suspicious! Open it."

"I go away for the weekend, and I get gifts? I clearly need to do it more often!" I unraveled the ribbon closing the bag; the flat box opened with a pleasing click. A bangle with three charms sat inside it.

Celo moved to sit at the edge of the sofa, picking up the bracelet and fastening it around my wrist. I raised my arm to eye level and looked at the spoils glittering against my skin.

He took hold of my hand, the leather cuff I had given him

on his wrist. "A bracelet, for a bracelet." His fingers picked each charm as he explained. "One for every place you'll find me—a cocktail for what I do, the São Paulo charm for my city, and the diamanté snake for where I live. The *Butantã* is also a study center for snake venom antidotes and vaccines. It's not far from here. I used to love that place when I was a kid. I will take you there some time." His eyes were so intense on me, I could feel my cheeks warming up, changing color. "I don't usually buy people gifts for no reason, but I thought it would be nice for my girlfriend to carry something I gave her."

His head touched mine, his long dark hair falling over his face. I fiddled with the charms between my fingers.

"So is that what I am? Your girlfriend? Strange... I was under the impression you didn't date," I teased.

He smiled. "I might have to introduce you to the other girlfriends. There's one living in my closet and another under my bed. But I must warn you, they'll be jealous. I've never given them anything. It might get nasty."

"And here was I thinking I was just gonna have great sex with this fit bloke I met on holiday... damn it." I smiled too wide, too pleased to make the teasing convincing. He smiled, satisfied, understanding I liked it.

"Great sex, huh?" he teased back. But the smile slowly drained from his face and was replaced by a light frown on his eyebrows.

He pulled me closer and kissed me. Then held my face with both his hands, looked me straight in the eye like he wanted it to mean something, and whispered on my lips, "You know there's only you, right?" His eyebrows screwed in some feeling I couldn't name, but it was intense and dark, like him.

I nodded.

"So don't bolt on me, ok?" He said it so quietly, I almost didn't hear him.

Another nod.

We looked at each other for a long while; an uncontrollable urge to kiss him came over me. My arms wrapped around his neck, fingers twisting into his hair and pulling him closer, body moving towards him until I was astride his jeans. I kissed him hard, deep, wanting. Leaned on him until his back touched the back of the sofa—my hair dropping over our faces and blocking the light as if someone had closed the curtains.

His hands found the hem of my top, got into the back of my jeans, fingers reaching for my backside but not quite succeeding. And I made the kiss deeper, wetter, rubbed my hips on to him. Hands going under his tee, nails trailing his sides and moving towards the front. His muscles contracted; he gasped. The fingers inside my jeans dug into my flesh. His hips pushing on to me, trying to rub on me even harder than I was doing to him.

He tried to kiss me, but I didn't let him. Instead, I kissed the corners of his mouth, pulled his tee off his body, ran my lips down his neck, breathing, brushing, but not kissing. He smelled so good. All masculine, clean and sexy. And as I rubbed my face on his neck, bottom lip dragging, devouring the scent of him, his skin got covered in goosebumps, breathing getting harder.

He pulled my top over my head, kissed my neck, my breasts… and my body went fluid. The more he kissed, the more I wanted, the more I rubbed, the more I wanted him to want me.

You see… rewards are earned. When a man does something you like, you should reward him. Show him what behavior gets him your most special treats. And being made the official girlfriend definitely made the rewards list.

So I kissed his neck… shoulder… chest… nipple while I knelt on the floor. His stomach, bit the side of him, unzipped his jeans. Before I could pull them off, he removed a condom from his pocket and placed it on the sofa. His eyes on mine the whole time as I stripped him of his pants.

My hands rubbed their way up both of his thighs and the first kiss went on the inside of his knee. Then higher and higher until my tongue was gliding over the crease on his hip, and across his stomach. His anticipation throbbing against my collar bone.

He gathered my hair, not pulling or pushing, just holding it in a ponytail so he could see my face. And I made sure I was looking straight at him, eye to eye, when my fingers wrapped around him and my tongue ran all the way under and up his length. His lips parting, breath speeding up. Eyes struggling to stay open as I kissed, licked and worked him over and over.

He tried to sit up, pull me up by the elbow. I brushed his hand away, pushed his body back onto the sofa. He let me do it for a moment, but as I licked and sucked harder, he let go of my hair and held on to my face with both his hands, sitting up and leaning over to kiss me so I wouldn't finish him off.

His mouth tried to capture my skin as I stood up. Full palms squeezing my backside, lips kissing my stomach before his digits made light work of freeing my legs from their denim.

Hungry fingers grabbed my arse, the back of my thighs, pulling me to kneel astride his lap. Hand reaching for the condom, splitting the packaging open with his teeth, and rolling it down in place, then returning to the back of my thighs to elevate me to position.

One arm wrapped around me, palm anchored on my backside, keeping me slightly suspended, fingers grabbing chunks of me. The other arm wrapped up my back, hand holding on to the back of my neck. Kisses wet, deep and full of meaning.

I could feel him, throbbing underneath me, rubbing on my skin, tingling my nerve endings with the promise. His hand on my neck traveling down my front to cup one of my breasts; his lips, tongue, teeth, playing with my nipple.

And I lost my patience and guided him into me. Slow at first. Enjoying the fullness, trying to feel everything, every thrust, every inch, every nerve ending being stroked. Until he leaned back into the sofa, palms full of my hips, pulling and pushing me faster. My hands holding on to the back of the couch, his mouth still playing with my nipples.

My body started to tingle with the fizz that starts at the center and radiates out, but just when it was getting good he pushed himself off the sofa, tightened his arms around my waist, stood up and disengaged.

"No! No, no, no!" I whined at the sudden stop.

He smiled. Smug, almost like a dare. Knowing exactly what he had just done.

I didn't have much time to complain. Arms tight around my waist, he carried me, then put me down by the side of the couch and stood behind me, teeth nibbling on my shoulder, leaving a wet line all the way to my earlobe. One hand on my stomach, the other on my neck, he slowly bent me over the arm of the sofa until the side of my face was on the seat. Pinning my legs in between his, palm flat running from my neck down my spine until it settled at the edge of my hips.

And he came back into me. Slow, gentle, watching my reaction, gauging how far he could take it. Nails clawing at the skin at my waist… hips… arse. Giving me smacks that were more for noise than sting. Grabbing hands full. Reaching deep, gaining momentum, hitting all the right places. I pushed on my tiptoes to get him to the right spot, and he kept it close, increased his speed.

His body not drumming into me but coming and going with steady intensity. Filling me entirely, stroking all my nerve endings. The friction building and sparking something inside my body that was made to spontaneously combust. Creating a feeling like peppermint cream on your skin, sour gummies on your tastebuds, tingling, setting your senses alight.

My body exploded in tremors and shivers that traveled their way up my spine all the way to my skull, stronger than before, making me whimper. Blood rushing to my brain and making me light-headed, turning my legs into jelly. The front of his body pushing deep against the back of my legs releasing aftershock waves that raised goosebumps all over my skin. His breath coming out in a gush, grunts sounding like a purr.

For a while he just stood there. Warm fingers snaking down my back, around the curve of my hip, up the back of my leg, over my backside and up my spine. And I didn't want to move. My body completely relaxed despite the slightly unnatural position it was in. But he thought better of it, hands scooping me up like a doll and bringing me to stand so he could smell and kiss my neck.

"I gotta go clean up," he said planting a kiss under my ear, arms tightening around my body, one hand squeezing one of my breasts, body coming undone from mine.

By the time he came back, I was lying on the sofa. So at peace and relaxed that I didn't move when he lay behind me—one arm going under my head, the other around my body and in between my arms. Bodies naked, face buried in my neck like the lost piece of a jigsaw that just found home. Fingers intertwined with mine, my bracelet glittering on top of his leather cuff.

♥♥♥

Coming back to Lu's was incredibly anticlimactic. Work had piled up and I needed to get my head out of yesterday's memories to focus. My mother wanted a call. Those always started well, but always ended badly. Ryan wanted to know when I was coming to visit. As the weeks went by, he started to wonder if I was going to deliver on my promise. He was keen for me to meet my sisters. Felipe was checking in. Lu wanted to know if I was still up for Thursday.

I had just put the phone down when it vibrated.

> **Celo**
> Forgot 2 say, next 2 days we've a lot on prepping 4 Thurs. Gabe's band playing again. Assuming u & Lu r coming? Bjs.

> **Me**
> We are. Lu has become Gabe's biggest groupie, but she will never admit to it. 😏 By the way, you know 'bjs' means blowjobs where I come from, right? Xx

> **Celo**
> Bjs (beijos) means kisses here. But I like ur version better. Happy 2 cum & oblige if u offering. Love that thing u do w/ ur tongue. 😉

Typing… He seemed to take a while.

> **Celo**
> Think Lu's more than groupie 2 Gabe. He's good 4 her. It's about time she got over Alexandre. Bjs

> **Me**
> 'Cum' also means something else where I come from. 😈 Oh, I think she got over Alexandre plenty. xx

> **Celo**
> She hasn't dated anyone since. Stop trying 2 talk dirty 2 me. I've 2 work u know. Bjs

> **Me**
> Just like you didn't date anyone ever? 😔
> What was your excuse? 😏 P.S. The day I talk
> dirty to you, you'll know about it. xx

He read my message but didn't reply. He still showed as online for a moment, then went offline. Maybe I'd cut it a little too close to the bone. When the phone vibrated a few minutes later, I had to admit I opened it with a level of relief.

> **Celo**
> Not true. I'm dating YOU Lewis. Sounds like I
> need 2 get acquainted w/ ur talking dirty
> skills. Bjs

It made me smile. I looked at the bracelet on my wrist. He was indeed dating me. Officially, apparently.

> **Me**
> [Picture of my boobs in the blue French lace
> bra he likes] I'm less of a talker, more of a
> doer. Xx

> **Celo**
> That's mean Lewis. U know I'm working. Bjs

> **Me**
> [Picture of my behind on the blue French lace
> he likes] 🐎 Enough for you? Xx

> **Celo**
> Keep sending me these pics when I'm working
> & I'm gonna ve 2 slap that. Bjs

> **Me**
> [Picture of my lower half bending over] I might
> like that. Xx

Celo
U killing me here. I've got 2 focus u know. Will end up w/ the wrong fucking order. Bjs

Me
[Picture of one of my nipples spilling over the blue lace] I like when you focus on these. And if you're going to fuck anything, it better be your girlfriend. Xx

Celo
Now I've a problem. I've 2 do orders and paperwork but all I can think about is u bending over my desk. Bjs

Me
Want me to come over? Xx

Celo
W/ that blue lace? Bjs

Me
[Picture of me in said lace] You mean this one? Xx

Celo
Hell yeah!

Me
Would love to. But I'm working, sorry. Xx

Celo
U ARE trying 2 kill me. Bjs

Me
What can I say? I'm irresistible like that. 😉 xx

> **Celo**
> That, u definitely r. Now, please... If u not coming 2 take me outta my misery, u need 2 let me work. Already can't think of anything else. Bjs

> **Me**
> Good. I'll see you in a couple of days. Xx

> **Celo**
> Fuck me, u're so mean Lewis.

> **Me**
> It'll be my pleasure. Looking forward to it. Xx

When we walked into Eight, I had not seen him for a couple of days. He spotted me as soon as I walked through the doors, grin spreading, lighting up his face, his expression soft.

The band was still setting up, but the bar was already busy. Lu waved at Celo and Leo, then pointed towards the band. I nodded; she turned and walked away. When I looked back, Celo was saying something to the other bartenders, pointing at a couple waiting to be served, his eyes still on me.

He nodded for me to follow and walked to the opposite side of the bar. By the time I walked around to where he was, he had walked towards the back of a corridor and had a door open, waiting for me. I walked past him and into the room; it looked like his office.

Before I could take it all in, he turned me around and kissed me. Deep, wet, his arms hugging me like a boa constrictor, one hand squeezing my backside. In my heels I was as tall as him. When he was done kissing me, his forehead touched mine, arms holding me tight, eyes closed. My arms wrapped around his neck.

"Hello there, boyfriend." His eyes opened, he smiled. "I missed you too."

Celo took a step back, looked at my outfit, hands rubbing my waist from the front to the back repeatedly.

"You look so sexy, Lewis. Like an English JLo." Full palms squeezed my behind. "It's mean. I have to work, you know. And I've had your little messages in my head for two days." His voice was raspy.

"I'm glad you like it." I bit his lip. "You will also like what I have underneath."

He grumbled. "You *are* mean." Then he let go of me and opened the door. "Now get out, before I forget where I am." As I walked past him, he smacked my arse. "Gabe asked me to reserve a table at the front. I'll send your drinks." I nodded and headed straight to the table.

The band started playing, the space filled to bulging, and I couldn't see the bar from where we sat. But every time our drinks were about to finish, new ones turned up.

"How does he do that?" Luciana shouted over the music as a new round of drinks landed.

I shrugged.

There were people everywhere, inside and out. The music and chatter so loud, Lu and I could barely hear each other.

Halfway through the set, while Gabe drank a bottle of water, all the other band members left the stage. But he stood at the center in the limelight. Caio sat next to me, leaning in so he could speak in my ear, and I leaned into him so I could hear him. "You're going to want to understand this next song."

"*Essa próxima música vai pro meu foguetinho mini,*" Gabe announced from the stage, hand raising and pointing from his nose to Luciana. She almost spat out her drink, eyes huge looking at him, frozen on the spot. And everyone else looked at her.

"He says this next song goes to his pocket rocket," Caio shouted in my ear.

Gabe slid his hands down the arm of the guitar and started playing—his thumb tapping the strings in rhythmic intervals after so many notes. Without the band behind him, the room echoed with his guitar skills. He looked down at it, giving it a half smile, and after a short intro, his smooth voice filled the speakers.

Caio started translating. Something about a regular boy falling in love with a posh girl. And how she had made him spend all his money and didn't give him a break. The lyrics were sung in little bursts, Caio staying close to my ear to translate them in time. Gabe was originally focusing on his guitar, but then his eyes focused on Lu. She tried to look unimpressed, but the fond smile on her face gave her away.

Then out of nowhere, Marcelo appeared in front of Caio and I. Hands clenched into fists next to his body. Looking straight at Caio, he raised both his eyebrows at the same time but didn't blink.

"I was just translating the song for her," Caio shouted over the music.

"Thanks. But I got it from here," Celo shouted back. His face said nothing, but his eyes were locked on Caio.

Raising both his hands up in the air, Caio got to his feet. Celo moving sideways to let him through but staring at him all the way until he had walked past him. His head turned back to me slowly, body following, and he took the seat next to me. One of his arms going across the back of me, hugging me to him.

He gave me a peck on the lips. "You want to understand the song?" Closer than Caio, he didn't have to shout.

I nodded.

The music had built to a more energetic crescendo. Celo continued translating... Something about how the posh girl didn't make it easy for him. But I wasn't really paying attention because, in between words, Celo started kissing my neck and rubbing his nose on it like he was smelling my perfume, and I couldn't focus. He touched his forehead to mine, his eyes open, staring straight at me, hand on my neck, thumb rubbing my cheek, like he was trying to transmit the lyrics via telepathy.

The song ended, the place erupting in applause. "I need to go back to work." He looked almost disappointed, kissed me, and stood up, disappearing into the middle of the crowd on his way back to the bar.

Lu sipped her drink. "Can you believe that guy!" A finger pointed at Gabe.

"Oh, give over! You loved it!"

She took another sip and shrugged like it didn't matter. Her grin too big to make the gesture convincing.

"I told you he was jealous of Caio." Her smugness was annoying.

"How did he even see that?"

Lu raised her eyes and nodded her head towards the camera on the ceiling. "He sat us right under the camera. There are three big screens hanging from the ceiling in front of the bar. They can keep an eye on everything while they're working, including outside. That's how I think he knew when our drinks were almost finished."

I didn't know what to say to that.

"Celo is many things, but if there is one thing he is not, it's stupid. That boy doesn't stitch without a knot at the end of the line."

"Is that another one of your sayings?" I laughed.

CHAPTER 13

Luciana

Pepino stormed into my office like a tornado on his path to destruction.

"Did you know about it? Did you know?" His voice on the lower, louder pitch he assumed when angry.

I got up from my desk and walked past him to the door, my assistant standing apologetic and confused on the other side. He'd bypassed her without giving her the time of day. I nodded at her, hand gestured that everything was fine.

"What are you doing here? When did you get back? We weren't expecting you back for another week." I tried to keep my voice calm.

"Don't change the subject! Did you know?"

"What are you talking about, Pepino? I know a lot of things." The door clicked shut.

"Marcelo and Paige. Since when has that been going on?" It wasn't a request; his face was red with anger. "Don't even try to deny it. I have a fucking picture!" He threw his phone at me.

Angie... The bitch! Not to be kicked to the curb and outdone, she had sent him several pictures of Marcelo touching his forehead to Paige's at the bar the night he blew her off, his hand on Paige's hair, eyes looking into each other's.

"Fucking son of a bitch, I can't believe he took her from me!

And you!" His angry finger pointed at me. "You knew all along! Some cousin you are!"

I narrowed my eyes at him, my voice changing to stern. "Keep your tone down. This is my office, not a whore house." I walked back to my desk, crossed my arms. "To be fair, you guys had a fling years ago but never dated, and I don't control Paige. I have no say on who she chooses to date. It was also not my place to tell you, Pepino." I tried to keep my voice down. "Celo stepped on your toes, he should tell you. But Angela clearly couldn't wait to smear shit all over the walls. Are you not at all curious about what's in it for her?"

"She has been more loyal to me than you ever were." He hissed at me, words dripping with venom; my calm was making him more agitated.

"Don't be ridiculous. The only reason she's shit stirring is because her ego is bruised; it has fuck all to do with you. That vindictive cow only wants to see Celo burn. And who are you to talk to me about loyalty? You let him keep that viper as a pet after what she did to me."

"I can't believe he was hanging around me while he was trying to screw her! Right under my nose!" He was so obsessed with his grief; he didn't hear a word I said.

"You know damn well it wasn't like that. Did you seriously cut your business trip short for this? I bloody hope you didn't walk out of our deal with the Chinese to come fight over a woman who's made it crystal clear she isn't into you. Your father will not be impressed."

"Oh! Nice try. But the deal is done. I closed it before I came back." He huffed. "You were in on it, weren't you? Of course, you were! He's been crashing at yours, hasn't he?" He leaned over, grabbed me by the arm, spitting the words at my face like a curse. "Ain't that cute!" The last word dripped in sarcasm and the blood of unsuspecting babies.

I pulled myself free. "Now, you're just being ridiculous," I spat at him. He was beginning to test my patience. "You and Paige were never together. You never dated. As a matter of fact, if you had stopped trying to get into her knickers yourself and looked around for long enough, you would have noticed she was into him. It was written all over her damn face! And to be fair to him, he did try to stay away from her. He didn't even speak to her properly, Pepino! When have you ever seen him do that? You tell me, you're closer to him than I am."

Pepino's eyes were throwing daggers at me. He knew I was right.

"Think about it for a second. When was the last time you saw him with anyone? Easter, Felipe! A month ago! Does that sound like your old love rat of a friend to you? I'm telling you. If you'd paid enough attention, you would've seen something was up. And what do you think you can do? At the end of the day, it's her choice. You can't force her to date you!"

"Are you really going to try defend that double-crossing son of a bitch?" His voice raised. "He will just use her and throw her away like he does to everyone else!"

I shrugged. "What do you want me to do? He's what she wants."

Pepino collapsed in one of my chairs, head on his hands. I leaned against my desk.

"For what it's worth, I do think he really has feelings for her. If he didn't, he wouldn't have gone against you. He considers you a brother. You guys have been friends since primary school. I don't think he would upset you just for the sake of it."

"Shut up!" His voice reached a whole new level of loud.

My eyes narrowed. He was really starting to press my buttons, but I didn't want to test his temper. For all his prim and proper, Pepino could be a loose cannon when he was upset.

"When?" His eyes were on the floor, head in his hands, elbows supporting the whole thing on his knees.

"When what?"

"For how long has he been screwing her behind my back?" It was just an angry whisper, pain written over every word.

"I don't know. A couple of weeks maybe."

Pepino snorted, his eyes darting from side to side, mind working, putting things together. The sigh came with a headshake, his nose and eyelids getting red, eyes now fixed on the floor.

"I've been speaking to her the whole time I was away."

"Paige sees you as a friend. She doesn't think she owes you anything, and she has always made it clear that you were just friends. She feels no need to explain herself to you."

His eyes turned to me, tired, hollow, then angry. "*You know* that's not true. What she has done is dangle the carrot and keep me on ice." He was silent for a minute. "I've also spoken to him while I was gone." The words hissing through his teeth.

I shrugged. "I wouldn't tell you over the phone either. Not when you are supposed to be on the other side of the world closing one of our biggest deals of the year."

He leaned back on the chair, his body going limp in the seat like a deflated balloon, head turned up, eyes staring at the ceiling. For a long moment he said nothing.

"For what it's worth, I'm sorry, cousin. I really am."

I reached over to touch his shoulder, but he brushed me off and stormed out of my office. If I knew Pepino, he wasn't done.

This whole thing was still playing on my mind by the time I met Gabriel for a drink; he smiled when he spotted me. But it must've been written all over my face, because he noticed as soon as I got closer and stood up from his bar stool like he was on high alert.

"What's wrong? What happened?" His hands

automatically reaching for me, eyes scanning my face as though he was trying to diagnose me.

"The proverbial shit has hit the fan." I stared at him until he put the puzzle together. It took him a minute to remember our past conversations about the whole Marcelo-Paige thing.

"Fuck. Felipe knows."

I nodded.

"How did he find out?"

"Courtesy of Angela—the scumbag. I can tell you, he's not a happy bunny. Kind of destroyed, actually."

Apparently satisfied there was no imminent danger, Gabe sat back down, pulling me with him till I was standing in between his legs.

"Is he back?" He reached over, grabbed a toothpick, and spiked an olive.

"Over a week early. Apparently, he managed to close the deal with the Chinese a week ahead of schedule." I could feel the headache coming, pressed my fingers to the spot to alleviate the pressure. "I guess he was into Paige a lot more than we all thought. And he had hours to marinate on it, sitting on a plane, going stir-crazy." I felt tired; my shoulders ached.

"Did you give Celo the heads up?" Another olive was slaughtered.

"I have no sympathy for him. Serves him right for giving that viper wings. I told him many times she wasn't worth the bother. You know, the picture she sent Felipe is over a week old. She only sent it to him when Celo put a label on it and called Paige his girlfriend."

"You really don't like this girl, huh?" Two olives were pierced through their bulging bellies with one swift prick. I pressed the middle of my forehead harder.

"Wouldn't pee on her if she was on fire. Angela is always scheming, trying to get one over people. And it's all so senseless! There's never any need or reason for what she does. She does it because she can."

He dropped the toothpick, lowered my hand out of his way, pressed his thumbs to the middle of my forehead, and the rest of his fingers to the pressure points on my temples.

"You think she is doing this because she is in love with Celo? Ha! She just doesn't like that he's chasing someone else. And if he was in love with her, she would be treating him like shit. That is what she does. Nasty piece of work that woman."

Gabe moved his hands to rub gentle circles on my temples. I closed my eyes, hands resting on his lap.

"Are you going to tell Paige?"

"She'd have a fit! She gets uber annoyed every time anyone talks about Felipe like they were a thing, or like she has to justify herself to him. To be fair to her, she has made it very clear, many times, that she had no interest in dating Felipe."

"But you feel guilty?"

"No. I'm not the one sleeping with the girl he's after. I just feel bad for him, you know? It sucks to be into someone that isn't into you." My voice sounded melancholic, more than I intended it to, more than I thought it should. "That's exactly why I don't get attached to anybody."

"Anybody?" The rubbing stopped. I opened my eyes, his eyebrows were raised, his eyes skeptical.

"Nobody." I looked him straight in the eye. "And that's precisely why you have so much fun with me." I smiled, flirting, trying to change the topic.

"So...you're just using me for my body?" he said in mock outrage. "God will punish you." Sounded like a joke, but he let go of me, crossed his arms, and leaned backwards on his stool. The action making him look stronger, arms more defined, his black and grey rose tattoo more visible.

I shrugged, no hint of an apology.

He seemed to think for a second, then shrugged. "That's

fine by me." His drink disappeared in one gulp. "I don't mind being abused by good-looking pocket-rocket blondes."

I smacked his arm. "Pocket my arse!"

He grinned at me, both his arms wrapping around my waist, big palms flat on my back. His eyes stared at me for a minute, first with a playful smile, but slowly it faded to a more serious face.

"You know we are nothing like them." His eyes narrowed. I could smell olives and *Guaraná*.

I rubbed circles on his arms but said nothing. Gabriel came across as playful and nonchalant, but he was far from stupid. He could read people better than I could, and despite my bravado, had unfortunately gotten under my skin and gotten to know me fairly well. I was under no illusion. He indulged me. Letting me pretend that our thing was just a fling, nothing more than several one-night stands that curiously seemed to happen with the same person. He knew how to play me, and he handled me the same way he handled his guitar—with skill and expertise.

After a pensive silence, he raised his eyebrows twice, like a geek trying to be sexy, and I laughed. He kissed me. Slow and meaningful, tasting of salty olives.

"You hungry?" I could feel his lips move against my skin rather than hear him.

"Not really."

"Leaving?"

"Perfect."

He knew me far too well.

CHAPTER 14

Marcelo

I'D BEEN WATCHING HER SLEEP FOR A COUPLE OF HOURS.

Paige was sprawled on the bed—her back bare, sheets around her hips and legs, breathing slow and deep. She was so beautiful. Had that strange, unassuming, simple type of beauty, even asleep and painted in the blueish-grey light the middle of the night brings. And when her eyes were open, it was like she could bewitch you, hypnotize you, because they were so freaky looking.

Of course it had to be her. Of course, the one that rocked, fucking capsized my boat, also had to be the one Felipe had fallen hard for. When you're as lucky as I am, of course 'the one' would be someone you shouldn't want and would break some cosmic rule by having. It was like I'd been cursed. A damn omen.

And the irony wasn't lost on me. Four weeks ago, I knew how she flicked her hair, rolled her eyes at Lu like a sister, bit her lip when she was nervous, and had a thing for pastel colors, but we had never spoken properly. And now she was here... my girlfriend, in my house, on my bed, naked, fast asleep.

Just over four weeks, that's all it took. That's all it took from the moment we started talking in the pool, for her to demolish my resolve and have me going to war for her. She looked all

227

cute and innocent shrouded in white sheets, but she had come into my life like a bulldozer, wreaking havoc, smashing anything left standing. And I was about to lose everything that meant anything to me for a woman that would get on a plane and leave me in a few short weeks.

I had come undone.

Fallen prey to the damn virus. Exposed my jugular, that's what I did. And as much as I would like to believe in happy endings, I knew how this would end. Something was going to cut my throat.

And yet… right now, with the smell of sex in the room and her skin under my fingers, I just couldn't bring myself to regret it or care. For some bizarre reason, it made me think of the mermaid tales—all the sailors said to have jumped to their deaths and died with a smile on their faces—because right here was my mermaid. I knew I was walking the plank, and I knew damn well that as soon as I hit the water, I was gonna sink and drown. But I'd keep walking because she was calling my name.

I kissed her forehead, fingers chasing the outlines of her hair, her face without thinking. She was magnetic and I was made of nickel.

Her eyes opened. Slow, long blinks. "You can't sleep again, Lewis?" Her words dragged with sleepiness, whispered rather than spoken, with the huskiness of a voice that hasn't been used for a little while.

It always made me smile when she called me that. I shook my head with the smallest movement required.

She lay on her back and flicked her arm over and under my head so I could lay on her shoulder. I did as she wanted, our lower halves a tangle of legs. She planted a kiss on my forehead, then her nails trailed up and down my back, drawing circles, lines and waves. Her other hand scratching my head, playing with my hair.

I hugged her tighter, pushed my nose in her neck to breathe in the scent of her skin. And just like that, all my unease was forgotten. I don't even remember falling asleep. But I did so before her, because the last thing I remember was her messing with my hair.

The next morning, the whole car journey back, she held my hand, played with my fingers. Held it to her face. Laughed and talked nonstop. It was like a parallel universe. Even the colors and the light were different. But as soon as I dropped her off, someone pressed play on reality at the exact moment the car door shut. Everything seeming a little more threatening and duller at the same time.

I could feel it in the pit of my stomach. This was the calm before the worse part of the storm. I was in the eye of a hurricane.

And my gut was never wrong.

I had just put all the tables and chairs out on the sidewalk when I saw Felipe entering the bar, face like thunder. I didn't know he was back from China; he wasn't meant to be.

"Hey man, when did you—"

He cracked me one. Right across the fucking face.

Ambushed, I lost my footing, stumbled backwards, tried to defend a second blow, but the punches just kept on coming. I just about managed to push him off before he pinned me against one of the pillars.

"I'm not fighting you, dude," I shouted, adrenaline kicking in.

"Too bad." Felipe came at me stronger, like a fucking demon, his face twisted with rage. I tried to defend my head as much as I could without hitting him, but a few of the blows connected. Disorientation hit me like a pile of bricks and brought me to my knees. And all I could see then was his foot. All I could do was hold on to his legs. He wavered but, rather than lose balance, the fucker bent over and continued to punch me, yanking at my hair so he could get to my head. Then he was off me.

Leo had one of his arms twisted behind his back, Felipe's face pinned to the counter by the neck. He spewed a string of curses and threats at Leo, reaching out, trying to use his weight to knock him off balance, but Leo was bigger, built like a tank.

"What are you doing, dude?!" Leo shouted. "What the hell?!"

"Let go of me or I will fucking kill you, do you hear me!"

"I'd love to see you try. I will let you go when you calm down."

I struggled to get up from the floor. My eyes were blurry, my ears ringing, I just about made it to my feet.

"I'm not fighting you, Felipe," I tried to say, but the words didn't come out right.

It hurt to breathe. Standing upright did me good, though. My eyes cleared a little. I could taste blood. Wiped my mouth and the back of my hand was covered in it, so I spit it out.

"You double-crossing son of a bitch!" Felipe was still trying to overpower Leo.

"Man, if you don't calm down I'm calling the police." Leo pressed his face harder on the counter. He had never needed to use his jujitsu skills, but today they came in handy.

"Fuck you! You..." Felipe said pointing at me. "You rat. You couldn't wait for me to be out of the country, could you? You piece of shit."

"I know I should've cleared the air with you first, Felipe." My chest started to throb. "But you talk like she belongs to you. You were never together."

That seemed to anger him even more. He swore, twisted, and thrashed against the counter.

"Calm the fuck down!" Leo pressed his face harder, twisted his arm higher up.

230

"Ok, ok!" Felipe shouted, no doubt triggered by pain and probably the fear of having his arm broken.

I spat more blood on the floor. Leaned forwards to pant, that hurt, leaned backwards, that hurt even more. Something cracked. Everything hurt, but my face was starting to feel tight like an overstretched rubber band. I walked around, trying to breathe through the pain. Felipe had gone quiet. The whole situation seemed to have de-escalated.

"I'm going to let you go, dude. Don't do anything stupid." After a minute Leo loosened his hold and in a split-second Felipe was free, flying at me with the speed and strength only rage can grant.

I deflected his punch and landed one open palm uppercut on his chin, Felipe falling backwards and hitting the floor.

"I'm not taking any more of your shit. Don't make me hurt you, man."

He got back on his feet, shaking his head, off balance. I prepared to rebuff him; this was going to hurt like a bitch if he came for seconds, but he seemed to think better of it. When we were younger, he had always had the temper, but I was the better fighter. I was the one who had to scrap to survive; he just had a big mouth.

"This isn't over!" he said through his teeth, pointing an accusing finger, turning and stumbling towards the door.

"I love her, Felipe. And I'm dating her. And she agreed to date me."

He stopped dead where he was. Then turned around slowly, unsteady. For a moment he said nothing, then he started laughing.

"Well, ain't that cute!" He sounded out of breath. I spat more blood; my ribs were killing. "I feel sorry for her if that's the case. Because, if I remember well, the people you love either end up dead or figuring out what an omen you are and leaving you."

231

It was below the belt, and it hit exactly like he meant it to. Harder than any of his punches. Then he turned around and stumbled out.

"Do you think he will be ok? You hit him pretty good there," Leo asked, following Felipe across the front of the bar with his eyes.

I spat more blood on the floor and tried to support my ribs with one of my hands. "And you worry about him?"

"True. He hasn't gotten laid in a while, has he? While you seem to have stolen the last cookie in his packet and been at it like a rabbit." Leo had this theory that frustrated men were angrier and fought harder. He wasn't wrong. They used to do it with horses, so they raced faster.

"It wasn't his damn cookie. It was just the cookie he wanted. It's not the same thing."

I walked to the bathroom while Leo cleaned all the blood from the floor. My face was covered, red gunk running from my nose to my mouth, dripping from my chin into the basin and onto my clothes. My hair a mess, sticking to the blood. I lifted my shirt, the movement shooting pain down my body; one side had already started to bruise. Washed the blood from my face, just to have some of it replaced with a fresh outpour. Had to do it standing up, because I couldn't lean over without pain shooting through my middle. My shirt now covered in red. My eyes had started to swell. I had to hand it to Felipe, he had minced me pretty good.

"Damn! You look a mess, dude. You really need to go to the hospital." Leo had come to assess the damage.

The seconds were ticking by real slow. The longer I waited, the more it hurt. I tried to help Leo shut down the bar, but I was just smudging blood everywhere. Sitting was uncomfortable, lying down was uncomfortable, breathing was uncomfortable, and now that the adrenaline was wearing off, my ribs, my face felt like they were about to burst. The towel full of ice was now dirty with blood and, as the ice melted, it was dripping everywhere. I could feel the swelling increasing, the skin getting tighter.

After they rushed me through emergency, I told Leo that I wanted him to go back and open the bar. But truth be told, I just didn't want him here, staring at me, wondering how the fuck I got myself minced by the guy I considered a brother. I knew it was moronic; Leo wouldn't judge me. But it didn't mean I didn't.

"Do you want me to call anyone? Marisa? Paige?"

"For what?"

"They will be mad if you don't call them. What you gonna do anyway? Hide for a month until your face goes back to normal?"

"Leo, give it a rest. I don't need a fucking lecture. What I need is for you to get your ass back to the bar and make sure it's open and making money. Call anyone that is not working to see if you can get a replacement for me."

Leo shook his head, sighed. We'd had the same conversation for the last two hours. "Fine. Have it your way. But I'm telling you, they'll be mad." He stood up to leave.

"Leo?" He turned around. "Thanks for having my six."

He smirked. "I look forward to my pay rise."

I started to laugh but it hurt. "Get outta here."

CHAPTER 15

Paige

VISITING HOURS WERE OVER. I PACED MY FRUSTRATION UP AND down the corridor while Lu tried to convince the nurse that we needed to go in.

"They suspect he has a concussion, so they're keeping him overnight. He fractured a couple of ribs and according to the nurse his face is a mess."

"Can we get in or not?" Nothing she said made me feel any better.

"She will sneak us in as a *goodwill gesture*," Lu said, making air quotes around the words. "She just needs a little time to get rid of her supervisor and we, flower, need to find a cash machine."

"Is he in pain?"

"A little, but they gave him some painkillers."

I was fuming. I had tried to get hold of Celo all day and he had ignored my texts and calls. So I walked into Eight and Leo had told Luciana not only that he was in the hospital, but that he would let Marcelo himself explain what happened. As soon as we walked out of the bar, Lu turned to me...

"Don't freak out." I looked at her annoyed. "I think I know what happened to him."

"What?"

"The good news is—he wasn't in a car crash or shot, otherwise Leo would have told us."

"Lu, cut the crap."

"I think he got in a fight with Pepino. And if he's in the hospital and Pepino is not, it's because he let Pepino beat him."

"What are you talking about!?"

"Pepino came to my office today first thing. He knew about you two and he was furious."

"So he gives himself the right to put his brother in hospital!?" I said, irritated. "I swear to God, Luciana, if this is true… I'm not even joking." I stumped my way around the taxi and got in.

Now we stood here, handing the nurse some hundred reais to break into the ward outside visiting hours. She led us into his room, his eyes were closed, and he half sat on the bed. His lip was busted, he had a cut on his cheek taped together with small medical strips, one of his eyes had swollen something chronic, and both of them had started to bruise. His long hair, now tied back, looked a mess. I wanted to cry.

The nurse whispered something in Portuguese at the door. "She said he had some strong painkillers because his ribs were too uncomfortable," Lu, whispering still, promptly translated. The door closed, the nurse walked away, Luciana stood by the door.

Slowly, I got near his bed and reached for his hand. He opened his eyes. Well, one of them. The other he could barely open.

"What are you doing here? How did you find me?" I was so upset looking at his face, my brain couldn't cope with anything else but staring.

"We went to Eight, twisted Leo's arm, and bribed the nurse," Luciana volunteered too quickly behind me. She sounded nervous.

Tears started running down my face.

"That bad, huh?" He tried to tease, his words slurring, hand raising to my face and cupping my cheek. "It looks worse than it is." But he sounded like he didn't want to move too much or it would hurt. "You should have seen the other guy." He tried to laugh but stopped himself.

"I hope you kicked his arse." I sniffled, wiped my nose, my eyes. "What happened? Who did this to you?"

"I got in a fight."

"With whom?"

He looked at me but didn't answer. After a minute he shook his head.

"Was it Felipe?" He didn't respond. "Was it?" Silence.

"Drop it, Paige."

"Look at you! Just look at you! Why are you protecting him?" My voice high-pitched, getting louder as I got more upset.

"Paige…" Luciana tried to bring me down a notch.

"Who was it, Celo?"

"I'm really tired," he said, trying to turn his back on me and clearly struggling.

"Don't ignore me!" He shuffled on the bed until he could give me his back, the motion clearly causing some discomfort. I tried to touch his shoulder, he recoiled.

"I'm tired. Please go home."

I felt numb. Luciana came behind me, one hand on each of my arms, and maneuvered me out of the room.

"Seriously? I paid three hundred reais so you could argue with him?" Lu said, staring at me disappointed.

"He doesn't want to tell me who it was!"

"And you think now, when he feels his face just got put through a cheese grater, is the right time to argue with him about it?" She hissed, a hand squeezing my wrist. "Seriously? I know you're upset but have some sympathy. Do you think this is easy for him? What do you want him to tell you? That he got his arse kicked because of you? Or that he let Felipe give him a beating because he feels guilty dating you? Have a little tact!"

A nurse appeared in the corridor then and said something in Portuguese. Luciana replied. "We need to go. Visiting hours are over and we overstayed our welcome."

CHAPTER 16
Marcelo

I woke up with someone touching my hair—soothing lines down my scalp, fingers rubbing circles on my hairline. In the haze of sleep and painkillers, I thought it was my grandmother. Then I turned, opened my eyes. The rubbing stopped.

Angie was standing there, hand mid-air, eyes wide open full of shock and pity.

The first one I didn't mind, the second made me mad.

"That bad, huh?"

She recomposed her face. "You still look sexy, babe. It'll add to your street cred." She winked at me.

"Thanks for coming back. Did you bring the clothes I asked?"

"It's all in the holdall. Are you sure you should be leaving the hospital?" She sat at the foot of the bed, swinging one of her legs back and forth.

"It will take six to eight weeks for my ribs to heal. There is nothing they can do for that, so they're sending me home."

"And the concussion?"

"They watched me for long enough, said I should not exercise for a week, but I'm all clear to go home." I sat up—my ribs shooting pain through my torso as though a knife was shoved to the hilt on my side—and slipped out of the bed to avoid a repeat.

"Well... that's a shame." Her tone made me turn. She was giving me one of her stares, the one she used to give me when she wanted to get me naked.

"Doctor's orders." I stood up and walked to the holdall on the chair. "It wouldn't be any good anyway. I'm stiff like an old man." I tried to lean over to grab the bag but couldn't. Pain shooting up my side, knocking me out of breath. Frustration got a groan out of me. "Sorry, can you..." I pointed at the bag. She moved it to the bed and sat next to it looking at me.

"You washed your hair? There is no blood on it."

"One of the nurses helped me shower earlier."

"Oh... was she fit?" This is why I liked Angie. There was no judgment, no tiptoeing around her. I didn't have to watch my mouth or what I did. There was no danger that I would break or ruin anything. It was just... easy.

I snorted, but even that caused me pain. "If I wasn't mangled like a car wreck, I might've enjoyed it. But I was too busy trying not to move too much." I reached over my shoulder and tried to untie the hospital gown. I couldn't do that either.

"Hey, come here. Gosh, did you look at that nurse funny, was she trying to put you in a straitjacket or something? What the hell is this knot!" She struggled with it for a moment. "Ok, done."

I stripped and tried to get to my underwear, but I couldn't lean over. Couldn't do that either.

"Allow me." Angie hopped off the bed and knelt down, then pulled my underpants down slowly while looking straight at me. Her hand rubbing up my thighs, reaching out to touch me. I stopped her. Shook my head.

She sighed, got to her feet. "Sorry, I forgot you have a girlfriend now. That is *so* lame!" Her voice had disdain all over it. She didn't really want to do anything; she was just testing if I would let her.

I had told her on the phone, ages ago when she had asked to see me, that I was dating Paige. Angie and I were never a thing, but we treated each other with respect and had always been crystal clear about what we were—fuck buddies. Well, now just buddies, I guess. But she clearly wanted to test my resolve.

I shoved one foot through the clean pair of underpants and then the other, trying not to bend over and not quite succeeding. Pain. It felt rude to let her stare at my cock when I wasn't gonna let her play with it. Even worse, to let someone else do it when I had just claimed the boyfriend title of my own accord. These things were supposed to mean something. And truth be told, if the roles were reversed, and it was a dude staring at Paige's naked privates the way Angie stared at mine, he would be the one on the hospital bed.

"Why is she not here with you, anyway?"

"It's complicated." I shoved the tee over my head, ribs aching. It was manageable.

"Yeah... everything seems to have gotten complicated after she arrived." I shoved a pair of shorts on. Barely managed. Angie leaned over, invading my field of vision to make me look at her. "Don't you miss when things were simpler? Before she got here?"

I stared at her but didn't answer. She had a point, but I wasn't sure I agreed with it. I wasn't sure I disagreed with it either.

"And honestly... dating the same person? Are you not going to miss it?"

"Miss what?"

"The excitement! Things get boring when you're with the same person."

"I have never been with more than one chick at a time, Angie."

"Yes, you have. We've been hooking up for years while we also see other people, so things don't get boring."

"No, I haven't. I have never had more than one woman in my life at a time. I've never done long-term. You know damn well you and I have never dated. That was always our deal. No commitment, no strings, just fun when we needed some."

"And now you're going to try and be with someone indefinitely? That's a bit of a stretch, don't you think? What makes you think you're cut out for it?"

I dropped my flip-flops on the floor and zipped the bag. "Come on, let's get the hell out of here. I can't stand the smell of this place."

Walking through the hospital to the car park was a pain. Worse still were the looks I got. Black eyes look worse before they get better. From day three you normally look like the Phantom of the Opera. I was on day two and Felipe had minced my face beyond recognition. Even with my hair down covering some of the damage, everyone stared, wondering what had happened. I had never minded people staring at me, but I hated this. These fucking pathetic pity looks.

By the time we pulled up outside mine, Marisa's car was parked in front of the garage gate. My stomach turned like I was going to vomit.

"I think that's my cue to leave." Angie knew damn well that, like Lu, Risa had no love for her.

I clicked the gate open, Risa's brake lights flickered, Angie's car came to a stop. "Thanks for the lift," I said, struggling to get out of the passenger door. She lowered the passenger window while I picked up my bag from the back seat. Shooting pain.

"Once the coast is clear, call me."

I walked up the drive just as a heeled shoe stepped out of Marisa's car. She stood behind me, not saying a single word, while I unlocked the front door. This was going to be worse than I thought. I dropped the bag on the coffee table and walked to the kitchen, bracing myself for the wrath she was about to unleash. She was going to tell me to leave her family alone, stick up for her son. Probably give me a lecture on loyalty.

"Marcelo, look at me."

Didn't really want to. But saying no to Marisa, when she spoke in this tone, was suicide.

Her heels tapped the floor as she walked towards me and pushed the hair covering my face behind my ear, holding my chin with both her hands, eyes analyzing the damage. She sighed, let go of me and stepped back. Her disappointment so thick, my mouth felt like paper.

"I see I'm going to have to have a word with Felipe." Her voice was hard.

"No, you don't." My words almost didn't make it out. I felt thirsty.

"It's my job to educate my children, no matter how old they are. Not yours. Now, you…" Her finger was on my face. I was about to get shredded, lose the little I had left. "How dare you end up in the hospital and not call me? Not call anyone from our family!" She was mad alright, but that was not what I thought she was going to say. It confused me for a minute.

"I hate to state the obvious, but we're not family. Your family did this to me." It wasn't an accusation. I wasn't sure I'd heard her right; I was trying to understand. Maybe Felipe had knocked my head harder than I thought.

"God help me, Marcelo Rissi Costa, I *will* slap you myself! Wipe that attitude off of your face this very instant!" she hissed at me.

242

And she damn well would too. It was never a good sign when she called me by my full name. Like a child, I stared at her shoes. Twenty-seven years on my back and she could still whoop my ass just like that.

"Why didn't you call me?" She was mad but her voice was pleading, almost sad. "I'm *not* happy with this whole debacle. You should have called me, and Felipe had no right to do this. You two are brothers!" We weren't. She called us that, said she had three sons, but I was more like the cuckoo in her nest.

I felt drained. "You don't have to do this anymore, Marisa. I'm a fucking grown man, my granddad isn't here to see it, and I don't have any interest in taking control of the company."

Her silence was so heavy, it became constricting. Her head turned sideways. Now, I'd really done it. She was going to shred me.

"Watch your mouth!" That came out through her teeth as a threat. More silence. "Is that what you really think?" It wasn't anger. It was worse. It was disappointment. "After all the years you have known me, you really think I'm here because of the business?" She stared right at me. "I brought you up as my own son since you were eight!" Her eyes filled with tears. "I gave you everything I gave my own children: you went on vacation with us, you had a bedroom in my house, you were in the hospital with my husband and son when I gave birth to Freddie! And you think I did this because Rogério worked for your grandfather? What do you take me for?" Tears rolled down her face. Felipe's punches hurt less. I moved away from her; I couldn't watch it. "You know this is wrong." Her voice caught. "You know you're talking out of fear and insecurity. What are you trying to do? Push everyone you love away?"

I had no answer. And I couldn't look at her. Just stared at her shoes.

"So let me set the record straight for you." Her voice was

hard. "Your grandfather was like a father to me. He was *my* father's best friend, and he looked after *us* when my father passed away. They owned the business *together*. I don't need you to have access to it. I have inherited my own shares. I took you into our lives because I loved your granddad like a father, and you like a son. How dare you think I am here because of money?"

Of course, she was right. Marisa was a good person. And she *was* the closest thing I had to a mother. Kinder to me than the woman that put me in this world just to make me suffer. I just always felt out of place, like I didn't belong.

"I'm sorry, Risa. I didn't mean to upset you or cause any problems." But I had always been a problem. The skinny kid that turned up on her doorstep, starving for a family, and never left.

Her hands had balled into fists, body stiff, face irritated. Marisa hated losing composure. She caught herself, closed her eyes, took a deep breath, forced her shoulders to relax, both palms hovering flat above the floor. Then she wiped her tears, straightened her clothes, and looked at me, her face different, softer.

"You're sorry for what?"

She waited. I didn't answer.

"For finally falling in love like a normal human being?" She was pressing a nerve. Risa had nagged me about this at length in the past. At some point, even suggested I went back to therapy, worried that something in me was broken. "If I knew it would take a girl from another country, I would have shipped her here myself. The life you have been living, not allowing yourself to love anyone, not allowing anyone to get close to you, pushing everyone away, that's not normal, my son. I'm *thrilled* you finally found someone you thought was worth putting your guards down for."

Anger boiled to the surface. "And look at where that got

244

me." I raised my shirt and opened my arm so she could see all the bruising on my ribs. "Happy? Because that is what love does to me, Marisa. It hits me like a fucking train and leaves me for dead."

She gasped, her eyebrows arching in the middle. Seeing all the bruises on my body was upsetting her. I pulled my tee back down.

"That is not true." Her voice was strained but calm. "I'm here and I love you. I have loved you as my own since you were little. You have a family. People who love and care about you. We have not hurt you or left you for dead. You are one of us."

"That is the thing, Marisa, I'm not one of you. I'm not one of anything."

Her chin lifted; she entwined her fingers in front of her lap. Her voice calm but sharp and assertive. "You *are* one of us. Whether you like it or not. Whether you fight with Felipe or not. *Because I said so.* I don't care if you disagree. It's not up to you or up for discussion. You don't get to choose who I love or who feels like family to me. That badge is earned. You have it pinned to your chest whether you like it or not." She walked to me and hugged me. Anais Anais—I could recognize her perfume anyplace. She had smelled the same since I was a kid. "And I will be here, reminding you of that every day if I have to. Because that is what family does."

Marisa's hugs used to work like a cure. When I was a kid they fixed everything and made everything better. But now I just felt more broken, more problematic, more of a burden.

She let go of me, stood looking at me, and sighed. "This fight between you and Felipe is stupid." She straightened my hair, my tee. She'd done this too since I was a kid.

"It's not. I broke the code."

"That is the most ridiculous thing I've ever heard. That girl had made it very clear, in front of our whole family if you

245

don't remember Easter, that she did not share Felipe's intentions. I saw the way you looked at each other. It's her right to date who *she* wants to date. So what are you guilty of to deserve this punishment, huh? That she loved you back? God forbid you should be so lucky!? And please... do bear in mind that you have as much control over that as Felipe did, which is to say, *none at all*. If Felipe had any sense, he would have withdrawn like a gentleman and let her be. But for some reason, that is beside the upbringing I gave him, he thought it was better to send you to the hospital. That is not on you or on her, that is on him."

Risa sighed, her shoulders hunching. She seemed to feel as tired of the whole thing as I was. Everything in my body ached, even my brain. My neck itched; I rubbed it.

She placed both her hands on my chest. "We are your family, and you are not less than anybody. You are loved, wanted, and you deserve to be happy." She had chanted this at me also since I was a kid, like she was trying to reprogram me. Whether it worked and stuck to me like she intended it to was something else, but the words were familiar and comforting all the same.

I nodded. I just wished I could believe them like she did.

She kissed my cheek. "I will send you some food; you need to eat. And I'll call you later to check how you're doing. Don't you dare ignore my call."

Another nod.

I heard her heels tapping the floor, the front door opening and closing, heels against the path to the drive, her car purring to life. The gate opened as she reversed out, and I waved at her from the window. Tiredness took hold of me. My will to live gone already and it was only midday.

Someone knocked on the door. "What did you forget?" I shouted before I opened it. Paige was standing there. "How... how did you get...?"

"Garage gate." Over her shoulder I could see that it had only just closed fully.

I turned my back to her and went back to the kitchen. Great! All the women in my life were falling on me like bricks. Like I needed any more casualties.

I went to the cupboard and started making her some of her tea; I couldn't face her. Last time I saw her she wanted explanations; I had none to give. Neither did I want her staring at me like everybody else. The loser whose face kissed a bulldozer.

Her arms appeared under mine and wrapped around me, gentle without squeezing me, her thumbs rubbing my chest up and down. My hands went still, the warmth of her body slipped through my clothes like a warm shower, relaxing my muscles, freezing the thoughts in my brain. She kissed my shoulder, my neck. I rested my head backwards on top of hers, breathed in her perfume. I could also recognize this one anyplace.

We stayed like that for a while—her chin resting on my shoulder, our heads touching, my hands holding on to hers on top of my chest, until she wiggled herself to stand in front of me. I avoided her eyes, didn't want to see in them what a hot mess I had become.

She kissed my mouth, kissed the cut on it; my cheek, the cut on it. Her lips touched my eye, forehead, other eye, down the other cheek. It was like she was trying to administer some sort of medicine, like her kisses would cure all the bruises on my face.

"Are you going to look at me?" she whispered so close to me I could feel her words on my lips. And I did. She smiled and kissed me.

It started gentle, but it became hungry. I was so drained and so empty, I wanted her comfort, I wanted it all. And I kissed her so hard that I started to taste blood. The split on my lip had reopened. Frustration got another grunt out of me. I couldn't even do that. Couldn't even kiss the one person that could make me feel better.

Paige raised a hand to her mouth, wiped the blood from it, and laughed. "Are you trying to initiate me into a blood cult or something?"

"One can only try." But the frustration was getting the best of me.

I tried to get a paper towel to wipe it off...

"Leave it." She stopped me from going anyplace.

Her hands found the hem of my tee and started to pull it up towards my head. I knew what she was doing. She knew I got shredded because of her and we kinda had argued at the hospital. She was trying to make it up to me, make me feel better, give me what she thought I wanted. She didn't need to. I didn't really know what I wanted either.

I stopped her hands. "I... I can't. My ribs..." I had no words for my frustration. Touched my forehead to hers wishing my thoughts could jump into her head to explain what I was feeling.

She shushed me and kissed my lip, just a brush, and I let go of her hands. Gently, slowly she removed my shirt. Flipped me over so my body was the one against the counter. She kissed my shoulder, chest, right down the middle to my bruised ribs. Administering her medicine to all the black and blue parts of my body. Electricity rising up my spine, numbing everything.

Paige stepped backwards, bending at her hip, her kisses going lower, her ass sticking out in a curve with her waist that made me want to smack it and grab a piece. I couldn't reach it, but I grabbed hands full of her dress. It started lifting slowly like the curtains to the best show ever, a level at the time, teasing me, until I could see the whole thing.

This woman was going to be the death of me. Not even

bruised and broken I could find the strength to walk away from her.

She had kissed me all the way down. Pulled me out of my shorts and was doing the thing with her tongue that sent me insane. Her mouth was around me, but I had no patience. I pulled her up by the elbows, twisted her around and bent her over the island.

Now I could reach and touch everything. And it was all mine. I had paid the price, and she was mine, no one else's. So I grabbed at it, her curves filling my palms; squeezed hands full and slapped it. One side of her face on the counter, she smiled, stretching her arms up to the edge above her head like she was giving me permission.

I wasn't polite.

Didn't get her in the mood.

Had no concern for her getting hers either.

I pressed her face against the counter, held her by her neck, her hair, pinned her arms behind her back, and I owned her. It was fast, intense, short, and just about all my battered body could take. Everything wrapping into one—pain, pleasure, possession, frustration, and Paige.

We stood there linked, her body still bent over the counter, both of us out of breath, hair covering her face. Realization slowly sinking in of how rough I had been, and I was worried. I needed to see her eyes. I swiped at her hair frantically, pain shooting up my side like a constricting band. I just couldn't get her curls out of the way, and when I did, her eyes were closed, my blood smeared over her face, but she smiled.

Relief.

"You ok there, Lewis?"

"No." I laughed, but it had no humor. "My ribs are on fire." She laughed with me. But acknowledging it brought the pain into focus. It wasn't just the ribs. My face throbbed, head hurt, I could taste blood. "I think I need more painkillers."

By the time I came down the next morning, she was making me breakfast. Her hair was down, and she was fully dressed. That was odd. Paige always had her hair up in the mornings and she never got fully dressed until we were either leaving or it was mid-morning. She also had one of my sweaters on over her dress. It wasn't cold.

"How you feeling?"

"Sore." I reached for the painkillers as she plated the food and put it on the kitchen island.

"Eat something before you take those. You're not supposed to take them on an empty stomach."

She took a seat next to me and smiled. But as she was about to start eating, she moved her hair over her shoulder, and I saw it—round edges on her neck.

The cold started in the pit of my stomach and slowly spread to the rest of my body.

I reached over and moved her hair out of the way. Four perfect finger marks were imprinted on the side of her neck.

Paige looked at me. Eyes anxious.

Gently, I took hold of her wrist and pushed the sleeve of the sweater up. There were more marks on her arm. It made me pause, stare at them. They were the exact same thickness as my fingers.

She was looking at me, but I couldn't look at her.

Didn't really want to see it or need the confirmation, but I ran my palm up her thigh, lifting part of her dress. There were bruises there too.

All the places I had grabbed hold of her the day before.

By tomorrow, they would go darker and look like she had also been in a fight.

I placed my elbows on the counter, mouth touching my hands, arms supporting my head. My eyes closed, remembering how rough I had been, taking out my frustrations and anger on something... someone that deserved anything but that.

"Hey..." She moved out of her stool, a hand touching my arm, the other combing my hair, her body touching the side of mine. "You didn't hurt me. I just bruise easy, and I didn't want you to worry."

I didn't move.

"Celo, look at me." Paige touched her forehead to my temple, her body invading my space, but I still didn't move. "Hey... listen to me," she whispered in my ear. "You didn't hurt me. I promise you, I'm fine. I know I bruise easy, and it always looks worse than it is. I covered it up because I didn't want you to worry."

When I didn't respond, she pulled one of my arms, wrapping it around her waist. I looked at her then. My thumb automatically rubbing up and down her back.

"I'm so sorry. I'm so, so sorry." It came out as a whisper. "I didn't mean to do it," I said, kissing her forehead, but the apology only made me feel worse. It was the same apology I got when I was a kid and got beaten in the haze of someone else's anger. The people who said it never meant to do it, but they always did it again.

"I'm fine, I promise. Everything is fine. Don't worry about it, ok?"

I nodded. She smiled. I didn't.

It wasn't fine. Not by a long shot. I had never done that. Not to anyone. Definitely not to her. There were quite a few occasions when, overexcited and in the middle of hot sex, we had been quite heavy handed with each other, but I had never bruised her skin.

There was only one other time she bruised like that that I knew of. Back then it had just been on her arms. But these? These were all over her body to the point she had covered them up.

I was no stranger to her. She was dating me, trusted me, had just tried to be nice and comfort me. And I had done worse. I *was* worse.

Paige leaned in and kissed me. "Please don't worry about it, ok?"

On what planet did you hurt someone, and they were more concerned about what you thought about it than the fact you had hurt them? It was twisted and I knew it only too well. I had done it myself when I was little. Feeling like it was me, it was my fault, that I'd done something to deserve it. Then trying to please the people that hurt me, because the rejection, being ignored or feeling unwanted, was worse.

Her forehead touched mine. She gave me a few more kisses, brushes on my lips.

But this is what this sickness did. Turned you into someone you didn't want to be, made you accept things you shouldn't accept.

♥♥♥

For the next few days I kept a low profile. Didn't really want anyone seeing the wreck that was my face. Nobody had seen the fight, and I didn't want to have to explain. It also didn't look very professional to turn up for work looking like a purple quilt. So I had been doing some paperwork, sitting on the sofa, propped by cushions like an old man, when Paige came in.

"Your eyes look better," she said, kneeling on the seat and planting little kisses all over me. This had become a habit of hers. Every time she came to see me, she would kiss each one of the bruises on my face. Almost as if she felt responsible for them and was trying to apologize with every kiss. One week after the fight, and the worse bruise had started to go down. I still looked like a damn pirate, with an eye so bloodshot and purple, it looked like a black eyepatch, but at least I could now open and see through it. Damn miracle Felipe didn't fracture my eye socket or break my nose.

I put the laptop down to let her kiss me. And in return, I kissed her wrists and her neck, where you could still see a shadow of her bruises. She felt responsible for mine, but I was one hundred percent guilty of hers.

The kisses on her neck made her get covered in goosebumps. I touched her face, her eyes sinking into me, eyelids heavy, blinking slowly. We just stared at each other while I caressed her face, admiring her complexion. I hadn't really put my hands on her since I marked her skin.

After the fight and me getting rough with her, things had changed, and we were a little awkward around each other. She trying not to cause me pain, me trying to keep my frustrations to myself. Which meant I was up for the greeting kiss and hug, but not anything else. I could tell she wasn't happy with the distance, but since I was mangled, she didn't push.

Neither of us spitting out the words that hung between us like a bitter aftertaste. I didn't tell her the fight with Felipe and losing him as a friend had really gotten to me; or that I let him beat my ass because I felt guilty I was dating her. She never admitted she let me get rough with her because she felt it was her fault I got mangled. And I didn't mention a word about feeling like a monster when I saw all the bruises on her skin, or that I had scared myself when I realized what I was capable of doing, what I felt justified to do. Neither of us said the words weighing us down, both of us bearing our battle scars on our skin.

She smiled and leaned over for more kisses. Gentle but full of want. As they got wetter and merged into one, her body moved, and she sat astride my legs. A vision of her bruises flashed in my mind, and I stopped the kiss, rested my forehead on her shoulder, hands rubbing up and down her thighs.

"I'm sorry. My ribs are still really painful," I said without looking at her. "I stopped taking the painkillers. Didn't want to get hooked on them." It was half of the truth. The other half was that I was still really mad, and I wasn't sure I would keep it to myself.

She sighed, trying not to take my 'no' as a rejection but not quite managing to. "It's ok. I get it." She kissed the side of my face, but her eyes were sad. "Would you like a drink?" I shook my head. She got off me and, without another word, headed to the kitchen.

I'm not sure she wanted sex. I think she just wanted the reassurance that things would go back to normal. That *we* were still *us*. Being physically affectionate was just her way to reach out and check we were still alive after the avalanche of shit. And I wanted to. I wanted to let her erase it all. But the last time she tried to comfort me, she ended up covered in bruises. It just didn't feel like I deserved such kindness. If I let her come any closer, she would have to release all my demons before she could vanquish them. But my monsters weren't fairytale ghosts. They were a horror film haunting—lurking in the shadows waiting to prey on the unwary who dared to cross their path. And there would be no escape for her if she did.

I heard a cupboard open and close. The kitchen faucet clicked, liquid filled a cup.

A phone buzzed. I thought it was mine, but when I picked it up, it was Paige's. The notification on the home screen said: *It's time to check in for your flight to London. Reference: 5958071.*

The fridge opened and closed. A bottle of something clanked against the countertop. A spoon banged on two sides of a cup like a high-pitched bell.

My insides dropped as though they were full of stones. Felipe's words ringing in my ears: *"They find out what an omen you are and they leave you."*

The fridge opened, something being put back on the rack,

and it closed. Footsteps got closer to the lounge. I put the phone down where I found it. Paige came back into the room, the bracelet I gave her rolling down her arm as she took a sip of her tea.

My mind was going at a hundred miles an hour. She had said she was staying in São Paulo for three months. That time was almost up. But I thought… I thought she would change her mind. I thought she would want to stay. She told me she didn't really have a reason to go back. Promised she wouldn't bolt. But that was exactly what she was doing. As soon as I screwed something up, she bolted.

She stopped before crossing the room, eyes nervously looking at me. "Lewis, are you ok? You look a little pale."

Autopilot kicked in, I forced a smile, nodded.

She covered the rest of the distance and came to sit next to me. "What are we watching?"

My mind had gone blank. I should've asked questions. Was she really going? When? And was she coming back? But instead, I just smiled. "Whatever you want." Couldn't face asking her the question that would confirm I was getting what I deserved, and she was leaving me.

She spent the whole afternoon with me. Watching a film, laughing, talking like she wasn't planning to rip my chest open. And I walked through it like a zombie—smiling on cue, responding when spoken to, kissing when kissed. While my head ran through everything I could've done differently. Calculating all the odds stacked against me that I had chosen to ignore. Trying to curse the day I had given into this sickness, but not quite being able to.

Everything in black and white, drained of color. My insides in a panic so great, I was literally paralyzed. If I didn't ask, she wouldn't confirm it. If she didn't say the words, it wasn't real. If I stayed in denial, I could lie to my brain and spare myself the excruciating pain of losing. Losing something that mattered. Losing someone I didn't want to lose when I had already lost or was at serious risk of losing everyone else that mattered to me.

But this is what happens when you give into this damn virus. You lose control and give someone else the power to rip you open.

Which, inevitably, they all do.

CHAPTER 17
Paige

"HOW IS THE PATIENT?" LU ASKED, FLICKING THROUGH THE papers, eating a piece of toast.

"I'm not sure."

She dropped the toast on the plate and folded the papers. "What do you mean?"

I walked across the kitchen and sat opposite her. "At first, he was ok. Black and blue, and in physical pain, but ok. He gave me the keys to his house; we even had sex."

"Gosh, what are you two? Bunnies? I mean… Christ! Fair dues to him for delivering the goods when he's in bits!" Her head tipped to the side. "Freaking weird, but admirable." She shrugged.

"Focus, Lu."

"You said it, not me!"

"Anyway… it's now been what? Almost three weeks? His ribs are still a bit sore, but the bruises on his face are almost gone. Yet, he hasn't left the house. Has gone quieter and quieter… He's withdrawing, doesn't talk much, squirms when I touch him, and just about tries any excuse to move away when I get close to him. It's weird!"

Lu was going to say something then thought better of it.

"Spit it out, Lu. I feel like I'm going insane and imagining it."

"Have you ever considered…" Her face went soft; she was trying to spare my feelings. "That maybe… he blames you. For what happened, I mean."

Gabriel walked into the kitchen, topless and barefoot, kissed Lu's head and went to the fridge. Of late, he had stayed at Lu's quite a few nights.

"At first, I thought maybe, yeah. But I don't think it's that. You see… when he finally lets me hug him or kiss him, he holds me so tight, it's like he missed me. But he is like a ghost. The other day, I went to see him, the house was a mess, and he was lying in bed in the dark upstairs. It was two in the afternoon. Leo said he was checking in with him every day at first but hasn't spoken to him in days now. He also said the fight was vicious. That at some point Felipe was kicking his head when he was on the floor."

"Wait… Leo doesn't speak English. How did you get all that out of him?"

"Out of everything I said, that's what you focus on? Seriously?" She was starting to annoy me.

"We will get to the other stuff in a minute, but seriously, how did you get all that out of Leo?"

"He speaks basic English; I speak basic Portuguese. We complemented the rest with Google Translate. Now, focus Lu! What do you think?"

"Maybe he's depressed." Gabe's voice hovered over us like the oracle. We both stared at him. He shrugged. "What? I'm right here, I can hear you."

"You think he's depressed?" The thought really upset me.

"What happened was a big deal. It was rough stuff. If he's shutting down and letting things slip into chaos… yeah, he could be depressed. You see, men are not like you ladies. You get upset, you talk, you cry, you get it off your chest. Men hold it all in, bottle it up. Sometimes we can compartmentalize it. You lock it in a room in your brain, throw away the key and, as long as the door stays shut, you're alright. But sometimes it festers, and it drags you under. Most men only know how to express their feelings in three ways: horniness, anger, and rivalry. Outside of that, when we feel shit, we punish or obliterate ourselves. We don't know how to do anything else. If you start crying, everyone thinks you're a wimp. And a lot of the time you just don't feel worthy or you're too scared to fuck it all up, but if you talk about it or come across like you don't have your shit together, you're weak. So you have no choice but to keep it all bottled up. That's when some people start to self-medicate, so they don't feel anything."

Lu and I stared at him blankly. I could hear the crickets.

"What? I've been reading up on toxic masculinity." He shrugged and drank orange juice from the carton.

Lu looked at me, lips pushed together, unimpressed. "He comes out with these pearls of wisdom and insight, like he's the Dalai Lama, then he goes and drinks from my bloody juice carton." She turned to him. "Like an oversized piglet that hasn't been trained to drink out of a glass."

"You love me."

She turned back around. "You wish."

He walked over, placed the carton on the table, hugged her, and kissed her face multiple times. She couldn't keep it straight and smiled.

"Your bravado doesn't fool me, pocket rocket. I know you love me."

"Don't flatter yourself, you giant piglet."

He buried his face in her neck and started to make pig noises. Ticklish, Lu kicked the table, the juice carton flying and spilling on the floor.

"Now, look what you made me do!"

I leaned down to pick it up, blood rushed to my head, and I felt instantly dizzy, out of balance. Gabe grabbed me before I face-planted on the kitchen floor.

"You alright there, Paige?"

"Ooh!" I tried to steady myself. "I think I did that too quickly."

Both Gabriel and Lu stared at me.

"I'm not sleeping too good. Most of the days I feel like I have a hangover, even though I haven't drunk a thing."

"Are you sure you're ok, flower? Maybe we should have you checked by a doctor?"

"Don't be ridiculous! I'm fine, honestly. It has just been a complicated few weeks. That's all."

❤❤❤

I stared at the nurse blankly. Lu stared at me, mouth gaped, eyes so big they didn't look like hers.

I'd been feeling dizzy for days. That morning, I was just feeling hot and exhausted, like I couldn't keep my eyes open. Then everything seemed to waver, and the room lost its gravity. Next thing I remember was Lu holding me in the recovery position. She thought I was anemic or had low blood sugar levels. I hadn't had breakfast, but even after I had eaten I still didn't feel any better.

"Maybe you're missing all the potato starch you eat in the UK," she teased as she took me to the doctors. Lu always used to joke that the English were very versatile when it came to potatoes. "You eat them in more ways than there are colors in the rainbow," she used to say.

I didn't understand it. "It's not possible."

"It is veree possibill. You havee sex, yes? Withee your boyfriendi, yes?" The doctor had the thickest accent I'd ever heard on a Brazilian.

"Yes, but—"

"Then it is possibill."

"But I don't think I'm late. My period isn't very regular."

"Still possibill. If the periodi is not regular, it is veree easee to calculatee wrong."

The doctor said a couple of other things, none of which I heard. She handed Lu a leaflet. We both walked out in shock.

"She said you're at least three weeks, five if your dates are right. You'll have to do an ultrasound to confirm it. You have been dunking the biscuit with him for what? Six weeks? So, what? He knocked you up the first time you broke into the cookie jar?"

I couldn't get my head around it.

"He either has athletic swimmers or you get pregnant looking at underpants hung out to dry. And you guys clearly missed the concept of wrapping it up. Jesus!"

"But we *do* wrap up. Every time."

"Clearly not *every* time. Was there a time you didn't?"

I had to think. Shit! "There was just this once."

"Like I said, athletic swimmers or pregnant at first sight."

We sat in the car, not saying anything.

"Just so you know, abortion isn't legal in Brazil. So you will have to fly home if that is what you want to do. But I really think you should talk to Celo first."

I didn't know what to say. We had been dating for just under two months. Most of which he had spent locked in his house in self-imposed exile.

Lu dropped me off at hers before heading back to work. "Think about what I said, flower. You really need to tell him before you make any harsh decisions."

I nodded.

After she left, I sat in my room for an hour, staring at my computer screen trying to do some work. I was freaking out and I didn't know what to do. Our relationship had been two weeks of bliss and four of drama. We never talked about the future. I didn't even know if he wanted children or had any plans to have them. I had no idea how he would react, especially now that he wasn't well.

But Lu was right, I should tell him. Before I shat myself, I called an Uber.

As soon as I set foot in his house, I knew something was off. There was a car parked out front that I didn't recognize. I picked some fabric off the floor at the entrance to the kitchen—Marcelo's tee. Two glasses were on the island counter, one had lip gloss so thick on it, it looked like paint. I turned around, eyes scanning for anything else that was out of place, and I spotted it.

A pile of flowery pattern abandoned at the bottom of the steps.

Then I heard the moaning.

Cold spread through my body.

It was like I was watching a horror movie. As if my soul was hovering over the scene, watching it from above. I started walking up the steps, the moans getting louder, rhythmic. Someone was murmuring, like a ghost whispering through the empty house.

My feet dragged down the corridor, a pair of wedges were lying abandoned down my path, first one foot, then the other.

The moaning now vivid, real.

I couldn't breathe, my head felt dizzy. The door to his room was open.

And there they were. Marcelo naked in between Angie's legs. She, moaning like a porn star in a bad movie, still wearing her bra, one of her boobs hanging out of it.

The air escaped my lungs in such a rush it felt like someone had punched my gut. I felt nauseous, covered my mouth not to be sick, lost my balance, and the door banged against the wall.

Marcelo moved his head from the other side of Angie's neck, and half suspended himself on his arms to look towards the door. His eyes widening as soon as he saw me. His face changing color, going from tanned to white. He just looked at me. Vomit rose in my throat, and I had to clamp my mouth harder not to spew it out.

Then he moved, looked at Angie, down to where their bodies connected, like he was confused. As though he didn't know how he got there. And I couldn't take it anymore.

I turned around and walked down the corridor, tripping over the wedges. The nausea taking over. I bent over at the top of the stairs, swallowing it back down, taking deep breaths, holding on to the wall, worried I was going to collapse. Sickness subsiding after a second and anger taking hold.

I was pregnant. I was pregnant with his baby, and he was here, fucking someone else.

I was the girlfriend he didn't want to touch, but that whore… that cheap tart!

How blind was I?! Lu had told me! She had warned me off him, begged me to leave it alone. And I had seen it with my own eyes! All the women he paraded around like toys, fucking them in bar toilets then coming back to sit at the table like nothing had happened. How naïve, how stupid was I?! Stupid, stupid idiot believing they didn't know him like I did. They didn't see the besotted way he looked at me, the way he played with my hair, the way his hands were always on my body. He did the same to them all!

At the bottom of the steps, I bent over and gasped for air. A photo of him smiled at me from its photo frame on the bookshelf. And it all came out like an avalanche. The anger, the sobs, the scream. I picked up the photo and threw it against the wall, pulled the free-standing bookcase towards the floor.

It wasn't enough.

It was hurting me, and I wanted something to break like I was breaking.

I hated him. God, I *hated* him.

And I let it rip.

Marched over to the sofa and pulled the baseball bat from its mount. I wanted to beat something, someone, until it was bleeding and broken. I smashed everything and anything in my path.

It wasn't enough.

So I went over to the kitchen. I wanted to break everything. Wanted everything around me to suffer. To understand how I felt. My vision was blurred, and when hitting and smashing wasn't enough, I screamed. I screamed until my lungs hurt. Picked up the frying pan hanging above the cooker and threw it towards the window.

Then I saw him.

Standing at the bottom of the stairs. Dressed only in a pair of jeans. His eyes wide like a child's. His skin pale like mine. He looked straight at me.

Take a look, prick. Take a look at what you've done to me. I walked towards him; I wanted him to see me. I wanted him to see my pain. *Go and add that other notch to your fucking bedpost.*

At first his face was blank. Then it cracked, his straight eyebrows arching. Pain twisting his expression. His eyes blinked but his eyelids didn't touch each other, he looked like he was going to cry.

Now you understand. I loved you. I love you! How could you do this to me?

Even after everything, just the sight of him, of how upset he looked, made me feel better. His presence working like relaxing hot water on sore muscles. Sobs spilled out of me without any control, my hair falling over my face and covering me in darkness.

Why did you do this?? Why did you do this to me??

I felt tired. Almost too tired to breathe.

Then I saw her.

That fucking tart. Standing just behind him in her shorts and bra, like they were a couple, and I was invading their privacy. She crossed her arms, half smiling at me, the bitch! How long had she been fucking him behind my back? Had they ever stopped fucking?

I would not give her the satisfaction. So I took a deep breath, and I made sure there was no pain on my face. Just raw, plain rage. I looked at Marcelo, grabbed the bat with both my hands and swung it right into the flat screen. The smashing sound working like a comforting lullaby.

He didn't stop me.

Oh! But he would pay. I walked out swiping every surface, throwing everything on my way to the floor. Outside, the first swing of the bat went on the back light, then the other. I could hear Marcelo screaming, but I couldn't care less. I went around the car looking for things I could smash and when there wasn't any glass left uncracked, I started on the bodywork.

"Stop! You stupid bitch!" Marcelo's scream cut through the haze created by my rage.

I threw the bat at him, but it never found its target. My arms, my shoulders, body and soul aching. And I had had enough. I had to leave, to be as far away from there as possible. As soon as I walked out of the gate I broke into a sprint. I wanted it to hurt. Wanted the pain to be physical. Wanted it to burn in my lungs, on my legs.

I arrived back at Luciana's building dripping in sweat and out of breath. The porter let me in, but came out of his hut alarmed, trying to see what had happened to me. He started asking questions in Portuguese; I was too tired to bother trying to understand him. Out of breath and with my lungs burning, I waved him off and took the stairs. By the fourth floor I had to stop. My legs could go no further. And I broke down. My sobs loud enough that I'm sure the whole building could hear me.

"*Dona* Paige?" the porter shouted from downstairs. "*Dona* Paige?" The voice disappeared after a while, and I heard the doors close.

I don't know how long I'd stayed there, head on my knees, folded like a ball, crying on the steps. Eventually, I ran out of tears to cry, and the sobs became muffled. From under my arms I could see feet. Someone tried to speak to me in English, but I didn't respond.

A hand touched my arm. "Paige?" It was Luciana, in her most soothing voice. The porter must have called her.

I looked up, my eyes felt so sore. My body felt heavy. Everything ached.

Luciana took one look at me, and she knew. "Bastard." She touched my head like I was a scared child, rubbed under my eyes like that was all it would take to erase all the tears I'd cried. "Come on. Let's get you cleaned up."

CHAPTER 18

Marcelo

MARISA SAT ON THE CHAIR NEXT TO MY GURNEY IN THE emergency room. A bloodstained kitchen cloth wrapped around my foot. I had cut a gash on my sole when I tried to walk over all the broken glass to stop Paige from smashing my car.

This was my second visit to the hospital in less than a month. I was on a losing streak.

"Are you going to tell me what the hell is going on? Why does your house look like an explosion site?"

I could have lied, but she would hear about it anyway. If not from me, from someone else. "Paige... she caught me... and Angie..." Marisa's head tilted to the side. "Having sex."

"Marcelo!" My name came out in a gasp, her eyes shocked, eyebrows bunched together in disapproval. "Angela Gurgel, that woman is a bad omen."

"And I'm like a virus that wrecks and kills everything it touches. We are a right pair." I felt so much agony, I could've scratched the skin off my face.

"You're not a virus. But that woman is an opportunistic parasite."

I wanted to scream, but instead I laughed.

"I thought you were in love with Paige."

Love. The weight of the word made me drop my head,

stare at my hands. Guilt and regret ripping my guts out, filling me with nothing but despair and anguish.

Risa could read it on my face. "Then what did you go and do something like that for?" Her voice exasperated.

"Because I'm tired," I spat at her. Anger boiling to the surface. "I'm tired of feeling that if I turn left, I lose. If I turn right, I lose. I stay with her, she'll wreck my life. Just for the privilege of dating her I had to declare war, get my face minced and split the fucking family. And I'm scared shitless of the day she boards that plane and goes back to England because something in me is ripping just thinking about it. But I'm not with her and I'm fucking miserable. So I can't win! And I'm tired of always being on the wrong side of the damn table, on this endless streak of bad luck! It feels like I'm trying to hold on to foam and it's slipping through my stupid fingers."

"So you break her heart and push her away? Because *that* will make you less miserable, right? You self-sabotage and wreck everything yourself, because *that* will solve everything." Marisa's eyebrows were raised, her arms crossed.

I sighed. She was right; I was just trying to wreck what was left of my life. I had kept it together, under wraps, and it had all come undone. Paige... I was so happy at first, but then my world had set on fire, and I had almost lost the only family I had left.

I knew it was coming. I knew it was the price I was going to pay for dating her, but it didn't make it any easier when it happened. And now... after everything I'd done, after putting everything on the line for her and burning all my bridges, she was leaving me.

"She's leaving me anyway, Risa." The voice I heard wasn't mine. It felt like an echo, like someone else had said it.

Marisa frowned, her head jerking to the side. "What makes you say that? Did she end things with you?"

I shook my head without looking at her. My eyes, my head felt heavy.

"Then how do you know this?"

"I saw it on her phone. Her return flight is booked. She's going back to England."

"You went through her phone?" The words were pronounced one at a time, full of disapproval.

Another head shake. "It flashed on her screen when she left it on the sofa."

"When was this?"

"A couple of weeks ago." I had spent two weeks waiting for her to come and tell me she was leaving. Dreading the day she did. The anticipation eating at my soul, dragging me under like I was drowning.

Marisa stood up and paced up and down. One hand on her stomach, the other tapping her thigh, thinking, putting things together.

"Celo, that doesn't make any sense. I know for a fact she has been talking to Marta and Lu about extending her stay."

I looked her in the eyes then.

"Last week, Marta told me that Paige has a ninety-day tourist visa. That she had to extend it or leave the country by the end date, or she would be fined and banned from returning for six months. We even laughed about how extreme the whole thing sounded. Last I heard, Paige decided that once her visa was up, she was going to visit her dad in Denver for a couple of weeks, so she'd get another ninety-days when she got back in the country."

I shook my head. "Her flight back to London is booked, Risa. I saw it with my own eyes."

"That's the thing. She can't enter the country unless she has an exit flight booked, Celo. She has to prove that she has no intention to stay past the ninety days. It's one of the conditions for her visa."

269

The coin dropped. "What are you saying, Risa?" I knew exactly what she said but my brain was refusing to accept it. The real meaning of it, the consequence, too catastrophic to even consider.

"I'm saying that I don't think she was leaving. The flight you saw was her original return flight. I'm pretty sure she changed it earlier this week."

My eyes blurred. Head pounding as if someone had thrown a brick at my forehead. I saw my hands raising to my hair in slow motion. And when they got there, my nails dug into my scalp.

"What did she tell you when you asked her about it?"

Risa's words tore into me, ripping flesh like an axe hitting the bullseye. Realization knocking the air out of my lungs. Nobody could hate me more than I hated myself right then.

For a moment nothing happened. No words were spoken.

Unable to do anything else, the frustration exploded out of me, and I kicked the end of the bed on repeat, bloody towel and all. Pain radiating up my leg, the movement also triggering the deep pain in my ribs. The rag gaining a new shade of crimson. Because physical pain was better than this mind fuck and it gave me some release.

"Hey! Hey! Stop that!" Marisa held my knee down on to the mattress.

Alerted by the noise, a couple of nurses came running in. Both of them holding on to my wrists and my knees, and I let go. My body went limp. Tired, spent, I stared at the ceiling. My eyes filling up and spilling over. And my mind went blank. Completely empty. Not one single thought in it. I burned the fuse. And it was done. Finished.

After a few minutes of the nurses speaking to Marisa, and me staring at the ceiling, they left the cubicle and Risa sat down on the gurney facing me. One of her hands rubbing soothing circles on my arm.

I hadn't asked the question. I didn't want to know. Didn't want to hear Paige tell me she was leaving, even though I had convinced myself that she was. And I... I needed to find a way to survive it.

But she wasn't. She wasn't leaving. She was trying to stay.

I closed my eyes and remembered her face—the screams, the tears, the sheer hurt twisting her features. I hadn't stopped her trashing the house because I felt I deserved it. But now I kinda wish she had taken the bat to my head instead. What a fucking moron! How could I be so stupid?!

"Celo, why didn't you talk to her when you saw the message? Something else is going on, isn't it? What is it?" Risa's voice was soft. Her hand rubbed up and down my arm trying to comfort the truth out of me.

For a while I didn't say anything. Unsure if I truly wanted to admit out loud what had really been playing on my mind. But I had already shot myself in the foot, I might as well continue the onslaught.

"Because I didn't blame her. After the fight and me getting rough with her, things weren't the same. *I wasn't* the same." My voice was failing me. Cracking and breaking under the weight of everything like I was. "I figured she probably realized how fucked up I am and decided I wasn't worth the trouble."

"After you got rough with her? What are you talking about? What did you do, Celo?" Risa sounded concerned.

"After I came home from the hospital, she came to see me." My head filled with memories. Her hugging me, kissing my face. "She could tell things had shifted. I think she was trying to make it up to me. She knew I got minced because of her." Flashbacks filled my mind. "But I was *so mad and frustrated*, Risa."

It took me a few beats to build the nerve to say it. Marisa waited, but her expression told me she didn't like where this

271

was going. I covered my eyes with the palms of my hands. Didn't want to see the disgust on her face after it all came pouring out of me.

"She was trying to comfort me, make me feel better. But I don't know what came over me, I didn't measure how heavy my hands were. And I hurt her. The next day she was covered in bruises all over. She covered them for days after. I picked the most beautiful thing I had and dragged it down to the mud with me." The more I told her, the weaker my voice had become, the harder my palms pressed into my eyes. "After that I wouldn't touch her. I was worried, you know…"

"That you were like your mother." Marisa's voice sounded monotone, as if her mind was somewhere else, remembering a distant memory.

I brought my hands down, nodded. "That I wasn't in control of my temper. I didn't want to hurt her, Risa."

Saying it out loud made me feel even worse. Like an animal, a damn monster. As if something toxic was lurking just under my skin, confirming just how much of an omen I really was.

"A week after that I saw the message. So I just thought it was my fault. That what happened had made her change her mind."

I heard Marisa take a deep breath and sigh. "Was Paige upset? After it happened, did she say or do anything?"

"I was upset. She was calm. Apologetic. Like it was her fault. Like she was the one that did it to me. In what fucking world is that right? It turns my stomach just thinking about it." The agony hit a new level of high as though I had bugs creeping all over my body. I wanted to smash something, break something, gouge my eyes out. "Love is not a good thing for people like me, Risa. I'll just twist it and make it into something ugly. I'm not good for her. Nothing good will come out of this. She deserves better and she has figured it out."

Another sigh. "People like you what, Celo? You just had some really bad things happen to you and you have a lot to work through. That doesn't make you a bad person. And Paige knows that. That's why she let you do what you did. She was letting you blow off steam. I know you, and I knew your mother. You're nothing like her. I know that if Paige had done anything to let you know she didn't agree with what was happening, you would have stopped."

"I want to think so, but I don't know. I keep on thinking… did she? And I was so out of it, I ignored it. Doesn't make it right, does it?"

"No. But she clearly wasn't distraught or upset with you because she was happy to come back. Paige is no quiet flower. If she was unhappy, she would've made it known."

I stared at the ceiling. Feet throbbing, ribs aching, head hurting. But I deserved every bit of pain.

"I was so happy, Risa." The words rasped out of my throat. "Paige was like sunshine, you know, made the color of everything brighter, warmer. For a minute I even believed it was a good thing. That my luck had changed, and things were looking up." My eyes were leaking like an open tap.

"*It is* a good thing, Celo."

I shook my head. "Not for cursed people like me, it isn't. It tips the balance, puts me in debt with some fucked up, twisted cosmic force and I have to pay."

"You're not cursed." Marisa's voice was whiny, her hands tugged at my arm like she was rebuking me.

"This whole thing was messing with my head. Even before it happened, I was already losing sleep thinking about it. I knew it was coming. I knew it was going to cost me. I thought I'd lose everything. It was only a matter of time before everyone got tired of being torn and picked a side." Crying wasn't going to help anything, so I rubbed a hand down my face. The agony was still there, ripping at my edges, clawing at

273

me like some underworld demon coming to collect my soul. "Then I saw her message. And I was convinced she was leaving me because something is wrong with me."

My eyes were revolting against my will and spilling over. I focused them on a point on the wall, without blinking, so it would stop.

"I thought I'd lost her already. So what difference would it make? I just wanted… I wanted to stop thinking, feeling shit. I wanted to feel back in control." My voice felt like a recorded message. An echo of something or someone long gone. "Things with Angie are just… easy, you know. I don't care what she thinks. I can't hurt or disappoint her… What I do doesn't matter. My head, my life was spinning at a hundred on a bend. I just wanted to stop thinking, that's all."

I heard Risa sigh. She was sighing a lot. "If only that was all it was. We could all call you an idiot and leave you to it, but that's not all, is it? That's not really what is running underneath all this."

I didn't answer.

"Trauma can do that to a person, Celo. And that's what it really was, wasn't it? The perfect storm. The trifecta—violence, fear, and abandonment. Making you feel you're worthless and undeserving. That bad things happen to you because somehow you did something to deserve them."

She squeezed my arm.

"Your fight with Felipe was brutal! Here is someone you love, and you thought loved you like a brother, but when you did something he didn't like, he hurt you so bad you were in the hospital for more than a day. Whether you accept it or not, this brought all your fears to the surface, didn't it? That you're somehow less and undeserving, because it was so easy for him to flip on you and beat you within a whisp of consciousness. Someone you've known your whole life."

I stared at my hands. Marisa's voice was soft, careful.

274

"You were upset, heartbroken, and worried you'd lose the people you care about. Then you saw the message and the abandonment kicked in, didn't it? You were so scared of being abandoned, that you didn't even entertain the conversation. You went straight into thinking that you must have done something to deserve it. That it is you who is not worthy of love and affection unless you give people a reason to give it to you. You have always struggled with that."

Marisa was unwrapping my old wounds one strip of gauze at a time. And she was making more sense of my life than I ever did, while twisting her fingers in all my old sores. It was fucking uncomfortable, if not outright painful, but she wasn't saying it to hurt me.

"You were upset, and you wanted comfort, but rather than talking to the people who really care about you, you pushed everyone away and went looking for it in the one person that would only make everything worse. I'm not going to lie to you, this is a mess. I wish you had talked to me, talked to us, talked to anyone, before you smeared the proverbial excrement on the walls."

I laughed. It was either that or crying. Only Marisa could talk about something so fucked up and not curse.

I stared at the wall for a minute. "What am I gonna do, Risa? I fucked it up something chronic. I don't think I can fix this. Paige and Felipe will never forgive me." It came out as a whisper, hopelessness swallowing me whole.

"Son, sometimes all you can do is breathe through it and put one foot in front of the other for a little while, until it eases up. Things always have a way of sorting themselves out. Today, Felipe is angry and irrational. But he'll fall in love with someone else and things will resolve. Maybe not tomorrow, maybe not next year, but they will find balance. And Paige... You need to go and speak to her. You need to apologize and tell her the truth, like you just told me. If it's meant to be, you guys will work it out."

Neither of us said anything for a while.

"If Rô had done what I did, would you forgive him?" I felt hollow, the words echoing inside my body.

Risa's hand moved from my arm. "I did."

My eyes snapped from the wall to her, and I realized she was staring at her wedding rings. "What do you mean?"

"He cheated. A long time ago. And I forgave him. But not before I made him grovel. My self-respect wouldn't allow me to take him back unless I knew he understood how bad he hurt me. And I only took him back because I was convinced beyond doubt that he was genuinely repentant and wouldn't do it again. It almost broke us."

I sat up. "But… you and Rô are like—"

"Humans," she interjected, her thumb rubbing over her rings. "Full of flaws and problems we don't share with everyone. Doesn't mean we have a bad relationship. Just means we have a normal one and we have to work hard to make it work." Her gaze returned to me. "Fairy tales don't exist, Celo. You don't fall in love, marry somebody, and everything is a dream from then on. You have to work at it. Love is actually a choice and an action, not a fleeting feeling. You have to decide you love someone come hell or high water. It's a choice. And you have to work like hell for it."

I did not see that coming. Risa and Rô were one of the few couples I knew who held a burning flame for each other. I had seen them as a rare anomaly. Something that many aspire to have, but only a few find. As it turns out, it was all smoke and mirrors.

A sarcastic laugh came out of me. "Why would anyone in their sane mind choose this shit? I have seen love do nothing but turn people into something they don't want to be, make them accept things they shouldn't accept."

"I think you're confusing things, Celo." A hand touched my face, then squeezed my arm. "You need to understand some things...

"The first is that love doesn't happen in a vacuum. You *can* love the wrong people. And not all people are good people. Love itself isn't toxic, but people can be.

"The second is that even good people make mistakes. You can have great relationships, with people that on occasion mess up and drive you insane. Doesn't mean they don't love you and you don't love them. Just means you're human. And humans are not perfect. We'll all mess up occasionally. But when you have a good person, the good far outweighs the bad.

"And the third is that loving and being loved is in our DNA. It's something we need to survive. Deep down you know this. That's why you miss being part of a family and you're never alone, you're always seeing someone. You need it, crave it even, but you fight it like it's trying to kill you.

"And yes. When you love and invest in relationships, sometimes you get hurt. Sometimes they leave or you lose people. But trust me when I tell you, life is a lot poorer when you don't have it. The good moments, the laughs, touching, sharing... They are what living is about. That's what turns merely existing into a good life.

"Now, things might not have run smooth, but do you regret loving your grandparents? Do you regret loving me? Do you regret dating Paige? Talking to her, touching, kissing, hugging her? Sleeping with her, waking up next to her in the mornings? If you could have all that love for years of your life, despite knowing that one day we will all die, would you really prefer to live without it?"

I knew the answer. Many times I had tried to walk away, make myself regret, but wasn't able to.

Neither of us said anything. Both of us staring at different walls.

277

"Maybe I'm the one who is toxic." My voice broke. I sounded weak. It gave me even more agony.

"And that's really the root of the problem, isn't it? You feeling like it's you. That you are lesser and undeserving and that's why things always end badly for you. But that's just *not true*. People don't love you because you're perfect. They love you despite your flaws. If someone loves you, they just do. They might not even be able to explain why. And you *are* loved. By me, by Rô, Freddie, Lu… the rest of our family. Even Felipe. And I think Paige loves you too."

"Not anymore, she doesn't." I felt so tired. There was no energy left in me.

We stared at each other until she stood up from the gurney and straightened her clothes.

"Rome wasn't built in a day, my son. You can only tackle one problem at a time. We will fix your foot, then sort your house; then if you love that girl, you will have to go and do some *serious* groveling and show her that you really mean it when you say you're sorry."

I knocked on Luciana's door. Luckily, the porter was used to me and had let me in without phoning the apartment. I wasn't sure Paige or Lu would have done the same if they had the choice.

It had been four days since it all went to shit. Paige hadn't picked up her phone or replied to any of my messages.

At first, my arrogance told me it was for the best—rather cut it off at the root now; it was going to save everyone a lot worse in the long run. I even went back to work. Telling myself that was better than admitting I had fucked it up beyond repair, and she didn't want anything to do with me.

But then the bottom dropped off and I was fucking miserable.

It was driving me insane; I saw her ghost everywhere. Thought I had it under control, then someone walked into the bar in a green dress. Caught it from the corner of my eye and for a minute I was actually happy. Went to do some paperwork and remembered kissing her in my office. Woke up rubbing my hand on the other side of the bed looking for her. Thought I could smell her perfume on some clothes I hadn't washed. That fucking green and red box of shitty tea staring at me from the cupboard... I had thrown it in the garbage. Then fished it out and put it back in the cupboard. Even Leo told me to sort my shit out. Apparently, my mood swings were giving everyone whiplash.

I wasn't expecting forgiveness, but I was happy to settle for just seeing her. Not seeing her, not hearing from her at all was worse than when I could see her and couldn't do anything about it. The few glimpses I could steal back then were better than this fucked up nothingness.

Luciana opened the door and, as soon as she took one look at me, tried to shut it on my face. It didn't work. I shoved my boot in the way of the door. The foot with the stitches. That was gonna hurt.

"Nice to see you too, Lu. Is Paige in?" I went for casual, but forceful.

"No. She's not. Get your damn foot out of my door." She spat every word at me like a cobra spitting venom, pushing the door harder, leaning her weight on it. She wanted it to hurt.

"Lu, please. I really need to talk to her," I pleaded. "Please, Lu. I need to see her. Just... just tell her I'm here, ok? I want to at least apologize. I even brought her flowers." I tried to show her the bouquet through the gap in the door.

"Oh! How nice! In that case..." she started sweetly, "why

don't you go give them to that whore you were screwing?" Then she shoved the door harder on my foot.

"Ok, I deserve that." I leaned my head against the doorframe, my foot throbbing, and gave up any pride I had left. "Please, Lu. I haven't been able to sleep, I haven't eaten. I really need to see her. Please…" I was begging, I'm not gonna lie.

"Aw! My heart bleeds for you." She leaned all her weight into the door. Fuck me, that hurt.

"I'll be here all day if I have to, Lu. At least let me apologize. If she doesn't want to see me after that, I will go and I will leave her alone."

"Oh! I would love to! I would love to see her tell you to get lost herself, but she's not here. She's gone." Luciana opened the door the whole way and waved me in with an over-exaggerated gesture, my foot tingling with the sudden rush of blood flow. "You can check for yourself if you don't believe me."

I stared at her. Fuck off energy rolling off her in waves that could physically slap me. "What do you mean 'she's gone'?"

"I mean that, thanks to you, she has gone back to England, you arsehole. Actually, I don't even know if she did go back to England. She just picked up and left. I came home from work, and she was gone." Her sarcasm and anger made her voice melodic.

Cold ran through my veins, my mind scrambling for a solution. "Did she leave a number or an address?"

"What part of 'she picked up and left' isn't clear to you, arsehole?" She waved her hands dismissively at me. "Go on now, go cause some more heartache somewhere else."

"When… when did she go?" It came out rasping, getting caught in my throat.

"Yesterday. What do you care?"

For a minute my mind went blank, my arms and legs felt numb, and my ears were ringing.

CHAPTER 19
Luciana

I have never seen anything like it! The color literally drained from his face like someone had pulled the plug under his chin. He walked to the balcony like a zombie. And then...

Lost. His. Shit.

Petals and flower stems flying everywhere as he trashed the bouquet on my garden table, then kicked my chairs. Marcelo was always such a poker face, but the scream that came out of that man wasn't human. The neighbors trying to find out where the commotion had come from, everyone hanging off their balconies on high alert, looking for the source of danger.

Once he had obliterated the flowers, he limped back into the flat, sat down on a chair, hunched over, and put his face in his hands, grabbing fists full of his hair, breathing like he had run a marathon. Then I realized he was actually crying.

Now, I had seen him do many things, even fistfight, but I had never seen him cry. Not even at the funerals. Whenever he was upset, he just looked angry. This was disturbing. For a moment I didn't know how to process the information.

I walked to the drinks' cabinet and picked a bottle of *cachaça*. What I was looking at was so out of sorts, I thought we both could do with a stiff drink. I placed the glasses in front of him on the coffee table. He let go of his hair but didn't look at me. Tears running down his face without him blinking, dripping on the floor.

"I don't get it. I don't get how you can love someone the way you seem to love her and cause them so much pain. Love is indeed a bitch."

He straightened himself in his chair. I poured two shots. I drank mine, he didn't touch his, so I drank his too and poured another two shots.

"You know… you look like she did the day she caught you with that whore. I think she ran from yours all the way here. She was so distraught, the porters thought she had been assaulted somewhere in town. They were so concerned, they called me at work. I got here just before they called the police."

He didn't move. But his eyebrows screwed together, the muscle in his jaw poking out then back in. I drank my shot, he didn't drink his, so I drank that too and topped up the two glasses.

"And here is where I get really confused. Now you're here, looking like you were the one that got assaulted somewhere. So my question is: why? Why did you do it, Celo?"

There was no answer. He just stared at the shot glass, his eyes now blinking but the lids not touching. He looked sleepy.

"You know, I called it. I did. She had you at hello! You were smitten even before the two of you got together. I saw the way you used to look at her when you thought no one was looking. The way you pissed her off to keep yourself at an arm's length for Felipe's benefit, but your hands balled into fists every time he tried it on with her. And how that gradually made you grumpy as hell. Got to a point that it was making you melancholic, didn't it?"

He didn't move, didn't look at me.

"For as long as I've known you, you never dated anyone. But you put a label on it with her. So what *the fuck* happened?"

283

He continued to stare at his shot glass like all the secrets of the universe were to be found at the bottom of it.

Frustrated with his silence, I changed tact. "For how long were you fucking that tart behind her back?"

Eyes filled with offense flicked towards me then. "I wasn't."

"Really?"

"Really." His tone and his eyes dared me to challenge him. I didn't. "It was just the once."

"How unlucky!" Yes, I was being a bitch. As much as I felt sorry for him, he had done it to himself.

His eyes tightened for a moment. Then he shifted, reached into his pocket, pulled a packet of cigarettes out, shook one out and lit it. I scowled at him. He'd quit smoking three years ago, after he opened Eight.

"You know, everybody keeps telling me that this was good. That me finally letting someone in was an amazing thing…"

He mumbled, staring at nothing. His voice was very raspy, he sounded tired.

"That I should open myself up, talk to people, tell people how I'm feeling…"

He took a long drag of his cigarette, let the smoke escape through his mouth, breathed it back in through his nose, then flicked the ashes in his shot glass. I wasn't sure if I was annoyed he was smoking inside my flat or because he was wasting perfectly good high-grade *cachaça*.

"But it isn't. Love is a sickness. An illness that drives you insane and stupid. A virus I told myself I would never catch."

Another drag, more ashes went into the glass.

"Nobody knows this, but I know where my mother is. I tracked her down when I was eighteen." He stared at nothing, his thumb rubbing on his lower lip. "The P.I. found her through her medical and police records."

This caught me by surprise. He never spoke about his

parents or his memories of them. Not even once. Today was apparently a day for firsts.

"She was black and blue, covered in bruises. Still with the same douche bag she was with when I last saw her. She looked old, you know, like she had aged thirty years in the twelve I hadn't seen her. Rough, rugged, bruised, and full of sores on her face."

More smoke got blown out of his nose.

"By then that piece of shit had broken her arm twice and a few of her ribs too. He was a mean fuck..."

His voice was distant and detached, almost disappearing in its raspiness.

"And he *hated* me. I'm not his son, so he couldn't stand me. He gave me my first black eye. I was only five and she lied for him, told everyone I had fallen off the monkey bars head first. Like she ever took me to any. I reckon he was the one that told her to get rid of me."

More smoke went in.

"But she was my mom. I asked her, I *begged* her to come with me, told her I could look after her."

Smoke came out. He looked at me then.

"She told me she couldn't. I asked why. She said she'd never leave him. That she loved him, and she knew he loved her. It made me sick. Then she gave me this"—he pushed the lighter at me—"told me she wanted me to keep it."

I picked it up. Marcelo always had it with him, and he was always playing with it, even after he'd quit smoking. It was silver and had his mum's initials engraved on one side, the words '*com amor*'—with love—on the other. His fingers had rubbed over it so often that the letters had all but vanished. I passed it back to him. He played with it for a second, flipping it between his fingers, then put his cigarette out in the shot glass, pulled another out of the pack and lit it.

"My grandparents would have done anything for her. *I*

would have done anything for her. But she was *so in love* with that piece of shit, she dropped everything for him—her health, her family, her son. I went back twice after that. She gave me the same answer every time."

Swirling smoke was all around him.

"She overdosed not long after that. I think she did it on purpose. That asshole took great pleasure in telling me which cemetery she was buried in. I gave him a black eye that day. Then I ran, scared he was going to kill me."

Smoke was irritating my nose, my throat. I started coughing. He didn't seem concerned.

"Everyone used to give me this look, you know, this *pity* look." He spat the word with disdain. "The poor kid who got dumped on someone's doorstep like garbage. And all of that because she loved that piece of shit. That was the day I decided that wasn't going to be me."

He looked down at the lighter, rubbed his thumb over it.

"Maybe that's why Paige and I got on so well—the two family fuck ups revolving around your perfect family. And now, I'm here... declaring war on the only family I have left, getting my face beaten to a pulp, and having my house trashed. All because of a woman. Doing exactly what my mother did. And for what?" He snorted. "So she could get on a fucking plane and rip me in half. Love is amazing, my ass. My life was much better before she bulldozed it."

I stared at him for a moment. He didn't look at me, flipping his lighter, bellowing smoke all over my lounge, lost in his pity party.

But I was in no mood to be charitable.

"Let's see... where should I start... First of all, that waste of space might be your mother, but she wasn't your *mum*." He frowned but didn't look at me. "*Marisa* is your mum. She has looked after you for longer and loved you more than anyone. *Out of choice*, may I add, *not* pity like you seem to think.

"Second of all, how dare you compare my best friend to your pathetic excuse of a biological mother and her shitty choices in men!?!" He had really pissed me off. "Paige is nothing like her. She would have been good to you, and you know it. The only reason she got on a plane was because *you* broke her heart. Stop talking about it like she did it out of cruelty. *You* put her in that fucking plane yourself.

"Thirdly, as well as an arsehole, you're a *fucking moron*! You've spent your life crying over that fuck-up of a woman and taking her stupid moronic choices as the truth that guides your life, while ignoring everyone else around you who loved and cared for you *after* she did the one decent thing she ever did for you and let you live with your grandparents. And by the way, she didn't love the douche bag. What she loved was the drugs. You've spent *so* much time living in your past, you let your present and future pass you by. You want to pick someone for Christ as an example, at least pick someone worth following.

"Fourth… you didn't declare war on your family, you declared war on Felipe's ego. *Another* fucking moron who didn't know how to take a fucking hint! Paige was never interested in him. That's why the whole thing fizzled out in the first place. She told him more than once that she didn't want anything to do with him. And she only kissed him drunk and upset because you had hooked up with that other tart on the beach.

"And last, but definitely not least, in my extensive list of why you're an idiot, stop smoking in my fucking house and wasting my good *cachaça*."

He laughed. It was more of a scoff, and it was sad, but the smile stayed on his face.

"Why are you still here anyway, telling me all this shit? If you came here looking for sympathy or a pity vote, you came to the wrong place. As far as I'm concerned, you are the arsehole that cheated on my best friend, stunk my flat out with your cigarettes, and kicked my chairs."

His smile got wider, he shrugged and looked at me. "Risa is always nagging me to talk to someone. I knew you were going to be the right one."

"Oh yeah? And how did you figure that, arsehole?"

"Because you've always called me on my shit and told me the truth like Risa does. Everyone else puts this soft voice on and tries to give me cuddly advice." He went back to flipping his lighter and staring at nothing, his face going sullen. "She's not coming back, is she?"

Then I too was sullen. "I don't think so. Would you, if you were her?"

Marcelo's forehead creased. He dropped his second cigarette inside the shot glass, then leaned over to look at me, eye to eye.

"You talk about me? We're just the same, you and I. Since Alexandre did what he did to you, you have been doing the same thing I have. Using sex for comfort. Sabotaging all the good people out of your life and keeping everyone at bay. So don't you sit there pulling the fucking righteous on me, because I know you. We are one of the same." He wiggled his finger in between him and me.

Arsehole! And worse still, I couldn't deny it. The idea of getting hurt and being manipulated by someone again petrified me. Romantic love was one of those things I'd rather live without. It complicated everything. It made me vulnerable.

"Do you wanna hear another reason why you're a fucking moron?"

He was still staring right at me, enjoying my discomfort, no doubt. "Do your worst, pocket rocket." His voice was flat and low. He called me that because that was Gabe's nickname for me.

288

"Your little viper of a friend… the one that was only too happy to drive you home from the hospital and play nurse with you…" His eyes narrowed. "Yeah! Marisa told me. She was the one that got your arse kicked in the first place." His forehead twisted into a deep frown. "How did you think Felipe knew about you and Paige, huh?" Celo sat back in his chair, head tilting. "The night you blew her off at the bar, in front of Paige, she took several… I will say that again for your benefit, *several* pictures of you and Paige, touching foreheads, smiling at each other. A week later, she sent them to Felipe. She only sent the pictures after she heard you had made Paige your girlfriend."

I let that sink for a minute, his hands turned into fists, his jaw pushing against his skin then back in.

"She set the trap and watched you and Felipe fall into it like the two idiots that you both are. Things with her are so… *easy*, aren't they?"

His eyes turned away from me in staccato, his head following until I was staring at his profile—his jaw working, mind putting the pieces of the puzzle together, his chest rising and falling like he was breathing harder. Touché, idiot.

We sat there silently fuming with one another until out of nowhere he moved. Leaned his elbows onto his knees and looked me right in the eye, knocking the shot glass out of place and spreading ashy *cachaça* on my coffee table. If I didn't clean that fast enough, it would corrode the varnish.

"I *need* to talk to Paige, Lu. She won't reply to my calls, emails, nothing. She blocked me out of everything. I need… I need you to convince her to let me talk to her."

"Good luck with that!" I laughed. "First, I would need to get past the Gates of Hades." Celo looked at me confused. "Kate, Paige's mother. She hated that Paige came to visit me, and I'm willing to bet that I'm officially black-listed now that I sent her daughter back as a single—"Oops! Bloody *cachaça*!—"hot mess."

Marcelo's eyes narrowed, his head tilted. He saw my hesitation. "What are you not telling me, Lu?"

For a fraction of a second I felt guilty not telling him that Paige was pregnant when she left, but I wasn't ready to admit to it. It was all his damn fault.

When I didn't answer, he persisted, "I need her address, Lu. If she won't answer my phone calls, I need to know where she is."

"I don't know where she is, and I don't have her address."

He cocked his head, his eyes looking at me skeptical.

"After we finished uni, her mother got a job in London, and they moved house. I don't know where she lives now."

"You need to find out. Please, Lu. I'm *begging* you."

"You don't get it, do you? She didn't just cut *you* off. She cut off *everyone* that would remind her of you, that is connected to you. That includes *me*. I haven't spoken to her since she left. If she's back in England, she landed over there hours ago, and she hasn't answered a single one of my texts or calls. Even though I told her not to date you. You didn't just... fuck it up for yourself. You fucked it up for everyone else." He stared at me trying to read me. "Paige won't speak to anyone until she is ready to do so. That's what she does when she's upset. And I have no idea how long it will take."

"You have to help me, Lu. I will do *anything* you want."

"I don't have to do shit. I'm not helping you get her back when you are just going to bring chaos into her life. If you want any help from me, you're going to have to sort your shit out first."

He nodded once, firm and certain. Then stared at me unblinking, eyes pleading with me.

"Stop stinking out my house. Let's go to the balcony before you set off the damn smoke alarm."

CHAPTER 20

Luciana

10 June

Me
Hey flower, came back and you're not in. Have you gone out? How rude of you not to invite me! 😜 xx

Me
Flower, it's late and I'm getting worried. Can you give me an update? I can see you read my message, so at least you're not dead. 😕 xx

Me
Just seen your things are all gone. 😳 Have you gone back home?!xx

11 June

Me
Woman, this is not funny. Can you please at least let me know you're ok? xx

12 June

Me
Paige, if you don't at least let me know you're ok I'm going to declare you as a missing person to the British Embassy and the Police. xx

12 June

Celo
Thanks 4 yday Lu. Sorry I kicked ur chairs. Tell me if they need replacing? Sorry Paige is upset w/ u 2. I know u 2 r close. I deserve it, u don't. Did she reply?

Me
Nothing. I have just threatened to report her as a missing person.

12 June

Paige
I'm ok. x

13 June

Me
Thank God! 🙏 I was about to lose my mind!
Now I want proof of life. I'm not going to trust
3 words that could have been typed by your
murderer. What Brazilian saying were we
talking about in Ilhabela? xx

> **Paige**
> Throw me against the wall and call me a
> lizard. X

13 June

> **Celo**
> Hi Lu, anything?

Me
She said she's ok. That's it.

> **Celo**
> Nothing else?

Me
No. Not so far. How you doing?

> **Celo**
> Shit. But it's my own fucking fault.

Me
Marisa said your house is a bomb site.

Celo
It is. She broke everythg she could. Car is in the garage 2.

Me
Good. Serves you right.

Celo
I know. I deserved it. I don't want 2 keep bugging & annoy u. Will u let me know when she replies?

Me
Sure.

14 June

Me
Why didn't you tell me you were going? Did you go back to England? I could have taken you to the airport. You didn't have to run away like you were escaping prison. 😔 Xx

15 June

Me
I can see you received and read my messages you know… 😔

16 June

Celo
Hey, how u doing? Gabe said u dating.

Me
Hey. We are. Is he telling everyone? 🤣

Celo
No. I asked if u r still seeing each other. He said u dating. Happy smile on his face, poor bastard.

Me
Hey! Watch it!

Celo
Sorry, lucky poor bastard.

Me
Yeah... Cause that's better. 😅

Celo
I'm happy 4 u. It was time. Lu... Did u hear anythg from her?

Me
No. 😔 She's not responding. I think this might take a while.

Celo
Understood

Celo
I miss her, Lu. Feels shit.

> **Me**
> I know. I miss her too. Felipe still not talking to you?

> **Celo**
> No. He'll b loving this. He said I'd fuck it up.

It had been two weeks since Paige left and none of us—not a single one of us—had heard anything from her. Not even Mum and Auntie Risa, who had messaged her to know if she was ok, after the news spread that she had left the country following Celo's shenanigans. There were no social media posts, no messages, emails, nothing. It was like the earth had swallowed her whole.

Mum was still upset with Celo. She really liked Paige, and she only forgave him because she could tell he was genuinely cut up over it. Risa was disappointed with both Celo and Pepino, but she was playing Switzerland, trying to help both of them move past it. Pepino was still not talking to Celo and me. A now that Celo had messed things up with Paige, he was definitely feeling the better man. And poor Freddie was completely out of the loop and lost in translation. Every time he asked where Paige was or when she was coming to visit, Celo stared at his feet and went quiet for half an hour. It was like Hurricane Paige had torn through my family at scale five and we were all picking up the pieces and trying to rebuild our lives after the disaster. Exactly as I thought would happen.

But I knew it was unfair to say that. This hadn't been Paige's fault. All she did was visit her best friend and fall in love with a guy. Everything else had been my family's fault. I'm pretty sure to her it felt like Hurricane Brazil had destroyed her life. Who would've thought a trip to see your best friend could've caused so many problems?

I popped into Eight at lunchtime to check in on Celo. Over the last two weeks we had become close friends. Both of us missing Paige and bonding over feeling guilty about what happened, wishing we had done things differently. Celo had also become close friends with Gabe. Pepino's absence had left a gap, and Gabe and I seemed to be filling it. Not to mention that I had been instructed by Risa to keep an eye on Celo. She was worried about his low moods, even though he had gone back to doing therapy and had a prescription for them.

"Hey, love rat."

"Hey, *patricinha*."

"How are things?"

"Same shit, different day. You?" He started making my usual drink.

"Busy as usual. Are you coming out with us on Thursday?"

"I'm not really in the mood to party." He had been keeping a low profile ever since Paige had left.

Then he looked at me, his eyes sad. He had stopped saying the words, but the question was the same.

"No, I haven't heard anything."

He nodded, sighed, his eyes dropping to the floor momentarily. He gave me a second look. I knew the second question too.

"No, there is still nothing on socials."

He nodded and placed my drink on the counter.

We'd been chatting for quite a few minutes when we both clocked Angela's car parking across the street. Celo opened the glass washer and started to unload its contents, drying them, and placing them on the shelf above the bar, but his demeanor had changed. Neither of us said anything.

"Hello there, stranger!" Angie walked in with a smirk on her face, flirting. By now, she would've heard Paige left the country. "Luciana." She nodded at me, her eyes sparkling with the realization I was there to witness her slithering around Celo like a python. She loved pushing my buttons knowing I wouldn't come off my heels for her.

I didn't respond.

"What you doing here?" Celo said without looking at her, his voice monotone.

"Oh, you know… It's been a while since I saw you. Thought I would check in. Maybe we could catch up?" She leaned over, trying to flash her cleavage at him and give him her puppy eyes.

He snorted but didn't look at her.

"You're not still mad at me, are you? It wasn't my fault your psycho ex turned up and started smashing stuff."

She said it for me to hear, and she definitely knew Paige was out of the country. Celo smirked and looked at her. She smiled at him wider, her flirting so outrageous she was flashing like a fire alarm.

"You have some balls; I'll give you that." He said the words slowly, his voice smooth like silk. His hands had balled up, but she had completely missed it and took his smile for flirting. He walked to her, placed his hands on the counter and leaned down so he was staring her right in the eyes. She grinned, pushed her boobs together with her arms as though she had him hooked on her line and was wheeling him in.

"You're right. My girlfriend being upset wasn't your fault. What was your fault was Felipe turning up here and almost putting me in a coma, just so you could get what you wanted."

The flirt drained from her face. And I wished I had popcorn to watch this with because I'd been dying for the day Angela got some much-deserved karma.

"And you know what irks me the most, Angela? You did it, then you turned up at the hospital like you didn't know anything. Came to see me almost every day, playing my understanding friend. While all along… you knew exactly why I got ambushed." Celo stood up straight, his hands off the counter. "You wrecked my life, messed with my family, but now you have the fucking face to turn up here like nothing happened."

This was better than a movie! I wish I had filmed it.

The viper recomposed her face. "I have no idea what you're talking about, babe." She crossed her arms over the counter, still flirting with him. Gaslighting at its best.

"I saw the pictures you sent Felipe with my own eyes, Angela." I couldn't resist. The opportunity to push a knife in was just too good to miss. Her face dropped. Her eyes going from me to Celo. I sipped my drink.

Celo leaned forward. "Liar." He said it slowly, like he wanted her to read his lips. "You thought you were *such* a smart-ass, didn't you? But you wasted your time. You and I are *done*. So lose my number and forget I exist." He walked back to his glasses. "You are not welcome here. Nobody here will serve you or your friends. So do yourself a favor and never come back here. I will have you thrown on the curb by Leo in front of everyone if you turn up here again."

Then he turned his back to her and walked out from behind the bar to place wine glasses on the tables.

She stood there stunned. Then her eyes shifted to me, and I couldn't resist. I smiled, waved goodbye to her, then gave her my middle finger. Childish, I know. But I'd waited years to do that.

CHAPTER 21

Paige

I OPENED THE DOOR AND PUSHED MY BAGS IN. THREE MONTHS IN São Paulo and three weeks in Denver, but I was back exactly where I started and none the better.

This is what you get when you try to run from your problems. You jump from the frying pan into the fire. I remember thinking the exact same thing when I landed in Brazil, as if I had a premonition.

The flat looked exactly the same. There was a level of comfort in that. It felt like home still, despite everything. I would only have time for a shower and a cup of tea before I had to leave for my appointment at the family clinic. The sooner I resolved my predicament, the sooner I could move on with my life and leave the whole thing behind me.

I dragged my bags down the corridor to my room. It looked exactly the same. Everything looked the same. The only thing that was different was me. And that… was worse for wear. I'd come back with more baggage and bruises than when I left.

The visit to the doctors confirmed that I was pregnant, but I had to wait another week for the ultrasound appointment to confirm how far along I was, so they could actually give me my options.

"This might be a little cold," the ultrasound lady told me as she rubbed the cool, viscous gel on my stomach. "Let's see what we have here."

The screen was black. But as she started maneuvering the machine over me, gel going everywhere, a picture started forming.

And then I saw it.

It already looked like a little person, a massive head with little buds for arms and legs. Floating inside what looked like a black egg.

"Ok… just taking some measurements. Won't be a moment."

I couldn't take my eyes off the screen. I wasn't expecting it to look so real.

In denial, I had avoided reading or searching anything about it. I didn't want to know. It would be over soon. All I had to do was go through the motions, get the appointment, agree to the procedure. Get rid of it so I could shed the memory and get on with my life.

But there it was, in the little monitor of a darkened hospital room. And then I noticed…

Its little heart beating.

Clear as day on the screen, the bright white spot flickering like a little light.

"So, it looks like this little cutie is around nine weeks old. And everything is as it should be. No anomalies, everything normal. Do you want to hear the heartbeat?"

I realized my head was nodding too late, and the lady reached out and increased the volume. This little beat filled the room, fast and short.

My baby.

And something in me broke. I burst out crying.

By the time I got home, I had been walking for over an hour.

"Paige?" My mother's voice came from deep inside the flat, triggered by the noise of the door opening.

"Yes."

"In the kitchen."

As soon as I walked in, she started talking, moaning about some design project she was working on that wasn't going according to plan, munching on a piece of toast.

"Mum?"

She stopped talking to look at me. "Are you ok, poppet? You don't look so good."

She had been surprised but happy when I got back. Things between us were still raw but, for the last week, we'd made a sport of avoiding the subject and pretending everything was alright. She didn't mention it; and neither did I. I just didn't have the energy.

"When you found out you were pregnant with me, did you consider a termination?"

That halted her mid-bite. She put the toast back on its plate and came to sit down next to me at the table.

"Are you ok, Paige? You look ill."

"You didn't answer my question." I didn't look at her. Just stared at my hands.

She took a deep breath. "I would be lying to you if I said I didn't. It was far from the ideal situation, and I was freaking out."

"What made you change your mind?" It came out husky, crackling, like I didn't have enough air to speak.

"Something just clicked. You became my baby and that was that. From then on, I knew I was doing it. I knew I was becoming a mum. I don't think I can explain it. You wouldn't understand."

"I understand." My voice barely louder than a whisper. I took the ultrasound picture out of my pocket and placed it on the table. "I understand."

For a moment she didn't say anything, just looked at the picture. And for the second time that day, I burst out crying.

"Oh poppet!" She hugged me. One of her hands cupping my head. It was tight and, despite our war of wills, it felt like home.

"Look at me," she said after a while, holding my face away from her and wiping my cheeks with her thumbs. "It'll be ok. You'll be a great mum. There is no need to cry."

She hugged me and told me everything was going to be fine until I stopped crying.

It wasn't a magic wand; it didn't fix what had broken. We still had a lot to work through. There were still a lot of questions that needed answering. But it was a start. And right now, I needed her. I needed the woman that had wiped my tears every time I had come home running with my tail in between my legs. I needed my mum, my family.

CHAPTER 22

Luciana

10 July

Me
Ok, it has been a month. Just checking in. Seeing how you doing? I miss you, flower 😴
Xx

10 August

Me
Hey flower, it has been two months. Yes, I've added the date to my calendar. I'm keeping score of how long you ignore me. 😔 I miss my bff. 😢 xx

10 September

Me
Yep! I'm going to send you a message every month for the rest of my life if I have to. Because you don't give up on true friends. How are you, flower? xx

10 October

Me

I have news. Gabe and I are dating. Can you believe it?! I'm a girlfriend!! Who would've thought! 😄 Well… actually, it's old news. We have been dating for four months. I was waiting to tell you when we spoke. I hate that I can't just call you and talk to you. I feel like I have lost my sister. 😢 And it's not even my fault. xx

10 November

Me

I'm now upset with you. I told you not to date him. I told you he would fuck this up. You dated him anyway. But now it's me you don't speak to. I have done nothing to deserve you cutting me off. I feel like I'm being punished for your choices and his. It's not fair. xx

24 December

Me

Merry Christmas, flower. 🎄 🎅 I miss you. Xx

25 December

Paige

Merry Xmas hun. I missed you too. 😌 Sorry I have been a bit of a shit friend. Had a lot going on. How have you been? How is Mr. Lu? Is he still alive? Xx

305

> **Me**
> OMG! You're alive! Mr. Lu is alive and kicking, surprisingly. 😅 How have YOU been? Are you back in London? Xx

> **Paige**
> Yeah… I'm ok. Too long to text. Can we video call? I miss your crazy Brazilian sayings. 😅 I'm having withdrawal symptoms. Xx

Straight after, the phone started ringing with a video call. Her face looked different somehow. A little rounder, her lips fuller.

"Oh my gosh, oh my gosh! I can't believe you finally called me back, you cow!"

She laughed. "Going straight to the insults, are we?"

"Of course! I will be taking the grudge to the grave with me. How dare you not speak to me for months on end!" The quicker we got the elephant out of the room, the quicker I would have my friend back. "How on earth are you? Where have you been!?!"

"I'm ok. How are you? Sill a girlfriend?" Her eyes were bright, she was smiling, her face was soft and her voice high-pitched. She was genuinely happy to see me.

"Still a girlfriend. Six months now, can you believe it?!"

"I can. He'd be an idiot if he didn't find a way to convince you to date him. You were so totally smitten with him and he with you."

"The band is really taking off too. He's playing in bigger and bigger venues."

"Look at your proud girlfriend glow! You turned into a proper groupie." Her smile was genuine, like she was happy for me. "That's great. He's a very talented musician, he deserves it. How is the love of my life—Freddie?"

"He is so big, Paige. Like a little bean stalk. Has gone a bit skinny too after his growth spurt. It was his birthday in November. He asked about you, if you would come. I think he's still in love with you."

The corner of her lips raised, her head tilted, and she gave a deep blink. The look that always told me she had a soft spot for Freddie. "He is the cutest. Tell him I miss him and happy birthday. He's seven now, right?"

I nodded.

"How are your parents?"

"Mum is being Mum. Every so often she asks me if I heard from you. She'll be happy we're back in touch. Dad… well, he is still living like he's from another planet." I looked at her with the look I gave when I wanted to tell her something was a different breed, and we both giggled.

Paige nodded. "Send them my love and say Merry Christmas to them for me."

"I will."

There was an awkward silence. I could tell she was thinking whether or not to ask about the others. So I volunteered the info.

"Pepino still hates me. He's gone traveling and didn't come home for Christmas. Risa is fuming. And Celo has been very quiet. He's not been the same since you left. All about his work these days and thinking of opening another bar." She nodded, her face going serious, but didn't say anything. "He's also gone back to doing therapy." I threw it in there to gauge her reaction. She heard me but decided to ignore it.

"Felipe hates you for what?"

"Because, apparently, I'm a shit cousin for not making you fall in love with him, and allowing you to date someone else."

Paige shook her head, her eyebrows frowning. "That's ridiculous. And so childish, not to mention pretentious."

"I know! He's just being a moron. But I have hopes he'll

307

come to his senses. I think he kicked such a sting about it, that he dug himself into a hole and now he's struggling to get out of it. Being a man, he's double the idiot. You know we are the superior sex." She laughed. But then things went a little quiet. She was tiptoeing around something. "What about you? Are you seeing anyone? Did the dance company take you back? Tell me everything."

"No. My priorities have changed a bit."

"You know I'm gonna have to ask what you decided to do in the end. About getting knocked up, I mean."

"Yeah… about that…" She moved the phone, placed it somewhere a little higher up and stepped away from it.

Her belly was… huge.

That's why she looked different. Her face was rounder, lips fuller, boobs bigger and her belly the size of a tent.

"That was what changed the priorities," she told me, turning sideways so I could see just how big her belly was.

I didn't think she'd keep it. When she left in a hurry, this is what I thought she had left to do. And I was completely lost for words.

"That's the same baby, right?"

She burst out laughing, shook her head. "You make it sound like I stole a random baby from somebody."

"Oh my gosh Paige! I don't know what to say. And that takes some doing! I'm in shock. I honestly didn't think you'd keep it. I thought that was why you left."

"I know." She sat back down. "Please don't say anything to him." Her voice went lower, like she was whispering, and she avoided looking at me. "To anyone. Not even Gabe. This is why I didn't want to talk to you." Her whole head dropped like she was apologizing. "I know it's a lot to ask, asking you not to tell him. And I didn't want to lie to you."

The call went silent. I was literally just staring at her humongous bump. I couldn't believe it.

"Are you not going to tell him?"

She looked down at her hands.

"Paige, you have to tell him. This is like déjà vu with you and your mum."

"I know. That's what everyone keeps on telling me. Even my mum."

I had to double-take. I thought Kate would be a hardcore never-tell-him campaigner. "What? Stop the bus! *Your mum* is telling you to tell him?"

"Ironic, isn't it?" Her eyebrows raised; she nodded. "After everything I said about it, about her, here I am. In her shoes, doing the same thing."

"Fuck me. If that isn't life being a bitch and slapping you in the face, I don't know what that is."

"I considered terminating it, even went to a clinic. But I couldn't go ahead with it. I don't know why. You would think the last thing I would want would be to be pregnant with his baby, after everything. But I just couldn't bring myself to do it. She's not just his baby. She's my daughter too."

"Wait! Did you just tell me it's a little girl?"

Another nod; she smiled. This one from ear to ear.

"She's a little *queen*!" My voice went incredibly squeaky. We both placed an imaginary crown on our heads. "How far along are you now?"

"Almost eight months. I'm about to pop. Quite literally!" She laughed, as if she was laughing to be polite when something is supposed to be amusing but it's not actually funny. "I'm sick of being pricked and prodded. My back is killing and I'm hot all the time, even though it's winter here. She also plays football with my ribs, and I can't sleep."

"And how is your mum? How is she about this? How are things with you two?"

"It's been a bit of a shock to everyone. In all honesty, it has been a bit of a shock to me too. We haven't really spoken about our fight. I can't do it right now, Lu. I need her. She's my mum and I can't do this on my own. So at the moment, we're both pretending it didn't happen."

"You're not on your own. You have me. You have all of us. There is no way Celo will drop the ball with his kid either. He always wanted to be part of a family. If you tell him, he will one hundred percent support you both. And Risa... she'll be the most overbearing grandma ever."

Paige avoided looking at me. Her hands wrapping around her belly and protectively rubbing it.

I decided not to push. "I'm still shocked by the fact Kate's on camp tell-him. What the hell happened there?"

"I'm not sure. And get this, her and Ryan seem to have become kind of friends. I think she still has the hots for him. Both of them think I should tell him. Especially Ryan."

"I think so too, Paige."

"I probably will. Just not now. I don't need it right now." Her eyebrows screwed together, and her eyes dropped to the floor. She still sounded heartbroken.

"When are you going to tell him? I hope not when she is twenty-four!"

"No. Maybe when she's twenty-three." She smiled, but the smile didn't reach her eyes, and she looked down to her bump.

"I'm going to be an auntie. Gee! Hey, wait! That means she will be born in the same month as me!"

"Yeah. She's due on the 4th of February."

"You know what that means? That she is *the best type of queen*."

Paige smiled.

"If you don't make me her godmother, after not speaking to me for months, I will never speak to you again."

"I missed you, Lu. Like, I really missed you as my friend." Her voice went quiet. "But I didn't know what I was going to do. I still don't. And I couldn't tell you. I couldn't ask you to keep a secret this big."

"And what changed? The baby is still here. And Celo still doesn't know."

"I missed you. It's hard going through all this shit without my best friend to be my conscience." Her face went red. "I'm an emotional wreck by the way. I cry at everything."

"Don't you dare open the waterworks on me! It will be the two of us crying. But flower… you'll have to tell him. You can't do this to your little girl. You know what it feels like not knowing."

"I know." She wiped her tears. "But I'm so angry still, Lu. I can't even put into words how angry I still am." She looked down at the tent pitched on her abs, one of her hands rotating over it in a big circle.

"Far from me to advocate domestic violence or anything, but you are going to continue to be angry until you slap him. Like, a proper one that makes him pivot on his feet. You vented your anger at his stuff, but you didn't vent it with him." Paige laughed. "You know, in Brazil we say that if the dad makes the mum angry, the baby is born looking like him. Don't do this to your poor kid. Slap him already and let her look like you."

"I think it's a bit too late for that. I've spent seven months being mad at him. Please don't say anything to him. I'll tell him. I promise. I just need a bit more time." She wouldn't say his name. Had not said his name or acknowledged it our entire conversation.

"Before she is eighteen?"

"Before she is eighteen."

"Before she is one?"

She hesitated. "Before she is one." A hand rubbed the full three-sixty around the bump. "I can't run from this one, can I?"

311

"No, not really. But maybe that's the point? Maybe it's time you stopped running."

CHAPTER 23

Marcelo

I HAD STAYED AT MY OLD ROOM AT RISA'S SO I COULD OPEN THE presents with Freddie first thing in the morning. He and I were just watching his favorite Christmas film when my phone buzzed. It was Lu. Over the last few months, we had become really close friends and unlikely allies. She was grieving over the loss of her closest friend, I was grieving over my fuck up, and we both wanted the same thing.

> **Lu**
> Spoke to Paige today. You better have your shit in gear lover boy. I'm telling you.

Reading her name made me sit up straight. Cold ran down my spine. It had been almost seven months without anything. Not a fucking word, not a single post on social media. Even Marta and Marisa had messaged her, wishing her a Happy Christmas, and she hadn't responded. Everyone still asked about her, even Freddie. On his birthday, he had asked in front of everyone if she was coming. Everybody's eyes turning to me, then Lu.

I had hired a P.I. He'd found out she had left on a flight to Denver; and another one had confirmed that she'd landed in Denver. But after that, things became impossible. Lu didn't know her father's full name and nobody had any idea of where she had gone after she landed.

I walked out of the room and called Lu; text wouldn't be quick enough. She answered my call in one.

"What do you mean, you spoke to her?" I had seen Lu the night before at our family Christmas meal, and she had told me she still hadn't heard anything back.

"Hello to you too. Exactly what I said."

"Like... on the phone, over text, what?"

"Video call."

"You *saw* her?" Something in me tightened. Agony and relief all at the same time.

"Yeah."

"Where is she?" I sounded tired, even though I wasn't.

"Now, in London. But when she left here, she did go to Denver."

I nodded as if Lu could see me. Neither of us said anything for a second. I didn't want to ask how she was. Half a year is a long time. When she left she was mad at me. I was honestly scared of the answer. For all I knew, she had moved on and was dating someone else.

"You're a lucky son of a gun. I have a feeling we will be seeing her sooner rather than later. And I'm telling you Celo, you better be on top of your shit and on your God damn best behavior—cleaner than a virgin nun on Easter week—by the time she comes back."

"My life is a temple. Any cleaner and I would be a monk. What do you mean 'when she comes back'?"

"I don't know yet. But I don't see how she won't be back."

"Stop giving me breadcrumbs, Lu. What are you not telling me?"

"Nothing. I just wanted to make sure you have your shit together. Like you promised me. God help me, she comes back around, and you fuck this up a second time, I will kill you with my own bare hands."

"You know I'm doing everything I can, Lu. Now, stop dangling the damn carrot." I was starting to lose my patience. "Can I speak to her or not?"

"I'm pretty sure she will be calling you. Eventually. I just don't know when."

This was like driving home after a very long trip. You're tired but forcing yourself to keep your eyes open because you're almost home, but the road doesn't seem to end. One hour feels like thirty.

"Can I not just call her?"

"No. She said she needs more time."

"She's still mad." I don't know why I expected her not to be. It was easier for me to get over it, I was the one in the doghouse.

"You are going to have to be patient with her. Let her work her way through it. I'm pretty sure it will all rush to the surface once she speaks to you too."

"I know." The call went quiet. "I'm tired of waiting. It's honestly driving me insane. But I've waited seven months. I can wait a little more." Just saying it took all my energy.

"At least you know she will call. That's better than silence, no?"

"Is it?"

CHAPTER 24

Paige

AMBER LOOKED LIKE A LITTLE DOLL WHEN SHE WAS SOUND ASLEEP. And, God help me, she looked just like him. Either that damn Brazilian saying was right, or destiny had played a real cruel joke on me, so I wouldn't forget his face.

Everyone, including my mother, was telling me I should tell him.

The irony... I had begrudged her so much for not telling me. Had even seen it as her being cruel to me; said horrible things to her. It had almost shattered our relationship beyond repair. Now, here I was. In her shoes. Contemplating making the same mistake. Talk about 'if the shoe was on the other foot'! It made me understand her reasons more than she'd ever know.

Every time I looked at my baby, it made me think of my own father. She looked like Marcelo the way I looked like Ryan. And she was in danger of growing up like I did—wondering why she doesn't look like me, why she doesn't look like anyone in our family. Wondering where her dad is; why she doesn't have one and, if he knew about her, would he come looking for her? Feeling like she's missing something.

As I stood by her cot, watching her sleep, I knew I didn't want that for her.

I now knew my father and spoke to him regularly. But to

316

me, he was Ryan. To my half-sisters, he was *Dad*. Even though I had spent time with him in Denver, that word felt wrong coming out of my mouth. We didn't know each other enough; we didn't have the history. We didn't have the bond I witnessed him having with my sisters. And he told me he felt the same. He didn't feel at liberty to hug me and kiss me like he did to them. He knew nothing about my childhood, hadn't driven me to school, watched my dance recitals, or given me a curfew I subsequently broke and got grounded for.

When I met him at twenty-four, I thought knowing him would fill the void. But in Denver, watching him with my half-sisters who grew up with him, I realized that we'd never make up for the lost time. What we had both lost, we would never regain. He was in my life, but he was just… Ryan. He wasn't my dad. He was just my father.

I envied my sisters. And I didn't want that for my little girl.

I wanted her to have her dad. I wanted someone to dress as Santa Claus for her at Christmas; teach her how to ride a bike; clap like a lunatic at her dance rehearsals; hug her when she had her first heartbreak and tell her that all boys stink. All the things I fantasize about having when I was a little girl. My baby was just a month old; she could still have all those things.

I had been thinking about this for days.

Before I lost my nerve, I called him.

By the time it had rung twice I was losing my resolve and considered putting the phone down, but he picked up.

"Hello?" The answer was in English. He knew it was me.

His voice was the one I remembered talking to me at night, whispering in my ear. My eyes filled up. My stomach twisted into knots. I felt sick and an overpowering urge to cut the call. But I looked at Amber—asleep in her cot like a little doll. This wasn't about me. It was about her, and I loved her more than anything.

"Hello?" He said it again.

"Hi."

TO BE CONTINUED…

ACKNOWLEDGMENTS

I could not have written *Playing with Fire* without the support of my family and friends.

Ian, my partner, who got thrown a curveball when I said I wanted to quit my job to become an authorpreneur. Despite the initial shock, he never once tried to convince me not to do it. Instead, he ordered a hydraulic standing desk and a walking machine so I wouldn't have to sit all day. You are a gem, Adamson.

My daughter, Natalha, who grew up hearing me talk about books and watching me write this novel—and who occasionally got fed some questionable meals when I was in the zone and didn't want to stop reading or writing. You are my treasure and my anchor, Babu.

My dear friend Janine, the first person to ever read the complete draft—and the one who called me from her holiday to say I'd broken her heart with that ending and she hated me. She was right. The ending needed changing.

Phil—the second person, and the first bloke, to ever read my manuscript—who is not a romance reader and wasn't ready for all the spice, but who still got really invested in the story. You getting sucked into it, despite not reading romance, convinced me I had a good plot.

Tai, the Brazilian from São Paulo who fact-checked my writing. She is the reason the Paulistas—people from São Paulo —won't come after me with pitchforks.

Maria, whose feedback ensured my characters weren't psychopaths, had depth, and that they internal struggles made sense from a psychological perspective.

Helen Hawkins, a fellow romance writer who, by a twist of fate, became my Romantic Novelists' Association New Writers' Scheme reader; and later—by another coincidence—my editor. She is the reason you can read this novel without thinking I butchered the English language—even as a foreigner. And if you find any mistakes, they are mine. I edited her edits. Sorry, Helen!

My mum, brother, and sister, who have heard about this book in minuscule detail but still love me. And my dad—bless his soul—for insisting I learn how to type properly so I could "use all my fingers, not just two" when I was eleven. You were right, Dad. You didn't know it then, but it made all the difference.

And last but definitely not least, God. Yes, The Almighty. For blessing me with a creative mind and grit. For creating the opportunities that led me to become not just a writer, but an authorpreneur. For He truly has a plan for all of us: "plans to prosper us and not to harm us, plans to give us hope and a future" (Jeremiah 29:11). I can assure you I don't deserve His blessing or His grace (depending on where you are, you might think all the spice in this book is a good case in point), but He has given it to me anyway. Because from Him comes the deepest, most unconditional love I have ever experienced. If you're looking for love... He is it.

ABOUT THE AUTHOR

Paola Santana is Brazilian but lives in Liverpool, England. Like her main character, she came to visit and had her heart stolen by a local. When she's not reading or writing, you can find her talking about books on her website and social channels - P.S. So Bookish. *Playing with Fire* is her debut novel.

CONNECT WITH PAOLA ON SOCIAL MEDIA

instagram.com/ps_so_bookish
tiktok.com/@paolasantanaauthor
facebook.com/PSSoBookish

PORTUGUESE TRANSLATIONS

Pg. 7
Minha casa é sua casa.
Literal translation: my house is your house.
Figurative meaning: please make yourself at home.

Pg. 26
Sertanejo Universitário
Style of Brazilian country music dancing

Pg. 27
Sertanejo
Brazilian country music

Pg. 30
Saudade
The feeling of missing someone or something akin to homesickness

Balada
Figurative meaning: slang for nightclubs or bars with international music, parties with a certain type of music, or a party with dancing that normally happens at night

Pg. 31
Patricinha
Figurative meaning: preppy, sometimes rich and spoiled young woman—think Alicia Silverstone in *Clueless*

Pg. 32
Ele chega, faz e acontece.
Literal translation: he arrives, does, and happens.
Figurative meaning: a man that has presence, makes things happen, and leaves a mark.

Pg. 38
Cachaça
Brazilian distilled spirit made from fermented sugarcane juice and normally containing 40% alcohol. Also used to make the traditional Caipirinha cocktail.
Author tip: if drinking Cachaça neat, look for a golden one instead of clear liquid. It will go down a lot smoother.

Pg. 39
Micos
Type of small monkey native to Brazil

Pg. 41
Alô
Literal translation: hello—greeting used specifically when speaking on the phone

Pg. 49
Vem cá
Come here

Pg. 66
Tanajura
Type of big leafcutter ant that has a bulbous posterior
Figurative meaning: affectionate slang for anything that is
bottom heavy, including women

Pg. 74
Bumbum
Polite, child friendly word for buttocks—equivalent to 'butt' in
America and 'bottom' in the UK

Pg. 80
Garçon
Waiter/server

Pg. 81
Vem nadar
Come swimming (with me)

Não... minha gravata!
No... my tie (necktie)!

Eu te faço outra, vem
I'll make you another, come

Pronto? Um... Dois... Três... e... já!
Literal translation: ready? One... two... three... and... go!
Equivalent in English: ready, steady, go!

Pg. 95
Se eu deixar, você vai arruinar minha vida, né?
If I let you, you're going to ruin my life, aren't you?

Pg. 99
Pegada
Showing affection with intent—a caress that squeezes and grabs; kissing that leaves you breathless

Pg. 101
Problema
Problem

Pg. 105
Hey, cê ainda quer entrar no campeonato de volley?
Hey, you still want to join the volleyball competition?

Meu, vamo lá
Dude, let's go

Pg. 106
Dona Flor e Seus Dois Maridos
Reference to a classic Brazilian novel that was turned into film—*Dona Flor and Her Twos Husbands*. Written by Jorge Amado, it tells the story of a widow who remarries but is then visited by the ghost of her first husband. The reference is normally used to hint at a love triangle.

Pg. 111
Vamo lá assistir o outro time?
Let's go watch the other team?

Pô mano, agora não, né?
Bro, not now.

É o último jogo, meu. Vamo lá ganhar, depois cê volta. O quê que ela vai fazer? Fugir? Pra onde? A gente tá nunha ilha, mano.

It's the last game, dude. Let's win, then you come back. What is she going to do? Run away? To where? We're on an island, bro.

Meu, toma cuidado com o que cê fala! Acho que ela entende mais do que a gente pensa.

Dude, be careful with what you say! I think she understands (what we say) more than we think she does.

Pg. 164
Nada pra mim, obrigado.
Nothing for me, thanks

Printed in Dunstable, United Kingdom

65448733R00190